Keagan's Fury

KC McGee

Pengate Publishing

Keagan's Fury

Pengate Publishing

www.pengatepublishing.org

Book Design: Akasia Marsh

Cover Design: Jiovonte Marsh and Linda Moua

ISBN 9780999893166

Table of Contents

Light

After that night I was able to feel the dark spirits around, with no fear in my heart for them, my wings would come out spreading, I'd begun to fight them off and send them back to where they belonged. Our family grew to know and respect things we could not see. The twins were going off to college, and Keagan was entering high school. He was very excited he'd talk about it every day, he couldn't wait.

He wasn't into sports nor did he have any interest in any clubs but Michael convinced him to join a gentleman's club called GQ. He had to wear a suit and tie two days out of the week, Monday and Friday. Although Keagan didn't like the thought of being in the club, he did it to please Michael.

He was so excited to be in school he wore his glasses and his clothes very neat. We were taken back by the kids around the school with their pants hanging down and their shoes untied, by looking around I was starting to feel like Keagan may have a hard time fitting in, he wasn't at all the bad boy type, we went from class to class meeting his teachers. Keagan would be in all advanced classes this year, and he would also be in the band he would play drums.

I was looking forward to him going to school and making friends the twins were also looking forward to this. "I'm ready for school mom," Keagan says grabbing his backpack from the table. The first day of school has finally arrived. "I hope you will enjoy your first day," Michael says to him grabbing his coat from the chair. "Now son remember, if you don't understand something ask the teacher, don't be foolish and miss out" Michael walked toward the door blowing me a kiss.

Keagan went to the car quickly after that. "Mom hurry," he says waving me over to get into the car as I locked up the house. "I'm coming son," I tell him walking down the front porch pathway. We drove to the high school which wasn't very far from our house. As we arrived in front of the school, we could see from the car that we were very early. The parking lot was empty, and there was only, but a few parents parked out front with their children waiting. I began to park. "No, No, mom you can let me out here," Keagan told me.

"I can wait with you son." "Oh no, mom that would be embarrassing," he says lifting his glasses from his face. "Okay," I say to him with a smile. "I will see you later then, will you walk home or should I pick you up," I asked as I began to pull off from the sidewalk. Keagan looked over to the other side of the street and then back at me, "Mom I would like to walk" "Okay son, I'll wait for you at home then," I tell him waving my hand, driving away. I could see Keagan standing holding his backpack straps close to his chest.

Wow, my son's growing up. I thought as I drove away. I went home to do some housework leaving Keagan at the high school. "Hey GQ," a voice said out loud to me pulling my backpack down, I almost fell to the ground with it as I turned around to see who it was. I grabbed my glasses and stood up straight fumbling to hold onto my backpack as well. "Who do you think you are GQ?" Oh no it's one of the jocks, he stood before me very tall and strong looking, I was afraid for a minute trying to remember never to show fear as my dad had told me.

"My name is Keagan," I said with a frown. "No your name is GQ, and if I hear you repeat Keagan or Kurgans I'll punch you out," the young jock said to me pulling my shirt close to his face. "I grabbed hold of my glasses again. "Listen my name is Keagan Phillips, and I am only going to respond to that," I tell him looking him in the eye. I could feel my throat swelling as I told him but I couldn't show fear I laughed out loud.

"Are you for real, GQ?" He asked as he twisted my shirt with his fist. I pulled back from him staring into his eyes. "Listen my name is Keagan Phillips, and if you can't call me by that name then just don't call me at all," I tell him snatching my shirt from his grip and walking away. He stood there staring at me holding his fist out as if to threaten me. I walked over to the front office I stood by the office door straighten out my clothes as more and more people showed up for school. I stared at the jock from afar hoping he wouldn't come back over to me to start trouble.

I watched as more and more of his friends showed up, I could see him talking to them about what he was planning to do to me. He pointed and smiled and balled his fist at me as he talked to them. I was still showing no fear as the bell rang and everyone walked into the school. I went over to the board to write down my classes as I took the pen and paper from my backpack I was shoved. "GQ" He said loudly nodding his head smiling. "You think it's over huh," I stood up in front of the board and began to write down my classes as I watched him and his friends walk away.

I went to my first class it was science the teacher was a woman named Mrs. Byrd "Hello class welcome to your first day of school at Kennedy High I am your Science teacher Mrs. Byrd please pay close attention to me today for what you hear I will not repeat, take notes if you have to" She was very stern, she also wore glasses hers with a dark-rimmed box cut glass squares, she wore a red scarf around her neck and nice slacks and shoes with a pink and red top. I listened and took notes, soon the jocks began to walk in laughing and joking loudly as Mrs. Byrd gave instructions for class.

She looked up from her desk as they made their way into the seats of the classroom. "Hello gentleman, thank you for joining us today, each one of you who walked in late will be giving me thirty minutes of your time after school today, Mr. Fredrick Hall, Mr. Matthew Johnson, and Mr. William Marshall and Mr. Shelton Brown, I will expect to see you there on time after school" She said to them looking down through her glasses. "Sure Mrs. Byrd, we know the drill" One of the jocks said aloud to answer her, they all laughed loudly.

When class was over I walked over to my assigned locker to put my backpack away my next class was gym. As I walked closer to the gym I could see down the hall the jocks were standing all around talking to the girls as they entered the gym rooms. "Look who it is" The jock said as I approached the gym room doors. "It's GQ." "Ah yes and you're Mr. Fredrick Hall, nice name," I tell him pushing my way through the crowd of jocks. "This one is fearless," one of them said loudly. I continued walking toward class. It was smelly in the locker rooms.

We all lined up to meet our new gym teacher. He was a big tall man he stood over us by at least three feet. "Hello class, I need complete quiet" He said with a paper and pen in his hand. "When I call your name stand up and walk over to the front of the gym locker room doors" He said pointing at the doors. "Welcome to Kennedy High, My name is Mr. Stewart, I am retired Marine drill sergeant I will show no mercy, if you think you can slack off in my class and not participate; you will be my favorite student, I will pick on you every day with no shame. I don't have anywhere to be after school for those of you who think you can come to class not suited up and ready for gym."

"I will meet with you after school every day until you can get it right, again I have nowhere to be after school" He began to call out names he was wearing sweat pants and a school shirt with his name embroidered on the front of it. I watched him listening for my name to be called. "His mustache was grey and black as if he was older but he didn't look too old at all. By the time he called my name almost everyone was in line staring back at us sitting in the bleachers. "Mr. Keagan Phillips," he yelled out. I stood up and walked over to the line taking my place in back of a young lady with red hair.

She had freckles, she smiled as I walked by her, I smiled back. We waited patiently as Mr. Stewart called name after name. When he was finished he walked over to the front of the line and stood in front of us. "I will be handing you a pair of shorts, a shirt and a pair of sweats these things are to be worn every single day of the week unless otherwise instructed not to be worn. They will be taken home by you every Friday to be washed and brought back on Monday, I will do locker inspections every Friday and will expect you to keep them clean and dirty sock free." Mr. Stewart walked back and forth up and down the line checking us out from head to toe.

We then were instructed to place our gym clothes in the lockers and meet him at the field in no less than five minutes; I rushed to my assigned gym locker and placed my gym clothes inside. I walked quickly going out to the field I didn't notice anyone around as I got closer to the door, I fell tripping over Fredric's leg I fell flat on my face. "Hey GQ watch your step," he says laughing walking away with his friends following. They all pointed and laughed. I stood up and wiped myself off. Is this really happening to me, I thought as I joined everyone on the field, Mr. Stewart was waiting with more instructions to follow.

"How many of you are going to do a sport, please raise your hand," He said raising up his hand, "Come on, track and field, volleyball, basketball, football" The minute he mentioned football all of the jocks raised their hands. "You guys don't need this class you will check in with Mr. Bell the football coach as early as tomorrow morning don't come back to my class and talk to your counselors about changing your schedule," he said loudly. The jocks were all relieved to go to the counseling office. I sighed with relief, I was just thinking of all the crap I'd have to put up with if those guys stayed in my class.

Mr. Stewart gave us strict instructions about his class, when it was over we all went away talking about how tough Mr. Stewart seemed to be. I walked through all of my new classes not engaging in any of the conversations that were going on until the red-haired girl came over to me. "Hey, do you have Mrs. Green for English?" She asked me. I looked down at my paper and shook my head yes. "Oh good me too" She said throwing her backpack over her shoulders. "So what period do you have Mrs. Green" She asked me. "I have her for fifth period, I love English I can't wait" I tell her rolling my eyes back. She laughed.

"Oh you're being funny, my name is Reese Hanson, how about you what's your name?" She asked holding onto her pen. "My name is Keagan Phillips" I tell her. "Okay well nice meeting you," she said running off to talk with her friends "See you in English class" She yelled back at me. I walked toward my third period class it would be history class. As I entered class there they were, the jocks standing at the doorway waiting, playing around as people walked by them to enter the classroom they spit something at them. "Hey it's GQ," Fredrick said to me as I began to enter class, the teacher wasn't in class yet so everyone was either standing at the door or talking at the desk, when the bell rang everyone ran in and sat down.

The teacher came in soon after everyone was seated. "Hello class, welcome to US History, my name is Mrs. Blanchard, you can call me Mrs. B for short if you like." She said standing in front of us she wore a short skirt with a black top with a green scarf draped across her shoulder and a pair of black boots that went to her knees she was younger than all the other teachers I'd met today, she explained to us that her class would be the best history class. "I will be giving a test every Thursday and will expect you all to get every question correct."

She spoke with a country accent as if she was from Texas or Georgia I liked the sound of her voice. I listened intensely as she gave us instructions' until the bell rang for the next class, the jocks left class quickly, and I placed my notes into my backpack and went for the door. As I stepped out into the doorway I walked forward and fell over onto the ground with my backpack flying over my shoulders I looked up and there was Fredric laughing alongside his friends. "Have a nice trip GQ," he said pointing at me. "Mr. Fredrick" Mrs. Blanchard yelled out. "You come in here right this minute," she said helping me to my feet. "Are you okay, Keagan?"

"I am Mrs. Blanchard I'm just fine," I tell her picking up my backpack from the ground. I walked away holding my back pack in my hand, I could see Mrs. Blanchard from the corner of my eyes still scolding Fredric. I walked quickly to the next class looking back and straightening my glasses and shirt. Wow what a day this has been, I thought as I walked quickly as the second bell rang. "Hello a voice said from behind me. "You in a rush, friend?" I turned around it was my old friend Jason from middle school.

"Hey what's up man," I said to him shaking his hand. "How's your first day going?" He asked. "It's going okay I guess," I tell him as we walked together toward class. Just as we approached the classroom door there was Fredric and all of his friends, he must have walked the back way around to the class. I began tell to Jason to watch out for these guys but just as I opened my mouth they all ran up to him and high fived him laughing and joking he walked away with them, I continued walking, I wanted this day to end now I was done, I walked into class there was Reese, she greeted me with a smile, she sat surrounded by a group of her friends.

"Hey this is Keagan," she said loudly introducing me to everyone in her group. "Hi," I said. "Nice to me you" Soon the teacher walked in she was a browned skinned beautiful lady she walked in smiling shutting the door behind her. "Hello everyone, welcome to Advanced English. How's everyone today?" She asked. "I will be your teacher this year and for all of you who are familiar with Kennedy High I've been here for over fifteen years I am a stickler for all the rules and in this class I do not accept late or unfinished work, so please don't try and get over on me."

She went on talking about the class rules as notes were being passed from person to person every time she'd turn her back to write on the chalk board. The girls would giggle every time. I was busy taking notes when I was suddenly hit on the back of the head with a notebook; it hit me so hard my ears rang. Mrs. Green turned around quickly. "What was that noise?" She asked. Everyone turned to me and pointed, I knew my face had to be as red as my tie. I looked up at her holding my ears. "Keagan," she said looking at the paper on the desk to make sure she get my name right, she walked over to me.

"Are you okay, what was that noise?" She asked again. "It was the sound of a book hitting him over the head" Reese spoke out and said. "Really who hit you" She asked. "Mrs. Green I didn't see who did it" I told her. "I saw who did," Reese told her pointing at Fredrick. "You come here" She said crossing her arms. "Mrs. Green I was picking my book up from the floor and I accidentally hit Keagan, man I didn't mean it, I'm so sorry," he said looking over at me. "Fredrick is it?" She said to him. "Yes."

"I will not tolerate any misbehaving in my classroom, I don't believe in any of that, if you are in this class and you do something you shouldn't be doing, I will only give one warning, make this your one warning" She said looking at him crossed. "Now sit up close," she pointed at a desk closest to her and made Fredric sit in it. He was so upset he just stared at Reese and I while we continued listening to Mrs. Green's instructions. When the bell rang I stayed behind putting my note book inside my backpack, Reese stayed with me watching me nervously. "Keagan are you okay," She asked, "I noticed you holding your ears."

"Yes, I'm fine;" I said taking my backpack and walking toward the door. "Are you okay, you look nervous?" I asked her. "Well I'm a little scared now, those guys are really horrible." "Oh you shouldn't worry about them, they'll get theirs soon enough," I tell her. "I won't let them hurt you, Reese," I tell her as we walked to our last class. "Well I have GQ this time, how about you, what do you have?" I asked her. "I have an Avid class." "Is it close, I will walk you," I tell her. "Okay great," she said holding onto her shirt looking nervous.

"Why aren't you afraid of them?" She asked me. "I don't scare easily," I tell her laughing and putting my glasses up with my fingers. "If I show them that I'm afraid then they'll pick at me forever don't you think?" I asked her. She shrugged her shoulders. "I guess you're right," she said as we approached her classroom "It's an Avid Media class, I want to be a journalist when I grow up," she said smiling at me. "Great that sounds just great Reese," I said as I walked away leaving her to go into her class.

As I waved goodbye to her I watched as someone pulled her by her hair toward the back of the door to the classroom, I ran back toward her class. "Hey let go of her," I yelled out. "You mess with my boyfriend, you mess with me!" The girl said holding onto Reese by the hair. I grabbed her hand. "Listen no one messed with your boyfriend except for me, let go of her hair right now," I tell her pulling her hand out of Reses hair. "Oh it's you huh, GQ? Yeah, I know about you, we'll deal with you later," she tells me walking away smiling.

She wore a black chain around her neck and dark make up all around her eyes her clothes were purple and black. She had on black military boots; she looked as if she should have already completed high school. I gave Reese her backpack and walked her to her seat. "Keagan if you don't come back here after class to meet me they will get me after class" She said appearing to be really afraid. "Don't worry Reese I'll be here right after class okay" I tell her. "I have to go," I had to run to my last class.

It was a meeting for the GQ club, but I didn't want to be late. I ran all the way there. When I arrived everyone was taking their seats in class and the leader of our GQ group was standing in front of class at the podium. "Everyone, welcome, this is our last class of the day, My Name is Mr. Cain and I will be your GQ instructor. I will be selecting two members of the club this first week one to be the President the other to be the vice president. There are no favors in this class, we are a gentlemen's club, and we are to act as gentlemen at all times especially around campus."

I watched the clock as he talked and passed around instructions and clothing samples. We were to only wear sweater vests and slacks on Mondays and Fridays, we would be doing debates at other schools and demonstrations and recruiting for the incoming freshman. The class was going by slowly we all were asked to stand up and give a short presentation, introducing ourselves and explaining why we joined GQ I was the last one to be picked to go up for my presentation. "Hello My name is Keagan Phillips, I joined GQ because it was important to my dad I'm also looking forward to building structure around the school."

I smiled and sat down quickly. "Keagan, that was a little too short for a presentation, I want you to go home tonight and work on it, come back tomorrow with a better answer for me" Mr. Cain told me handing me more papers to study" The bell rang quickly after my presentation I jumped from my seat grabbing my bag. I walked trying to shove my way through the crowd to get to Reese, once I broke through the crowd I began to run, I ran so fast that I could feel the wind cutting against my face and blowing into my ears.

I didn't stop until I reached her, when I got to her class I could see her standing in the doorway she stood taller than the crowd surrounding her with her red hair blowing in the wind she wasn't hard to spot. She yelled my name and waved. "Keagan," I made it to her. "Hi, see I told you I would make it, where do you live, are you getting a ride home?" "No, I walk home," she said clutching her backpack on her shoulders "Where do you live?" She asked me. "I live about three blocks from here, I told my mom that I would walk today" I tell her.

"I live about five blocks east of here near the grocery store," she tells me. Just when we began to walk toward the front of the school we were surrounded by a big crowd of jocks and other students they were all wearing black. "So where do you two think you're going," Fredrick said grabbing onto Reese's backpack, I looked at Reese, she was so afraid she clutch her hands together and cringed with her head down low. "I grabbed his hand from her backpack.

"Excuse me sir, Fredrick, we are leaving the bell has rang and it is time to go home," I said holding his hand. "Unless you're planning to walk us both home my suggestion would be for you to move away from her," I tell him looking into his eyes. Reese began to cry, I took her by the hand and we walked through the crowd, I had to push our way through as they shouted to Fredrick. "Ah man you're just going to let him talk to you that way." He followed behind us as we walked soon we were through the crowd with the path cleared ahead of us, I didn't feel comfortable holding Reese by the hand I hardly knew her but she was so upset.

I continued to hold her hand until we made it to the hill away from the school. "I will walk you at least halfway Reese and then I have to be going or else my mom will worry," I tell her. They were still trailing us, I was afraid to leave Reese so I walked her further. "Hey GQ, what's the matter, you and ginger afraid" He yelled out. "Just ignore them, Reese," I tell her. "Keagan there is something you should know about them," she said as I let her hand go. "Yeah what is it?"

"Well, last year in junior high they would fight anyone who would get in their way, they have a private club to they do awful things to people and no one not even the teachers can do anything about it," she tells me. "And now that we are on their bad side they won't stop until we either join their club or we allow them to treat us how they want." "Reese, we don't have to do any of that, I will take care of it, I'm not afraid of them at all and you shouldn't be either," I tell her. We stopped at the top of the hill. "I live right there," she said pointing at the apartment building near the grocery store.

"Thank you so much Keagan for walking me." "No problem, I just have to find my way back," I tell her. "It's that way," she said pointing toward the sidewalk ahead. "See you later alligator," I tell her as I began to walk back towards the hill. As I walked back toward the school I noticed several of the jocks following me, I plan to run home once I get to the school I had to make up some time before mom began to worry and come looking for me, I thought as I got closer to the school.

Soon as I had passed the school I began to run when I was snatched back from behind I turned to look behind me and suddenly I was on the ground looking up at Fredrick. "So you think you're going to come to my school and do what you want, he placed his boot on my throat. "You better watch your step GQ or you'll understand what I mean by my school," he said kicking me as they all walked away I got up and dusted myself off. I picked up my backpack and began to walk quickly home.

I looked behind me over and over again to see if they would come back. They laughed and yelled out things as they walked away. I began to run looking at my watch it was already half past three I knew my mom would be worried if I didn't walk through the door soon. I ran all the way with the freezing cold wind hitting my face. This was a long day I thought as I cut around the corner to my house. I ran faster and faster soon I could see ahead when I approached my house there was mom getting into the car; she turned and looked at me.

"Where have you been son, I thought you were lost" She said holding onto her keys. "I'm sorry mom, I had to stay after to help someone in class" I told her. I couldn't tell my mom what was happening in school because she would worry. I waited for her to come toward the stairs and we walked into the house together. "So tell me, how was your first day at school?" She asked. "Um I'd have to rate it a six," I tell her smiling. "Just a six son, well tell me who'd you meet, what were your teachers like." "Okay mom, but can we talk about it over some kind of snack?" I ask her. "Sure, look what I have waiting for you" She said pointing over to the table. "Wow mom thank you" She made my favorite peanut butter and honey sandwich and milk, I sat my bag down took my shoes off and sat at the table with mom, I tell her all about my teachers; I only want to tell her the good things about school I don't want to talk to her about the jocks.

"Did you meet any friends," she asked well there weren't many students from my old school because it was private and most of them went on to the private high schools but there was one friend that came along to public school with me, Jason but he hung out with the jocks so I didn't tell mom about him. "I did meet a nice girl," I told her taking a bite of my sandwich. "Her name is Reese, she's very nice mom" I say drinking my milk.

"Oh a girl huh," she says smiling. "No mom she's just a nice girl that's all" I told her putting my empty plate into the sink. "Do you have homework?" She asked. "On the first day mom, no way," I told her picking up my backpack and going to my room. The house seemed so quiet and empty without the twins around. I sat in my room quietly, I wondered what Reese was feeling about her first day I feel a little responsible for her troubles with the jocks. I didn't want her to be in trouble with them.

I lay in bed daydreaming about what happened today I had my hands behind my head staring up at the ceiling. I wondered how long this would go on, and if they would pick on me everybody, I was falling off to sleep when I hear my mom calling out for me. "Keagan, come down here for a second please" She called out. "I jumped to my feet and went for the door. "Yes mom I'm coming" I told her going through the door. I ran quickly down the stairs to find her. She was in the kitchen cooking dinner.

"Hey mom what's going on?" I asked. "Well I was down here alone, I thought you could join me, maybe keep me company." "Sure mom, no problem," I tell her pulling out a chair from the dinner table. "Mom, how are you?" I say to her as she continues chopping onion s on the chopping board. "I'm okay son, how about you, are you sure there's nothing else that went on in school today, maybe something you might want to share with me?" She asked I reached over the counter for an apple after taking two bites I turned to her with my mouth full.

"No mom, there's absolutely nothing I'd like to share," I ate my apple and watched as mom cooked. I daydreamed a little about Reese maybe I'd run up the hill in the morning to meet her. I thought just to make sure no one attack her. Mom had everything cooking on the burners; when she finished, I went back to my room to finish my nap before dinner. I fell off to sleep easily thinking about my day tomorrow, I'm not afraid of these people at all, but I know Reese is and that worries me. In my sleep I dreamed I was in a dark tunnel I ran through the tunnel breathing hard trying to find my way out, but there was no way out.

As I ran, the tunnel began to get smaller and smaller as if it was closing in on me. The walls were coated in wet mud, I tried to dig through, but it didn't work, and so I ran through as fast as I could so that the tunnel wouldn't close in on me. I began to hear chanting and crying. Soon I was out of the hole in a room filled with only darkness and a flame of fire surrounded by Fredrick and all of his followers. I stood behind them watching until one of them saw me. She waved for me to come closer.

I walked up slowly to see what it was that they were looking down at, their eyes were still as if no one else noticed. I was in their circle they chanted as I went forward to look down; they grabbed me by the arm and threw me down into a hole of darkness. I yelled out as I went flying down into the tunnel, I must have been screaming out loud because I was woken up by mom, she was shaking me.

"Keagan what's wrong, wake up Keagan." She said shaking me and looking into my face. I was sweating and breathing hard; "I'm up, I'm up, I said sitting up in bed. "What wrong Keagan talk to me?" She yelled at me. "I just had a dream mom that's all; it was just a dream," I told her. "Are you sure it wasn't a nightmare, you were kicking and panting as if you were running away from something or someone," she said. "Yes, mom a nightmare," I told her standing to go to the bathroom, what did it all mean I thought as I washed my face.

I walked from the bathroom back into the room "Mom is dinner ready?" I asked. "Yes Keagan," she said staring at me "Well let's go eat mom, stop worrying I'm okay," I pulled her from the bed by her hand. We walked down to the kitchen when dad came in; mom greeted him with a kiss. "Hello Michael, she said as we walked into the kitchen. "How was work sweetie, what smells so good?" "It's dinner Dad," I told him sitting at the table. "Hey son, what about that first day of school?" Dad asked.

"It was school Dad nothing special," I tell him as I placed my napkin over my lap. We started dinner off with a prayer, and Dad said the blessing as usual. We began to eat, "so Keagan do you want to share your nightmare with us?" Mom asked. I shook my head no. I didn't want to recall it. I ate quickly and asked to be excused. "Son, are you okay?" Dad asked. "I'm fine dad, I just want to get my things ready for tomorrow," I told him as I push in my chair carrying my plate over to the sink. I walked over to the stairs to head up to my room when the doorbell rang.

"I'll get it Dad" I yelled out. I opened the door just crack. "Hello, how can I help you?" "Hello son, are your parent's home?" The man asked he was wearing a suit and tie he looked clean. "Yes, sure hold on a sec," I told him closing the door. "Dad, mom the doors for you," I yelled. "Coming son, be right there." They yelled out I could hear the sound of the dishes being placed into the sink. I began walking up the stairs as they went for the door. I stood near the top stair to listen in on who this guy was.

"Hello, how can I help you?" Dad asked him. "Oh hello sir, how are you, I'm detective Albertson," he said flashing his badge. "May I have a word with you?" Sure Dad said inviting the man inside as soon as I was able to get a good look at him everything around him went black. Mom and Dad's voices began to fade, he stared at me as he talked to them, and I couldn't move nor could I hear what this man was saying. He handed Dad his card and began walking out giving me a stare before they closed the door on him.

"Keagan, Keagan," mom said as she turned to me. "Are you okay son?" I sat down on the stairs with my head down. "Keagan" Dad yelled at me. I looked up at him "Yes, I'm okay, hey Dad who was that man?" I asked. "He was some detective; he wanted us to be aware of some strange things happening around the neighborhood. Apparently, there have been a few break-ins, and the burglars are destroying the homes, and taking all of the pets, dogs, cats, even fish, he said." Dad said with a grin.

"There was something about that man Dad," I told him standing up holding on to the rail on the stair casing. "What do you mean son?" Mom asked. "I don't know maybe I'm just a little tired," I told them heading for my room. When I made it to my room door, flashes of the man went through my mind only there was a face on his face. As if it was ripping through his to stare at me, there was also fire all around it and darkness. I closed my door and slammed my body across my bed. I lay on my stomach and hugged my pillow tight, that guy was no detective. I thought as I lay there thinking of him.

"Mr. Albertson, huh, I doubt it, I thought. I went into my closet to set out my clothes for tomorrow; I wanted to wear these new boots that Dad bought me. They were like work man boots; I would wear them with jeans and a sweatshirt long sleeves. The sweatshirt was orange I loved these fall colors; I thought as I looked my clothes over. I took my clothes off and headed for the shower. After that, bed and tomorrow round two, Jocks versus Reese and me, I thought as I showered.

I pictured Reese's red hair and her wonderful smile she was the most beautiful girl I ever saw. I washed quickly and hopped into bed; tomorrow I'd meet her at the top of the hill I thought as I fell off to sleep. I woke up the next day to the smell of dad's coffee brewing through the house. "Keagan, get down here you don't want to be late now, do you?" Mom yelled out to me. "I'm coming mom, give me ten minutes I'll be right down," I told her jumping from bed to the bathroom. I washed my face and brushed my teeth quickly.

I threw on my jeans and sweatshirt and wrapped a scarf around my neck; I threw on a matching hat and grabbed my backpack heading for the door. "Mom I'm ready," I told her. "No, son breakfast first," Dad says tipping his cup of coffee to me. "You can't function on that brain alone; it's healthy to eat something every morning. It won't even take long," he tells me smiling. "Do you have your schedule? I'd like to see all of the classes your taking." "Dad, I only have one paper with that information on it, and I need it for now. I'm not familiar getting around school yet." I told him handing him the schedule.

"Oh, it's okay son, I don't need it. I have my way around this." "Dad, I like the classes I have, please don't change any of them," I ask him scarfing down my breakfast. I drank my juice as fast as I could; I wanted to get to school so that I could rush up the hill to meet Reese. When I finished, I grabbed my backpack and threw it over my shoulders. "Mom I'm ready to go," I said. She took one last sip from her coffee cup and we rushed to the door.

"Mom do you think you can drive a little faster today? I want to get to my first class early to help my teacher set up," I told her. I couldn't tell her that I would be leaving school grounds, she would worry. I thought as she drove slowly to get to school. When we pulled up, I kissed mom on the cheek and stood at the curbside waiting for her to drive off. I watched as she faded into traffic after there was no sign of her I began to run for the hill. With my scarf flowing against the wind I ran as fast as I could to meet her, once I was at the top of the hill I stood there at the top hoping to see her soon.

I looked at my watch over and over, I was to be in school by seven fifteen, it was now six fifty, and I wondered where she was. I looked all around, there was people driving all around me staring in suspense that I was just hanging around alongside the trees and the sidewalk. I looked straight ahead at the apartment building it was now six fifty-five and still no Reese. I turned to look down the hill and there at the bottom of the hill I see Fredrick and all of his friends laughing and playing around in front of the school.

It was now seven and still no Reese, I would go inside the apartment building to ask for her but there was so many I didn't know where to start. I stood there with my head down, I needed to get back to the school soon, and Reese was nowhere in sight. I just began to walk toward the apartment building to see if maybe I would catch her coming out from the front entrance. I looked down the hall it was empty one little old lady and a man walking hand in hand towards the front. When they came out I approached them to ask about Reese.

"Excuse me, please can I ask you a question? Do you happen to know a young lady living in this building by the name of Reese?" The man looked at the women and then back at me, I looked down at my watch it was now five after seven by my clock. "Son, we do know Reese, what do you want with her?" He asked. "I was just hoping to walk her to school," I replied anxiously. The man looked down at his watch. "Reese usually leaves by six thirty, all though she doesn't have far to walk, smart girl she likes to get ahead of everyone," He said with a smile. "You must have just missed her," He said, holding his watch in his hand. "Well I didn't get here until around six-fifty," I told them.

"You should hurry off son, it's almost time for that school bell to ring now," the man said. I looked down at my watch again and it was already seven ten. "Oh no, I'm sorry sir, ma'am I have to go," I said running away. I ran as fast as I could to get down that hill, my scarf flowed alongside me as I ran. I just made onto the campus when the bell rang; the crowd scattered all around going to their first class.

I was still running as fast as I could to make it to my class on the other side of campus, as I turned the corner to my class, and there she was standing at the door of her classroom. She stood there looking afraid; Fredrick was standing over her with his hand against the wall. "Hello Reese," I say to her waving my hand. "Hey GQ, do not say another word to her, or I'll do more than just pull her by her hair." Reese stood the against the wall, she didn't say hi back she just stood there looking frightened, just then my first-period class teacher came out of the classroom, Mrs. Byrd.

"Is there a problem here?" She asked me looking at Fredrick. "No there's no problem," I said staring into Reese's eyes. I could tell she didn't want me to say anything; she walked off to class with Fredric looking scared. I could tell she didn't want to go with him; he wrapped his arm around her neck and looked back at me as they walked into the classroom. I sat down in front with the rest of the students and Fredrick sat in back looking back at me every chance he got.

I couldn't understand why Reese wouldn't speak to me, I knew she was afraid, but she displayed so much bravery yesterday. I thought as Mrs. Byrd began our assignment for the day, "Today I will be assigning science partners; no you don't get to choose." She shouted as everyone began to exclaim who they wanted to partner with, "this will be your partner all year long, and each assignment must be completed by the both of you once a month. Projects are due on time and completed with the opinion and ideas of each partner.

Responsibility will be equally divided between partners!" She went on talking as I watched from behind. Every time I turned around Fredric was whispering into Reese's ear; I try to catch her looking at me I wanted to see if I could see what was in her eyes. I could tell she was very uncomfortable with Fredric so close to her. Mrs. Byrd talked us through the assignment for the day and at the end of class she read off who would be partners with who, she started reading by row, I was sitting in the second row and Reese two rows behind me, I hoped to be partnered with her. Soon it was my row.

"Keagan Phillips you will be partners with Reese Hanson, Reese move up front," she said to her tapping on her desk. I couldn't help myself; I looked back at Fredrick and laughed. Reese moved up front and sat next to me; she was still acting strangely. I leaned over to her and whispered. "I waited for you this morning" I whispered, again she didn't say a word just a nod. I leaned back into my seat continued writing what was on the chalk board, when I heard Fredric talking to another student behind me.

"Yes, he's a loser," He said pointing to me laughing, I turned and stared at him. When the bell rang I waited for everyone to walk out, Reese and I were last to walk out of the door; she walked as if she was afraid. "Reese" I called out. She acted as if she didn't hear me, but Reese was so close I knew she could hear me. "Reese, what is it?" I asked following quickly behind her. She turned to me and pointed. I turned to look at what she was pointing at; it was Fredrick and his friends rushing toward us. "GQ, how about I warned her not to talk to you," he said rushing into my face grabbing my scarf.

"Warned her! I said to him holding onto my scarf trying to pull it from his hands. "Yes she's been warned, and now you, don't you dare talk to her again, or you'll be sorry," He said standing directly in front of me straightening out my scarf around my neck with a smile. "See GQ we are from around here, you don't get out much huh, you keep butting your head into things around here, and I'm afraid you're going to end up back at that private school where you came from." He said smiling with his friends laughing all around him.

"I'm not afraid of you Fredric and Reese doesn't have to fear you either," I told him as he began to walk away with his crowd of friends. There were teachers watching all around but no one said anything to him. The bell rang for the next class; Reese went walking ahead of me looking as sad as she did this morning. I don't know what he did to her or what happened between now and yesterday, but I could tell she believed he would hurt her.

So I waited all day I had lunch alone watching her sitting at the table with her friends as Fredrick watched us intensely waiting for one of us to speak to one another so that he could cause a scene. I waved at him every time he'd look my way. With a smile I waved. Classes went by slowly Fredric was in almost all of my classes, and I couldn't get Reese even to look my way all day. When the bell rang at the end of the day, I walked through the crowd slowly wondering what happened.

I walked past her last class to see if she was there, she was she was still sitting in class after everyone had gone. The teacher handed her some papers she took them and began to sort through them, I needed to get her attention let her know that I was still there waiting, but she didn't look up, I went to the door of the classroom. "Come on, in son," The teacher said to me "How can I help you, you must be here for Reese, your no student of mine," Reese looked up quickly and then back down, she shook her head no. "I was just wondering if she needed me to walk her home" I said to the teacher, Reese looked back up at me.

"No not today," she said with a frown. "Okay, well maybe tomorrow then," I said to her walking away. I began my walk home in disappointment; this was so puzzling, Reese is not talking to me anymore, I know she's afraid of Fredrick what did he do to her? I wondered as I walked alongside the trees planted in the sidewalk. It was fall; I could hear the leaves crunching underneath my feet as I walked, suddenly I felt like I was alone.

When I began to hear yelling and screaming, the trees began to shake as if the wind was blowing one hundred miles an hour it startled me. I began to take off running when I was snatched from behind by my scarf; it was Fredric he twisted my scarf around his arm choking me and pulling me closer to him. Suddenly I was surrounded by a crowd; he twisted the scarf tighter and tighter pulling me right up to his face. "Hello GQ, what you think I didn't notice you disobeying me."

I tried twisting around to get away from him, but soon suddenly more of his friends jumped from the trees, he had the scarf wrapped around his arm so tight that I couldn't breathe. I stared into his eyes as he pulled me to the ground I kicked and moved my arms all around to let him know that I was going to fight back. "GQ you better give it up, you can never win, you will never win, what I say goes around here, I say stay away, you damn well better stay away." Fredric's eye color changed as he talked to me from blue to red, I looked him in the eyes still trying to shake my way from his twisted restraints.

When he finished warning me, they all surrounded me, and he stood up still holding me by my neck with the scarf. "Get him" He yelled at them as he let go. Soon they all began to kick me while I lay on the ground trying to catch my breath. I curled up in a ball so that they wouldn't get the best of me. When they stopped, I turned and lay flat on my back. They all ran away, but Fredric stood over me looking down at me. "See GQ; it's going to be this way until you get it." He said he spit down on my shirt than wipe his feet on my stomach; I covered my eyes.

When he removed his boot from my stomach I waited to hear him walking away, he grabbed my hands from my eyes, laughing so hard. "GQ, you're a funny guy," he said walking away still laughing. I laid there taking deep breaths before I got up. I looked all around I could see by the sky that the sun was soon to go down. I had to hurry home before mom would come looking for me. I can't let her catch me down like this. I stood up and began dusting myself off, I was covered in dirt and tree leaves.

I went over to the tree and picked up my backpack. I held my side as I walked down the sidewalk. As I walked, I took the scarf from around my neck and wiped my face and hands. I walked as fast as I could to the house hoping that mom wouldn't catch me outside. I needed to get past her to clean up before she could see me like this. As I walked, I could hear footsteps following closely behind me, but I had to ignore them. I had to get home quickly; I did not look back. When I made it home, I peeked through the trees near the house to make sure mom wasn't outside.

It was clear; I went to each window around the house to make sure she wasn't downstairs when I didn't see her I opened the door with my key slowly. I crept in trying not to make any noise at all. "Keagan is that you?" I hear mom yell from the guest room downstairs. "Yes, mom it's me I'll be right back down after I change," I yell out to her as I dropped my backpack to the floor and began to run for the stairs. I made it; I started changing my clothes immediately clothes were flying everywhere I took the scarf from my pocket and tossed it along with my pants into the closet.

I grabbed an old sweat suit from the drawer and threw it on. I ran into the bathroom and began washing my face. I thought I could hear mom coming over and over again. I moved around so quickly that the noises seemed closer than they were; my neck had a red ring around it from the scarf. I took a sweatband and put it around it the same color as the sweat suit. I checked in the mirror one last time for any scratches or bruises that mom would notice before walking out of the room.

As I walked out of my room going for the stairs the doorbell rang. "I got it Keagan," mom yelled to me. I began walking down the stairs as she opened the door. It was Reese; my eyes opened wide what was she doing here? How did she know where I lived? I thought as I stood in the stairwell. "Keagan, do you know this young lady?" Mom asked me with the door cracked open only wide enough for me to see Reese a little. She waited for me to say something; I stared at her with hesitation.

'I was unsure about whether or not I knew her; Reese was so mean to me today. "Keagan, do you know her?" Mom asked again; I shook my head yes. "Well come in young lady" "No mom I'll go out there and talk to her," I told mom, running towards the door in my socks and sweat suit. I went out shutting the door behind me. "Thanks mom I yelled back at her. "What are you doing here, how did you know where I lived?" I ask her.

"I followed you," she tells me looking all around. "Can we please go inside, it's not safe for us to talk out here" She said nervously. "No, out here is fine, what is it that you want?" I asked her. "I just wanted to tell you sorry, I saw what happened, I'm sorry Keagan, but they're so dangerous. They'll kill me if I ever talk to you again." She said with tears in her eyes. I laughed. "Kill you, are you sure, I mean those guys are just bullies, they don't scare me, and I thought they didn't scare you either but I was wrong," I tell her. "I'm not afraid of them, you shouldn't be afraid either, I told you I wouldn't let them hurt you," she shook her head no.

"Keagan it's more than what you think it is, you can't beat them," she said looking around. "Beat them, beat them at what?" "Keagan just be careful please, they won't stop until you do what they want you to do," she said walking away from the porch. "You don't believe me Keagan, but it's true they're dangerous so be careful," she said. She ran away quickly looking all around as she ran. I waved bye to her and went back inside. Mom was sitting in the front room waiting for me to walk past. "So, is there someone trying to threaten you?" She asked.

"No mom it's nothing, don't worry I can handle it, she's just overre-acting," I tell her, standing by the stairs. "Keagan, do not get into any trouble," she said. "Mom, I can handle this on my own it's no trouble I promise," I walked upstairs to my room and sat on my bed. This has been a very tough couple of days, I thought as I began to take my homework from my backpack. I started to work on it then laid it across my chest and lay back on the bed. I looked up at the ceiling shaking my head thinking of what happened today. Today was a horrible day, but from what Reese says I guess it could get even worse. Whatever the case I won't let it scare me I'll be at school tomorrow, and I won't fear him.

Fighting

Reese never was the same I'd watch her at lunch take her food and go out to the lawn, she'd sit under the tree and eat, I wanted so desperately to talk to her but Fredrick was always watching her, and I knew she would do what he wanted. Fredrick was in all of my classes he'd throw things at me now calling me GQ, every day it began to be his ritual pushing me when he could or throwing things across the room at me. In science, Reese was my partner, but she barely spoke of anything outside of class work. I tried every day to get her talking about other things.

The school's homecoming game was coming up; I wondered if she had a date. We were also having parent-teacher night; all of the parents were to come to school to meet the teachers. My mom couldn't wait to go; I was a bit afraid that she'd see that the jocks were not friends of mine or how alone I was at school. It seemed that Fredric had everyone afraid to talk to me outside of school work, which was fine I preferred being a loner anyway there was hardly any pressure for me to fit in anywhere.

I sit alone at lunch and I walked to class alone hardly anyone spoke to me besides the teachers, most of them loved having me in their class, I participated in everything just for the fun of it. I walked home today with a crowd following behind me, I didn't know what their destinations were, but mine was soon coming up they walked behind me close, I turned to look back at them from time to time only to find them staring back at me. "Are you guys from around here?" I asked as I began to get closer to my house.

No one said a word; I didn't want to go to my house, it seemed they were following me, maybe watching for where I lived, there was five of them all dressed in black hooded sweatshirts and blue jeans. "There you are." One of them said pointing at my house. I shook my head yes. I wondered how they knew I'd never seen them around before not even around the school. I stood by the trees on the corner waiting to see if they would budge but they didn't "Aren't you going home Keagan?" The girl in the crowd asked. I shook my head yes.

"Hey, who are you guys, what do you want, why are you following me," I asked them holding onto my backpack straps. They looked at each other and began laughing loudly. "Really? Who are you guys and what do you want?" "Man you're something Keagan, just go home, you'll find out soon enough," The taller one said still smiling. I had to use the bathroom so badly. I shook my head at them and began walking across the street; they stared at me as I walked across the street when I reached the porch I looked back, and they were gone.

I looked all around for them; they left. I went inside the house; I took a deep breath at the door tossing my backpack over to the hallway. "Keagan is that you" Mom yelled from the kitchen "I'm in here" I followed her voice down the hall only stopping to go to the bathroom before going into the kitchen to see what mom was doing. "Hello mom, how are you today," I asked grabbing an apple from the bowel on the table, taking a bite. "I've been having a great day son," she tells me "How was school today?"

"Mom, school is school, I have a project due this week but other than that I only have homework for three classes" "You never told me, son." "Told you what mom?" "Well, you never explained to me who the girl was, what did she want that day? Is she a friend?" Mom went on, and on I chewed at the apple watching her talk. "Mom she's not a friend, just a girl from school who needed my help before, that's all," I tell her sitting down on the stool in front of her. "She needed help with school work or something else," she asked.

"Mom, do you think we can talk about something else?" I asked her I felt sad every time I thought of Reese, she couldn't talk to me, she was so afraid of Fredric and all of his friends that she didn't even look at me at times. Just as I was about to go upstairs, the doorbell rang. "I'll get it, mom," I said walking toward the door. I cracked it open, and there she was. "Can I come in" It was Reese "What is it Reese," I asked her opening the door wider as she walked forward.

"I have to talk to you." She said closing the door. "It's important, I know you don't want me here, but I need to tell you what Fredric is planning to do to you next week." "Reese, I don't know how many times I have to tell you, I am not afraid of Fredric or any of his buddies," I told her standing at the door with my hands tucked inside my sweatshirt. "I know you aren't but please listen to me Keagan" She said loudly. "Shh," I said with my finger to my lips I didn't want mom to hear her talking about this.

"My mom is in there," I told her grabbing her arm taking her toward the living room. "Why are you here Reese, you don't talk to me at school, you won't allow me to walk you home, I mean I just don't get it, what do you want from me, you don't even believe me when I say I can protect you" I said in a whisper "I know Keagan I'm so sorry Keagan, I have to do what he says, everyone does" She tells me looking around my house. "You have a beautiful home" She said "Thank you Reese would you like to take a look around" I asked her.

She shook her head yes. Just as I began to walk her around to look around the house mom peeked her head into the living room. "Hey Keagan who are you talking to honey" Mom said. "Reese this is my mom, mom this is Reese, a friend from school; she just wanted to come by to find out the homework assignment for tomorrow" I told mom. "Can I show her around the house mom?"

"Sure son go right ahead, how about I make you two a snack," mom said. "Reese it was very nice to meet you" She said walking back into the kitchen. "It was nice meeting you to Mrs. Phillips" Reese and I walked through the kitchen into the backyard, I wanted to show her the pool. "This is great Keagan, do you think I can come over and go swimming sometimes" Reese asked taking her shoes off and rolling up her pants leg sitting on the curve of the pool. "Sure, can you swim" I asked her. "Of course I can," she said frowning back at me.

"I bet you can swim well huh" She said to me. I shrugged my shoulders and smiled. Just then mom came out with a plate of snacks. "Here you go" She said placing the plate onto the patio table, she stood by watching us for a while before she began with her questions. "So Reese honey, what grade are you in, do you live around here" She asked "I'm in ninth grade, yes I do" "How long have you lived around here?" Mom went on asking questions I sat down at the patio table watching her grill Reese.

I smiled at Reese and winked I could tell she was uncomfortable. "Mom don't you have dinner on" I asked her. "I do son, again Reese it was really nice to meet you" Mom said walking back through the glass door to the patio. I walked over to the pool where Reese was sitting. "I bet you didn't see that coming did you" I asked her laughing "You are so lucky Keagan" Reese said standing to get up from the pool. "Lucky, you think so huh." "Yes, I only have my father," she said rolling down her pants grabbing her shoes from the ground.

"My mother left me when I was a baby; I don't even know what she looks like." "There are no pictures or anything?" I asked her as we walked back into the house. "No my dad says it's better for me to never know what she looks like, he doesn't want me going looking for her, she's been a prostitute my whole life," she said sitting on the stool in the kitchen putting her shoes back on. She leaned down to put them on I couldn't help notice that she had a big blue bruise on the back of her neck.

"Reese, what is this?" I asked pulling her hair up over her neck to get a better look at it. She stood up really fast flinging her hair back around her neck to cover it again. "Keagan it's nothing, don't worry about it," she said walking toward the front door. "Hey I have to get home, maybe I'll come back tomorrow," she asked as if she was questioning me. "Sure why not," I said to her walking behind her to the door, I opened the door for her. "Thank you so much, Mrs. Phillips, for the snacks," she yelled out to mom from the door. "No problem," mom said from the kitchen.

"See you again soon Keagan," I stood on the porch and watched as Reese ran as quickly as she could through the pathway near the trees. I watched her until I could no longer see her hair waving in the wind; just as I was turning to go back into the house I see them again. The group of people who walked behind me today, they waved to me smiling. I waved back looking all around to see if there may be someone else was watching me at the door. As I walked into the house mom was watching from the window. "She's nice Keagan, is she in trouble?"

"I don't know mom," I tell her walking up the stairs, mom kept looking out of the window but she didn't ask me about the crowd across the street. I looked down at her from the top of the stairs, she was still looking out. "Keagan, promise me something," she said as I started for my room. "What's that mom," I asked "Promise you'll tell me if you are in any trouble," She said still looking out of the window. "Mom, I can handle things myself, I'm in no trouble," I tell her smiling walking toward my room door. When I got inside my room I sat on the bed. It was quite except for my fish tanks water bubbling.

I lay back on the bed to catch my breath that was nice of Reese to visit, but wonder why she's coming over here now I thought as I fell off to sleep. I dreamt of a dark room, this time people were screaming in there, I reached all around the room to find a way out, but there was no way out. Soon in the dark room, I could see eyes all around me red eyes but no faces. I was afraid. Still, I kept searching for a way out.

Finally, I turned to a hole in a wall I ran for it, but it was closing fast so I ran as fast as I could. By the time I reached the hole, it was only big enough for me to fit in. I was afraid to go into the hole not knowing what was inside, but with the eyes following me along with all the screaming, I have to go inside it. I ran as fast as I could and began to jump into the hole, just then I was awakened by mom. "Keagan, Keagan," she called out to me. "Wake up son, I have an appointment, are you okay here alone or would you like to come along."

I was staring at her not responding just thinking about jumping into that hole. "Huh, Huh mom, what is it?" I asked her. "Son, are you okay?" She said sitting down on the bed beside me holding her purse in her lap. I sat up to catch my breath; I wiped my eyes with my hand. "Mom, I'm okay," I said standing in front of her. She stood up and stared "Okay Keagan I'll be back soon son, can you please keep an eye on dinner for me" She asked walking out of the door. "I will mom," I said going to the bathroom to wash my face.

After washing my face, I went downstairs to check mom's food. It smelled so good in the house; I went into the kitchen to see what was in the oven and the pots on the stove. Mmm, just like I thought when I opened the oven. Mom had a pot roast in a bag; she had whole corn on the cob and mashed potatoes. I took a spoon full of mashed potatoes and walked away from the kitchen. I walked with the spoon in my mouth toward the front room. When I entered the front room the doorbell began to ring over and over again as if someone was in trouble.

I took the spoon from my mouth and went to the window to see who it was. It was that detective from the other day I thought as I cracked opened the door. "Hello sir, my parents aren't home," I told him. "Hello son, I'm not looking for your parents today, I came to see you." "Me, what can I help you with sir?" I asked him surprised. "Well son we are looking for a young girl, her father said she didn't return from school this afternoon, have you seen her around?" He asked holding out a picture for me to look at, I took the picture from his hand, and it was Reese.

"Yes sir, I know her, she was here a little earlier." "She was here?" He asked me. "Yes, she came over a little after school. We talked and hung out by the pool and she left." "Did she say where she was going, son?" "Yes, she was going home she said she was late, I watched her run all the way through there," I said pointing to the pathway by the trees. He looked over near the pathway. "She went running through there?" "Yes sir, she should have made it home by now."

"Son if you see her or if she should come back here, please call her family or me?" He handed me his card and walked towards the door pointing to the other man in the car to get out. He began to walk toward the pathway. I closed the door and went to the window to see where he was going or if he would find something. I watched him as mom pulled up. She came in the house carrying a bag of groceries. I helped her at the door. "Keagan, was that the detective from the other day?" She asked as she walked in.

"Yes, mom he says that Reese didn't make it home yet." "Really? Did she say that she would be stopping off somewhere?" "No mom she was going straight home, a matter of fact, she said she didn't want to be late. I should have walked her mom; I think I should go looking for her." "Son if they're already looking they don't need your help," mom said going in to put away her groceries. "Keagan I don't think you should get involved," she said. I ran upstairs to change my clothes and get a jacket, as I was running back down there was a quiet knock at the door.

I peeked out of the window. I didn't see anyone at first, but soon a head popped out from the side of the door, it was Reese. I opened the door right away. "Reese," I said grabbing her in. "Where have you been, a detective was looking for you. Your dad is worried, why haven't you been home yet?" I asked her. She shook her head no. "I can't go home Keagan, they followed me here, they know that I was here, he'll make me pay." She said with tears rolling down her face. I took her by the arm gently guiding her upstairs.

I didn't want mom to know she was there. "Shh," I said putting my finger to her lips. "Don't say anything more?" I tell her as we walked quietly up the stairs. "Keagan!" Mom yelled from the kitchen. "Yes mom I'm here, I'll be up in my room!" I yell down to her pushing Reese into my room. I look down over the railing to make sure mom wasn't coming up. When I went back into my room Reese was looking all around the room, tapping on the fish tank. "Okay Reese, what's wrong? Why didn't you go home, what in God's name is the reason a detective is looking for you?" I asked her in a whisper.

"No detective is looking for me Keagan, believe me." I looked at her with a frown. "There is Reese, here's his card." I reached into my pocket and handed her the card. She looked it over and tossed it on the dresser. "Keagan the sooner you figure this out, the better. They want to hurt me now because I disobeyed them." Reese said playing around with the fish tank. "Disobeyed them? Reese you're beginning to creep me out, what do you mean, are they threatening you?" I asked her. She just kept playing around with the fish.

"Are they threatening you?" I asked her again. "Of course Keagan," she said turning her head to me. "They want me to stay away from you; they said that if I am seen near you, they will make sure I pay for my sins. They are all in this together it's hard to tell which of them are not a part of Fredrick's group," she said. "Fredrick is a bully, my father taught me never to be afraid of bullies, once they see you're afraid they will pick at you forever," I told her. "They're different from bullies Keagan, this is different," she said sitting on the bed.

"You have a nice room, Keagan," She said looking all around. "Yes, thank you, so tell me more." "I moved here with my father ten years ago; we use to live in a nice house like this one until my mother." "Your mother?" I asked. She just stopped talking and began to cry loudly. "Reese, no, it's okay please don't cry, I can't take the crying," I told her grabbing a Kleenex from my nightstand. "I'm afraid," we both looked toward the window, it was dark by now, and I needed to get her out of my room before mom called me for dinner and dad showed up.

"Reese, I know you're afraid, but you have to go home, your dad is probably worried, and my parents will come up here to check on me," I told her standing to my feet. "Hey you need to call home, wait right here I'll get the phone for you, you can call your dad. Tell him you're safe and that you'll be on your way home soon okay." She shook her head yes. I ran out into the hallway to grab the phone from the hallway chest. I ran back into the room. "Here you go Reese," I said handing her the phone. She was sitting with her hands folded in her lap. I reached out to give her the receiver.

"Thank you," She said taking it from my hand. She dialed the number slowly and put it to her ear. "Hello, dad" She said softly. "I'm at a friend's house studying dad, I know, yes dad, I know, I will be there real soon don't worry okay dad." She handed me the receiver back and lay on my bed. "Keagan I'm so tired, can I lay here a while please?" "I don't know; my parents don't even know that you're here," I told her nervously. "Reese, this has to stop, you can't keep running from them," I told her standing over her near the bed. "It won't stop, I should have kept my mouth closed, if I'd done so, they would have never come after me.

"There were this sister and brother last year at our old school; they tried to go against what Fredrick and his friends wanted. They came up missing; they walked to and from school, Fredrick and his friends tortured them every day. No one said a word to them, no one made them stop," she said putting her arm around her head. "Reese maybe they changed schools or moved, what do you mean they were never seen around here again?" I smiled at her, it all seemed unreal, Fredric and his friends were all very scary, but to make people disappear, I didn't' t think that was possible. I thought as I watch her from the chair in the room.

"Keagan, Fredrick, and his friends are bad news; they don't fight fair, if you cross them they will make sure you pay, they have this thing going, almost like a cult. They get together and chant and play these stupid, dangerous games. Their objective is to make other people feel pain. The pain they feel is a sacrifice; they get a thrill from watching other people suffer from the pain. I know you find it hard to believe but it's real, I have every right to be afraid," She said standing up from the bed.

"I'm leaving now," She said to me going for the doorknob. I ran in front of her grabbing the doorknob. "Wait for a second; I have to look out first, I don't want my mom to see you coming from here, I'm not allowed to have girls in my room yet." I told her opening the door slowly to peek out. "Come, come," I tell her pulling her close to me. "You have to be quiet okay," I tell her as we began to creep down the stairs. I was so scared that mom would see her coming from up there. I looked over toward the kitchen the whole time we walked. I could hear mom in there moving around the dishes, as soon as we reached the last stair, the door swung open. "Hello, son, who's this?" I was startled by dad walking into the door.

"Hi dad we were just leaving," I told him holding onto Reese by her wrist. "Are you in a hurry son, Hello I'm Dr. Phillips, and you are?" Dad took her by the hand and kissed it. "Nice to meet you, sir, I'm Reese." Just then mom stepped out of the kitchen. "Reese, a detective, is looking for you, did you just get here?" Mom asked wiping her hand with a towel. She turned her head to me. "Mom she's been here for a while" I told her. "Well why haven't you gone home sweetie, I'm sure your dad is going bananas worrying about you, right?" Mom asked her. I looked over at Reese.

"Mom she's leaving now," I told her. "It's dark out, do you live far?" Dad asked. "Yes she does dad, that's why she has to go now." I told them trying to get her to the front door. "Well, why don't you stay for dinner and afterward I'll give you a ride home," Dad said to her smiling. "Would you like dinner?" Mom asked. She shook her head yes. "Good, well I'm going to wash for dinner, I'll be right down," Dad said walking to put his coat on the hanger then going up the stairs to wash. "Yes well Reese, did you call your dad and let him know that you're okay?" Mom asked.

"Yes mom, she called her dad already." I told her as we walked into the kitchen, we sat down at the table, and mom began to spread the food all around the table preparing for dad to join us. When he came to the table, he began to say grace by holding hands around the table blessing the food. "Thank you, Lord for blessing us with a guest this evening, thank you for allowing us to have food to eat lord. Please continue to bless us every day in the name of Jesus we pray amen."

After dad said the blessing we began to eat quietly, Reese took little to almost nothing on her plate. "You're not that hungry tonight?" Mom asked her as she took a spoon of food to her mouth. Reese shook her head no. "Mom she's not that hungry, it's okay," I told her drinking my juice. Reese began to eat faster with her head down. "Do you live close?" Dad asked. "Yes, I live near the school, it's not far from here sir, I can walk really," Reese explained. "No hun, it's dark out, and I'd like to make sure you make it home safe," dad told her.

"It's okay Reese, I'll be riding with you and dad," I reassured her. We finished up dinner, mom said her goodbye to Reese, she thanked her for dinner, and we drove off into the darkness to get Reese home. "Turn left dad after the hill to the school." I told him as we drove along the street; Reese looked scared watching the street from the window. "Pull up over there dad," I told him pointing to the apartment building next to the grocery store.

"I'll walk her up dad wait in here," I told him getting out opening the car door for Reese. "I think I can make it from here," She tells me walking away from the car. "Hey now, I want to see where you live, I'll come tomorrow with mom to pick you up, for school, how about that?" "Are you sure Keagan? I can walk," "No, it's no problem Reese." We walked down a very dark hallway and up the stairwell to Reese's apartment. "Here we are Keagan, this is my place, I would invite you in, but I know my dad's angry at me."

"Oh no, Reese I understand, another time maybe." "Yes another time Keagan, thank you so much, see you tomorrow then." "Yes, I'll be here 6:45 am okay," I told her walking away to the car. I hear her open the door and go in. When the door shut, I began to run to the car, just as I made it through the dark hallway three dark shadows flew past me knocking me to the ground. I fell to my knees I stood back up quickly preparing myself for the worst I could feel the cold air coming from them. I began to run to the car after watching them fade into the darkness of the hallway.

When I reached the car, dad was waiting with the music playing softly on the radio. "Hey Keagan is everything okay? You look terrified," he said turning the knob of the radio all the way down. I hopped into the front seat. "Are you okay son?" He asked me again. I shook my head yes, "I'm okay, dad let's get home," I told him. On the way, home dad began to talk to me about having a relationship. "Son, when I was your age I dated more than one girl, I guess you can't say I dated them. I was curious; I went out with different girls, every Saturday a new girl. I was quite the prince," he told me.

"Is she your girlfriend son?" He asked. "No dad I said shaking my head around quickly. "Well son it looks like that's where you're heading; she ate dinner with your family, that's usually big for a girl you know," he said smiling. "No dad she's just a good friend," I told him as he pulled up into the driveway of the house. "How's school son, have you made any other new friends beside Reese?" He asked. "No dad, I have so much to do at school."

We got out of the car and walked up to the porch; dad put his arm around my neck and walked with me into the house. "Son, you know you can talk to me about anything, right?" He said holding me tight. "Right dad, I know I can talk to you." "You're going to go through a lot of changes, you're in high school now make me proud son, "He said as we walked in laughing and smiling "Michael, that detective came by while you were out, I told him that you had given Reese a ride home."

"Really, why would he come back here I wonder?" Dad said. "I don't know Michael, but he didn't seem happy that she had been here," Mom said walking back into the living room. "Goodnight mom, goodnight dad," I told them as I walked up the stairs. I thought about what Reese said about the detective is not who he says he is. Maybe she's right, why would he look for her here? I wondered as I began to get ready to take my shower and to bed. I stood looking in the mirror at myself I was beginning to get facial hair and more hair all over my body. I took off my shirt and turned the light brightly on the mirror.

I rubbed the hair on the sides of my face on one side the hairs looked as if they were growing in white on the other side. They looked as if they were growing in black as if I had two different colors on my face I took a   flashlight from the drawer to a closer look. Oh no, what's happening to me I thought, frowning at the mirror I threw the flashlight down, what is the problem, what's happening to me? I stood in front of the mirror with both my hands down on the dresser looking shaking my head.

I can always shave them off I thought as I took a harder look at my-self. Then I looked down at my arms, wow, I have muscles I thought I stood back smiling at myself. Yes, muscles, I thought as I began to flex my arms like the bodybuilders I see on TV. I turned and flexed and turned and stood still, I picked up the flashlight from the dresser again and turned my back to the mirror. I flashed it on me and looked at myself from the back, that's when I noticed that I had a huge spot of white hair on my right shoulder.

It was thick I held the flashlight closer. Oh my goodness, what's happening? I shined it on the other side there was nothing on the left side it was smooth, I felt all over for any hair there was none it was smooth, I began to panic, I looked harder at the patch of hair. "Mom, Dad, please come in here!" I screamed out I stood there holding my hand to my shoulder blade on the patch of hair when mom came running in with dad following behind her. "What's wrong son, what's going on?" Dad said. "Mom, dad, look at this," I told them turning around to show them my back.

"Mom, what is it?" I asked frantically. "Oh son, don't panic." Dad said turning me around to look at the hair; mom rubbed her hand over it while dad looked it over with the flashlight. "Son, it's just hair after a while when it all grows in you'll find out what it's there for." Dad said turning the flashlight off. "Dad, what do you mean?" Mom looked at dad with worry on her face. Dad checked the other side of my shoulder blade for more hair, he rubbed and rubbed for any sign of it, but it was smooth there was no hair on my left shoulder blade anywhere.

"Let me show you something son," dad said removing his shirt. He turned around and showed me his back; he had two patches of white hair on both sides of his back. "See son it runs in the family," He told me. "Come, come touch it." I shook my head no. "It won't bite you, come over and feel." He said grabbing my hand trying to pull me in close to his back. "No dad, I'm okay, do you shave it, why do you have white hair there?" I asked all at once.

"Son, we will talk about that soon I don't want to scare you now, but there's more you need to know. I don't want to tell you; I want you to learn what it means in time." "Dad, what do you mean in time, what is going on, will I look like an old gray-haired man soon or what?" I asked them in a panic. "Oh my goodness dad, just tell me what this all means?" I asked him in a panic again. "Son, calm down please," mom said rubbing my back.

"It doesn't mean anything yet son, just be patient time will tell." They both hugged me and said goodnight, leaving me with little to no explanation to why this was happening. I was so upset I didn't even want to take a shower anymore; I fell across my bed with my face to the pillow and wandered off to sleep when I woke up the next day I was freezing. The room was so cold, I wrapped myself in my blanket and ran to the thermostat on the wall to turn the heat up, and I sat wrapped in the blanket on the chair at my desk looking at myself in the mirror.

I looked over at the clock, oh no I have to get ready; I told Reese that we would pick her up soon. I rush to my closet to get my outfit for the day. It was chilly, so I needed to dress warm I wore my blue sweater, blue jeans with a blue and white scarf. I wore suede boots, they looked like hiking boots, but they were fashionable. I threw on a T-shirt to wear underneath my sweater and dressed quickly trying to make it out of the door to get to Reese before it was six thirty. I rushed with my backpack down to the kitchen to greet mom good morning.

"Good morning mom," I said grabbing a piece of toast from the pile of toast on the table. She turned to me, "Good morning son." She looked as if she was shocked, "son, you need to go back up and wash your face, it's not clean." She tells me with her hand on my cheeks. "Did you brush?" She asked. I shook my head no. She pointed toward the stairwell "Go back, get it done." She said in a stern voice, "But mom I have to get to Reese before seven, or she will leave for school," I told her dropping my backpack running toward the stairs.

"Call her son, and tell her you're running late," she says to me. "I don't have her phone number mom." "Are you walking or riding with me?" She asked. I washed my face and brushed my teeth as fast as I could watching the clock the whole time, this was beginning to be a very tough morning, I thought as I finished running down the stairs. "Mom, I need you to give us a ride to school, I want to make it to her before she leaves," I stood at the door waiting for mom to grab her bag.

"Mom hurry," I said opening the front door for us to go out. We got into the car and drove off to get Reese when we made it to her apartment building I thought I might have missed her because there were the old man and old lady again going for their morning walk. I got out of the car and walked toward the entrance of the apartment building. "Hello son, don't worry she's there waiting." The old man said pointing down the hallway.

"Thank you, sir," I told him running past, I didn't even have to go too far Reese was waiting by the stairs. "Good morning Reese," I said reaching out for her backpack. "Good morning Keagan," She says walking beside me. "We are running a little late, are we walking?" She asked me "No I told you that my mom would drive us there" "Okay, but could she take us around back toward the gym?" She asked. "Sure that should be no problem," I told her opening the car door for her.

Mom drove us to school quickly, she dropped us in the back at the gym, Reese began to run as soon as her feet hit the ground it seemed, and I ran behind her, Reese "what's your hurry? We're at least ten minutes before the bell." I told her rushing to catch up with her as she turned the corner to the back of the gym. She pointed up at the trees. I looked up, and there I saw Fredrick and his friends covering the trees. They all stood on the branches of the trees shaking the leaves off them and yelling, throwing what looked like hard acorns from the trees.

"Hey GQ nice to see you like blue too," Fredric yelled out to me laughing. I nodded my head at him and continued to walk by, Reese walked ahead of me clutching her backpack tight. "Reese!" I yelled out. Just then Fredrick did a flip from the tree and fell to his feet right in front of her snatching her backpack from her tight clutch. "So, you like playing with fire, don't you?" Fredrick said with his hand on Reese's face. He grabbed her cheeks and squeezed them so tight they were turning red.

He pulled her in close to his face, his eyes changed, and he blew into her eyes "Open your eyes, Reese before you find yourself in too deep." He said sticking his tongue out at her. I took my backpack from my back and ran for him grabbing him by the shirt, pulling him from her face standing in between him and her. "You want to pick on someone? Try me, Fredrick," I said holding onto his shirt as tight as I could. "Don't you ever touch her like that again! I said pushing him so hard away from me that he almost stumbled to the ground.

He stood back, and his friends began to surround us. "No, No not here, not now," Fredric told them with the wave of his hand, he began laughing. "Come on, yes GQ has a pair." He laughed as they followed him toward the school. I picked up Reese's backpack and helped her put it on and picked mine up and strapped it on. I stood in front of Reese, "Are you okay?" I asked her; she was holding her face on both sides as if she was hurting, tears rolled down her cheeks, she shook her head no.

"Let me see," I told her moving her hands away; she was bleeding on both sides of her cheeks. I immediately took my scarf off and wiped the blood from her face. "Reese, I'm so sorry, don't worry" I told her, the bell rang, we had to get to class, and I walked her to the nurse's office before going to class. When I made it to class, I was late; my teacher made sure I remembered never to be late again. She gave me a verbal scolding about being on time and told me that I would have detention after school.

I tried to explain to her that I had to escort a friend who got hurt to the nurse's office, but she didn't want to hear that at all. "Be on time to my class or suffer the consequences?" She said in front of everyone. "Next time we call your parents!" She said. I worked through that class as quickly as I could. I ignored Fredric and his friends the whole time. Just thinking, I want to get to Reese before she went to her second class to let her know that I have to stay after school today. When the bell rang, I ran out looking for her.

I spotted her at the end of the hallway rushing toward her other class. "Reese, Reese!" I yelled out to her. She turned and looked back at me stopping for me to catch up to her. "Hi, she said smiling, "Are you okay now?" I asked her. "She is for now," a girl said standing behind us. "She won't be later," she said laughing. "Reese, I have detention after school today, do you want to wait for me, or do you have to get home quickly?" I asked her walking beside her. "I have to get home, but I think I should wait for you."

"Okay then, I will see you after your Avid class at the hill by the tree in the middle of the school right?" "Yes, she said walking into her classroom. I ran quickly to my next class; the day was going by so fast I could barely concentrate on what was going on in class when Reese was in the class with me I was fine. I didn't worry at all about if she was okay or not I knew she was fine she was there with me. When we got into science class we worked together on our project, I whispered to her during class.

"What happens to me if I don't go to detention today" I asked her "You might have to see the principle and do school ground clean up for a week" She tells me smiling "That doesn't sound so bad, I'll take it" I said her smiling back. When the day was finally over I ran to the hill in the middle of the school to wait for Reese; she came out smiling "Keagan guess what?" She said excitedly "What happened?" I asked. "I'm getting an A in my Avid class."

"Good Reese, what are you going to do to celebrate?" I asked her. She looked over at me and smiled as we began to walk toward the entrance of the school. "I'd like to go swimming in your pool," she said smiling. "Swimming, Reese it's freezing out." "Your pool is warm, right?

It doesn't matter; I just want to get in and swim, can I?" She asked. "Sure why not," I told her we walked outside of the school toward the hill to get to her apartments. When we reached the top of the hill, I could see Fredrick and his friends waiting for us there. Reese began to get nervous.

"Reese don't worry, I will handle everything, you just get to your house, okay." I told her looking at her; she shook her head yes. "Be careful please Keagan." She said as she began to run toward the side of the building "GQ!" Fredrick yells out. "Are you ready to be as brave as you were earlier today; he ran up toward me and stood in my face. "What's with you Fredrick, I have never done anything to you, what do you want from me?" I asked him. He slapped my face as hard as he could "Yes, I was just saying how wonderful you are" He said laughing.

"You came to the wrong school, you don't belong here," He said slapping me again. My face began to burn as if there was a fire set to it. I looked around at my surroundings trying not to get as angry about him hitting me. "Oh, you can't hit now huh?" He said slapping my face again. "I won't stoop to your level Fredrick; you're so tough aren't you," I said to him as he slapped me over and over. "Is that all you have, you're so weak." I told him as he hit me over, and over I stared him in the eye. I could see the fire in his eyes; he was angry at the fact that I didn't budge.

I smiled and laughed at him I thought about how his hand must feel in those gloves. "Tough one huh," he said smiling standing back away from me. He waved his hands up as if he was calling someone over and looked to the side of the building then he whistled loudly. "Katy, come now!" He yelled, he grabbed me by my shirt and pulled my head around to the look down the side of the building. "See you have to live with that," he said as he pulled my face back around to look down the side of the building. It was Reese they had her by her hair while one of them stood back.

The one he called Katy began to throw her leg back as if she was going to kick her in the face. Reese was crying and yelling at me. "Keagan please, please!" She said holding her hands out waiting for the kick. I couldn't believe what I was seeing; the thought of that happening brought my spirit into a rage. I snatched Fredrick's hands from my shirt and began to kick and hit at him; I ran so fast away from him and his friends they couldn't catch up. As the girl began to kick Reese, I grabbed her leg and twisted it backward trying not to break it; I flung her forward.

She hit the wall; I pushed Reese out of the way of them covering her body with mine as they all ran over to me angry with fire in their eyes because they couldn't catch me "You bastard!" Fredrick said standing in my face his eyes were red as if they were bleeding. I could feel my left shoulder blade aching as if I hit it somewhere. It felt as if something was ripping through my skin, just then the police showed up. There was two of them, they got out of the car and stood at the entrance of the side of the building. "What's going on here?" The policeman asked.

Fredrick stepped back fixing his jacket. "Nothing much sir, just a small disagreement," he explained. "Is that all son?" He asked looking at me, Reese shook her head yes. They began scattering around, helping the girl from the ground they held her by her arms carrying her toward the street. "Listen this is private property back here, I don't want to catch you guys back here ever again." The policeman said. "Get out of here, if you don't live around here don't come back or I will arrest the lot you, do you hear me?" He said waving his hand around looking angry.

Fredrick's friends ran off into the darkness; the policeman came over to Reese "Are you going to be okay young lady?" He asked her. She shook her head yes, I helped her to her apartment where her father was waiting at the door. He was very old; he stood in the light of the doorway with a frown wearing a bathrobe and what looked like long pants underneath. He had a full gray beard and bright blue eyes just like Reese. "Son, what are you doing?" He asked me as I helped Reese to the door. "Sir there was an altercation with some guys from school; she just has a couple of scrapes and bruises." I told him handing her over to him.

"Reese, I will see you tomorrow then?" I asked. "Yes, will you be picking me up?" "Yes six forty-five, is that good?" "Yes, thank you." I walked down the dark hallway my left shoulder stung and burned so badly. I tried rubbing it as I walked down the hallway but it was like a razor, or a knife stuck in my shoulder blade. Oh no, they cut me, I thought. I began to run I needed to get home before mom did, today she volunteers at the Red Cross so she wouldn't be there too early I thought as I ran home. I ran so fast I could feel the wind cut my face, it was frigid. When I made it to the corner near my house, I noticed that the same guys from the other day were standing on the corner watching the house again.

I slowed down as I turned to the house, just to get a closer look at them. Yes, they're the same guys; I wondered why they were waiting there. Did they want to rob us or something? I slowly walked toward them, "Hey, how's it going," I said passing by them. I wanted them to know that I was watching them too and that I'm not afraid of them. I walked across the street to the house still turning back looking at them, when one of them ran over to me. "Hey man," He said with a smile "You don't have to worry okay, we're here for you."

"For me? Okay very funny" I said walking to my door "We'll see you later man," the guy said. I turned the key to the door; I walked in holding my shoulder, boy did it hurt. As I ran upstairs I began taking my shirt off; it stung so badly I stood at the mirror. What now? I thought as I grabbed the flashlight from the dresser. I turned around with my back to the mirror to look with the light. Oh my God, I thought, there was black, really thick hairs sticking out of my shoulder blade. It was as if I was growing hair like a porcupine; the hairs were sharp like knives and steel.

They covered my shoulder blade but stuck out. I ran my hand over them carefully trying not to cut my hand; I fell to the floor dropping the flashlight. What was happening to me? I thought I reached over to my right shoulder to see if it had grown the black hairs, but there was still a patch of white hair lying flat to my shoulder, not at all like the other side. I held onto that hair with my arm crossed over my chest. It was all so confusing, what was happening to me? I stood to my feet to look into the mirror at both the patches of hair on my back I wanted to shave them but the hair on the left was like steel.

There was no way I'd be able to shave them off I thought as I reached for the shaving cream. I sprayed it all over both patches; I will try. There is no way I will be able to have these two different patches of hair on my back, especially with Fredric around. I thought as I began to take the razor to my right shoulder blade, I went over it hard. Scrapping it as hard as I could, I could hear the scrapping it sounded as If I was raking the pavement. I went into the bathroom to run the razor over the water to make sure it was coming off, but nothing. I shaved over, and over it, no white hair came off in the razor it only made the skin bleed.

I began to try the other side, I scrapped the razor across the skin leading up to the black hair, and the razor twisted and broke off the stick. It didn't even go through the hair at all. I threw the stick to the floor; my right shoulder was still bleeding I took toilet paper from the roll to cover it. My left shoulder blade was still stinging and burning. I went back into my room to sit on the bed. I just sat there thinking; I would have to show mom when she comes in, maybe she can help me shave it, maybe I need to see a doctor. I thought as I waited for mom to get home.

I was so confused about what all this meant. I went to the window to look out at the trees. God if there is something you want me to know, if there is something you need me to do, please help me understand. I knew one thing, I knew that if I had any problems I needed answers so I could pray. That was something mom and dad always taught me to do. It was clear now that I needed to know something because I'm being attacked by Fredric all the time and it's getting worse. Fredrick is determined to defeat me in every way possible; it seemed impossible to run from him. I thought as I looked out of the window waiting for mom.

When mom came in she went to the bathroom downstairs; I ran down to wait at the door for her. When she opened it, she was startled by me standing there. "Oh Keagan, you scared me," she said clutching her chest. "Why don't you have a shirt on son, aren't you cold?" She said walking into the kitchen. "Mom look at my back, look there's hair on the left side now but it's black mom, it's sharp like a knife, what's happening to me, mom?" I said turning my back to her for her to look at the hair. She moved back turning on the hallway light. "Let me have a look son," She says holding my shoulder over into the light, she rubbed one hand over the right side up and down. Then she began to rub the left side.

"Ouch Keagan, I'm bleeding, when did this happen? Does this hurt you?" She asked me, going over to the bathroom sink to run the water over her bleeding hand. "I have to call your father, the hair is like sharp knives," She said with a frown on her face. She walked up close to me, grabbing at my face; she took my face in her hands moving it all around. "The hair on your face is a different shade on each side also Keagan, did you notice that at all?" She asked me looking confused. I shook my head yes. She walked away to the kitchen. I could hear her praying out loud. "Lord please cover him, be his guidance through it all." I went back up to my room and came back down she was still praying, I had on a big sweatshirt.

Something that wouldn't stick to the hair on the left side; I went into the kitchen to find mom on her knees at the table still praying. "Mom, please get up," I said to her. "Praying might not be the answer." She looked up at me with a frown and began to stand on her feet walking toward me. "Son there is nothing that God cannot fix, absolutely nothing," she said to me. "Mom, God can't fix everything, sometimes he leaves things up to us here on this earth," I told her. She began to cry "Lord, my son," she said. I took an apple from the bowl on the table; I walked up to my room to wait for dad to come home, I could tell that mom was just as confused as I was.

She was crying and praying for hours before dad showed up. "Keagan, Dad yelled, to me to come down as soon as he entered the house. "Son, come down here please." I wrapped the apple core in a paper from my desk and threw into the trash by my bed. I went out to greet dad, "Hi dad, how was work?" "Son, come down here please," he said in a stern voice. I walked down to him slowly. "Son, are you okay? Let me see your shoulders," he turned me around pulling up my sweat-shirt. "Take that off for me, son," I took it off. Dad looked over my back with a small light from his pocket.

"Un huh, un huh," he said as he looked me over. "Son, does it hurt you at all?" I shook my head yes. "Only this side," I told him putting my hand on my left shoulder. "When did it come out, what was going on when it came out?" He asked me. I couldn't tell him that I'd been fighting, especially the part about the police. "I just was a little upset about something after school, and that's when it happened, dad." I told him putting my sweatshirt back on.

"Dad, I just want them off, is there something you can do?" I asked him "I will try something later, are you sure that there was nothing else going on with you that may have caused this to happen?" "No dad, nothing," I walked away to my room. Dad went to the kitchen to find mom. "Michael, what's happening to him?" Mom said crying I could hear her from the top of the stairs. "We just have to remember that he was born into this world, nothing happened to him, but he was born of us. We need to pray about it; he was born of this world, he may be going through a transition phase that may be conflicting of two worlds. We have to let him be; he has to learn what it all means on his own." Dad told her.

I went into my room; born of this world, conflicted I thought, what does it all mean? I fell asleep on my side thinking of Reese, that fight, and Fredric. I'll figure it out myself. That morning mom was standing over me watching me sleep. I woke up to her looking at my back. "Mom, what are you doing?" I asked her covering my back up with the covers "I was just looking over your shoulder, Keagan the black hairs are gone" She tells me. I opened up my eyes jumping to my feet. "What?" I began to feel over my left shoulder.

"Mom, they're gone, yes!" I said jumping all around. I washed my face and brushed my teeth getting ready to get Reese for school. Mom walked out of my room smiling. "See you downstairs son." She said closing the door; I rushed into my closet to find my outfit for the day. I would wear black today a black turtleneck sweater, and black jeans with black sneakers. I put a T-shirt on underneath my sweater; I wrapped a red scarf around my neck. I took one look in the mirror, brushed my hair up with gel.

I spiked it making it stand up straight through the middle. It was about six thirty-five by the time I got breakfast. We left the house a little behind; I knew Reese would be waiting. We pulled up in front of the building; I got out and ran to get Reese. She was standing at the top of the stairwell with her father; he was still in a robe with pants underneath. "Son, we didn't formally meet," he said reaching out to shake my hand. "Hello, I'm Mr. Hanson; it's so nice to meet you, thank you for taking care of my Reese."

"No problem sir, is she ready?" I asked him. Reese came walking out with her backpack in her hand I took her backpack from her hand carrying it. "You look nice today Reese," I told her. She was wearing a sweater dress it had lots of colors in it. Red, orange, green and blue, she had on yellow tights and black boots. She looked so nice; I couldn't stop looking at her and smiling, her red hair was back today, away from her face, it seemed that her eyes were sparkling, they were a beautiful blue. We walked to the car together smiling.

"You look nice today too." She said to me as we approached the car "Hello Mrs. Phillips," Reese said entering the car. "Hello Reese, you look beautiful today," mom told her. "Thank you," she replied. We made it to school again ten minutes before the bell rang. Mom drove us to the back of the school again; it was always quiet in the back except for the trees whistling in the wind. There was no one else around; we waited around in back on the bleachers for the bell to ring, we sat and talked.

"Well, I guess that fight messed up your swimming plans huh Reese?" I said to her smiling. She shook her head smiling back. "You know we can try to do it again today if you like," I told her looking down hoping she'll tell me yes that's what she wants to do. Just then we heard the rumbling of the bleachers as if there was a herd of bulls coming down behind us. We stood up to look; when we turned around, there was Fredrick and his friends running toward us.

They ran so fast that we didn't have time to run. We turned to look, catching us off guard they ran between the both of us, with their arms spreading out knocking us on our backs to the ground. We fell flat on our backs to the graveled pavement of the field. It was a hard fall knocking the wind out of us; we both had to catch our breath. Reese was coughing loudly; I was gasping for air. Fredric leaned into my face standing over me backward.

"You think you're her guardian angel GQ? You better be ready to call on all of the angels in heaven to protect you. You're going to need them all," he said as the bell rang. He stared down at me with his red eyes smiling. "You sucker," he said as he stood back and began to walk away. I tried to get up when he ran back putting his boots to my throat.

He spits at my face, then they all began to spit at us as they went walking away laughing.

Parent Teacher Night

Reese and I made it through that day okay, we went through our classes trying not to acknowledge what Fredrick and his friends had done to us that morning. I could tell that it was getting to Reese, although she tried very hard to get over it; I could see in her eyes that she was hurting. I sat in the back of her in English class; we had to take a test that day. She was handed the test sheets to pass around to the class. Reese got up from her seat to pass them around; she moved slowly around the tables passing them from student to student.

Fredrick and his friends mumbled nasty names at her as she passed them around. Reese put her head down in shame, I felt bad for her I knew she was still upset over what happened that morning, so I raised my hand to get permission to go to the bathroom. I had to do something to make Reese feel better; the teacher permitted me. I had to pass Fredrick to get to the door, when I passed him I stomped on his boot hard, watching to make sure the teachers head was looking at the chalk-board.

I knew that he would try and make me pay later, but I wanted so badly for Reese to believe that we will be okay; I wanted her to know that we don't have to be afraid. She looked over at Fredrick's face when I stomped on his boot; his eyes opened wide. She could tell he was surprised; she shook her head no at me as I walked by to get to the door. "Mrs. Green, I need to go to the restroom." I heard as I walked out of the door, it was Fredrick asking for permission to come after me.

I walked back through the door and went to my seat when Mrs. Green turned around from the board I was back in my seat. "Keagan, did you go to the restroom? That was a quick restroom run," she said smiling at me. "Mr. Fredrick put your hand down; you won't be excused to go to the restroom, the bell is about to ring in ten minutes, hold it!" She told him. He looked at her with a frown then over to me; he winked at me, I smiled back.

When the bell rang, everyone stood up and began walking toward the door. I noticed Reese still sitting in her seat; I walked over to her. "Reese, what's wrong, are you going to class?" "I am, I just have to wait here until the bell rings," She tells me with her head down on the desk. I put my hand on her back and began to rub it. "What's wrong Reese are you sick?" I asked her. "No, I'm just tired of being afraid, do you see how everyone looks at us Keagan, they hate us, and they hate me." She tells me crying.

"I'm tired of running from them; I'm tired of being afraid all the time." "Reese you don't have to run or be afraid, I promise I will never let them hurt you," I told her with my hand on hers. "Are you having the same troubles with them?" Mrs. Green asked. "I'm not afraid of them," I told her. "Reese came to me before class started, she told me that you two have been running from them since school began she told me that you've been trying to help her, but she's still afraid. You two need to tell your parents and the principle, maybe that will help," she said going through her paperwork.

"Have you two been starting trouble with them at all?" She asked No not at all, I told her frowning. "You should just try and avoid them." "How can we? They're everywhere," Reese told her. "Come on Reese," I whispered to her taking her backpack from the floor. The bell rang; I took Reese by the hand, walking her out. "Thank you so much, Mrs. Green." "Sure Keagan, you two are such good students, just try to avoid them, they can't tease you if they don't see you," she tells us as we walk out of the door.

When we get into the hallway, Reese was still crying. I pulled her hair back from her face; I wiped her tears with my scarf. "Come on where getting out of here; I tell her grabbing her by the arm running toward the entrance doors to the front of the school. "Where are we going?" Reese asked. "Come on don't worry," I told her running with her backpack in one hand and her other hand in mine. We ran through the schoolyard; we had to duck and hide to pass the teachers standing outside.

We crept past quietly. "Don't say a word, Reese," I told her holding her hand tighter. "Where are we going?" She asked again as we began to slow our run down to a walk when we made it through the school, we made it to the front sidewalk. I didn't want to go toward the hill near Reese's house, nor did I want to go toward mine, but I thought what would make Reese happy now. She would love to go swimming; she's been asking to go all week, I thought. I pulled Reese by the hand; we went running through the pathway toward my house.

I didn't know if mom would be home today or not when we made it there I stood across the street by the trees watching for her car; it wasn't out front, it could be in the garage. "You wait here," I said to Reese. "I'm going to check something." I walk across the street to my house. I went around to the back to look into the windows; I jumped over the fence. I looked in all the windows I climbed the tree to the balcony on top to look into moms room I didn't see her at all. It was clear; I was so happy I jumped down and took off running to get Reese.

"Come on," I said as I ran toward her crossing the street. I grabbed her by the hand running with her back across the street; I couldn't get my key out fast enough. "Keagan, are you sure, is your mom here?" She asked as we walked into the house. "No, she's not; she must have gone out somewhere." I told her placing our backpacks on the floor near the doorway. "Hold on," I told her going to the kitchen, I wanted to get an apple from the bowl, before reaching for an apple I noticed there was a note for me sticking out from the bowl.

"Hi son, I've started volunteering today, I'll be home in time to cook you dinner, don't worry." Good I thought, we have some time, I went back to the front room to get Reese she was gone. I looked all around the front room. "Reese, where are you?" I heard a noise in the living room I went in to find her standing by the window looking out. "Keagan your house is so nice, you are so lucky," She tells me. "Luck has nothing to do with it; my parents worked hard," I told her taking her by the hand. "Come on; you want to swim don't you?"

Reese's eyes opened so, wide as she smiled. "Keagan, I don't have anything to swim in," she tells me. "Follow me," I told her running up the stairs. "I have something," I told her walking into my room. "I have these and these," I said pulling shorts and tee shirts from my dresser drawer. "Just grab any one of them you think you can fit into, the bathrooms over there, you can change in there," I told her, sitting on the bed. "Thank you so much Keagan," she says running into the bathroom. She came out dressed in my gray tee shirt and my blue shorts. "Is this okay?" She asked me spinning around.

"Where do I put these?" She asked holding out her clothes to me. I took them and sat them on the bed. We went down to the backyard to the pool. Reese ran and dived in, she went underwater, when she came up, she gasped for a little air. "Keagan, aren't you coming in?" She asked me, I shook my head no, I was too embarrassed to take my shirt off in front of Reese I have that white hair over my shoulder blade, she'll probably think I'm some kind of freak. I thought as I watched Reese swimming around the pool, she smiled every time she came up for air.

"Why don't you want to come in?" She asked me floating around on her back. "I just don't feel like swimming today, I swim all the time," I told her leaning back on the patio chair. "You're missing out on all the fun," She said splashing water on me with her feet. "Hey, cut it out I said her standing to my feet laughing. "It's so good to see you are smiling Reese," I told her. She swam around the pool while I ate my apple watching as the hours went by. I had to have her come out before mom came home.

"Reese, would you like to get out soon? I can make you something to eat," I told her walking through the glass door. I needed to get her a towel to dry off with; I ran upstairs to grab her clothes also. I handed her the towel and her clothes. "What are we eating?" She asked. "I can make tuna fish sandwiches, do you like tuna?" I asked her. "Tuna, do you think we can eat something different?" She asked. "I don't like tuna at all," she said drying her hair. "Okay, how about salami, turkey, and cheese?"

"Salami huh," "yes salami, don't you like salami?" "I do," she said with a smile. "I like it with green peppers and lots of cheese," She tells me. "Is there a bathroom down here somewhere?" She asked me. "There is, go down the hall and turn to your left." She took her clothes and went down the hall. I went into the kitchen to start the sandwiches. She came back quickly dressed in her clothes, holding my shorts and T-shirt out to me. "Thank you so much Keagan, I haven't been swimming for a long time," She said to me.

"I used to swim every summer at the recreation center until they took the pool out," she said taking a seat at the bar near the kitchen. "Do you cook with your mom sometimes?" She asked. "No, I watch her though, she loves cooking, I can make a sandwich though." I told her putting mayo on the bread. "Would you like to help me? You can if you like," I told her. "I can cook you know, I cook for my dad all the time." "Oh yeah, what do you cook?" I asked her. "I cook burgers, fries, meatloaf is one of my favorites to cook," she said smiling.

"I wish my life were different; I wish I had a mom to cook for me." She said looking down at the floor. "Did your dad ever talk about her; maybe tell you what she was like before the drugs?" I asked. "She couldn't have been all bad Reese, I mean she had you." She shrugged her shoulders. "Reese do you have any other friends beside me?" I asked her. "Yes, but they all go to Madison High school; they live in the houses across the hill, not many kids live in our apartments. Before we lived here we were in a shelter downtown," she told me.

I handed her a sandwich and took mine over to the bar stool to sit down beside her. "What was that like, I mean was it scary, the shelter?" "No I had my dad, see he was on drugs too, he cleaned up when they told him he would lose me." "Does he work now?" I asked her. "Yes he was a biologist before the drugs, now he works at a pharmacy at night," she tells me. "He doesn't make a lot of money, but he tries his best to make me happy," she told me eating her sandwich twisting around in her stool. "How about you, what school did you come from?" She asked me.

"I was at St. Vincent Christian Academy." "Huh?" She said nodding her head up and down. "Why did you come over to Kennedy High?" She asked. "I don't know if I had to guess I'd say my parents wanted me to be closer to home. St Vincent Academy was so far away." I told her eating my sandwich. "How far was it from here?" "We had to cross that big bridge every day; I can't say how far, but it took us a whole hour in the mornings when I was in middle school," I told her.

"Do you miss your friends there?" She asked me. "A little," I told her getting up from the stool. "Oh, I want to show you something." I put my plate away and went over to the living room; I went to get my photo album to show her my friends. "Here we go," I said sitting back down on the stool slamming the book down on the counter." "What's this?" Reese asked. "It's my photos," I opened up the album and skimmed through them fast page by page. I didn't want her to see the photos of me when I was a small boy; I just wanted her to see the ones of me in middle school.

"Wait, wait, you're going too fast Keagan, what are those?" She asked putting her hand toward mine stopping me from turning. "No, not those" "Just one Keagan, I just want to see this page, where were you?" "We lived in Africa for a while; I don't remember it much." "Really Keagan, Africa?" "Yes my dad went there for work some time ago, okay enough let's look at these," I told her flipping the pages to my class photos from middle school. "See there I am, these are my friends, Mica, Ben, Tim, and Sharon," I told her.

"You were so funny here," she said pointing at our Halloween photos, "yes that's one of my favorites," I told her. Just then mom came through the door. "Hello son, hello Reese, how are you two doing today, you made it home before me today Keagan did you come straight home?" I shook my head yes. "I have some bags in the car; you want to get them for me?" She asked handing me the keys. "Sure, come on Reese you want to help?"

"Sure why not," she said getting up from the stool. "Be careful Keagan; I have eggs in one of the bags," she says. We went to the car to get the bags out when I noticed the guys across the street. I looked down at my watch to see what time it was they seemed to be watching the house every day around this time. It was 2:45 pm by my watch, and usually, I'd be walking down the pathway by then. I grabbed a couple of bags and Reese grabbed a couple too, we went walking towards the door.

"Keagan! One of them yelled from across the street. I looked over at them. They all waved back at me. "How are you, man?" One guy asked I didn't reply. "Do you know them?" Reese asked, "No, I don't, I don't know them at all, they keep showing up there as if they're waiting for something, do you know any of them?" I asked her. "No, I've never seen them around before" She said walking slow staring back at them. We placed the grocery bags on the table for mom. "Thank you, son, thank you, Reese; will you be having dinner with us tonight?" Mom asked.

"Mom, remember, parent-teacher night is tonight." I told her forgetting that I skipped out on school today. "Yes son, I remember I will cook dinner, we'll wait for your father, and then head over to the school," she said to me. "Reese, will your parents be going to parent-teacher night?" She asked. "Yes, there's only my dad, I believe he is going, can I call him?" "Sure honey, go right ahead," mom told her. Reese walked over to the den area to use the phone.

"Is she okay?" Mom asked. "She's fine mom, why do you ask?" "She has a couple of scratches on her cheek." "Oh she has an unruly cat," I told her looking over at Reese as she walked back into the kitchen to sit with mom and I. "Did you speak with your dad, is he coming?" Mom asked. "Yes, is it okay if I ride with you guys to the school? My dad is going to walk over; he'll meet us there." "Oh, no problem sweetheart" Mom said walking over to Reese; she put her hand on her face.

"What are you using to heal these scratches?" She asked her. Reese looked surprised at mom's intrusion of her face. "I um, no, I haven't tried anything at all Mrs. Phillips," She said nervously. "Mom's a nurse Reese she's just a little bit worried about your skin." "You have such beautiful skin I think I have something in the cabinet that you can use every day that might heal it fast; it won't leave a scar." Mom released Reese's face; she walked away to the bathroom to get Reese the ointment for her face. "Reese I'm sorry, I hope she didn't scare you," I said. Reese was holding her face she looked a bit shocked.

"I'm fine Keagan, your mom is great, I don't know what to do about these," She said to me. Mom came back in with the ointment on her finger; she carried the tube of the ointment in the other hand. "Here you go honey; this is just what you need." She began to rub the ointment on the scares, Reese stood still. "Thank you very much, Mrs. Phillips," she said. Mom handed her the ointment. "Here you go, use that on your face every night, and every morning, your face should heal in no time, and honey you should get rid of that cat." She said walking away.

"Cat ma'am?" Reese said. "Yes, the cat," I said before mom caught my lie. "That unruly cat that scratched your face yesterday" I said mom turned to me; she looked at me with a frown. "You do have a cat, Reese?" She questioned. Reese shrugged her shoulders and nodded her head at the same time. Mom walked back into the kitchen to finish up dinner. "Why did you lie to her?" She whispered so that mom couldn't hear. "I don't tell her things like that she'd worry." I told her, walking her back to the backyard to sit on the patio.

Mom was making a pasta salad my favorite, Reese rolled her pants leg up and sat down with her putting her feet back into the water. "Don't you want to join me Keagan? The water is so warm," She said grabbing my feet. "No I'm fine over here," I told her. "Do you think they'll be there with their parents tonight?" I asked Reese. "Yes, they'll all be there; no one will miss this night." "Why are you so sure?" "Because I know they will come, they might even come just to taunt us more," she said. "I sure hope they don't," I said. "Thank you Keagan, thank you again for today," Reese said smiling at me.

"No problem, I'll let you swim again if you promise me you won't allow them to get to you again, they just want you to feel that there is no other way to be. They're mean and hateful, what they're doing to people is wrong. Everyone's so afraid of them; I refuse to be," I told her. Mom called us in for dinner. "Is dad here mom?" I asked. "No son he will meet us at the school also, he's running a little late tonight," she tells me as we began to take our places at the table. "Do you like pasta Reese?" Mom asked her. Reese shook her head yes.

Mom served our food, we said grace. Reese began to eat the pasta first. "This is so good Mrs. Phillips," Reese said, "Thank you, honey." "More mom" I said sticking my plate out. "Slow down son; there's plenty more." I shook my head. "I can tell you like it," Reese said smiling at me. "It is delicious," she said again to mom. When we were finished eating dinner, I went up to my room to wash my face and change into a nice sweater.

I had to figure out how I would keep any of the teachers from telling that I was missing today, so I walked ahead of mom and explained to them why I had to leave or try to cut them off whenever they try to ask about why I was missing. I thought as I changed. "Keagan, let's get going," mom yelled up to me. "I'm coming mom," I yelled back. We left the house soon after I was done. On the way to the school, mom asked a lot of questions. "Do you like Kennedy High Reese?" "It's okay Mrs. Phillips; I love my teachers." Reese tells her.

"Does Keagan have a lot of friends?" We looked at each other; I began to laugh. "No, mom I don't have many friends." I told her as we pull up to the school, there were cars everywhere, and mom had to park far away from the school. She parked on the hill we had to walk down to the school. On the way down the hill, we ran into Mr. Hanson. "Reese it's your dad," I said as we walked alongside the people walking to get to the school. "Hey dad, dad" Reese said walking fast to get to him. He turned to her, "hey sweetie" Mr. Hanson said grabbing Reese by the waist.

"Hi, I'm Mrs. Phillips, Keagan's mom, very nice to meet you," mom said shaking his hand. "Nice to meet you too," Mr. Hanson said. We all walked down the hill together into the school; everyone met in the auditorium for the assembly with the principle first. It was so crowded we sat in the middle section where we could see the podium. By the time the principal came to the podium the auditorium was full, people were standing everywhere; there was a big crowd.

The principal started off by telling us how we would be helping our parents out by taking them around to each class introducing them to our teachers. He explained that we would have ten minutes in each class then on to the next one. Parent-teacher night was only going to be an hour long when he finished explaining everything; everyone walked out slowly toward the outside starting off to all of our classes. Mr. Hanson and Reese walked alongside us to almost every class except for the ones we didn't have together. We made it through to the first two classes without any of the teachers questioning me about my absence in class today.

They explained the lesson plans and how they graded us, mom was still waiting for dad to show up. There was no sign of Fredrick or his friends anywhere; I sighed in each class with relief. We were in the fourth period when dad showed up and behind him walked Fredric with his dad, "Mr. Hall." We were all too shocked to see that Fredrick's dad was the detective, the one who came to our house looking for Reese. When the teacher began to talk about her testing scores and how she grades, Fredrick winked at me and smiled.

We all walked out of the class one behind the other. "Did you know that was his dad?" I asked Reese as we walked. She shook her head yes, the rotation for meeting the teachers was over, and we were to all meet back at the office for another assembly with the principle and the counselors. "Welcome back." The principal said greeting everyone back to the auditorium; she introduced the counselors one by one the head counselor was to talk at the podium.

"Hello fellow parents and students, I'd like to welcome you all again tonight to parent-teacher night once again. My name is Mr. Thatcher I'm the head counselor here at Kennedy high; we welcome you and your students. I'd like to talk about peer pressure and our tolerance policy tonight if you have a little time," he said looking down at his watch then over to the principle laughing. "I won't take too much of your time tonight, believe me, I would like to go home to my dinner," He said still laughing. "I'll go fast," he promised.

He went on to tell the parents that if ever their student should have any trouble or should need to come to a counselor for help they are there for them especially if they're having problems with any teacher or grading. He also explained the peer pressure and bullying would not be accepted. While he talked about that issue, almost everyone in the room looked around laying their eyes on Fredric and his friends who were all standing alongside the walls of the auditorium.

Reese made sure she didn't look at anyone she held onto Mr. Hanson's hand and looked down at it as if she was playing around with his ring on his finger. When it was over the crowd scattered toward the entrance of the school. "Would you like a ride home Reese?" Dad asked her. "No thank you, we will walk, it's not that far away." Mr. Hanson replied. "Hello, I'm Mr. Hanson; Reese's father, how are you?" Mr. Hanson says to dad. "Hello, I'm Dr. Phillips, I'm great, we love your girl," he said smiling at Reese. "She's such a nice young lady." Dad says as Fredrick, and his dad walked pass them looking over at us from the entrance of the school grounds.

"Do I know you?" The Detective says standing next to dad smiling. "Sure, you came to my house a couple of days ago, right?" Dad says shaking his hand. Mr. Hanson grabbed Reese by the hand and walked away with her quickly not saying a word to the detective at all. Reese didn't even say goodbye; she just walked away. I stood next to my dad and mom not saying a word. "Michael, I will see you at the house." Mom said kissing dad on the cheek.

"Come on son let's get to the car," mom said. As we walked away closer to the hill, someone tapped me on the shoulder. "Hi Keagan, missed you today in Science," Mrs. Byrd said as she walked alongside us. "Oh yes, I was a bit quiet today wasn't I?" I said trying to distract her from talking any further. "No, I mean you were out today weren't you?" She asked looking confused. "No I sat in back I was there Mrs. Byrd," I told her walking faster to the car. When we made it to the car mom was so quiet. "What's wrong mom?" I asked. "Keagan, I asked you not to get into trouble."

"Mom, I'm in no trouble I promise," I told her. "I did leave school today; I had to get Reese away from there, she just couldn't take any more of it." "What do you mean; she couldn't take any more of what son?" She asked starting the car up. "Mom they pick at her, they all do, it's not fair, and no one ever sticks up for her or anyone else for that matter." I told her. "Keagan you think you can help her all the time with that? Did she tell anyone? The counselor seems to want to help," she says.

"No one helps mom; their solutions are for it to be ignored and avoided, it's impossible to ignore it or avoid it, they are in all of our classes, I can handle it my way." I told her leaning back in my seat. "Son, if Reese isn't safe at school she needs to tell her father to go and talk to them, all of them. She needs to feel safe and so do you, do you feel unsafe?" She asked me looking over at me. "No mom I'm not afraid of them, I will not allow them to make me feel afraid," I told her. "Son, please don't get into any trouble, if you feel unsafe you have to tell the counselors and teachers, make them all aware of what's going on." She tells me pulling up to the house.

"Mom I'll handle it my way," I told her getting out of the car. We walked up to the front door. "Son, do not miss any more school and absolutely no fighting." She said before turning the key to get inside the house; dad pulled up right after us. When he came in mom was in the kitchen I could hear them talking about Reese and her father. "Yes Karis, he took off suddenly after the detective showed up, did you notice?" Dad said to mom.

"I did," she said, I stood at the stairs listening to them chatting about the school, soon after I walked up to my room. I needed a shower, after showering, I went straight to bed. I lay on my bed just thinking about how weird it was that the detective turned out to be Fredrick's dad, what a real trip I thought as I laid on my bed. No wonder why he thinks he rules the world. He thinks that he can do no wrong, I fell off to sleep thinking of Reese and her father running off the way they did. They both seem to be in fear of the Hall family; I didn't notice that Fredrick had a mom around.

I wondered what that was all about; I woke up the next morning rushing again to get to Reese. Today I would ask her why she and her father walk away from the detective and Fredric without saying hello. Mom and I made it to Reese's apartment at exactly six-thirty her father was standing with her in front of the building. "Hello Mrs. Phillips, thank you for picking my Reese up," he said waving his hand at us. Reese walked over to the car slowly looking all around her as if she was confused today. "Hi Reese," I said to her as she got into the back seat of the car.

"Hello Keagan, Hi Mrs. Phillips," she said strapping her seatbelt across her shoulder. "You look nice today," mom told her. Reese was wearing a red dress with black tights it was a long shelve dress, she always wore the same boots they were furry black flat boots, and she wore her hair up in a nice ponytail. "Are you okay today?" I asked her as we drove to the school." She shook her head yes, but was very quiet. "Mom, please drop us in front today?" I asked mom.

 I didn't want to go to the back of the school in fear of Fredrick, and his friends might be there again. I could tell that Reese was feeling bad this morning; mom dropped us right at the front entrance. More parents were dropping their kids off in front there was a lot of traffic. I reached for Reese's backpack when she got out of the car, and she pulled it away. "No Keagan, I can carry it today." "Okay no problem," I told her.

We began to walk toward the hallway near the hall lockers I looked at Reese. I could tell she didn't want to be there. "Reese are you okay?" I asked her. "I'm just fine Keagan, can you stop asking me that. Today I just want to be left alone; can you do that for me? Can you leave me alone?" She asked me looking cross at me. "Sure, I can do that fine." I told her holding onto my straps on my backpack. I walked away from Reese; there was still ten minutes before the bell.

I watched her walk to her locker, she took her books from her backpack and placed them in, when she finished she stood by her locker. I watched as a group of girls walked past, they began calling her names she turned her head to her locker putting her head down. "You nasty bitch, you're as nasty as your drug-addicted mother, whore!" They all yelled out nasty things at her; she didn't turn around she kept her head down.

One of them pushed her in the back; Reese didn't budge until the bell rang. I wanted so badly to run over to her to stop them, but she asked me to leave her alone, I have to respect her wishes. When the bell rang I walked to class, Jason came up to me. "Hey man, where have you been?" He asked. "I've been here every day. I told him walking faster to make it to class. "Man, Keagan, do you play any sports?" He asked. "No, I don't" "Well you should join the track and field team, I mean the way you run around here in a hurry all the time, man you'd kill on the team."

"Yeah," I said in shock to hear him asking. "Yes man, why don't you come down after school and talk to the coach," he said walking away in no hurry to get to class. "I'll think about that," I said entering my class. Fredrick and all his buddies were standing by the door. "I wouldn't try that if I were you," Fredrick said to me shaking his head. "What, the track team?" "You better stay in your place GQ, you're pushing it." I laughed at him and sat down in my seat the teacher began our lesson for today.

I took out my class book and began to listen to the teacher. I heard in the back of me the sound of the chairs moving all around; then I felt breathing on my neck. "Hey GQ, if you decide to join track and field you'll be sorry, see I'm the captain of the team," he whispered in my ear. I smiled at him turning back away to read with the teacher. "Did you get that GQ?" He said to me. I didn't respond to him at all. I worked through class ignoring anything he said to me, when the class was over I took my backpack and walked out.

I smiled at Fredrick the whole time walking out. I will show him out on the field I thought as I walked toward my second period class. "You better think about what you're doing, GQ," I hear him saying walking behind me. I went through every class today rushing through the lessons hoping that time would speed up when I saw Reese I didn't say a word to her. I figured if she wanted to talk to me she would I'd give her a bit of space, I thought.

When the last bell rang I walked down to the field in back of the gym, I looked around for coach Bell. I found him down near the bleachers talking to Jason and the other track and field runners. "Coach Bell, I'd like to join the track and field team." I told him stepping close to the crowd. "Son, this is a serious sport you have to practice and compete, are you ready for all that?" He asked me with his hand on my shoulders. "Can you run, son?" He asked me.

I shook my head yes. "There are a lot of different kinds of running in track and field, we have the track running, distance running, and long jumping, son, which one do you think you do best?" He asked me. I took one look at him then I looked over at Fredrick. "Coach Bell, which one does he do?" I said looking Fredrick in the eye. "Son, we're a team, there are no challenges here between us at the school, we work together to defeat other teams around the county." He tells me standing in front of me looking at Fredrick.

"I know that coach, I just think I could learn from him; he's the captain, right? What is better than having the best run against the best for practice?" The coach laughed. "Son, are you saying you're as good as Fredrick Hall?" "I'm saying I can be one of the best runners for your team, if you just give me a chance," I tell him folding my arms looking serious. "Okay son, enough talk." Coach Bell stood back from me and clapped his hands. "Hall, get over here," he yelled out. "You have a challenge today."

Everyone began to chant Fredrick's name over and over as we began walking over to the starting line. We stood side by side at the line while coach stood on the sideline giving instruction and holding his pocket clock. "Okay, I'm starting the clock, on your mark get set, go" He yelled out. We took off running I ran so fast that my shoe flew off I didn't look back, I didn't look over at Fredrick. I ran and ran to the finish line when I made it there.

I leaned over with my head hung down catching my breath, Fredrick wasn't far behind, but I smiled as I was looking back, oh my goodness Fredrick was behind me. I thought as I watched him slow to a complete stop before he made it to the finish line. He was kicking the dirt around; his friends ran up to him, they patted him on the back. "It's okay, it's okay he's finished, right Fredrick?" They said looking down at me.

The coach was standing still staring at the clock. I stood up and walked over to the coach looking at Fredrick smiling. "How'd I do coach?" I asked. "Son, I am baffled you are heaven sent," He said smiling. "You beat a record time son, if you can do this for me at every competition we will be the county's champions this year," He said walking out to the gym with me. "Son, go to the office, get a permission slip filled out by your parents, make sure you have a physical, congratulation son you just became a part of Kennedy high schools track and field team."

Coach Bell was excited; he talked to me all the way to the gym. "You, be here tomorrow after school son, get you some track gear they sell it in the sporting goods store downtown," he told me as I grab my bag from the bench of the locker room. "Okay Coach Bell, I'll be here," I told him as I walked out of the gym. I did it I thought as I began my walk home. I beat Fredrick; I smiled so hard it hurt as I walked down the pathway home, there was hardly anyone left standing around you could hear the school band playing for miles they were practicing for the homecoming game.

As I walked I thought about Reese I wondered if she made it home safe, just as I reached the corner near my house. There they were again standing on the corner watching the house; I nodded my head at them as I walked past. "Hey, Keagan, good going on the team." one of the guys say to me, I walked past them not saying a word. I don't know them, how did he know about the track and field run I wondered. When I made it inside the house, mom was cleaning all around she had a woman there to help her.

"Hello son, there's a snack on the counter for you if you like!" She yelled out to me from the bathroom. "How was school?" She asked I placed my backpack on the floor and walked into the kitchen; I took an apple from the bowl. "Mom I joined the track and field team today can we go out and get my gear?" I said walking into the bathroom. Mom was showing the women where she wanted her to clean. "Track and field son, are you up for that?" "Yes mom it's fun" I told her biting into my apple.

"Mom, who is this? I said pointing down at the woman with my apple in my hand "This is Cassandra, she'll be coming to the house once a week to help with the cleaning and cooking" "Mom, you hired a maid?" I said out loud. "No son, don't call her that, we'll call her our helper, I don't like the term maid." She said grabbing me by the arm pulling me from the bathroom. "Son I will be volunteering more, and I've decided to go back to work at the hospital, just assisting your dad." She told me.

"Mom, can we go look for track and field gear?" I asked her. "Oh and wait, I have to give you something." I said running over to my backpack. "Here you go, the coach says I need to get a physical and these permission slips have to be signed soon." I walked up to my room, mom followed behind me. "Keagan how's your back; have you the black hairs come back?" "No mom," I said reaching over at my back feeling around it.

"It's still smooth," I told her biting my apple. "Let me take a look," she said coming toward me. "Can you take your shirt off for me, son?" She asked. "Sure," I said removing my shirt. Mom looked me over; she stared back there for a while rubbing her hand on my shoulder blade over and over "This hair on the right, is it always here," she asked. "Yes mom, it's always there, I tried to shave it, but it's too thick mom." I tell her rubbing the hair.

"No son don't try to shave it, it will either fall off or grow out." She tells me, "Fall out mom?" "Yes son, don't be afraid," she told me. "There is nothing to worry about okay," she said walking away from my back. She went to the door, "I'll be done showing Cassandra around in a minute, then we can go get you that gear, okay son." She told me closing the door behind her. I nod my head at her eating my apple. She opened the door back quickly.

"Oh, son, I almost forgot, Reese called she left her number downstairs. She said for you to give her a call when you get in," she smiled and shut the door. "Thanks mom!" I yelled out to her. I stood up from the bed, I don't know if I should call her back, she said she didn't want to be bothered with me, maybe I shouldn't, I thought as I stood looking in the mirror. Sometimes Reese made me feel bad, I don't know how to handle it, she likes me than she doesn't I thought.

"No, I won't call her," I said out loud, I walked away from the mirror and went down to the kitchen to see if mom finished. It was getting dark; I wanted to go and get the track and field gear. I just wanted to see what it looked like; mom was standing at the door talking to Cassandra explaining to her the rules of the house. She handed her a key, "Come here Keagan," she said to me waving me over to her form the stairs.

"Say hi to Cassandra, she'll be here from time to time, get to know her, alright son." "Sure mom, nice to meet you, Ms. Cassandra," I told her. "Alright Cassandra, I will expect you every Tuesday and some Friday's alright, have a good night." "Good Night," Cassandra said walking to the door. We walked behind her escorting her out. When she opened the door, Reese was standing at the door just about to knock. "Hello Reese," mom said surprised "Hello Mrs. Phillips, Keagan, can I talk to you?" She asked.

I didn't say a word I was just as surprised as my mom, what was she doing here? I thought she needed her space today. "Keagan, can we talk please?" She asked again. "Sure come in," I said to her pulling her in from the doorway, Cassandra walked out with mom all the way to the porch. I walked Reese into the living room. "What is it, Reese?" I asked, "You're mad at me, I know, I'm so sorry Keagan I just hate going to school, I feel bad about being there every day. I can't give one hundred percent of my effort because I'm afraid all the time.

Even though sometimes you are there to protect me I still feel bad; no one likes me Keagan." She said crying, "Reese don't cry" I told her. "Keagan, mom said standing at the door "Are we still going to the sporting goods store?" I held Reese close to me, "Reese, honey, are you okay?" Mom asked. "Keagan, what happened to her?" She asked me. "She'll be fine mom," I said to her. "Reese, do you want to come with us to look at some track and field gear?" I asked her. She stood back, "you're running track now?" She asked.

"Yes," I said smiling, "I tried out today after school," I told her. "Do you know that?" "What Fredrick's the captain of the team? Yes, I know that that's why I tried out," I told her walking towards mom. "We're ready then?" Mom asked, "Yes mom, can Reese come along?" I asked her. "Sure as long as it's okay with her dad," mom said pointing to the phone on the counter. Reese knew to go call him to ask if it was okay. When she finished talking to her dad we left to the sporting goods store. It didn't take long for mom to get downtown.

It was so busy downtown; it took a long time to get a parking space, mom circled the parking lot for it seemed a long time to wait for space when she finally got one, we parked in the lot near a huge mall. "Mom can we walk around a little," I asked her. "Sure Keagan I'll be upstairs," she told me. Reese and I walked all over the mall there was a lot of people from our school there almost in every store we ran into someone from the school. They were all shopping for homecoming dresses and suits. "Oh Keagan, I forgot, homecomings in two weeks, are you going?" She asked.

"Only if you are," I told her smiling. We walked into a department store where we ran into the girls who called her names earlier that day. They were looking at dresses with their moms. Reese was so afraid that she started to walk out, I grabbed onto her by the waist "No," I whispered "You don't need to walk away, let's have some fun." I told her pulling her toward the dress section near them. "Reese, do you like this one?" I ask her, holding up an orange dress it was like an orange tutu, it looked like something Reese would wear.

She smiled at me; I began putting different dresses up to her body and spinning her all around. We watched them try on their dresses; they looked over at us from time to time giving Reese a mad look each time. "So Reese what do you say?" I asked her holding up a nice red and orange dress up to her body. "Would you like to go with me to the homecoming dance?" I asked her. Her eyes opened wide as if she was surprised at my question. "Keagan, you want to go with me?"

"Yes really, why not?" I asked her. "Are you sure?" She said covering her smile. "I'm sure, will you go with me?" I asked her again. She shook her head yes. "Okay then, pick a dress any dress, and I'll wear a tie to match it," I told her smiling. She grabbed the dress from my hand the girls stared at us with angry faces. They whispered and pointed at her. I made Reese smile and there was nothing they could do about it I thought as we stood in line to pay for the dress. Reese was as beautiful as anyone else; she just needed to be reminded of that at times.

We paid for the dress and went looking for mom. She was in the department store upstairs looking around, she had a hand full of items that she was about to buy. "Mom, do you need those things?" I asked her; she shook her head yes. "Son, did you find the sporting goods store down stairs? I don't see any bags from there in your hands," She said frowning at me. "I'm going now mom," I said laughing grabbing Reese by the arm "Meet you there in five minutes," mom said going to the register to pay for her things. Reese and I walked down to the sporting goods store, when we got there, we found that most if not all of Fredrick's friends work there.

I opened the door for Reese to go in, immediately she stepped back grabbing the door handle, she turned around to me. When I looked at the register there was one of his best friends Skylar, he was in his sporting goods work shirt with a nice pair of khakis. He wore his hair straight up in the air; he had pierced ears, I pulled at Reese to come back inside, she tugged at my arm to loosen my grip. "No Keagan, I can't," she said snatching my hand from her shirt and walked away. I followed her to the other side of the mall.

"Reese, Reese, don't be afraid, you can't allow them to make you run away all the time, stand up to them, and they'll back off." I told her. "What good is it doing for you Keagan, you're standing up to them, they still come after you, don't you see, they don't care, they won't stop," She said sitting on a bench outside of the electronic store. "Reese I have to go there to get my things, my mom will be there looking for me, please come with me" I asked her holding out my hand, she looked at my hand rolled her bag up with the dress in it and smiled.

"Okay Keagan," she said getting up to walk with me, we went into the store to meet mom she was standing around looking for me when I went in. "Son, where have you been?" She asked me when I approached her. "I've been looking for you mom," I told her smiling. "Keagan, I just seen you walk in the door." "Yeah mom I was searching around for you out there I told her looking around, we began to walk around the store looking for the gear I needed.

"Hi, can I help you find something?" Skylar asked us. "Sure we're looking for track and field gear." "Um let's see if you just follow me back here, I can show you some things that you might need to have." He said walking ahead of us, Reese and I kept looking back and forth at one another in disbelief; this was the same guy who spit on us the other day, the same guy who jumped from the trees with Fredrick to surround us. We couldn't believe our eyes and ears.

We walked to the back with him, I picked out a couple of tracksuits and track shoes to run in, he pointed us to the best ones to buy, by the time we went to pay for everything Reese and I were in a state of shock. "Thanks for your help, Skylar." Mom said looking at his badge. "You've been very helpful," she said taking the bag away from him. "No thank you, have a nice night," he said as we left the store. Not once did he utter any bad words at us nor did he look as if he was angry.

"That was pretty interesting," I said when we got inside the car. "Yes, that was," Reese said. Mom drove us home slowly when we were close to the house she asked Reese if she wanted to be dropped off, she shook her head yes. We drove to her apartments, I walked her up to her door, we said good night. Mom waited in the car when I came back she was waving a bag around in the air, I made it to the car. "Keagan, Reese forgot this," she said "Oh no!" I said grabbing the bag, running back up through the hall.

I made back to her door when I got to the door she was standing with the door cracked talking to someone. I stood back to wait for them to turn around to see who it was then, I went up closer to get a better look. She was standing there shaking; the guy had his foot in the door I ran upstairs. "Can I help you?" I said to the guy, "Yes go away," he said. It was Mr. Hall, the detective. "Reese, what's wrong?" I asked her; she shook her head holding it down, tears were streaming from her face. "Sir, what do you want from her?" I asked handing Reese her dress. "Sir, you should probably leave, her father's not home," I told him.

"Son, you should probably go home now," he told me, sticking his arm out waving me away with his hand. "Reese shut the door, go inside," I told her. She pointed down at his feet. "Sir, please go away until her father comes home," I asked him again. "Son, go away now," he said in a demanding voice. Just then, mom walked up. "Keagan, what's going on?" She asked. "Mr. Hall is here with Reese, he won't leave, her father is not here," I told her. Mom walked up to the door. "Mr. Hall what can I help you with?" As mom walked up she closed her eyes as if she felt pain; mom didn't say another word until she opened them.

"Mr. Hall, you should leave now." She told him walking to the door stepping in between it and Mr. Hall. She took the doorknob in her hand and moved Mr. Hall's foot with hers shutting the door closed. "Mr. Hall, if you want to come back and speak with her father, do so later; now she's alone, you need to leave," she told him leaning against the door. "Mrs. Phillips, I'm a detective I go in where I please." He flashed his badge in moms face, "You see this?" He said, "This is my pass to anywhere I please."

"Maybe it is Mr. Hall, but not without a warrant, do you have one of those?" Mom asked him. Mr. Hall stood back staring at mom. "You like trouble ma'am?" He asked her looking angry. "You just made some," he said walking down the stairs; he stared back at mom shaking his head. Reese cracked the door opened, "Thank you, Mrs. Phillips," she said sniffling she was still crying. "Reese, what does he want from you?" Mom asked her. She shook her head and shrugged her shoulders.

"Listen, Reese just go inside don't open the door anymore for anyone okay." Mom told her, "Keagan, let's go." We walked down the stairs and through the dark hallway, as we walked closer to the entrance to the gate we felt a strong wind of cold air blow past us that cause us to shiver. We began to walk faster to get to the car, when we got in mom turned the key fast and drove off. We made it home to found dad in the kitchen cooking dinner for himself. I walked up to my bedroom.

Mom went into the kitchen with dad; I stood on the stairs to listen to her explain to dad what happened tonight. "Hello Michael," she said with a kiss on his cheek. "Hello baby, where have you been?" He asked,

"Your son decided to join the track team at school, we went out to buy gear for him." "Looks like you purchase more than gear." he said laughing at mom. "Yes, but Michael the strangest thing happened when I dropped off Reese, that detective was there. I don't know what he wanted from her or her dad, but it looked as if he was intimidating her. She was crying; he had his foot stuck in the door to keep her from closing it." She told him as I started to head up to my room I hear her say.

"He's not who he says he is Michael, he's something evil," she tells him. "Something evil, I know baby, I've known for a while, he knows who we are also. Baby, he doesn't care, he'll come out soon." Dad said to her I could hear them talking about this man who claimed to be a detective, funny Reese said the same thing about him. He's not who he says he is; I guess he isn't if mom knows. I went to my room and began to study, after studying I ate dinner. I went straight to bed after that.

I couldn't wait to see Reese tomorrow I thought when I fell off to sleep. The next day I rushed to school hoping to see Reese. I looked for her in all of my classes, she wasn't in any of my classes today, so I waited for her at her avid class at the end of the day she wasn't there. I went to the class to ask her teacher. "Did Reese Hanson come to school today?" I asked her. "No, she did not, son, she's out sick, I hear," the teacher told me. I walked home worried about her I thought maybe I should go to her house to see how she was, but I didn't want to go unannounced.

I was walking home when I remembered that I had track and field practice today, I was so worried about Reese today I'd forgotten all about it. I turned and ran back to the school I ran in through the back way to be at the gym. I went inside the gym locker room to change my clothes, after changing, I ran out as fast as I could. Coach Bell was standing on the sidelines giving training instructions.

"Phillips hurry up, get out here," he said blowing his whistle after screaming at me. I ran onto the field and began training, I looked up into the bleachers as I did jumping jacks, and Reese was sitting in the bleachers. She waved at me; I waved back. "Keep your eyes on the field," coach Bell said out loud. After the jumping jacks, we were to run a circuit, we ran and ran for about an hour. When it was over, I rushed to change so that I could go and talk to Reese. When I came out of the locker room, she was gone.

I walked all around the school looking for her before I left. I even went halfway up the hill; there was no way she could have gotten home that fast. I thought as I began to give up I started walking home after looking everywhere for her. When I made it to the corner by my house, I saw her sitting on my porch waiting for me; I crossed the street quickly.

"Reese where were you today, why didn't you come to school?" I asked her. She shrugged her shoulders, "hey can I swim in your pool today?"

"Sure, only if you tell me why you didn't come to school today." "Okay it's a deal," she said standing up to go inside with me. We walked into the house together; I placed my backpack on the floor near the door and went into the kitchen to get an apple from the bowl. "Do you want one?" I asked Reese. "No thank you, I just want to swim," she said removing her shirt. She was ready to swim she had a bathing suit underneath her clothes. "Go on then," I told her walking her to the back glass door.

"Thank you Keagan," she said diving into the pool, I sat down on the patio chair eating my apple. I waited for her to come up for air. "Reese what is it with you, why are you missing school, you know that if you miss too much school, you'll receive bad grades right?" I told her, she was floating on her back. "I don't care anymore Keagan, I just want it to end," She said turning over going back under water. I stood standing over the water waiting for her to come up. "What do you mean you want it to end?" I asked her.

"I mean I don't care to be here anymore, you wouldn't understand Keagan because you don't know." She turned over and swam away from me; I heard something crashing down in the house. I dropped my apple and ran into the house, when I got inside there were dishes scattered all over the floor. There were glasses flying all around the room; I went into the kitchen to see where it all was coming from there was no one there when I ran back outside to get Reese she was gone.

Homecoming Dance

After that day I didn't see Reese, she didn't come to school the next day nor did she call me. Weeks went by before she turned up at school; she came back on a Wednesday. I was walking through the halls of school when I saw her in passing; it was like I hadn't seen her in months. "Reese!" I called out to her as she walked the hall; she turned to me looking confused. She didn't speak to me she walked past me with two other girls from class. I had almost every class with her; I tried not to worry too much about what was wrong with her.

Maybe she just wanted to hang out with the girls in her class; she wanted friends so desperately. I decided to wait for her to approach me; I didn't even talk to her in class. She chose a different partner in science to work with, at school everyone was talking about the homecoming dance. Who was going with who and what they were wearing, Reese had been giving me the cold shoulder for so long that I forgot that I'd asked her to go to the homecoming dance?

There were decorations everywhere, and the nominations were up all over the cafeteria for homecoming king and queen, I dared to say nominate me. I was standing in the hallway looking at the nominations when Fredrick came up behind me and slapped my glasses from my face onto the ground. He just flung his arm between the bulletin board slapping them off He laughed loudly walking by stepping on them. I looked down at my glasses after I watched him get to the end of the hallway I leaned down to get them from the floor.

"Hello, I hear someone saying to me from behind. I stood up quickly; it was Reese, she was standing behind me looking over my shoulder trying to see the board. "Bad break huh," she said smiling. I took one look at my glasses and back at her, "Yes, awful break," I told her putting the broken pieces into my pocket. "So, how about that?" She says pointing at the bulletin board. "This is Kelly my friend and Sara my other friend and Rose," she said introducing her new friends. "Nice to meet you all," I said waving my hand at them.

They all gave me a smile and a wave "So is our name up there?" She asked smiling "Uh no, I told her smiling back "You know we're lucky to be invited to such an event," I said to her smiling. "It's nice to see you, Reese," I told her nervously. "You too, Keagan," I began to walk away; I didn't want to overstay my welcome. Reese seemed to be different, more open, and happy even. "Hey Keagan, we're still going, right?" She asked me.

I hesitated, stunned and flattered at the same time. I shook my head yes. "Good, I really can't wait to wear that dress," she said walking away with her new friends smiling back at me. I went through the whole day thinking about Reese; I could hardly concentrate after the last bell rang I went straight to track practice. We warmed up for fifteen minutes before we had practice runs. Coach Bell always put me up against Fredrick or one of his buddies. Troy was fast, not as fast as me, but he did give me a run for my money at times, today I didn't feel up to running at all.

I allowed Fredrick to beat me when it was time for me to do a practice run with Troy I stretched before going to the starting line. I knew he would beat me today if he gets the chance and coach would allow him to start at the races on Saturday. I began to stretch when I noticed Reese sitting in the bleachers again when she caught my eye she waved at me smiling. I looked up through the sun and waved back, her friend Kelly sat close to her. I really couldn't allow him to beat me now; I shook my body going over to the starting line.

"On your mark, get set, go!" Coach Bell said out loud, holding his watch in his hand. I took off like I had a fire to my back trying to impress Reese and her new friend. I ran so fast I didn't even notice that Troy never left the starting line. When I made it to the finish line, I jumped up and down feeling great because I knew I'd beat him there, after catching my breath. I noticed Coach waving for me to come back to the starting line, I was so embarrassed I looked up in the bleachers, and she was gone, thank goodness, I thought as I walked back over to Troy and Coach Bell.

"False start son, you need to pay attention, you're a great runner, you just need to focus, son." Coach Bell said patting my shoulder; I looked around all over for Reese to find her standing at the gate entrance to the field, she waved at me smiling. "Son, let's try this again this time focus." Coach Bell said holding his watch in his hand. We were at the start again; coach blew his whistle, Troy took off ahead of me as fast as he could, I let him get ahead halfway through; I sped up and took off leaving him to try and catch me.

I made it to the finish line quickly coach came over to me smiling looking surprised. "Mr. Phillip, my goodness, you keep that up, we are for sure to going to be the season's champions at the games this year," coach Bell was so impressed he walked me all the way to the gym, talking about getting ready for the races. I hardly heard a word he said I was thinking about Reese the whole time; after getting dressed, I walked out of the gym I stood on the field looking around.

Maybe Reese would show up again, and we could talk about the homecoming dance, but I did not see her anywhere. I began to walk home; I walked fast trying to make it before mom when I reached the corner, there was the group of people who were always there after school. This time I'm going to ask them, I won't walk by and wonder anymore, this time I will ask them straight up, I thought as I walked toward them trying to build up enough courage to say what was on my mind.

"Excuse me," I said tapping one of them on the shoulder. "Hello Keagan, how are you today?" The guy said turning around to me. "I'm good, why are you guys here watching my house so often, what are you waiting for, do you live around here?" I asked them. The others looked at me smiling "Man Keagan, we're not doing anything here just watching the view, we live all around here," he said waving his hand all around. "Why do you stand here in front of my house? What are you waiting for out here; do you have any friends around here?" I asked them.

"Yes plenty of friends, you should see them all," the tall guy said to me smiling. "Just relax man we're not planning to rob anyone or anything like that," he said smiling at me. "Why don't you guys go somewhere else to hang out?" I said to them. "We would, but the view is so nice from here," he said looking directly at my house. I walked away from them with no questions answered; I wondered if they were the reason that happened in the house with the dishes.

Maybe they were there in the house, or maybe they're trying to scare us. I thought as I walked up to my door I looked back at them, they waved at me as I took out my key to unlock the door. I dropped my backpack on the floor when I got inside and went to the kitchen for an apple. I went back over to the window to see if they were still there, I peeked out just enough to look out only to find them still hanging out there. I stood there watching them they talk to one another laughing when they caught me watching they waved at me smiling. I shut the curtains shaking my head; I took my backpack and went to my room.

I sat at my desk and began to do homework. I had so much to do; the house was so quiet I turned on the music loudly so that I could break the silence in the house. I began working on my homework, eating my apple; I took my English homework out to start on it first. I worked on it for a while until I began to hear noises. I reached over to the radio to turn it down; I listen for where the sounds might be coming from, I opened my door. No sounds were coming from the hallway; I poked my head out to hear better, but there was nothing.

I shut the door and sat back at my desk, there it was again this time it was clearer, it was water splashing I quickly went over to my window to look out at the backyard. I see water splashing all over the sides of the pool, but there didn't seem to be anyone swimming. I looked up at the trees maybe something fell in the pool from the trees; I shut the curtain and started to walk over to my desk when I heard another splash. This time it was louder than the last time, I ran to the window. I snatched the curtain back to look out, this time I waited.

I stood looking out with the apple core hanging from my mouth; I leaned closer to the window to get a better look. The water was splashing everywhere, but there was no one, I took the apple core from my mouth and threw it into the trash I opened the door and ran down the stairs. I bet it's them; I thought as I dashed to the back glass door, I slid the door open to go out. As I stepped out, there was more splashing, Reese suddenly popped up from the water her red hair plastered to her head. She soared up from the water; I ran over to her. "Reese!" I yelled out.

"What are you doing here?" She swam over to the edge of the pool holding on to the edge catching her breath, "You told me I could come over and swim anytime, so here I am." She said wiping her face with her hand taking a deep breath. "I didn't think you'd mind," she said floating off to the other side of the pool. I followed her by walking on the edge of the pool. "Reese, what's going on with you, I mean you've been acting odd these days, are you doing okay at home? Is it Mr. Hall and Fredrick again?" I asked her.

I stood over her watching as she swam around the pool, she didn't answer any of my questions. She went under the water and came up only to come up for air. "Reese, will you answer me please?" I said to her getting down on my knees leaning over the pool edge. She swam up to me, "Well, which question do you want me to answer first?" She asked me smiling flipping onto her back. "Answer all of them, if you can," I said to her. "All of them at once, Keagan, you are funny," she said looking at me while she float with her head turned to me upside down. "You look funny upside down Keagan," she said smiling.

"I wanted to hang out with my other friends," she said. "I didn't know you had other friends," I said. "I didn't have any at first, but now I do, are you upset that I'm not hanging out with you instead." She said kicking water up over her head splashing it all over me. It was so cold. "Reese that water isn't heated, you should probably get out its too cold," I told her. "No, it's just fine, I needed to cool down, after watching you run like that, hey," she said flipping over really fast splashing me again with water.

"You are fast Keagan; you beat Troy, you know Troy and Fredrick are the fastest runners in the county as far as I know." She said looking surprised, "Do you think you can compete at the meets?" She asked me excited. "I will, Coach Bell already told me that he wanted me to compete," I told her. "Now, will you get out of there? It's too cold, you'll get sick," I told her reaching for her hand. "Okay," she said taking my hand, she pulled my hand fast, and I flipped over into the pool. I went all the way under, the water it was so cold, when I came up I looked all around, and Reese was gone again.

I went back underwater to see if she was underwater hiding for me, she wasn't there. I looked around the back yard to see if maybe she was sitting by the door, she wasn't. I swam over to the edge of the pool and got out. I was soaked, it was so cold I rushed over to the glass door, I pulled the door, and it was locked, oh no, how, I thought I didn't lock it behind me, there was no way I could have, it only locks from inside. I went over to the side door of the house to see if maybe there was a chance that it was unlocked. It wasn't; I walked back toward the door.

I stood there thinking; I am going to freeze out here, just then I tried one last time this time the door slid right open. I went inside, what was that? I thought while holding the door handle. I flipped the lock over twice while I shivered dripping wet. I opened the door and closed it, back and forth I couldn't tell why it was locked, just then I heard crashing coming from upstairs. I ran up to see where it was coming from, as I approached my room door, I could see something moving all around inside it was a shadow.

"Hello, is there anyone there?" I asked cracking open the door. I cracked it just enough for me to go in halfway, "Hello, who's in here?" I said out loud, I looked around the room, my closet door was opened wide, and my clothes were scattered all over the room. I stepped all the way in; I shouldn't be afraid, I thought as I entered all the way. My closet door was wide open; all of my clothes were off the hangers. I reached in and turned on the light and out pops Reese from the mountain of clothes. "Reese, you scared me!" I yelled out jumping back.

"What did you think that door locked on its own, why don't you have anything that I can wear besides sweats?" She asked me holding up a pair of my sweatpants, "why don't you wear what you came over in?" I asked her, "I swam in them, they're all wet," she tells me holding her shirt by the bottom with water dripping off it. "You're going to have to help me clean this all up," I told her, picking up the clothes from the floor. "I was planning to clean it all up, Keagan," she stood up from the pile of clothes on the floor and began to help pick up all the clothes. I grabbed a shirt and pants to change into I was still freezing, I went into the bathroom to change while Reese stayed picking the clothes up from the floor.

When I came back into the room, Reese was in my sweats and a T-shirt. She was hanging clothes back on the hangers, "I'll help you hold on a second," I told her hanging my wet clothes over the desk chair. "Where're your wet clothes, I can throw them into the dryer with mine if you like." I told her, while we worked on the pile of clothes, "Can we do this first?" She asked me, struggling to finish putting them away. She handed me her wet clothes, I flung them over the chair and continued to working with her to clean the clothes up. When we were done we walked down to the laundry room. "Would you like a snack?" I asked her; she walked beside me shrugging her shoulders.

I shrugged my shoulders back at her, "is that yes or no?" I asked her smiling; she shrugged them again, I placed the clothes into the dryer and escorted her to the kitchen. "Are you starving?" I asked her, "Yes I am," she said smiling at me. "I was thinking; maybe we can have some chips and cheese sandwiches, do you like cheese sandwiches?" I asked her. "I'd rather have something hot," she said. "Something hot huh," I said as I look through all the kitchen cabinets trying to search for something hot to cook up. "Well, we have, hot cereal, and hot tea, and we also have noodles, you can cook in a bowl, they're hot," I told her shaking the plastic bowl of noodles.

"I like those," she told me pointing at the noodles. "Noodles in a bowl it is," I said turning the tea kettle on to heat the water. "Keagan, do you think that I'm pretty?" Reese asked. I was stunned by this question, what should I say? I do think that Reese is pretty, but do I tell her? I thought as I went to the refrigerator to get us a drink. "Keagan, did you hear me?" She asked me. I leaned into the refrigerator door with my back to her. "What was that?" I said as I came out with a bottle of juice.

"Nothing, never mind," she said reaching over to the bottle of juice. I turned around and walked to the cabinet to get our glasses to drink out of, that was close I thought as I reached for the glasses. "Do you think I'm pretty?" She said again as I walked over to her with the glasses, I looked at her. Okay, here it goes, I thought as I walked over. "Yes Reese, I do, I think you're beautiful." I tell her trying not to look her in the eye; I sat the glasses down. I began to pour the juice into the glasses. "Reese, why are you asking?" I asked her.

"I just wanted to know," she said taking a sip from her glass. "Why, don't you think you're pretty?" I asked. She shrugged her shoulders again "You don't, or you do, what does that mean?" She shrugged her shoulders again. "Reese, do you think you're pretty?" She didn't even shrug her shoulders this time she just continued to sip from her glass with her head down. I didn't know what to do; I was all ready to laugh when I saw that she was crying, her head hanged down with her wet red hair hanging over almost into her glass.

"Reese, what's going on; are you okay?" I asked her, walking over to her pulling her hair back. "Keagan, I don't know," she said leaning her head back wiping her eyes with the back of her hand. "I thought I was okay until I overheard them talking about me." "Talking about you, what were they saying?" "It was nothing I guess; they were just saying they hated the color of my hair and the way I dressed." "I thought that you were all friends, don't they call themselves your friends?"

"No Keagan, I was introduced to them by Fredrick, he told me to hang out with them, and they'll leave you alone." "What do you mean Reese?" "I mean he'll leave you alone, he won't fight you anymore, and you and your family will be safe from them." "You're talking crazy Reese," I told her shaking my head. "No Keagan, you don't understand, you keep getting into it, and it's only making him angrier. He wants his spirit to cover the grounds he walks on." "His spirit," I say to her shrugging my shoulder.

"I think you have a serious fear of Fredrick and Mr. Hall for no reason." Just as I was getting up from the stool to walk over to her, the doorbell rang. I walked over to the door and peeked out "Who is it?" I yelled out through the door; there was no answer. "Who is it?" I said again; no one said a word this time, I went for the curtains. I peeked out; there was Mr. Hall, I opened the door. "Can I help you, Mr. Hall?" I asked with the door cracked.

"Are your parent's home?" He asked. I shook my head no. "What time do you expect them back?" He asked. "I don't know when they'll be back, maybe this evening," I told him closing the door slowly. He was trying to peek inside; I quickly cracked the door. "I'll tell them you came by, sir," I said as I completely closed the door. "Don't you see," Reese said coming from the kitchen. "They know I'm here," she said crying.

"So, they know you're here, so what, why are you upset?" "I can't be here; I can't be around you or your family." She said holding her hand to her mouth; she sat down on the living room couch. She put her hands on her cheeks and leaned over crying. "I can't believe this, I can't," she said standing up; she began to pace back and forth on the living room floor. "Reese, please be still, are you kidding? All this talk about spirits, Mr. Hall and Fredric, come on Reese, it's not that bad is it?" I asked her; she began to talk to herself, mumbling while she paced back and forth. I got up to go into the laundry room to get her clothes, when I came out she was gone.

"Reese!" I yelled out, "Reese where are you?" I walked all over the house; I went into the kitchen, then up to my bedroom, I even rechecked the patio. She was gone. I held her clothes in my hand; I went to look out of the front window to see if she was there. I looked out; she wasn't there she was gone, with three days left until the homecoming dance I wasn't sure whether Reese would still want to go. I took her clothes upstairs with me and folded them up I placed them on my desk. I sat down to continue working on my English homework, I began to work, and suddenly I hear loud crashing noises.

I stood up from my seat quickly; I ran downstairs to see where it was coming from, I went to the kitchen first. There was nothing; I backed out still hearing the loud crashing when I turned to the hall toward the living room. I thought my eyes were deceiving me, oh my goodness, oh no, I thought all of the furniture in the living room was turned over, and the windows shattered. The lamps were turned over; it was all in the middle of the room turned over in a circle. I went to the window to see if someone was there, mom is going to have a fit I thought as I looked out of the window.

The wind was blowing the curtains outward toward the front yard; it was like we were struck by a series of storms that blew out every front window. I turned around looking at the circle where the furniture was; I shook my head as I began to pull the pieces of furniture out of the circle. I took piece by piece back to its place in the living room. After getting it all done, I went back to the curtains and pulled them in. I tied them to the hooks near the window; I sat down on the couch waiting for mom, what would I tell her? I thought.

I had no explanation for the widows; she's going to think that I had a party or something, and maybe I won't get to go to the dance after all. I'll just tell her that I came home and found the house this way; I'll tell her that it was some crazed kids from school; I didn't know what to say. I waited for what felt like hours for mom to show up, I fell off to sleep. Finally, she did show up; I was lying on the couch holding onto one of her throw pillows. "Keagan, Keagan, what happened here?" She asked me.

I rolled over to her. "Huh, what is it, mom?" I said covering my eyes hoping that what I had fallen to sleep to was just a bad dream. "Keagan, what happened in here? "Keagan, why are all the windows broken? She asked running over to the windows. She crept through the broken glass trying not to step on it. "Mom, I came home and found the windows broken," I told her standing up. "Also the furniture was all thrown in the middle of the room," I told her. Mom grabbed the broom from the closet and began sweeping.

"No mom, I'll finish it," I said taking the broom from her hand. "Keagan, did you see anyone, was there anyone hanging around out- side?" Mom asked I shook my head no; I watched as mom went to the phone. She went to the cabinet to get the yellow pages to call someone to come out to fix the windows. I listened in while I was sweeping until I noticed through the window Fredrick and his friends from school coming down the pathway, laughing and talking.

They stood at the corner staring over at the house I stood at the window watching to see what they would do; next, mom came back into the living room she was still angry. "Keagan, can you tell me again how you think this happened? They will be here soon to repair the windows." She told me going over to each window spreading the curtains out for closure. "I'll take these down when they get here," she said looking out of the front window at Fredrick and his friends. "How long have they been here?" She asked me still looking out at them.

I shrugged my shoulders, "sit down son," she said waving me over to the couch to sit next to her. "Son, what's been going on at school, what's been going on with that guy?" She asked I turned away from her looking toward the window. I shook my head no, " Keagan; you have to tell us what's going on at school with those guys, we might be able to help." She said looking me in the eye. "Mom, nothing is going on, Reese says things, but mom I can handle it I'm not afraid of them, I'm not afraid of any of them." I told her spinning the broom around in my hand.

"Keagan, I understand that you're not afraid, my brave little young man," she said holding my chin up. "Mom, I'm not afraid of them, nothing about them scares me, it scares Reese and almost everyone else in the school, but not me." I said standing up holding the broom looking toward the window. Mom stood up next to me with her hand on my shoulders she turned me to the window. "Keagan, look out there, come," she said taking me closer to the window to look out.

"Keagan, son, look out there, look closer at those boys and girls, what do you see in them that you've never seen in anyone else?" She said holding my chin to the glassless window. I stare out at them; I didn't see anything different except around them was like a dark blacken fog.

"Mom I don't understand, what are you telling me?" I asked her, "Keagan, do you remember the time before you turned 13? Do you remember not waking for a while?" Mom asked I shook my head no, "mom," I said turning away from the window.

"I remember that time it was like I was in a dream, I didn't want to remember what happened to me then. I just know that whatever it was it made me stronger I'm not afraid of anything. I thought to myself as mom was looking out at the window I could tell she knew I was lying about not remembering what happened back then. I took the broom back into the kitchen and sat down on the stool and took an apple from the bowl.

"Keagan, listen to me," mom said coming toward me to get the broom, "you promise me, son, if there is something you can't handle, please come to us, we can help you," she said. The doorbell rang, mom walked over to the door, I snuck away to my room. It was the window repair guys. "Mom, call me if you need me!" I yelled at the top of the stairs; mom was too busy talking to the men that she didn't even hear me. I went into my room and sat down at the desk with my apple to finish my homework; I began to work on it quickly finishing up English.

Then math, I was working on science when the phone rang. I jumped up to get to the phone on the hallway amour. "Hello," I said quickly catching it before the person hung up. "Hello Keagan, it's me, Reese," she said whispering. "Yes Reese, how are you?" "I'm okay I guess, Keagan, do you think I can come over and stay with you and your family. My dad left town for a while, and I'm alone," she said whispering. "I don't know Reese; I'd have to ask my mom and dad," I told her.

"Who do you usually stay with when your father leaves?" I asked "My dad never leaves Keagan, he left me a note saying that he would be back, there was an emergency with his grandmother in Kansas," she said to me. "He had to fly out immediately; there was a storm out there," she said. I didn't know what to tell her; I never had anyone sleep over before, especially not a girl, mom and dad might not have it, I thought. Reese sighed I didn't say another word, "Keagan, are you going to ask them or not?" She asked me, I hesitated.

"Uh, Reese I'll ask my mom now hold on a minute" I told her going to the stairwell to yell down to mom. I can hear the men working on the windows loudly; mom stood close by watching them work "Mom is it okay if Reese comes over to stay a few days? Her father had to leave town in an emergency!" I yelled. She didn't respond so I yelled again, this time I yelled louder. "Come down here Keagan; I can't hear you!" She called out to me "Coming mom!" I yelled down to her.

"Reese, please hold on for a second I told her placing the phone down and ran down to mom, when I reached the bottom stair she stopped me. "Don't come down any further, I don't want you to get near the window glass," she said with her arm across my chest. There was window glasses sitting near the stairwell awaiting the men to place them in. "Mom, Reese's father had to go to Kansas for an emergency, and she needs a place to stay for a while. Is it okay if she stays with us?" I asked her.

"I don't know Keagan; I'd have to call your father and ask," she said. "Well can you mom, she needs to come over soon," I told her holding on to the railing. "I will call son, tell her you'll call her back soon," she says walking back into the living room with the men. I ran back up to get the phone; I put the receiver to my ear and Reese was gone, there was just a dial tone, I hung it up and tried calling back, the line was busy. I went back down to mom.

"Mom, you can call dad now?" I asked her as I walked into the living room to see how the windows were coming along, mom went to call dad. When she came back she gave me a thumbs up "It's okay mom" I said beginning to run back up the stairs to call Reese "Keagan, she can sleep down here in the guest room," mom told me in a stern voice "I know mom," I told her running up, I was excited to tell Reese I tried calling her again, but the line was still busy.

I wonder what happened; maybe she's on the phone with her dad, maybe she had to tell him what was going on, I thought as I held the phone. I would hang up and try again over and over again, the line stayed busy for a while before I gave it up, I thought I'd try one more time when the window guys left, it had been hours. I picked up the receiver and tried again, again there was a busy signal. I went down to see the windows. "Keagan, did you tell her?" Mom asked as we looked over the windows.

"I tried, but I keep getting a busy signal mom." "Maybe she's talking to her dad." "Maybe so, but it's getting late Keagan," mom said looking out of the window. "You're sure her father was already gone?" She asked me. "Yes, mom that's what she told me" I said to her standing to go to the window to look out for her. "Do you think we should go by and check on her?" I asked mom as I approached her at the window, mom turned to me looking worried.

"Keagan, we can go to her house, but I want you to stay in the car," she told me. "No matter what you hear, you stay in the car don't get out even if you hear yelling and screaming." She tells me grabbing her keys from the desk. We rushed out to the car mom drove there quickly as the sun was going down. When we arrived in front of the building the street lights were just coming on, the lights lit up at the front entrance to the apartment building. Mom turned to me with her hands in her lap she took a deep breath, "Keagan, you remember what I said?" She says staring me in the face.

"Don't you get out of this car, no matter what" She says again putting her hand on the door handle to open it. "I won't, mom I'll stay put, I promise," I told her leaning back in my seat. I knew that mom would be okay she didn't seem to be afraid of anything. I watched as she walked toward the front entrance of the apartments. She went inside, and down the hall, I watched until I no longer could see her in the hallway. I was anxious, but I couldn't get out, I looked down at my watch over and over counting the minutes and seconds that mom was gone, it had been well over fifteen minutes.

When I saw her again, she walked up to the car looking all around the building first before opening the door; she was carrying a bag with clothing falling from it as if she'd unzipped it and checked it quickly before closing it back. She got into the car and threw the bag into the back seat. "Keagan the door was open; the apartment was a mess, there was furniture turned over, things everywhere, I don't think she's safe where ever she is." "Mom, should we call the police?" I ask her, worried.

"No, Keagan, I don't want to alarm them if there's nothing wrong, we should take a good look around here for her, and if we don't come up with anything, then we'll call the police." Mom told me starting the car; we drove down the back alley looking to see if Reese would be there anywhere, then back down near the store and the back entrance of the building. She was nowhere to insight. "I'm going down the alley one more time; then we'll head home, maybe she'll call us again." Mom says making a turn back toward the alley; as she turned to go back to the alley, mom had to brake hard to avoid hitting three guys running from the alley.

They were laughing and jumping all around talking about something they'd done in the alley; one of them stared at mom as they ran past us. "We'll just go down there one more time," she said driving down the alley slowly, she slowed almost to a complete stop as we went further and further down the alley, she put her bright lights on. "You look on that side, and I'll look on this side," Mom said driving slowly "Mom!" I shouted. "Stop, please stop," I saw a girl lying on the ground ahead of us, I couldn't make her face or hair color, but I was afraid it might be Reese.

Mom pulled up beside her, and we both exited the car at the same time rushing over to the girl, we went up close to her and stood over her. "Reese, is that you?" I shouted, looking down at the girl she was wearing black stockings a red dress, she had boots with laces tied all the way up to her knees. She wore a black jacket with silver zippers all over it, and her hair was coal black, mom reached down and tapped her shoulders. "Young lady, are you okay?" She asked I stood there watching I didn't want mom to turn her over; I was afraid that she would be hurt.

"Keagan, we have to turn her over," she told me looking up at me. "I shook my head no and turned my back to her; I could hear mom pulling on her black leather jacket to turn her onto her back as if she was very heavy. I kept my back to mom until I heard a loud scream, mom had turned her over. I turned to look at what was going on, it was a girl her face was cut up, and blood ran down her face. She reached out to mom with her hands covered in blood.

"Keagan get in the car!" Mom yelled out to me, as I walked toward the car I began to see dark shadows coming quickly toward mom. She waved her hand to me to the car. "Keagan hold your head down toward the seat!" She shouted, soon she was surrounded by the dark shadows, I closed my eyes and hide only peeking up to see if mom was still standing as soon as they approached her. I put my head down to the seat of the car; I could hear the girl still screaming, it was awful. I could hear the gravel on the ground in the alley moving all around; they were growling and screaming horribly at the same time.

I was worried about mom; I was sweating with my head down not knowing if she was okay. I had to peek up, when I did, what I saw startled me the dark shadows were all around mom, but mom was not afraid, and to my surprise, she stood to face them with what looked like wings with lights on the tips of them. I was so stunned; I couldn't take my eyes off her until she looked at me, they attached her one by one.

I didn't know what to do my shoulders began to burn as if someone was cutting them open tears rolled from my face as I leaned my head down to the seat of the car, mom was out there alone, what do I do? I thought as I listen to the screaming and hollering of the chaos outside the car. I heard what sounded like the ground crack underneath the car to what sounded like thunder. I put my hands over my ears to escape the sounds I closed my eyes I felt as if my shoulder blades were opening I reached with one hand to feel them, there were hairs forming. Fine hairs like knives I quickly put my hand back to my ears I began to pray for mom.

"Lord, help her, please help mom." As I prayed, I began to get visions of my parents fighting in a church while I watched surrounded by eight small bright lights circling me. I saw myself watching them fight dark shadows from the stairwell in my house. I was not afraid in the vision, but confident enough to help them I saw myself taking control of the situation they were in, and the dark shadows went away. I took a deep breath, opened my eyes and removed my hands from my ears, it was quiet, no more sounds or movements coming from outside.

I dared to look up in fear of my mother hurt, but I had to check to see how mom was, I began to peek up from the seat only to find mom sitting in the driver seat I jumped, startled to see her there. "Mom, are you okay?" I asked her, "I'm fine son, just fine." She said turning the key to the car we drove off from the alley, mom was quiet. "Mom, will the girl be okay?" I asked her as she drove silently into the darkness, she didn't say a word we were almost home when she stopped alongside the street and looked at me.

"Keagan, you need to know something about us, I can't explain to you all that has happened in the past, but you need to know what could happen in the future. There are some things that we cannot explain about this life we have, do you understand son?" She asked me looking stern; I shook my head yes. "Your dad and I have been waiting for you to ask us things, we would like to know what you're feeling. We don't want you to be afraid of what you have; some supernatural things could happen."

"Things that others around you don't believe in, things they say you shouldn't believe in, we believe in God and the Holy Spirit, not everyone agrees with our belief, especially other spirits. Son, there are other spirits among us, and they don't like us. They cannot control what we have, so they try and defeat us, but you must always keep your faith in God strong. Trust that he'll come to your rescue in giving you the greatest strength to fight them," she told me.

"Mom I don't know what I believe in, I can't say I believe what you do." I told her looking out the window into the darkness. I didn't want to talk to mom about what I felt at the moment; I just wanted to find Reese and get home. "Keagan, do you have any questions about what just happened back there?" She asked me as she began to drive off. "No, not about that anyway, just about Reese, do you think she's okay?" I asked her as mom drove off to the house. "I don't know son, it looked like her house was broken into and a fight happened there, it didn't look good son, but we'll find out, hopefully, she'll call us soon." She said driving slowly to the house.

When we arrived home detective Hall was standing on the porch waiting for us, mom got out first. "Keagan you stay put," she said in a stern voice as I started to open my door. "Do not get out," she walked toward Mr. Hall. "Can I help you, detective?" She asked him with her keys in her hands; the detective looked crossed at mom. She walked right up to him to ask him again, "Mr. Hall what is it, is there something I can help you with?" She said again this time he shook his head yes.

"Ma'am, I need to know if you've seen Reese Hanson, the young lady who hangs out with your son, we've been trying to get in contact with her father." I wanted to get out and talk to him, but there was darkness all around him. Mom waved her hand at me. "Get out!" She yelled as she walked toward the house. "Son, don't say a word to him!" She yelled out to me as I opened the car door to get out. "We haven't seen Reese, we've been looking for her all night, but I know that you know that already!" She yelled out to Mr. Hall as we walked in the door of the house.

"See you, Mr. Hall," I said as mom closed the door, when we got in I went to the kitchen for an apple I sat at the table while mom went for the phone. She pushed the button for the answering machine, we listened for Reese, but she didn't leave a message. There were a few hang-ups, but no messages at all from her. While mom went to the window, I went into the kitchen to grab an orange and a drink of water. I was leaning over the sink with the glass when I noticed by the pool there were wet footprints as if someone had just gotten out of the pool.

I looked around so intensely that my cup overflowed with water, it could be Reese I thought, but I couldn't go out now, mom would be upset if we were looking for her and she turned up in the backyard. "Keagan, what's wrong?" Mom asked turning the water off grabbing my cup from me. "You're making a big mess," she said pouring the water back into the sink. I turned to her. "Nothing mom," I told her shaking my head. "I'm going to go up and take a shower," I told her backing out of the kitchen.

"Don't be long dinner will be ready in a few," she tells me rambling through the pots and pans underneath the countertops. I ran upstairs; I know that if that is Reese I would see her better from the window in my room; my shoulders were still burning from the hairs that had come out earlier that night. I took my shirt off as I approached my room door; I scrambled around the room rushing to the window. I pulled the curtains back and saw no one. The ground by the pool was wet with water; the footprints faded as I scanned the poolside looking for any signs of Reese.

She wasn't there at all; I lay on my bed hoping that she would call soon just as I began to smell the food cooking I fell off to sleep. "Keagan, Keagan, wake up son, it's time for dinner," it was my mom; the room was even darker than before. She reached over me to turn on the light over my bed. "You need dinner son," she said patting my back I sat up "Mom did Reese call or come by?" I asked. Mom looked back at me as she walked toward the door.

"No, she never called, she never came by, we can't do anything about it son." She said walking away, I stood up from my bed and went to the window to look for any signs of Reese. I sighed there was still no signs of her; I went down to have dinner, it was just mom and me tonight. Dad was working late; I sat at the table, I didn't want to talk to her about anything, I barely could concentrate on the meal. "It smells delicious mom," I told her looking down at the food on my plate.

"Why don't you taste it, maybe it tastes as good as it smells," she told me with a smile. "Mom, I really can't eat now, is it okay if I just have my shower and go back to sleep?" I asked. "Son, you have to eat dinner, you need nutrition son, what's wrong? I know you're worried about Reese, son, but it's really out of our hands. "But mom, what if something terrible has happened? Like the girl in the alley, what if she's in trouble?" I said sitting still waiting for her to answer back.

"Son, I know you can't help but to worry, you have to trust that God will take care of her," She told me. I look at mom I know that there is a God; sometimes I cannot do anything but pray to him for help myself because mom and dad believe that he can make things change. I'm having a hard time believing that he helps everyone. Reese and I have been getting pushed around at school now for months, and we're good students. We are not troublemakers, but it seems never to stop, and now Reese is gone missing, is God going to rescue her? I wondered as mom went on eating, I took a few spoons of mom's dinner, ate some veggies and gulped down my juice.

"Mom I love you," I told her going over to her to kiss her cheek. I knew if I did that she'd excuse me with no questions about finishing dinner. "Good night mom," I told her going up the stairwell. I took my shower and lay on my bed. I got up to put some Vaseline that mom had in the bathroom and rubbed it on my shoulder blades. I stood looking out of the window, I sighed. Where could Reese be? I know how much she wanted to go to the dance, why would she run away? She knows that she could stay here; mom and dad already gave the okay. I thought as I stood there rubbing the Vaseline on my shoulder.

I went over to the mirror to have a look; they were all bruised and red they burned like fire. There was a cut where the hair surfaced, big cuts as if my shoulders ripped apart. After rubbing lots of Vaseline on them I put a shirt over my arms, I lay on my stomach until I fell off to sleep. I dreamt that I was back in the tunnel again. I dreamt of all that I'd seen that night with mom with her wings. I was fighting to get out of a tunnel again, but this time I was surrounded by Fredric and his friends.

They all looked as if they could eat me alive; I woke up just as the fight began. My heart was beating so hard and so fast that I could feel it, I could hear it. As I sat up on the bed, I was so angry sitting up; I heard tapping at the window, Reese, I thought, I quickly went to the window to look out again. It was only the tree branches hitting the window I looked down by the pool. The ground was dry; leaves were blowing everywhere, I walked away going to the bathroom, I stood over the toilet to relieve myself after I finished I went over to wash my hands.

I looked in the mirror as I washed, I was startled by what I saw, so startled that I jumped, and my hand flung out and hit the toothbrush holder of from the counter. Oh my goodness, my eyes, I stared at my eyes they were white the pupils were completely white with a dot of darkness inside them. What had happened to me in that dream must have turned them. I closed my eyes over and over to see if they would change back, but they didn't I went to my room quickly so that mom wouldn't come out to check on me and see my eyes.

I went over to my mirror on my dresser; they were the same, I sat on the edge of the bed. What do I do now? I wondered after a while of checking over and over again; I decided to lie down. Maybe they'll go back to normal if I go back to sleep I thought. I closed my eyes tight hoping to fall asleep quickly I placed my hands over my eyes; I can't go to school with my eyes like this. While I was waiting with my eyes closed tight, I heard a tapping noise as if someone was throwing some-thing at the window.

I sat up; there was the noise again this time there were four taps like rocks hitting the window. I sprang to go to the window; it has to be Reese, I thought to open the curtain. I looked around outside near the pool; the tree branches were still hitting the window I didn't see a thing other than the branches. I began to shut the curtains and there she was, she stood under the umbrella near the pool she was all wet up. I knew I couldn't go to her while mom and dad were sleeping I waved to her to go near the glass door.

It wasn't going to be an easy task, but I had to get her inside it was a little cold out. I could tell she was cold she held herself as if she was shivering, I checked my eyes, they were back to normal. Then I twist the doorknob, creeping out into the dark hall trying not to make any sounds. I went to get Reese; when I made it downstairs, she was standing still at the glass door waiting for me with a smile on her face. I quietly turned the alarm off and slid the door open gently; I put my finger to her mouth as she began to speak, pulling her in by the arm.

I turned the alarm back on and escorted her upstairs guiding her through the darkness of the house. As soon as we made it up to my room, I heard moms door opening I shoved Reese in by her waist. "Keagan, is everything okay?" Mom asked me peeking out from her door "Everything fine mom," I told her "I was just downstairs getting a glass of water," I told her closing my door. "Sorry about the noise," I turned the light on to see Reese's face.

"Where have you been? We've been worried about you, my mom and I went looking for you," I said in a whisper. She stood back from me and shook her head as if she couldn't say a word she turned her back to me and began to remove her shirt. "Reese, what are you doing?" I asked in shock, she back up to me. "Look at me," she said whispering. I turned my head to her, Reese was bruised all over her back had black and blue bruises, covered from her hairline to her waistline.

"Oh no what happened?" I asked her. She shook her head with tears flowing from her eyes. "Keagan, can I use your restroom?" She asked. "Sure; I'll get you something to wear to bed, are you hungry?" I asked her. I didn't know what else to say; she wouldn't tell me what happened. I handed her an old pair of sweats and a T-shirt; she lay across my bed weeping until she fell asleep, I sat beside her holding her hand, the next day I explained to mom and dad where I found her, they didn't ask her any questions.

She stayed there with us until her father came back from his trip. We didn't go out; we just hung around the house. When I went back to school, Reese didn't show up at all and the dance was soon approaching. She did call me to tell me that she would meet me there even when I asked to pick her up. "Mom wants to take pictures," I told her, but she still refused to come by the house. When Friday came, I got all dressed up in my tux I wore an orange and green tie with a black suit, with long coattails. Dad insisted that I wear a hat with a black brim and an orange and green silk trim.

My shoes were Stacy Adams, with black, orange, and green specks. I looked like someone in the old mob movies; I knew that Reese was wearing the dress I bought her. I wanted to see her before the dance so badly; I was so anxious, my first dance I thought as mom drove off to the school. When we arrived the parking lot was full, there were so many people taking pictures, laughing and running around. I didn't see Reese anywhere.

"Mom, I will see you later," I told her as I got out of the car. I watched her drive off as I stood on the sidewalk looking around for Reese. I waited and waited, staring down at my watch from time to time. Soon I was the only one outside of the auditorium I could hear the music playing loudly. Just as I was about to give up and go to the dance, I saw Reese down the hill. Wow, I thought as she walked up to me slowly. She took a spin with each step smiling until she landed right into my arms.

"I bet you thought I wouldn't show," she said to me smiling, I smiled back; she looked so beautiful that it took my breath away. The dress was orange and green with some red it wrapped around her small, slim body just right, I took her by the hand, and we walked into the auditorium together. When we stepped in, it seemed that everyone watched as we took our place on the dance floor. The music was fast, but I held her hands to mine and moved with her slowly. We danced and danced until we were both tired and thirsty, when the music stopped we walked over to the refreshment table for drinks, she held her drink while I drank mine.

"Keagan, thank you," she said looking me in the eyes. "No problem, Reese." I told her throwing my cup into the trash. "I have to use the restroom, be right back," she says walking away. I watched the dance floor waiting for Reese to return. She took a long time, after a while I began to worry, especially when I saw Fredric and his friends going toward the bathroom hall. I rushed back there to see what was going on; once I made it through the hall, I saw the girls surrounding the girl's bathroom laughing.

As soon as I walked toward them they all turned to me laughing; they covered the entrance to the bathroom. As I walked closer they spread apart allowing me to push through the crowd. I walked up to the door to look in, and there was Reese covered in multi-colored bubble gum they had spit bubble gum all over her hair and her dress. She was slouched over the stall of the bathroom floor on her knees trying to cover her body. I ran to her.

"Who did this?" I yelled out to them; I tried turning her over to see her face, they all stood in the doorway laughing. Once I turned Reese towards me, she started screaming. She stood to her feet kicking off her shoes, and she ran to the door pushing through the crowd. I ran after her trying to catch her; she ran so fast into the darkness of the street I couldn't catch her. I began to run toward her house knowing that that's where she would turn up.

I ran as fast as I could hoping to catch her there, when I made it there I knocked on the door breathing heavily, trying to catch my breath. When Mr. Hanson answered the door, he was startled to see me there. What is it Keagan, where's my girl? He asked me looking around for Reese. "Mr. Hanson," I said trying to catch my breath. "I was there, she ran." "Wait a minute, wait, take your time." He said grabbing my shoulder, "ouch," he said pulling his hand away from my back, I stood back.

I could feel my shoulder splitting open it hurt so bad, I stood up straight and took a big swallow. "Mr. Hanson, Reese was attacked in the girl's restroom at school, and then she ran off. I don't know where she went, I tried to follow her, but she got away from me." I told him quickly. "Okay son, don't worry," he said shutting his door, he ran down the stairwell fast almost falling forward. "Reese!" He yelled out as he ran.

Boy, could he run fast I thought running behind him. I ran behind him for a while before I lost him in the darkness also, soon everyone would be coming out of the auditorium. I was so upset about what happened to Reese I could hardly stand it; I wanted to fight for her. I wanted to get them all I couldn't follow Mr. Hanson, so I began to make my way back to the front of the school. The front of the school was filled with students waiting for their parents.

Cars were pulling up alongside the schools parking lot picking up students off and on. I waited for mom or dad to show up for me I began to get angrier as I waited. Soon, Fredrick and his friends showed up "How'd you like that bubble gum?" Fredrick said to me laughing. I took one look at him; I could see a dark shadow covering him and his friends as they walked towards me, he walked up close to my face.

"Don't have anything to say GQ?" He said with a smile. I turned my back to him because I couldn't take any more, I couldn't respond, I was so angry, I folded my arms across my chest and waited for mom, I could see her pulling up alongside the curb. Fredrick came around in front of me and slapped my hands from my chest, "You are a sad piece of crap, you suck at life, die, you freak." He said to me staring into my face. Mom honked her horn over and over to draw everyone's attention. I pushed my way past Fredrick, when I got into the car she drove off quickly. "What was that all about, Keagan?" She asked me.

"Nothing mom, everything's okay," I told her as she drove toward the pathway where the trees were. I spotted Mr. Hanson walking with his hand on Reese's shoulder. "Mom, stop the car!" I yelled out. She stopped suddenly; I jumped out quickly. "Reese, are you okay?" I asked walking in front of them. "Son, everything will be fine." "Well at least allow us to give you a ride home," I told him standing in front of them with my hands extended out. Mr. Hanson looked ahead and saw that Fredrick and his friends were still standing in front of the school, and then he looked at mom.

"Is it okay?" He asked. Mom shook her head yes, they got into the car and we drove off to drop them off in front of the apartment building. After dropping them off, mom began to question me about Reese. "What happened, son?" She asked. I explained to her what happened to Reese as she drove. She shook her head. "Poor girl," she said as we pulled up to the house. What a night, I went straight to my room. I lay across my bed with my tux on; the night would have been perfect until they ruined it. Why? I thought as I fell off to sleep thinking of what Reese must be feeling. I thought of her in that dress, just the way she smiled that night with her hair pulled back from her face, she was stunning.

To Church on Sunday

After that night I didn't see Reese at all, she didn't come to school. I would sometimes go to her house after school, I'd stand at the door knocking, but no one ever came. I spent most of my days at lunch eating under a tree in the courtyard of the lunch area. There were a couple of classmates who would eat with me at times. A girl named Rae and her friends Spencer and Ian; they wouldn't talk much, only to tell me how much they admired my courage to stand up to Fredric and his friends. I would tell them that they needed to do the same thing, they needed to stand up to them all of them.

Fredrick would watch me from across the way; sometimes he'd walk past us and throw his trash at us. His friends would follow him throwing their trash as well. I'd get up and throw my trash back at them while Rae and Spencer even Ian would sit back and watch with fear in their eyes. "Don't, Keagan, you don't want to throw it back at them." Rae would say out loud as they walked past, I would throw it anyway. I was not afraid of Fredrick at all, and after what he did to Reese at the dance I wanted so badly to get them, all of them.

I've been thinking of ways and things I can do to get them. My mom said I shouldn't and to let God handle it, but I know that I could handle it my way. "Don't be afraid Rae, that's what they want you to do, they want you to fear them," I told her standing up staring at Fredric as he walked by, he smiled with a smirk on his face as he stared. I knew how I would repay him, I know that he wants to go to the championship races with the track team, but it will not happen for him.

I thought as I stared across the courtyard at him and his friends, yes that's what I'll do, I will run him right out of his leading start I thought, picking up my bag walking toward class. "See you guys later," I say to

Rae and the others as they followed me into the halls of the school. We all separated, I noticed ahead Reese waiting for me at my locker. "Hey," I said waving my hand hello to her, "Hello," she said with a smile as I walked up to her. "What are you doing here, where have you been?" I asked her eagerly waiting for an answer.

"I've been trying to go to another school outside the district, after the dance. My father decided that it wasn't a safe environment for me here at Kennedy High," she said smiling. "Keagan, I just can't take anymore, I'm tired of all the teasing." She was wearing a hat with a little of her hair hanging out of it. "I had to cut most of my hair off because of the bubble gum," she said sadly. "I'm sorry Reese, I should have been there for you, and I knew that they would try something. I just didn't know they'd do it at the dance. I'm so sorry, but Reese," I said in a whisper pulling her to the side as the second bell rang everyone else went into their classes there would be no more warning bells.

"I have a plan to get them back," I told her smiling. She covered my lips with her hand "No Keagan, there is no getting them back, you promise me you'll leave them alone" She said staring into my eyes. "Keagan this is much more than it seems, you have to stop trying to get them back, you can't win and even if you do they'll come after you and your loved ones they'll get you," she said with tears in her eyes. I pulled her hands away. "Reese, I'm not afraid of them, and you shouldn't be either, they are just like us," I told her.

"No Keagan, they are not at all like us, and the more you try and get them back." She stopped chattering, Fredrick walked up to us, and he was chewing what looked like a huge wad of bubble gum. He came right in between us and turned to Reese; he blew a bubble so big in her face that some of it stuck onto her eyelashes. I grabbed him by the collar of his leather jacket and swung him down to the ground. "You stay away from her!" I said to him pointing down at him. His friends helped him up from the ground; he began to laugh as he walked up to my face.

He put his arm up as if he would hit me, but I didn't flinch at all I stared him in the eyes. "You get a pass, for now, GQ," he said to me laughing. "Come on," he called out to his friends they all looked back at us laughing, there was darkness following all around them. I was so upset; I just wanted him to give me a reason to hit him, I was ready. "Close your eyes," I told Reese; she was reaching for her lashes to remove the gum from them. She stared at me speechless looking afraid.

"What's wrong? They're gone, don't worry, I'll help you get the gum off," I told her. She stood back away from me still speechless. "Reese, what's wrong?" I asked her. "Keagan, you're eyes." She said pointing to my eyes. Oh no, I thought, they turned again. I put my head to the ground, "Reese, I will see you later," I told her walking away quickly to get to the restroom before anyone saw me. I began to run as soon as the hallways were clear. When I got into the bathroom I ran into a stall at the end; there were two other people in the restroom.

I couldn't go out to look until they were gone, I waited to listen for the doors to open and close. I closed my eyes opening them and shutting them over and over hoping that they would change back. If they don't I have to find a way to go home before anyone else saw me, I thought as I waited. I wanted to beat Fredric today at practice; I needed to be there to beat him today. I sat down on the toilet seat taking long deep breaths hoping they'd change back. I could hear the bell ringing outside the door, and the halls were filled up with students walking by, some of them stopped in the restroom.

They came one after the other some of them even pulled on the door handle of the stall I was in, but it was locked. A few of them looked under the stall; I hit the door and yell out "I'm in here!" They'd say sorry and stand in front of the stall; I wasn't planning to leave at any time soon. I needed to get a look at my eyes before going back to class. Soon after the bell rang, I rushed, and I heard silence. I came out I checked under all the stalls before going over to the mirror. I walked up to the mirror to look; I closed my eyes tight, and then opened them with a deep breath.

I placed my hands on the counter, thank goodness; I said to myself, they were back to normal. I grabbed my backpack and began to walk out, I reached for the door handle, and it opened up swinging outward. Fredrick and his friends stood before me. "Where are you going GQ?" He asked trying to grab hold of my backpack straps. I pulled away from him, "I'll see you on the field today Mr. Hall," I say to him pointing my finger as I walk away.

He winked his eye at me as the door closed; I went to my class sneaking in while the teacher had her back to the class. She was standing in front of the chalkboard; I sat down behind a tall guy name Sam. I took my notebook and pencil out quickly trying to be as quiet as I could, as soon as I began to write what was on the board the bell rang again. I tried to get it all down as the classroom cleared for the next class; I stuffed everything into my bag trying to get out of there before the other bell.

Just as I made my way to the door, the teacher stopped me. "You owe me a little time after school Mr. Phillips," she said pulling her glasses down staring at me, I shook my head yes. "But, Mrs. Byrd, I have track team after school today, I promise when I finish I'll come right in, is that okay?" I asked her holding my backpack looking at her with a smile on my face. "You can do two extra pages of homework and an essay," she said with a smile. "Now go on before you're late to the next one." "Thank you so much, Mrs. Byrd, I promise I'll do it all," I told her running to my next class.

After GQ I'll have to go straight to track practice. I couldn't wait to get there. I rushed after GQ to change into my track gear, I was ready to get him, I ran down to the field to warm up with the coach. He was waiting anxiously with his whistle and stopwatch. "Keagan, today you can't make any mistakes, competitions next week." He said as I stretched my legs out, everyone on the team began to warm up. Fredrick warmed up alone near the bleachers; he winked at me the whole time smiling. Soon it was time, we all lined up side by side at the starting line, and the coach stood on the side with his clock and whistle.

"On your mark, get set!" He said out loud; I looked at Fredric making sure he stared back I winked my eye at him with a smile and with the blow of the whistle we were off. I allowed Fredric and the others to get ahead of me for at least a half of mile. Just when they thought I couldn't catch up to them, I soared toward the front of them running to the sound of the coach yelling for me to keep going. I ran past Fredric leaving him in the wind when I reached the finish line I jumped up and down sweating and panting to catch my breath.

The coach came over to me, rubbing my back, smiling, "son, you did good, you are going to the competition, you'll be my front-runner," he told me with a smile. "Thank you, coach, I won't let you down," I said to him standing straight up. I put my hands on my hips and turned to the bleachers to catch my breath; I saw Reese sitting in the bleachers with her girlfriends watching. She didn't wave at me; she just stared down at me in almost a glare, I waved to her to get her attention. "Reese!" I called out loudly.

She stood from her seat stared down at me as they walked away. I didn't let that make me feel bad, Reese does this a lot. I thought as I walked back to the gym to change my clothes. It would have been the perfect day until I heard what sound like thunder; the lockers began to move all around me shaking, like they were being knocked around the locker room. I hurried to tie my shoes as I sat on the bench, I grabbed my bag and stood up to run out of the locker room when I started for the door the lockers began to all fall over hitting each bench in a row.

Beside them smiling, stood Fredrick, he was angry; he walked to-ward me pushing every locker down with ease. It was if he didn't even touch them, they fell to the ground as he walked. "You plan to run as the front-runner GQ? What if you can't? What if you have no legs?" He yells out to me; I began to go to the door with my bag. "You still don't get it, do you GQ?" He said now standing in front of me, blocking the doors entrance; he came close to my face. "GQ you need to understand you're not helping yourself at all," he said staring me in the face.

"I can't keep reminding you of these things; I am not going to keep repeating what I tell you." I looked Fredric in the eye as he stared into mine with nothing but anger in them. I could see that he was holding back, there was a dark shadow standing over him, I closed my eyes. I didn't want to get angry with him; I didn't want to allow him to believe that I was afraid or even intimidated by what he was saying or doing to me, I smiled at him.

"Listen, Fredrick, let me by, you don't understand me, I am not afraid of you nor will I ever be, do what you have to. I will not fear you." I told him pushing him in the chest with my bag in my hand. I walked past him looking back at him as I went toward the entrance of the school. He stared back at me frowning this time, "GQ this is my last warning to you, you'll regret ever crossing me." He said as I walked toward the track to the back gate. I didn't think that it was over by far, I could see all of his friends coming from everywhere covering the school grounds.

They stood at the gate watching me, they stood by the locker room of the gym, and they were also standing by the trees outside of the gates. I strolled watching for them all around me. They didn't turn away they watched as I left the field. I didn't allow myself to think of them anymore; I wanted to see Reese. I began to walk toward the hill to her apartment building when mom pulled up. "Get in Keagan," she shouted. I stood by the car holding on to my backpack straps. "Mom, I was going to see Reese, I'm going to do some homework with her." I told her leaning into the car window.

"No; son get in the car, we have to get to the church today we are going to meet the preacher. We're meeting your dad there, get in," she said frowning at me. I got in the car; I placed my backpack on the floor. "Mom, why are we doing this now? I thought we didn't have to go to church to love God, isn't that what you've always taught me?" "Yes Keagan, I have always taught you that, but it wouldn't hurt our family to become a member to the fellowship from time to time," she told me as we drove into the traffic.

"Mom I think this is silly, why should we fellowship with anyone? Do you believe all that stuff about God?" I asked her. "Son, I do and you should too, he's real, you'll find out the truth soon enough," she told me as we pull up to the church. I reached for the door handle to get out. Mom grabbed me by the hand. "Wait, son, wait just a minute, your dad is not here yet," she said me holding my hand. "Look around son, is there something familiar about this place to you?" She asks me looking toward the church. I followed her looking over at the church; it didn't look familiar to me at all it was a little far out from everything.

It was white with a fence all around it, and lots of windows were the sun could shine in I guessed. "Mom, I don't understand why I had to come along with you to meet the preacher. I'm a kid what would he have to say to me but the same things, God is watching over me, and I should be careful what I do, right mom?" I said to her looking her in the eye. "Son, I know it's a hard thing to do, to believe in something or someone you can't see at all, but I want you to start learning."

"Start reading the Bible, it is sometimes a mystery to all people especially children, but son you have to admit, there are some great things all around us, which came to be, no one knows how they came to be or where they come from right? Don't you ever wonder?" she asked looking around. "Like the birds that fly look how many different species there are, and the trees look around son, they are all different. Can't you see, God doesn't do anything twice it's always different. Everything is different you know, there are people of all kinds, and different places, this place."

"What he's given us is a beautiful place, we all should be happy to live in it," she told me staring out of the window soon dad pulled up. "Mom I will believe in what I see, when God starts doing something different for me than I'll change how I feel, until then I don't know mom," I told her getting out of the car. "Hello dad" I said approaching him, he put his arm around my shoulder "Hey son how's it going today, how was the track meet" He asked as we walked toward the church "I will be starting at the track meet competition dad, I beat everyone, I'm the fastest on the team now" I told him as we entered the church.

Dad reached his hand out for moms and kissed her hand. "How are you, pretty lady?" He asked her holding onto her hand, mom blushed "I'm okay Michael," she said with a smile. We entered the church together with the doors closing behind us as I stood in front of the pews looking down at the podium where the preacher would preach I began to have a vision of something that happened there, it was mom and dad fighting there was darkness all around them and I was left on the floor of the church, there was lights, eight of them all around me.

I blinked my eyes as I saw before me the dark shadows attacking mom and dad. "Son, son are you okay? Dad asked tapping me on the shoulder. I stood back "Yes dad I am, can I sit down somewhere?" I asked. "No son the preacher's in the back, come on let's go and get this over with, I'm hungry," he said smiling. I followed mom and dad into the back room where there was an office. An old man was sitting at a desk with a smile on his face; he was wearing a robe with a purple scarf across his neck, he had a gray beard.

His head was completely hairless it shined as if he'd put oil on it before the meeting, he stood up as we approached the desk. "Hello welcome, welcome, please have a seat," he said coming around to pull a chair out for mom. "Hello, son," he said looking at me as if he saw through me. "Boy oh boy, does the Lord our God have plans for you," he said going back around to his seat on the other side of the desk. "It's so nice to see you all back in the house of the Lord," he said smiling back at us.

"It's been awhile, I'd like to talk to you all about some of our services before we get into membership if that's okay," he said looking at dad. "Oh sure no problem," dad said. "We offer a great teen program here we do bible studies field trips, we offer after-school programs and clubs for all ages. We also have our teen work for seniors program, where we pick a teen member of the congregation to go out to our senior church center and help out for a day, either by reading, or feeding or serving dinners to the seniors of our community. That one is one of my favorites," he said handing me a pamphlet.

"Please, look it over," he went on talking, telling mom and dad all about the service times. They offered an afternoon service and a morning service after all the talking he gave us a tour of the church. It was a nice size church there were statues and pictures of everything biblical that you could imagine. With lots of colors, my favorite was the statue of Mary crying it stood taller than all the others, and it made me think of what she must have been thinking with her eyes to the clouds like that. When the tour was over, he shook dad's hand and moms too; he grabbed me and hugged me. "Welcome son," he said with a smile grabbing my hand.

"By the way, my name is Pastor Kenneth Hall, welcome," he said smiling. Mom and dad walked toward the entrance of the door to leave the church; I followed slowly behind them looking back at all the statues and crosses in the church. I could see Pastor Hall standing from afar as I left watching, waving with a smile, far behind him stood darkness. I wondered if he saw what I did as he turned to go back to his office they were all around, but behind him was a bright light.

I walked out of the church to the car, mom and dad were already sitting in the car when I stepped out of the church, and they were having a conversation about Pastor Hall. "He's the detective's brother," Mom said to him grabbing at his hand "Do you think he knows," she asked dad "Knows what?" I asked as I sat in the front seat with mom. Dad leaned into the window helping mom to the driver seat. "I'll see you back at the house," he said kissing her on lips. "Son, don't worry about it, we're just talking," he said walking back to his car. Mom drove off, "Mom, what was he talking about?" I asked.

"Nothing son, what are you hungry for tonight?" She asked changing the subject. I shrugged my shoulder, "I think I'll have an apple for dinner," I told her knowing that she'd get angry. "Come on Keagan, what do you want for dinner?" "I'll just have this apple mom really," I said to her grabbing an apple I headed up to my bedroom. "I'm expecting you down here in an hour to eat dinner, son!" she yells as I walk up the stairs. Dad walked into the door as soon as I made it to the top of the stairs. He looked up at me as he walked in.

"Hey, Keagan, where are you going?" He asked me throwing his coat on the table near the door. I held my apple up to the air and smiled at him. "Just having an apple for dinner dad," I said walking to my room door. I had lots of homework to do I thought as I sat at my desk. I wondered about Reese; I wondered what she thought of the race. She watched so intensely from the bleachers, but she didn't say a word as she left the field, Fredrick seemed angry, maybe she was afraid to congratulate me while he was there, I thought as I began to do my work. I put on my headphones to listen to some music I liked to listen to it while I did homework; it was a little soothing at times.

It took me an hour to do history and an hour to finish up English, I began to beat my books to the sound of the music in my ears as I finished up, when I saw what looked like a dark shadow walking past the window in the light. I took my earphones off my ears and walked over to the window. I looked out to see if someone was there, there was no one. "Keagan!" mom yelled. "Dinners ready son, get down here!" She yelled from the bottom of the stairway. "Coming mom," I yelled back walking away from the window throwing the apple core into the trash.

I ran downstairs to the kitchen for dinner. "Hey, wash those hands," dad told me pointing at my hands. "You think I can have a piece of cake after this mom" I told her running for the bathroom to wash my hands. When I came out of the bathroom I saw Reese standing at the door "Mom; no one got the door?" I asked. "The doorbell didn't ring; I didn't hear anyone knocking." Dad said; I looked out through the glass at the top of the door at Reese, then I walked over to the window and peeked out. She had her finger hovering over her lips to shush me.

I cracked the door open. "Hey Reese, what's happening, what are you doing here?" I asked her she leaned into the crack in the door and kissed my cheek and with a whisper she said. "Congratulations to you Keagan, good luck at the meet." She walked down to the bottom of the stairs and waved goodbye, I was still in shock of her kiss. She looked around in both directions and began to run toward the trees in the pathway. I shut the door and walked over to the kitchen table; I sat down and began to reach for my drink.

"So, someone likes you huh Keagan." Dad said smiling at mom, "Yes, I guess someone does." Mom and dad both laughed at me as I ate my dinner fast. I thought about how sweet Reese was to come all the way over just to tell me how proud she was of me. I could still see visions of her flashing through my mind as her red hair blew in the wind underneath her hat as she ran from the door. I hurried up to my room to finish the rest of my work, all I wanted was a nice warm shower and to get to sleep so that I could see Reese tomorrow I thought as I hurried through my homework.

The next day I woke up so early that I beat mom and dad to the table for breakfast. I dressed in a red shirt today and jeans I wore my red and blue scarf to warm my neck, it looked like it would be a little chilly out from the window. When I made it to the table mom was standing in front of me with an apple in her hand. "Here you go son, have a good day," she said with a smile. I kissed her cheek grabbed my backpack from the floor and hurried to the car to wait for mom. I sat out there looking around at the trees blowing in the wind waiting for mom, when she came out it felt I'd been waiting for hours.

"Mom, I don't want to be late today, I'm hoping to catch Reese walking into school today," I told her strapping my seatbelt across my shoulder as she got into the car. "Okay, okay son, no problem you will make it I promise," she said as we drove away from the house. We arrived at school early there was hardly anyone there, I ran through the school through to get to the back I looked around every corner for Reese, she wasn't there I decided I'd wait at the back gate because she always came through the back.

It was fifteen after seven when more and more people began to show; I stood at the gate waiting until the bell rang, there was no sign of Reese anywhere. I saw a couple of her new friends walking past me; they smiled and waved as they went by "Hey has anyone seen Reese this morning?" I asked. No one seen her, I rushed quickly to my first class so that I would beat the bell. At the door of my class there she was standing waiting for me.

"Hello Keagan, I thought you'd never show," she said grabbing my hand, I looked down at her hand it was so cold. "Are you cold Reese?" I asked as we began to walk into class. She smiled at me and shook her head no. Class went by so fast it was a room full of laughter as we learned today about dissecting the brain of a sheep. Mrs. Byrd would tell us about every part of the brain, and what it did. We were able to touch it everyone was laughing and toying around with the sheep brain while Reese and I were busy writing down everything she said. While class went on quickly, I thought of how nice Reese was today.

She smiled at me as we worked on our project together, when we finished we walked out together. Reese took my hand as we walked through the crowd. "Wait for a second Keagan," she said pulling me toward the lockers down the hall. "I know you have to hurry, but I want to share something with you," she said digging into her backpack. She pulled her hand out quickly flashing a picture of us at the dance that night. "Do you like it?" She asked me.

I looked it over and smiled at her, "how nice; someone was so beautiful that night." I told her placing the picture to my chest. "I'll cherish this forever," I told her sarcastically. She slapped me on the arm, "Keagan you're so funny sometimes." She said looking me in the eyes I leaned in to kiss her on the cheek when I was shoved in the back; I fell into her chest almost knocking her off her feet. "GQ you still haven't learned the lessons I've been trying to teach you, have you? Fredrick said standing over me. I grabbed onto Reese to catch her fall after catching myself from falling.

I turned to Fredrick, I stepped closer to him thinking that he would see the look in my eyes and back off, but he came in closer. "Fredrick, I don't want any trouble, and I don't think you want any either, please leave us be." I told him staring him in his eyes soon the bell rang, everyone around us scattered, and Reese took off down the hall. Fredrick stood in front of me staring at me with a smirk of a smile. "You lucked out this time GQ," he stepped back.

"You need to listen to the sounds of my footsteps coming down this hall, every day I'll be watching for you," he said looking at me with a dead stare. "Sure Fredrick, I'm really afraid," I told him walking away still watching him from the distance. The second bell rang and I ran for it hoping that I would make it to my seat before I would be marked tardy. I sat down quickly sitting down in the chair so hard I shook the desk to the side nearly flipping it over "Good afternoon Keagan," Mrs. Blanchard yelled out as he began to write the assignment on the board.

Fredrick sat right in front of me for this class; he turned to me winking his eye. "See you later GQ," he said in a whisper with a smile. I made it through the class not acknowledging his presence when class ended through the rush after the bell rang I saw Reese rushing for the door with her friends trailing behind her quickly to get through the crowd in the hallways. I called out to her, she turned to look back at me, but she kept walking quickly down the halls, I didn't chase her this time. I walked on through the crowd to get to the front gate; coach told us that there would be no practice today.

I made to the front entrance of the school; it was a bit windy as I began to walk toward the trees of the pathway I walked quickly thinking about Reese holding my hand and being so comfortable with me that day. As I entered the crosswalk near my house, I noticed Reese waiting for me on the porch; she waved at me as I crossed. "Hello stranger," she said as I walked up to the porch. "What took you so long to get here?" Before I could answer, she walked up to me and kissed my lips.

"Let's go swimming Keagan," she said taking me by the hand pulling me toward my door. I set my bag down on the ground while I search my pocket for the keys, when we got inside I threw my bag near the door and went to the kitchen. "Would you like something to eat or drink Reese?" I asked her. She shook her head no "Are you sure you want to go swimming?" I asked her looking out of the window biting my apple. "It's a bit chilly out," I told her pulling the door to the backyard open.

"Oh come on, Keagan you're going to tell me you're afraid of little cold air," she said pulling her shirt up over her head and running out through the doorway. She was wearing a poke-a-dotted black and white swimsuit underneath her clothing; she came prepared to swim. I sat on the patio chairs eating my apple watching her swim. She swam back and forth going under the water for long period of times, then coming up splashing water all over the patio.

When she finished I went inside to get her a towel, when I came back out she was gone. I looked all over the house for her. I thought she'd gone to my room, but she wasn't there nor was she in any of the restrooms. I shook my head and went back to where we started, and I noticed her wet footprints in the pavement of the patio I followed as they lead me to the side gate of the backyard, she'd left from the side entrance. I shut the gate and went back inside. I threw the towel over my shoulder and began to walk up the stairs.

As I began to walk up the stairs they began to sway as if they were being pulled up from the floor; I held on to the railing of the stairs as they swayed. Soon the pictures from the wall began to shoot at me as if someone was throwing them at me I ducked. I held the towel up to shield myself from the pictures as they flew into me. I could hear them crashing to the floor as I tried to hang on to the rail it seemed to shake and sway as if to fling me around enough to make me lose my grip of the railing.

I held on as tight as I could while trying to hold the towel to cover me. Soon the railing felt as if it was splitting me apart and with one hard tug, I was flying. I held onto the towel as I began to roll down the stairs I laid on the floor looking up at the ceiling of the house, I closed my eyes listening for the shaking to stop. When it did I sat up there was glass everywhere picture frames broken up all over the house I quickly stood to my feet. I went to the kitchen for the broom; I swept the floor placing all of the glass in a pile in the middle of the floor I placed each picture near the pile when I had it all in a one big pile I went to find the dustpan.

I went back out to the front room, and the glass was gone and the pictures back up. I stood there looking all around the room, this was something that I couldn't explain nor could see the reasoning for what was happening. I took my towel from the floor and went up to my room; my room was dark I didn't bother with the light I laid across my bed covering myself with the towel from my head to my waist I covered. I took two very long deep breaths with my eyes closed. I fell off to sleep thinking about what had happened downstairs.

When I woke up, mom was standing in front of me. "Keagan, what happened downstairs, son?" She asked, I jumped up looking at her I was startled to see her standing there. "Mom I tried to clean it all up," I told her rubbing my eyes. "The broom is out, and the cabinets are all opened, were you looking for something son?" She asked me still standing over me, "I was just about to clean mom that's all," I told her standing. "Mom is dinner ready?" I asked her, "No son, we have church tonight." "Church on a Friday, no mom, I'm sure God wouldn't want us there on a Friday," I told her walking toward my bathroom.

"Keagan, God wants us to worship always, now get yourself together I'll be waiting for you downstairs, we'll meet your dad there," she said walking out of my room. I looked in the mirror "Church on a Friday," I said to myself in the mirror, as I turned from the mirror I saw a dark shadow pass by me going toward the door. I rushed down to be with mom. "Mom, mom," I yelled as I walked down the stairs. So that I wouldn't see it again, mom yelled back up to me.

"What's going on Keagan, why are you yelling?" She said looking up at me from the bottom of the stairs. "I just wanted to see your face, mom," I told her as I came down. "How was your day mom?" I asked her. "It was good, son, grab your coat it will probably be a long night, we'll be doing bible studies," she said holding her bible in her arms. We went to the car, mom drove off to church. When we arrived at the church the parking lot was full there were cars parked all the way around the church.

Mom parked on the side street a ways away from the church, and we walked up, looking around we weren't the only ones who had to park far we walked alongside many people going into the church. We met up with Mr. Hall, and Fredrick, all of his friends trailed behind him and Mr.

Hall smiling and laughing. They played around the whole time we walked; mom looked around for dad, I looked around for Reese I saw her friends standing around waiting to get into the church. It was a full house; people were lined up to get in to sit down, when we made it to the front entrance of the church there was a sign saying.

Tonight's Guess Speaker would be a great pastor from the east coast by the name of Pastor C. J. Brown, and along with him a mass choir, mom and I looked at one another. "Now we know why there's such a big crowd," she said to me grabbing onto my arm to walk in with her, she wanted to sit on the balcony of the church so that we could see everything from up top. We were escorted to our seats by the ushers and asked if we wanted a bible or a program, mom took the program and we waited for dad.

From where we sat, we could see everyone coming inside. Reese never came in, dad found us by mom waving her program and standing to her feet when she saw him enter the church, soon everyone was seated. The program began with the pastor of the church preaching about Job in Chapter 23. He preached about how Job was tested as he preached people were standing to their feet clapping.

When he finished the choir began to sing, I watched from the balcony. Fredrick and his friends were tapping one another and pointing up at me. When the speaker walked up to the podium to speak everyone stood to their feet applauding him. He took to the podium with his red robe on; he sat his bible down on the podium and looked around. "I came here today to tell you all something new, see; on my way here I was struck with a fever, suddenly ill but the devil is a lie"

"I knew I had to get here after that, I looked around at all of my saints, they asked me. "Pastor C. J. should we turn around the bus? I looked up at them and shook my head. See, I know why I'm sick, I know why I had to come. My Lord God sends messages to us sometimes in the worse way. See, this place, this church is his clinic; we all have a sickness in here." He went on and on pointing and explaining how God is a healer and how all things can be changed through him.

I listened to him intensely; he was so strong in his speech the church was so quiet, even Fredrick and his friends took notice. It would be an hour later when his speech was over mom and dad stood to their feet when he left from the podium. The whole church stood to their feet for him. I couldn't help to notice that all around Fredrick and Mr. Hall there were dark shadows they stood all around the pews where they sat, the pastor came back up to the podium and thanked everyone for coming out. He dismissed the church with the choir singing, Amazing Grace.

When the doors opened for everyone to go out there was a loud scream; people were running back into the door pushing and shoving their way back in. The pastor pushed his way out toward the door when he made it through he stood at the entrance of the door looking up, we all looked up. There was a pair of legs hanging from the door entrance of the churched they were dangling back and forth red stockings covered the feet of the legs.

The pastor went outside to look at who it was everyone followed; there were more screaming and crying, mom and dad ran to the front entrance, they began to escort people back into the church to sit down, trying to calm them. "Everything will be alright," they told them walking them inside. I walked around the crowd slipping past mom and dad to go out to see what the pastor was looking at; he had dropped to his knees in prayer by the time I reached the front steps of the church, the wind was blowing all around us.

I walked out. I turned and looked up, immediately I began to shake all over as flashes of what I saw began to run through my mind. It was Reese hanging from a rope around her neck her face blue, blood dripping from her mouth. I stood back; my body shook so bad I couldn't stand, dad ran to me, "Son, come to me, come in," he said to me I saw his lips moving, but I couldn't hear a thing I began to get angry inside. I screamed out to the top of my lungs so that everyone could hear. "God Who!"

The scream broke the glass in the church and people were covering their ears as I stood there screaming I felt ripping in my shoulder blades. My face felt as if it was on fire, I felt the hair ripping out of my face I put my hands to my face, the hair was like blades to my hands. They began to bleed, the pastor tried to touch me, I stood back screaming. I took one more look at Reese and I ran as fast as I could through the pathway. Behind the church, were woods all around; I ran through them crying, as I ran I could feel my body changing with every thought of Reese hanging there.

I began to run faster and faster, I ran until night and only than I would stop, sitting on the tree stomps surrounded by nothing but the night winds and the sounds of the night. My body was covered with the black blades of hair; I could feel the blades in my shoulder sticking way out. I sat there crying, why did Reese do this to herself? I closed my eyes and began to remember all of what she'd endured at school with Fredrick and his friends taunting her just because she was close to me. I thought about how she feared them, I began to run again this time I would run through the woods all the way home.

When I made it home the house was still dark, mom and dad must be out looking for me I didn't want to see anyone. I took the key from under the rock on the front porch and went inside to my bedroom, when I went into my room I cried I went to the bathroom mirror to look at myself. I was covered in black feathered like blades, my eyes were white with black only in the middle, I had short black wings hanging form my shoulders none of this bothered me, I took a look at myself and threw myself to the floor crying. Flashes of Reese hanging from the church would haunt me all night. I heard mom and dad come in yelling for me, I never answered them; they even came to the door knocking. "Just leave me, please!" I yelled out to them.

"Not now mom, please, not now," I yelled as they knocked. "Son, it will be okay," dad said as they walked away I laid on my floor crying all night Reese was gone. She was gone, there was nothing I could do about her dying, I thought as I cried. I was angry and hurt it felt as if someone ripped my heart out at that moment I looked up at her. There was no way I could allow Fredrick and his friends to get away with this I thought, crying. This meant war to me they have started a war, and no one would stop me from making them pay. I couldn't help for thinking about where we were; in this church where was their God? I thought as I cried, where was he?

Saying Goodbye

I laid there on the floor of my room on the hardwood; covered in my black bladed feathers listening as mom and dad knocked hour after hour trying to make me come out. I scraped my body around the floor thinking about Reese, mom and dad came back time after time. The light from the sun shined in through the window all day, then came the darkness of the night. My body stayed the same; I only would move to go to the restroom. I'd look at myself in the mirror and walk back out to the room, lying on the floor looking up thinking of Reese.

I asked myself could I have done something different as flashes of our time together came through vividly over and over again. I knew that Reese was strong, maybe I pushed her over the edge by making her stand up to everyone the way I did. Maybe I should have given into their constant bullying and teasing too. I laid there, tears rolling from my eyes. I carved with the tip of my wing a picture of Reese and her name over and over again all over the floor. When the sun began to come up on the third day, I sat in the corner of my room carving a puzzle on the floor.

Mapping out a plan to get them all back, for some reason, I think I'd have to start with Mr. Hall. I believe that he has a lot to do with their plan to continue their harassment. No one's afraid of him nor do they fear the law, which I found to be odd seeing as how he was a detective and Fredrick's dad. I began to circle his name over and over drawing arrows to all that surrounded him. I plan to get them all. I cried more thinking of Reese's body swinging from the church as it did that day. My heart ached with pain while I cried, I put my head down over my knee as the night grew long the wings became heavier.

I leaned onto the chair near the desk, the room was dark, I couldn't see around me. I looked out into the darkness at the moon shining brightly through the curtains on the window; suddenly I felt a hand rubbing my face. I jumped moving away slamming my wing against the desk, what appeared in front of me was shocking, a girl she was my age. A light shinned over her, she smiled at me, I began to talk, she put her finger to my lips as to shush me, "Hello Keagan, I'm Sage." She said in a whisper, soon six more voices began to speak one after another introducing themselves by name.

"I am Adam." "I am Matthew." "I am Ferris." "I am Kendall." "I am Tasha." "I am Peter." There was light all around them as they came closer to me forming a circle around me. They all reached one hand out to me touching the blades of my wings, Sage spoke first. "We are here for you, Keagan, Reese is fine now," she said putting her hand on the top of my head. "Let go of the anger, Keagan let go, you'll be ready when the time comes to defeat them. We'll be here to help you," she said. I kept my head down crying the tears dropped onto the floor of the map I drew of my revenge.

"Look up Keagan, look around; you have our light with you always, just look around." They all began to fade away as I looked up the light around them faded one after the other they were gone. I stayed in the corner weeping for a while before Sage appeared again holding my hand; she took my hand and rubbed it on the side of her face. "Don't worry Keagan, she's okay," she said. I closed my eyes; when I opened them, she was gone. Mom and dad knocked loudly on the door.

"Keagan! Enough is enough; you have to come out of there. It's been three days already, open the door son, right now!" Dad yelled out. I stood to my feet, and I walked over to the mirror to take a good look at myself before opening the door. I was all back to normal with some cuts and bruises, I took a wet cloth to my face and arms and wiped the blood. There were cuts on my shoulders where the wings had spread out. I took a shirt from my drawer and changed quickly before I opened the door.

When I opened the door mom and dad were standing waiting with the look of worry on their faces. "Son, we are here, there was no reason to take off like that and run away. We could have helped," Dad said putting his arm around my shoulders. "Son, I know how much she meant to you, and I'm so sorry," Mom said grabbing me by the waist and hugging me tightly. "It will be okay son, with God's help it will be alright." I cringed and pulled away from mom.

"Mom not now, I don't want to hear about God. Where was he when Reese decided to take her life mom?" I began to become angry all over again. "I'm sorry, I won't say another word," Mom said walking with me to the kitchen. "You need to eat something son, come on I have some warm soup for you," she said as we walked downstairs. We walked down to the kitchen to get soup I sat at the table, dad sat across from me, he stared at me waiting for me get my bowl of soup.

"Son, we have to talk to you about Mr. Hanson, he's getting all the arrangements ready for Reese's funeral. He asked if you wanted to speak at the funeral since you two were so close," he told me as I spooned my soup. I shook my head no, "I can't dad," I told him getting up from the table. "Son, where are you going?" Mom asked I shook my head and walked away toward the back sliding door. I wanted to sit outside in the fresh air. I sat down at the patio table and looked out at the pool; all I thought of was when Reese would come here to swim.

"Son, you don't want to hear this, but they're burying Reese in a couple of days. She's gone, and you have to let go of her, allow yourself to accept what happened. She's gone now; all you can do is pray that she had our Lord God to guide her through what she did." "Dad, I really don't want to hear what our Lord God can do, he takes people away, and he took Reese. He allowed them to harass her and scare her and now this," I said raising my voice looking out at the pool.

"Son, Reese made this decision she wanted to go," he says looking at me standing at the edge of the patio table. "No, dad you're wrong, Reese would never do this to herself. They taunted her and teased and it was all my fault. She kept telling me that she had to stay away from me, but I kept pushing for us to be friends. Now Reese is gone, dad, she's gone." "Yes son, she's gone, and there is nothing you can do to bring her back, so just pray. I know you don't believe that you should, but you have to pray, son. Pray that the Lord has welcomed her into the heavens and claimed her as one of his angels. She will need your prayers," he said walking away from me.

I stood up to go back into the house following dad when I entered the house, I could smell Reese beside me. Her scent covered the air around me. I began to smile. "Son, are you okay?" Mom asked. "I'm okay mom, I'm okay," I told her grabbing an apple from the bowel on the table. I felt better after smelling Reese in the room. "Son, what do you want me to tell Mr. Hanson?" Mom asked. "I can't speak mom, please tell him I'm sorry, but I just can't do it," I told her as I walked up to my room. "Are you going to taking a shower son?"

"Yes mom, I am, and I'll get my homework done." "Make sure you get things ready for tomorrow, I have a list of homework assignments that you missed in the past couple of days." I went up and took a shower, the hot water burned my shoulders and arms as it ran down my body in the shower. When I got out, I threw on my pajamas and sat at my desk to do my homework. There was assignment after assignment, from science to English.

I was swamped after missing two days of school. I fell off to sleep thinking about what tomorrow would bring, what would everyone be saying about Reese and the way she died. The next day I woke up early and dressed quickly for school. I went downstairs to eat breakfast. "Son, do you want me to drop you off?" "No thank you, mom, I need to walk," I told her. I wanted to clear my head.

"Son, before you go to school and cause trouble for yourself, please remember that this was a decision that Reese made on her own" Dad told me staring me in the eye "No dad your wrong, this wasn't any decision of Reese's, but I won't get into any trouble, I promise" I said grabbing an apple and going for the front door. It was a little chilly out, I began to walk through the pathway of the trees when I looked back to check how far I'd walked I noticed Sage standing at the end of the corner waving at me.

I waved back at her and continued walking toward the school, when I made it to school there was signs everywhere in front about suicide and crisis hotline numbers posted on every door of the hallway. I walked through the entrance near the office and there was Fredrick and his crew standing laughing and playing around as soon as he realized that it was me he looked at them and nodded his head signaling them to follow him. "So GQ, you made it back to school?" He said shaking his head.

"Sad how your girlfriend ended up huh, I told you I would make her mine, one way or the other," he said smiling. I began to walk away but I couldn't I turned to him so fast, grabbing him by the shirt. "You will regret what you did soon enough" I told him pulling his face close to mine, my eyes turned white, I could feel the blades of hair beginning to rise on my shoulders, calm, later, later I told myself letting go of his shirt. I laughed loudly.

"Yeah Fredrick, it's really sad," I said walking away taking a bite from my apple, I watched them as they all stood in shock while Fredric caught his breath and straightened his clothes. I smiled at them and waved as I continued walking toward class. Fredric came to class after me sitting behind me in every class, he whispered to me in English "Hey GQ, are you sure you want to do what you're thinking of doing, you know it won't be easy?" He whispered I turned around to him, whispering back.

"Fredrick this will be the easiest thing I've ever done, you and your friend should brace yourselves, I smiled at him fearlessly and turned back around doing my work. Today after school I will follow them to where ever they go. I thought as I worked on my class assignments. I will find them out, where they go, what they do and until they all suffer after what they did to Reese I will not rest. I walked home that day with a new feeling over me I felt confident, fearlessly, confident I waited for them to follow me to start trouble.

I wanted them to but they didn't, when I saw them walking on the other side of the street I crossed to walk behind them. I tucked my backpack away in one of the trees in the pathway. I needed my hands to be free as I walked behind them I watched as they played around, handing each other drinks of alcohol and passing cigarettes. I followed them through the streets than through the backwoods of the city, I watched them laughing and talking loudly until they came to a stop in the woods at a shack covered in mud and trees.

They all took a puff from the cigarette and went inside the shack; there were girls kissing one another and the guys joining in as they all went in together. I went to the side of the shack where there was a small window, it was covered in dirt, I took the sleeve of my shirt and wiped the window, they began to play loud music. They danced around the shack; some sat and watched the girls while others laughed in the corners smoking cigarettes. I watched them waiting to see if they would even notice me watching them. I stood steel waiting.

Fredrick turned off the music and walked into the middle of the room. "We have a goal tomorrow," he shouted. "We should be ready to take Reese in as she tried to move into the light of their savior," he said merely shouting. "She belongs with us!" They all began to shout; "with us, with us!" I stared in the window with my eyes pierced on Fredric, he wants to take her even when she's already gone, I thought. "We will have her!" He yelled with his head straight up into the air, when he stopped yelling, he looked down, then back up and with a twist of his neck he looked at me with a smile.

His eyes turned dark red, he pointed at me, and they all looked at me through the window. "Get him!" Fredric yelled out and they all began to run for the door. I took off running through the woods as I ran I thought about what Fredric said. I wanted to get him but not now, today I will just tease them as they did Reese. I ran around in circles so fast, they followed me racing to catch up, they screamed out as they ran behind me. Soon my body was changing in my anger; I began to run faster and faster.

As I ran I knocked trees down all around them making it easier for them to see me but unable to touch me, they grew more and more frustrated. I laughed at them; I could see them growing angrier. Soon they stopped and looked to Fredrick to guide them; he stood staring at me with a grin on his face "You!" He yelled out. "Yes me," I told him standing behind the trees I knocked down. "I'm here, come get me, Fredrick," I told him guiding him with my finger.

"You really don't want this GQ," he yelled out. I jumped over the trees launched my body toward him pushing him onto the ground with my hands to his shoulders holding him down in the brush. "I will make you pay for what you've done to Reese, and every time I see you taunting or teasing anyone, I will make you pay again." I told him looking him into his red eyes, I could see my reflection in them, he tussled trying to throw me off him, and I held him down by the shoulders even harder.

"You don't want to ever cross me again Fredrick, you don't want to know what I have in store for you." I told him jumping over him landing on my feet into the brush behind him; he got up from the ground quickly trying to come after me. I looked back at him and began to run as they all stood around looking shocked and confused at what just happened. I ran through the woods laughing to myself about their faces, I had them all afraid, they better be for what I have planned for them they better be very afraid. I thought running through the brush as I ran my body began to change with every leap through the brushes of the trees, when I made it through the woods I slowed down and began to walk toward the lights of the city.

The sun was going down as I walked toward the pathway to get my backpack I needed to get home before mom began to worry. I ran as fast as I could to the trees where I left my backpack. I picked up my backpack and began to run toward my house down the pathway. When I made it to the corner near my house I saw Sage from afar as I walked up, she waved and smiled I waved to her and continued to walk toward the house. I could see mom coming out of the door beginning to walk toward the car.

I ran up to stop her, I approached her from behind, she was startled. "Keagan, where have you been? I was beginning to worry," she said looking cross. "I'm so sorry mom; I missed a couple of days I had to stay late to catch up." I told her helping her back into the house carrying her bag. "Did you get caught up son?" She asked as we entered the front door. "No mom, a few more days I will be caught up." Mom went into the kitchen and began to look around for what she would cook tonight.

"Keagan, you must get ready we're going to the church tonight for the viewing of Reese's body," she told me. "Viewing, mom what is that?" "Well, they give this service for friends and family to see their loved one before the funeral services. They usually like to do it a day before the service," she said to me. "I'm going to cook something to take for her family." "Mom, I don't think I want to do that, I think I'll just go to the service," I told her walking up to my room with my backpack over my shoulder.

"Besides I have lots of studying to do tonight," I told her. I went up to my room and closed the door; I threw my backpack on the floor beside my desk and lay across my bed. I wondered if Fredric and his friends would be at this service, this might be a perfect chance for me to scare them some more. I thought as I laid staring up at the ceiling; no I think I'll stay here tonight I will see everyone at the service tomorrow I thought I fell off to sleep. I was awakened soon after by knocking at the door.

"Keagan, we're leaving for the services now, are you sure you don't want to join us?" She asked me. "Yes mom, I'm sure," I said in a sleepy voice. "Are you okay son?" She asked. "I'm fine mom, just sleeping," I told her "See you later mom," I said. As soon as mom was gone, I would go to the church but not to say my goodbye's to Reese. I wanted to see how many of them would show, this time I will follow them one by one to give them back a little of what they gave Reese.

I watched from the window as mom drove away in the car. I stood in the window with my hands in my pockets until she was out of site, then I went to my closet to grab a change of clothes. While searching around the closet for dark clothes, I found a pack of bubble gum sitting in a pile of clothes that I had in the corner of the closet. I picked it up and flashes of the night of the dance ran through my mind I was reminded of the gum they threw all over Reese's dress and hair that night.

I threw the pack of gum down, took the clothes and began to change when I was ready, I ran out of the house toward the church. The church isn't as close to the house as I thought, I ran and ran until I could see the church ahead there were lots of cars surrounding the church as well as a hearse. I could see people standing around talking, many of them crying, they were talking about Reese and all the things she was.

I hid in the back of the church I could see Mr. Hanson standing near the casket, he wasn't crying but the woman next to him cried loudly. Mr. Hall, Fredrick, and all his friends stood side by side together in a pew, three pews behind them. Mom and dad sat on the other side of them; the church was filled. When mom noticed me in the back she waved her hand at me to come over to her, I put my head down and walked outside the church.

When the preacher finished preaching about reasons everyone should get along everyone stood up while they waited for the ushers to escort them out from the pews they opened the casket and as everyone walked out they were able to look at Reese Lying still inside. I walked across the street and sat under the tree looking back at the church, my heart couldn't take it, my eyes filled with tears for Reese it was if it was being ripped out.

I held my head down on my knees thinking of her lying there when I heard car engines starting and traffic moving I stood up to see where Fredric and his friends were. I spotted the girl he hung out with, I watched her get into a car with her parents, and she would be first. I would get her first, I thought as I watched them drive off. Mom saw me she drove up to me. "Keagan, come on, everyone's headed to the burial grounds." "Mom I don't want to go, go ahead without me," I told her keeping an eye on the car with Fredrick's friend in it.

Mom waited for a while then rolled up her window and drove off. I stood watching everyone driving off when there was almost no one there I ran across the street to go back to the church as I was crossing the preacher stood at the door of the church as if he was waiting on me. I hesitated when I noticed him; he looked at me and waved his hand for me to come over. I didn't, I took off running toward the pathway I would go to the burial grounds to watch them put Reese there. But today I will start my war against Fredrick and all of his friends, I thought as I ran with the wind blowing so cold to my face as if it was cutting me.

I ran fast enough to catch up to her parent's car everyone was parking on the outside of the grassy area where they would lay Reese to rest. I stood in the back of the crowd waiting. When the preacher arrived, he walked over to the casket lying over the hole in the ground, as the preacher began to speak verses from the bible everyone stood up. Mr. Hanson threw dirt down, and flowers came after, by everyone who wanted to place flowers on her casket, mom placed her flowers down.

When he was done the crowd began to get smaller when they were all gone, I went over to Reese's casket.

I stood with my hand on the casket, how I wished she was standing there beside me smiling. I couldn't believe that she was inside the casket but she was and now I will lay them all beside her, I thought as I walked off toward the grassy pathway. It would be an hour before I spot Fredric's friend, they were all standing outside Mr. Hanson apartment. It was growing dark when everyone began to leave one after the other wishing Mr. Hanson all their best and offering there help if he should ever need it. I went inside and hugged Mr. Hanson I asked him quietly if I could go into Reese's room.

He said "sure, she always trusted you Keagan, thank you for everything." I went into her room and into her closet; I wanted the dress I bought her to wear that night of the dance. It was the only thing hanging up in the closet; I took it and stuffed it into my jacket pocket. I walked out through the crowd waving goodbye to Mr. Hanson, I waited to watch for Fredric and his friends to start down the alley, After Mr. Hanson closed his doors to the last couple wishing their condolences.

When they set off down the alley, I followed them from afar watching and waiting for them to split, when they all began to part ways I followed the girl, as she walked with Reese's obituary in her hand. She twirled it around, she walked through the pathway by the school, soon the wind was blowing heavier colder winds, and the trees were whistling waving back and forth. I thought about her laughing as she threw gum at Reese on the floor of the bathroom at the dance that night, my body began to change I began to run with the pain ripping through my back as the blades grew out of me like knives.

I ran and ran watching for her to get closer to the middle of the wooded area in the pathway, soon she spotted me running, and she began to run from me screaming loudly, I chased her down pushing her down to the ground. I grabbed her by the back of her black dress and turned her around to face me, I looked her in the eye, and I could see my reflection in her eyes. She shook in fear, I took my hand around her throat and began to choke her, I took the obituary and held it over her face she cried, gasping for air.

I could hear her trying to whisper help and sorry. "It's too late for you," I told her smashing the obituary over her eyes as I squeezed her neck harder, she finally stop stopped kicking and squirming. She kicked up the dirt from the ground it covered her boots when she lay limp. I took a deep breath and thought of Reese on that night she humiliated her, I took her by the top of her dress and sat her up; her body was so heavy. I took her dress off and ripped it down the middle tying it together to make a rope as her body lied limp sitting up against the tree.

I tied the dress watching her, when I went over to her to place it around her neck, holding her chin down to place the rope around and suddenly she lifted her head up, she gasped for air. I grabbed her neck quickly and squeezed it tight until her eyes rolled back soon she stopped breathing I tied the rope around her neck tightly. I took her toward the tree and placed her body down beside the tree. I took the dress from my pocket and placed it over her neck, it draped over her body, then I began to climb up the tree, as I climbed she began to squirm.

I wrapped the rope around my wrist and tugged at her neck as I went higher up the tree when I got to the top of the tree I began to pull her body up. As I pulled, I wrapped it around the sturdy tree branch hanging in the middle when she was all the way up, and the rope was secured I loosened it leaving her to hang. I climbed down from the tree and ran away, I didn't look back. I ran as fast as I could as my body changed I looked around with my eyes filling with tears for Reese. I began to think about Reese's body in the casket, saying goodbye to her wasn't easy and as I ran crying through the woods thinking of what I'd just done, living for her wasn't going to be easy either.

Fire in the Woods

On my way home, I smiled thinking of what would happen the next day. I ran past Mr. Hanson's apartment to see how many people were still hanging around giving their condolences. It was quiet walking through the alley; there were obituaries on the steps of the apartment. As I passed by I picked one up just to look at Reese's face; Mr. Hanson used a beautiful picture of Reese, she smiled in it showing her beautiful white teeth, her red hair pinned back away from her face.

When I made it home I saw that mom and dad were standing outside in the front door, it looked as if they had just gotten there. I walked up to the front porch and approached them from behind. "Hello mom, hello dad." "Hello, son," dad said turning toward me. "Where have you been?" He asked me. "I've been running at the field for practice," I told him with my head down. Mom grabbed my chin; "son look at me," she said looking into my eyes. "It will be okay, Reese will be in heaven with the Lord," she said.

I took her hand away from my face. "Mom, you don't really believe that, do you?" I asked as I passed them to get to the front door. As I walked in dad grabbed me by the arm. "Keagan, what have you done?" He looked down at my hands; they had dirt on them, my nails looked as if I'd been digging into something. "Dad, it's nothing, I've done nothing," I said pulling away from him walking into the house. I went to the kitchen and grabbed an apple from the bowel on the table and took a bite; I looked down at my pants they were covered with dirt, when mom and dad came inside they went into the kitchen.

"I'll be up in my room," I told them walking toward the stairwell. I went into my room and began to undress. I looked in the mirror at my back; there were cuts and blood running down my shoulder blades, the blood was drying. I went into my bathroom and turned the shower on when I came out there was Sage sitting on my bed, she startled me, and I jumped at the sight of her. She took her finger to her mouth to shush me, "Keagan, this isn't good," she said in a whisper shaking her head at me I turned my back to her.

"Leave!" I yelled out. "Get out of here please," I said not looking at her. I went into the bathroom to get into my shower. As I stood there underneath the hot water, I thought of what I'd done that day. I put my hands on the wall of the shower; I began to cry, I cried loudly, I cried for me, I cried for Reese, I cried for what I'd done to the girl in the woods. I cried so hard my stomach hurt; I sat down on the floor on the shower, I wept. When I finished I walked out of the bathroom, I wrapped up in a towel and lay across the bed.

I held my arms under my head; when I looked down at them they were covered in white hairs all over, I flipped over fast, and my legs were covered in them as well. I jumped up and ran to the mirror to look over the hairs. Oh no, I thought, as I rubbed the hair, a chill came over me, I turned away from the mirror and laid back across the bed, I wept for Reese a little longer before mom started knocking at the door. "Keagan, would you like something to eat, son?" She asked me.

"No mom, I'm okay!" I yelled out peeking from the crease of my elbow; I just wanted to lay there and wait for tomorrow, I sat up and grabbed my pants from the floor. I reached into my pocket to get the piece of the dress that I ripped off, tomorrow I will throw it at Fredric during lunch to give him something to think about I thought as I lean back looking up at the ceiling waiting for night to fall. When my room grew darker, I covered my face with a pillow to cry; the white feathers went away and came back again. I turned over onto my stomach, I drifted off to sleep, as I fell off to sleep I thought about tomorrow I tossed and turned.

When I began to dream, it was the darkness that made me open my eyes, but when they opened I was in the same tunnel as before in my dream, this time there was no way out. I ran in the dream from one end to the other trying to look for light; the tunnel grew smaller and smaller as if to squeeze me in; it was closing. I could hear screaming, moaning, yelling, there were lots of people; I couldn't see them, but they were there. I stood trapped; leaning on one side of the wall, rubbing my hands over the wall it was like wet mud. I hit it; the mud splashed all over my face and body, I yelled and screamed to get out as the mud kept splashing.

Soon there was a hole where the wall was, inside it shined a bright light, it shined like the sun. I squint my eyes with my hands up to them to shield them from the light; I tried looking into the light. My eyes burned like fire as I pierced them trying to focus them on what was in the light when I began to focus. I felt what felt like hands grabbing me pulling me backward, soon I was back into the darkness. I opened my eyes everything was black, pitch black, I couldn't see a thing I felt around again for the wall this time while feeling around.

There were nails, or what felt like knives cutting up and down my arms from the top of my shoulders to the tips of my fingertips I felt scraping. I yelled out each time the scraping would go up and down and back up again. "Someone, please help me!" I yelled out. "Please," I cried as I scratched at the wall. I yelled and yelled for what seemed to be an eternity as I was being scratched. I hit at the walls around me in the darkness, "Keagan, Keagan! Wake up son! Please wake up," I heard mom's voice, but I can't see her I can't touch her. I reached for her in the darkness.

"Keagan, son, please!" She yelled, "Michael, please come, please come!" I hear her yelling. "He won't wake up Michael, he won't move," she yelled out I can feel myself being shaken around by them. "Please baby, wake up." Mom began to cry as she held me to her chest, rocking me crying, I could feel her warm chest I began to stop trying to fight my way out of the darkness. I let go of my fears and became still, my body felt limp I slid down the wall in the darkness, I opened my eyes, I looked up at mom, she rocked me in her arms crying.

"Mom, mom," I whispered; she held me even tighter she was praying aloud while rocking on the bed crying. She didn't stop when I looked up, she continued to pray and cry and rock me. "Son, son," dad said sitting next to her on the bed he put his hands on my legs. "Son, what happened?" He asked me, I shook my head as if to say I don't know. "What time is it?" I asked sitting up still a little scared. "It's 6:45 am," Dad said looking down at his watch I sprang from the bed sliding between them; rushing for my closet.

"What's wrong now son, where are you going?" Mom said standing following me into the closet "I have to get to school mom," I told her grabbing my boots from the floor and throwing on a black hooded sweatshirt and my jeans. "Son, why don't you stay home today and hang out with us?" Dad said. "No thank you, dad, I have a lot of catching up to do at school, I missed enough already." I ran to the bathroom and slipped into my clothes, I sat at the foot of the bed to put my boots on, dad stood up over me.

"Son, try not to get into any trouble, I know you're still hurting over Reese, everything will be fine just allow it to work it's self out. Please don't try and get involved in any of it," he said before walking out of the door. I was still thinking of the dream, being in that tunnel of darkness and the light behind the walls of mud as I walked out of my room I looked back thinking of it just being dark, I ran down to the kitchen grabbed a fruit from the bowel on the table, I grabbed my backpack from the floor and ran out of the door before mom could come down to ask me if I wanted a ride.

I ran as fast as I could through the pathway to school, I thought about what I had done. I reached into my pocket as I ran making sure I carried the clothing from the girls dress, I held onto it   smiling thinking of what Fredrick would do when he discovers what I'd done. When I arrived at school the bell hadn't rung yet; I walked around campus looking for him and his friends. They were nowhere to be found when the bell rang I began to walk to my homeroom class when I saw Fredrick across the walkway in the hall.

He was surrounded by his friends; they were all laughing and joking around in a circle. I began to walk up to him when I noticed what was going on, he had a young boy hanging up on the door frame of the class by his backpack. He was hitting him with his fist as if he was punching bag hanging from a wall as his friends stood watching. I ran to the boy grabbing him by his legs to help him down from the door, as I took him down they laughed and joked. "Aw GQ you're just no fun," Fredrick said grinning.

He pushed me around as I struggled to get the boy from the door when I got him down and stood him up he took one look at me. "Thank you," he said shaken, as he began to run off Fredrick snatched him by his backpack. "Remember it's never over until I say it's over," he told the kid in his ear. "Now GQ, you really get a kick out of saving them huh," he said looking at me eye to eye. I didn't say a word I stepped back as the second bell rang I began to turn away from him; he grabbed me by my sweatshirt and pulled me back. I turned and looking him in the eye, I reached into my pocket, pulled out the piece of cloth I held it into his face; I pulled away from him dropping the cloth down in front of him.

I walked away looking back smiling as they all watched the cloth drop to the ground. I made it to homeroom right as the warning bell stopped ringing. Fredric walked in just as the teacher went to shut the door, boy was he angry, he was so angry at me. He couldn't take his eyes off me; staring as if he could burn me in my seat with his eyes, I smiled. I knew he had recognized the cloth from her dress; it tickled me to know that he was still awaiting my wrath in fear of what I'd done to one of his own.

Classes went by slowly, Fredrick didn't say a word in class at all, during gym, he didn't challenge me at all he was settled and calm. When the last bell rang at the end of the day I walked calmly through the halls to the front entrance of the school; it was loud people were running everywhere happy that the day was over. When I reached the end of the hall I noticed Fredrick and his friends waiting on the front lawn of the school, they all looked my way as I walked out to the steps of the hall.

I pretended I didn't see them waiting, I walked slowly toward the sidewalk in front of the school, just as I was about to continue to walk toward the path mom showed up. Oh no I thought as she pulled up alongside me I looked down into the car. "Hello mom, I'm walking today, remember?" I told her as she rolled the window down to hear me better. "Here just take my backpack home mom, I'm going to go check on Mr. Hanson today," I told her placing my backpack through the window. "Aren't you going the wrong way then son, Mr. Hanson lives up the hill, right?" She says looking at me through the window.

"I'm stopping by another friend's house before going there," I told her. "I'll see you later mom," I told her walking off toward the pathway, I watched as she waited a while before driving off slowly watching me from the rearview window. I waved at her as she drove away, when I saw that she was down the hill I began to walk toward the pathway near the entrance through the woods. I could see Fredrick and his friends gearing up to come after me. I would run them directly to the girl hanging in the woods, I thought as I waited for them to take off toward the pathway.

They all split up when we entered the woods; I ran through the middle near the fallen trees, where I could hear them scattering through the brush. I took off running as fast as I could toward the tree where I hung her. I wanted them to meet me there; I knew they would come looking for me. I ran until I could no longer see the sun, for the trees on the dirt path blocked it, and this was where she hung from the tree, I stood, waiting for them. I could hear them one by one coming closer to the dirt pathway they ran so fast the dirt kicked up behind them everywhere.

Soon Fredrick was standing in front of me; he looked up at the girl hanging from the rope then back down at me. I smiled at him with a smirk, when I turned my head to look away; he grabbed me by my sweatshirt. I snatched away from him and began to run, he sprinted behind me, and grabbing my shirt again. We scuffled across the dirt, tussling with one another. He tried to get a grip on my neck; I placed my arms in front of my neck and face to protect me from getting choked by him. He was so angry it was almost like he was growling; he turned red, his eyes were red the sounds he made would get louder as he tried to get a hold of me.

I pulled away from him dragging us both through the dirt far from the girl hanging over us. I turned him over onto his back and ripped away from his grip I struggled to get up from the dirt, I began to run as fast as I could when he jumped onto my back trying to pull me down. I stretched my arms out breaking away from his grip once again, I ran away as fast as I could this time through the woods. I could hear them all running behind me; they began to scream loudly as they ran, I ran faster and faster "GO!" Fredrick screamed out.

"You will not make it out of here today!" He yelled. I looked back at him smiling as he struggled to catch me. Soon I could see darkness all around him his face red as an apple, his eyes redder, it was as if smoke was coming from his body as he grew angrier at the fact that he couldn't catch me. I turned away from him to run faster ahead my body began to change as I ran when I turned to look back to look for him; he wasn't there. I could hear him around the woods; it was darker in the woods.

The trees surrounded me as I stumbled through the brush looking behind me into the darkness; I looked down at the dirt as I ran through the woods to find my way back to the pathway. The cold wind blew over my face as I ran through the darkness looking around for Fredrick. I looked back for him, I could hear him, but he wasn't there, I looked up ahead of me, still no Fredrick. When I looked down at the dirt there was a flash of light, it was so bright it hurt my eyes to look down at it; I covered my eyes with my arm and looked up.

There were bright lights everywhere I looked. The light was so bright it was like fire. There ahead I saw Fredrick standing in a flame of fire, he was grinning at me trying to intimidate me with the fire. He began to walk toward me with the flames following behind him; I walked backward watching him as he came closer to me. I turned quickly and ran from him; he ran behind me with a flame of fire following behind him. He stretched his hands out to me and fire shot out from his hands toward me as I ran through the trees to get away from him.

He hit the branches of the trees and they caught fire sending flames of fire all over the woods. I ran faster away from him; soon I could hear fire sirens as the flames sent smoke outside the woods signaling a fire. Fredrick became angrier as he couldn't catch a hold of me when I reached the end of the woods near the pathway I looked back at him grinning. "Maybe next time," I said running away through the pathway to get to the entrance to the streets. I didn't want to be there when the fire truck got there and discover the body of the girl hanging from the tree.

I ran all the way home it was dark when I got to the front door of my house I could see mom in the window looking out for me. I waved to her catching my breath as I approached the front door to go in. "Where have you been?" She asked as I entered the door. "I've been waiting for you." "I've been at a friend's mom," I told her walking toward the kitchen to get a glass of water. I stood over the sink drinking the water; sweat ran down my face on both sides.

I looked up at my hand as I drank the water, there was steal blades of black hair on them I quickly placed the glass down into the sink and covered my hand with the ends of my sweatshirt. I ran upstairs, when I got to my room, I took the sweatshirt off and stood in the mirror I was covered in black hair all over. I opened my pants to see if it was on my bottom half, it was; I was covered all over. I sat down on the bed; I wondered if the fire trucks discovered the girl hanging, I wondered what Fredrick would tell them.

Would he let them know it was me, I wondered as I lay back across my bed. I thought about what would happen next; smiling because I had once again got away with hurting Fredrick with no circumstances, I laid there thinking of Reese. Would she be proud of what I was doing for her, or would it hurt her, it felt good to me, I was defeating Fredrick, I thought as I laid there looking up at the ceiling. Soon I will get Fredrick to understand that people should be treated fairly no matter who you are his friends would understand too.

I begin to daydream about how nice it would be if everyone got along without having to deal with someone like Fredrick when there was a knock at the door. "Yes!" I yelled out. "There's someone on the phone for you Keagan," mom said yelling through the door. "I'll take it in the hall mom," I yelled back. I went out into the hall to get the phone. "Hello, this is Keagan," I said standing against the wall.

"Yes I know GQ, I want you to know what this all means, and I won't stop until I finish what you started." He hung up; I looked down at the phone then hung it up and went back to my room, I sat on the bed. I'm ready for whatever he has in mind, I thought as I leaned back across my bed, I'm not afraid of Fredrick, nor will I give into what he has in mind for me. I held my hands in back of my head and smiled thinking of what would come next.

When They Come Back

I made it to school the next day just in time for the bell to ring. I sat at my desk and took out my notebook when Fredrick and his friends walked in slowly. They were laughing and joking about something loudly, as they took their seats they all stared at me. I looked ahead at the teacher writing the assignment on the board, Fredrick made sure he got my attention somehow. He dropped his book down beside my feet and reached down to pick it up; when I looked down to see exactly what he was doing he stared at me and grinned. "Hello GQ," he said.

"Nice seeing you," he winked his eye at me and turned to the teacher. I knew right away, that meant trouble, what would he have in store for me today? When the bell rang for the next class, I didn't get up immediately, I sat in my chair and waited for the classroom to clear out, when everyone was gone I reached down grabbed my bag walking quickly for the door to get to my next class. Fredrick was standing at the end of the hall talking to all of his friends waiting to go to our next class. As I began to get closer to the classroom door, he looked up at me and winked his eye again.

I walked past him quickly going into the class taking my seat. The teacher began to write the class assignment on the board as I pulled out my notebook Fredrick reached over and snatched it from my hands putting his other finger to his lips to shush me. He turned over the pages of my notebook until he found a blank page, he began to write and draw pictures. I reached over to get my notebook, he pulled it away still drawing, and when he was done he placed it on my desk in front of me.

Shushing me again with his finger, I took the notebook and turned it over. I didn't want to see what he'd drawn; he reached over me and turned it back, winking at me. I looked up at the teacher, trying to turn the page back over as Fredric pulled it to keep it open. I didn't look down at the book soon the bell would ring, I watched as the teacher stood in front of the class explaining to us the assignment for homework tonight. When the bell rang, Fredrick grabbed at my notebook as I began to put it into my backpack.

He snatched it from my hand and dropped it open in front of me onto the floor of the classroom and stepped on it. I stood up not thinking about what I would see when I reached down to pick it up. On the pages of my notebook, Fredrick had drawn a picture of me hanging in the tree and a girl standing at the bottom of the tree pointing up at me. And surrounding us was flames of fire all around it, at the bottom of the page he wrote in big bold letters "Can't Wait."

Then there were just scribbles of with four words in the center of them, I ripped the pages out crumbled them to toss into the trash as I walked out of class. I walked down the hall to get to my next class in the hallway Fredrick, and his buddies waited for me. Dare I ask him what the note meant; I looked at them frowning and continued on to the next class. Toward the end of the day I readied myself for gym class, I knew that running track would be awful today.

If Fredrick had his way with me, he'd be making plans to get me in gym during track. I went into the locker room to change, Fredrick and his friends were already out on the field, the coach yelled at me as I began to walk out of the locker room slowly. "Phillips! Get out on the field, we don't have all day," he yelled. I knew he was angry when he called me by my last name. I rushed out onto the field still fixing my shirt, when I stepped onto the dirt track; Fredrick was all ready to race me. "GQ, you think you can hold back a little and allow someone of us regular track runners to win?" He asked lifting his eyebrows smiling.

"You're such a waste of skin GQ," he said grinning. "Hey Hall, a little less lip, a bit more focus, let's get started," the coach said anxiously. We all lined up side by side to get ready for practice. I stretched my legs up toward my back and leaned forward stretching them both. I jumped up and down in high jumps to warm up, soon the coach directed us to get to the starting line. Fredric and I stared at each other as we stood on opposite sides of one another; I looked forward after giving him my signature smile.

As soon as the coach blew the whistle, I ran slowly at first giving Fredrick and the others a head start. When I could no longer see their names on the back of the T-shirts I sped up to catch up, I ran so fast I could hear the wind whistling in my ears. I vision Reese standing at the finish line waiting for me to make it there. She was smiling and waving assuring me that I would make it there and she'd be waiting to give me that hug. She always said goodbye, I couldn't get there fast enough before I knew it, I was on the line in front standing alone.

I leaned forward with my hands on my knees catching my breath, I looked down the track, and Fredrick was trailing the other track runners as they all tried to make it to the finish line. When I stood up I turned my back to see where Reese had gone; this time she was in the bleachers waving. I didn't wave back or smile, I knew that she wasn't really there. The coach came over to me and put his hand on my back. "Son, you did good, make sure you run like that in competition, keep up the good work Phillips," he said looking at his watch still waiting for the rest of the team to get to the finish line.

I sat down on the dirt track to catch my breath. When everyone else made it to the finish line, I got up and went to the locker room to change. I change quickly before the other guys came in I took my bag and place it on my shoulders and began to walk out. "Leaving so fast GQ?" Fredrick asked when he came into the locker room. I didn't say a word I continued to walk out as I passed everyone else. Fredrick wiped his face and neck with a towel and threw it at me, his friends followed what he did wiping their faces and necks throwing their towels also as I walked past them; their towels hit me so hard in the face.

I didn't look at them I continued walking quickly out of the locker room. When I made it outside, I wiped my face with my towel from my bag. As I walked, I would be walking through the pathway to get home. I walked slowly looking up at the trees and clouds following me. As I approached the end of the pathway, I began to hear footsteps following behind me. I turned around, there was no one there, and I looked up ahead of me there was no one ahead.

I began to walk faster toward the end of the walkway when I hear more than one pair of footsteps; I didn't look behind me this time. I knew it was Fredrick and his friends about to come after me; I began to run toward the end of the pathway; when out of the trees I hear a loud thump to the ground. I turn around, and there was Fredrick, I turned back around to continue walking as though I didn't see him. Then another thump to the ground this time dropping down in front of me was the girl I hung in the tree.

She smiled at me shaking her head, I dropped my gym bag and began to split ways between them both back through the wooded areas of the pathway. I ran as fast as I could; taking off my backpack tossing it to the ground so that I couldn't be caught by them pulling it. I ran as fast as I could, listening for their footsteps, jumping over tree branches and pushing my way through the brush. It seemed I'd never get away from them, as I approached the middle of the woods I could see them standing, waiting for me to come out.

I slowed down, peeking through the trees; I pulled back the branches to look out before turning to go back the other way. I slowly let them go, the tree branches spread apart wide when I let go of them they slammed the tree's in front of them. As I started to turn to go back I felt blowing in my ear, I was afraid to turn I was stuck, I turned slowly to look. It was the girl I left hanging in the tree that day in the flesh, I was startled; she smiled at me winking her eye. I ran backward out of the brush; still watching her as I ran out.

Fredrick grabbed me by my shirt and pulled me up from the ground. "GQ, nice to see you, we thought that was you hiding out in there, you think you can get away from us so easily?" He shook his head as he held me onto my shirt. "Come over here Tessa, show GQ what happens to one of us when they try to get rid of us," he said waving her over with his other hand. I stood still wondering what he'd do I wasn't afraid at that moment nor was I angry my body didn't change. I feared that I wouldn't be able to protect myself from what would happen next.

She walked over to me; I could see the madness in her eyes as she approached me. I closed my eyes, what to do I thought. They had me surrounded and trapped; I could hear them chanting her on. "GQ, don't tell me that you're afraid now?" He shook me by the shirt. "You're afraid now, open your eyes, we have a big surprise for you," he said. I pulled away from him trying to break free from his grip, I found myself kicking around in the dirt as he held on to my shirt tighter.

I opened my eyes to see what was happening, and standing over me was the girl. Tessa, he called her, she reached down at my shirt grabbing me pulling me across the dirt. "You like trees huh?" She said dragging me across the dirt toward the big trees ahead. "You know what I thought about as I hung there waiting for them to come for me? You don't do you? Well I can tell you, I thought about this very moment," she said as she dragged me. I tried grabbing onto the stubbles in the dirt ground, but I couldn't catch anything. "Don't worry," she said as she pulled me closer to her boots.

"I may give you a break, I may take my time with you," she said as we approached the biggest tree standing, she stopped. I looked up at her; her black boots were covered in dirt, she was still wearing the dress I bought Reese. I tried pulling for the dress; reaching for it while she held my shirt. She looked down at me suddenly letting go of my shirt, she held up her boot from the dirt and began kicking me, first in the face. I fell backward, she continued kicking me in the back, everywhere she could she kicked.

Soon they all came over and began to kick and talk as they kicked. "How do you feel about this GQ? Where's that smile you wore for me earlier?" Fredrick asked still kicking me. I held my head down into my knees trying to protect my head as they went on kicking. I slid around in the dirt trying to move away from them; it didn't help. I began to see my blood everywhere in the dirt; it spewed out of my mouth with every kick. I closed my eyes; I was fading in and out of consciousness now looking toward the big tree.

I didn't feel the pain from all the kicking anymore, but I could hear their heavy boots sweeping across the dirt with every kick. Soon everything was dark. "There he goes," I heard Fredrick saying to the others, the kicking stopped suddenly I felt myself being dragged across the dirt. I could hear the sound of the dirt and rocks as they drug me across, my back began to hurt. I could feel my shoulder blades bleeding it felt like they were being cut open with a sharp knife.

I began to come to; I looked around as I was being drugged across the dirt, where were they taking me? I wondered. We were away from the trees inside the wooded area away from where anyone would notice us; it was growing dark out. I could see them all; two of them had me by the shirt the others followed behind them looking around. "Here," I heard Fredrick say, I didn't want them to know that I was awake they flipped me over onto my back. "This is it," he said. I peeked to see what it was that he called it. It was a well there was an old rope hanging from the top of it.

Oh no, I wonder what they going to do now, I waited, keeping my eyes closed. "You get that end, hey you come up here, and we'll get this end." He told them as he approached me looking down into my face; he grabbed the front of my shirt. "Okay on three, we all pick him up," he said to them. "One, two, three" Soon I was being lifted up "On three again we throw him" he said to them again.

"One, two, three" soon I could feel myself being thrown into the well. I opened my eyes as they threw me in, the well was dark, I couldn't tell whether or not it was filled with water until I splashed into it, it began to feel wet and cold, and it was freezing. I looked up, I could see that sun was going down; I could hear Fredrick and his friends walking away from the well laughing and joking about what they had done to me. As I floated there in the well, my body stinging from the kicking, I began to feel around the walls of the well.

I followed circling in the water hoping that there's nothing else down there with me. Soon I felt a pole I couldn't see how it looked but it felt strong enough to help me get out, It was so cold I was shivering trying to hold on to pull myself up. The pole was cracking I pulled up and slid down quickly, falling backward into the water, my hands felt as if they were bleeding with every attempt. My body felt heavy as I reached up from the water, I yelled out; "God help me!"

As I fell back down into the freezing cold water, I was beginning to get so angry I slammed my hands down the in the water clutching my fist. "Ah! Ah!" I yelled out. "Ah!" again and again. I tried to get out, my lips were quivering, I stopped yelling out. I held onto the pole allowing my body to sink low into the water to try and keep my body warm. As time passed the night came, the night moon lit up the well. I could see around a little better, I felt my way around more.

Soon I came upon stairs; I grabbed onto them and began to climb up, my bodies freezing every inch of the way. When I made it to the top I held on to the top stair I was shaking; my body quivered with cold chills as the air hit. I began to climb out, putting one leg over the wall when I hear footsteps. "Oh no, you don't." It was Fredrick. He looked down at me hanging onto the stair rail. "You're not getting out of there GQ," he said laughing. I looked up to see what he was up to, he was gone, but I could hear him scrambling around in the dirt. What is he up to? I thought quivering holding onto the rail.

"Here you go GQ grab onto this," he said loudly. As I looked up I saw a big rock barreling down on to me I held the stair railing pulling myself closer to it so that the rock will miss me. I began to get angry as he went back to get another rock to throw. "GQ, you can't win this race, give up or die," he said looking down at me. As soon as I looked up he threw the rock. I jumped from side to side dodging the rocks I became so tired that my hands slipped from the railing.

I fell back into the cold water in the well, this time I was so tired and angry I sank all the way down I went under so angry I yelled as I fought my way back up. I felt my body changing the black blades split my shoulders coming out my body began to get warm as I pressed my way up I was covered with the black blades. The bladed feather-like wings spread out of my back, I yelled out; "ah!" As I came up and before I knew it I was out of the water and lying on top of Fredrick looking him in the eye with my hands to his neck.

"It took you long enough," he said struggling to get out of my grip. We scuffled around on the dirt in front of the well trying to grab onto one another me on top of him than him on top of me. He laughed as if this was a joke to him, he was able to get loose from my grip, and run toward the trees. I ran after him following him into the through the trees in the darkness, Fredrick laughed loudly as I ran after him. When I caught up with him, he stood in front of me laughing.

"You're hopeless GQ; you have nothing for me after all this." I was so angry I flew toward him trying to grab him, but he moved fast I couldn't grab him. I could hear him, but I couldn't grab onto him at all; soon he disappeared into the darkness leaving me. I looked into the darkness of the woods to find him, I heard him everywhere. I followed the sounds I could hear him breathing heavily I turned to walk away; he kicked me from behind sending me to slide in the dirt.

I turned quickly toward him, I ran back to grab him, he began to play around laughing and stomping his boots to the ground. Laughing with every stomp of his boots the sound was so loud it hurt my ears. It was as if he was shaking the earth with every stomp; I covered my ears and began backing up. He laughed. "GQ you're so weak," he said pointing at me as I backed up. The sky was dark as I backed up; he came close when I turned and began to run toward the outside of the wooded area, I was stopped.

Something bumped my back so hard that I was still; I looked back, and there was Tessa, the girl I hung from the tree. She reached out her hand to me smiling. "I thought you'd never ask," she said reaching for me; I stepped back moving away from her again. She pounced forward lunging to grab me, I stepped back toward Fredrick he was laughing as if this was a funny joke. "GQ, what are you so afraid of, you have your wings, right?" He said standing in front of me; I was stuck in between them both, not knowing where to move next.

I looked up into the moonlight, I closed my eyes and began to run between them both going for the trees and brush ahead. I ran as fast as I could; it was almost as if I was flying, I was almost near the edge of the woods when I heard my mom calling out for me. "Keagan! Keagan!" I hear as I grew closer to the edge of the woods I ran toward her voice not thinking about what she would say if she sees me covered in these bladed feathers all over my body. I ran toward her voice, as I ran my body warmed, and the bladed feathers began to disappear.

I ran and ran and just as I reached the edge of the woods where I could see mom Fredrick tackled me to the ground. I rolled with him through the dirt away from where mom could see us. I began to fight him trying to get loose. "No, No GQ, this is not over," he said as he rustled with me to keep me down on the dirt. Tessa ran over to me and began to kick me with her heavy boots. "Stay down there GQ, stay down," she said as she kicked.

I balled up with my head to my knees; I could still her mom calling out to me. I couldn't allow her to come looking for me, it could be dangerous for her, I thought as I laid there trying to cover myself from being kicking. I looked up Tessa was still kicking while Fredrick had his back turned looking through the brush as if he was waiting for mom to come through at any time. I got on my hands and knees and crawled away as fast as possible my body changed again covering me with the bladed feathers.

I ran around them in a circle I struck Fredrick with my bladed wing he fell to the ground. Quickly I hit Tessa hard enough to fall on top of him. I hit them both over and over again as hard as I could with my bladed wings until they stopped moving. I could hear mom still calling out for me I ran into the brush of the woods grabbing all of the tree limb tree branches that I could to cover them with. I threw them over them and went running into the woods to get to mom.

Darkness

That night mom and I walked to the car in silence; I was dripping wet with water from the well. My body was covered in dirt as I drug my body in the heavy wet clothes behind her. She wrapped her arms around me as we walked on; mom opened the car door for me helping me inside. It was freezing, I shivered all over; we drove home in silence. I don't know how long mom had been looking for me, but I could tell she was tired, she didn't say a word to me at all until we reached the house.

"Keagan, I want you to always know that your dad and I know what you're going through. We totally understand, if you should need us at any time, please come to us. I know it's been hard since Reese died, you can't take on her fight; you can't bring her back at all son, she's gone." Mom took me by the face and held my head close to hers. "I want you to be okay Keagan; I want you to stay safe." I got out of the car and walked to the door, I was still shivering from the wet water all over me.

Dad walked to the door to greet me; he was wearing his robe it was well past bedtime in our home. I didn't say a word; I walked up to my room and lay across my bed. I was covered in dirt; I rolled around onto my side in the covers to get warm covering my head. I kicked off my shoes one by one; they hit the floor splashing water as they fell to the ground. I closed my eyes exhausted from the struggle in the woods. I fell off to sleep wet and dirty thinking of Fredrick and his friend Tessa. How did she come back here?

I vision her hanging from the tree in Reese's dress. I know that I hung her there; I know that she wasn't breathing when I left her there. I bashed her over the head and strangled her, how did she come back? I wondered as I fell off to sleep. When I woke, the next morning dad was standing over me. "Son, get up," he said pulling the covers from my waist. "You need a shower, and we need to talk this morning," he said as he went over to the window to pull back the curtains.

I shook my head no as I sat up. "What's there to talk about dad?" I asked as I began to lift my shirt over my head. "There's a lot to talk about Keagan, these guys that you keep getting into trouble with; what do they want from you?" He asked me staring out of the window with his back to me. "I don't know dad, I don't think they want anything from me, they just like hurting other people," I told him standing to my feet to remove my pants. "Well son, you need to stay out of it, you had your mom and I so worried last night.

She was out there searching the streets for you last night for hours; do you think that's fair to us? We don't want to find you dead, we don't want you to come up missing," he tells me looking over at me. As I began to walk away, he approached me, taking me by the arm. "Son let me look at those," he said examining the bruises all over my back and neck? "What happened there son, what did they do to you?" "It was a fight dad, they kind of got the best of me when I fell to the ground, they were kicking me all over, but I got up dad. I fought them back."

"Keagan fighting is not always the answer, this looks really bad, maybe you should come to the hospital with me for some x-rays," he said pushing down on my side. "Son, these look really bad, are you hurting there?" He asked. "No dad," I answered moving away from him. "I'm fine, dad really," I told him going to the bathroom. "Son, you could have a fractured rib or some broken bones. Well, I'm not going to bother you about it, if the pain should get worse, please come to the hospital to get checked out," dad went out.

I ran the shower water as I stood in the mirror looking over my body, turning sideways looking at all of the marks and bruises they left on my body. They were blue, red, black, and green; they were everywhere. They looked like shoe prints, I washed my face and brushed my teeth as the water ran. Afterward, I got into the shower. I washed the dirt from my body thinking about Fredrick and his friends, what I would do the next time I saw them. I became so angry just thinking of what happened that night in the woods.

The way they threw me into the well, I imagined throwing them into the well the next time, I will not allow them to get out, I thought as I got out drying myself with the towel. I thought about all the things I could do to get them back to make sure they know that I'm not afraid nor will I give up fighting this fight for Reese. I'll make them pay for what they did to her, I thought as I began to dress for breakfast. When I got to the breakfast table mom and dad had everything set up for me at my seat.

I sat down and began to drink from the glass that was placed in front of my plate. Dad snatched the glass from my hand. "Keagan, say grace before you eat please," he said looking at me crossed. "I'm sorry, dad," I told him placing the glass back onto the table. We bowed our heads down as mom and dad held hands dad began thanking God for our food. I peeked up at them, they really believe in this stuff, I thought as I watched them with one eye opened, when they held their heads up I smiled at them both.

"Amen," I said reaching out for the glass once again. I giggled inside at the thought; they thought our food was blessed by God, while I was eating dad began to talk to me about what happened in the woods that night. "Son, is there a reason why these boys don't like you, did you do something to make them dislike you?" He asked me eating his food. "Of course not dad, I've been nothing but nice to them," I said in an offensive tone.

"Dad, do you really believe that this maybe our fault, mine and Reese's?" I asked him with my hands to the table. "No son, I am not saying that you and Reese deserved any of it at all, what I'm saying is that you have to move on and forgive them. Reese is gone she won't come back and what you're doing, holding on to her spirit in such an angry way. Son, you have to let it go," he said putting his hand on mine. "I believe you can, son, you can let it go, God will take care of the rest."

I snatched my hand from him, leaning back in my chair, I looked over at mom, and she was holding her head down as if she was praying for me. "I understand dad," I said standing from the table, I took my coat from the coat rack by the door, and I walked out. I stood at the door leaning against the porch rail. They really believe that I can just allow this to happen; allow them to live in peace after what they've done to Reese. What they've done; they are still doing horrible things to everyone around them, and I'm the one who is supposed to forgive them.

I thought as I began to walk away from the porch, I wanted to walk through the pathway today I knew that I would run into Fredrick and his friends on the way. By staying on the trail near the street, I wanted them to know that I'd made it out and the next time we get into it they would be the ones inside the well, not me. I thought as I walked down the pathway near the street soon I could hear footsteps behind me; there was more than two pair of shoes. I didn't turn around to see who it was; I assumed right off that it was Fredrick and his friends.

I cut through the pathway out of the way of the crowded street, the footsteps followed me. When I reached the wooded area, I turned around quickly. "What do you want from me?" I yelled with my fist to the air as if I was going to hit first. "Shish! Do you hear that?" It was Sage; she was with three other girls. "Hear what?" I asked with a sigh of relief that it wasn't Fredrick. I was hoping to get to school today without having to fight my way there. "I don't hear anything," I said to her in a whisper.

She stood back and turned around slowly I turned my head to see what she was looking at. "There's nothing there," I whispered. "Listen," she said turning my head around to face the well. She began to walk over to the well smiling the two girls followed her over to the well. I stood back watching them; I didn't want to go near the well, remembering the night before down in the cold well. "No thank you, I have to get going," I told her beginning to walk out of the woods back toward the pathway to get to the street.

She ran behind me grabbing my arm to pull me back into the woods. "No Sage I can't go, I don't want to see," I told her pulling away. She looked at me with the saddest look on her face; she blinked her eyes as she turned around to go back into the wooded area. I began to walk back toward the street sighing as I turned away then I turned back around thinking of her sad face, I ran behind her. "Okay, okay Sage, I'll go," I said running to catch up with her. She walked slowly approaching the well it was beginning to get warmer out; I removed my sweatshirt and continued walking behind her.

Her two friends waited near the well looking at me smiling as they waited. When we approached the well they turned to look down into it, I stood back. "Come Keagan, come over," Sage said to me guiding me with her hand. I walked up closer standing in between them, I looked down, at first I couldn't tell what I was looking at then, I moved in closer to see what they were staring at when Sage grabbed me by the head and pushed my head forward. "See what I see?" She said holding my head down.

I opened my eyes wide to get a better look into the dark waters of the well soon five faces were staring back up at me from under the water; I turned to Sage. "What is this, why are they down there, who are they?" I asked her in a panic as if I should try and reach down to help them up. "Look closer," Sage said pushing the back of my head down toward the water, I opened my eyes up wider looking down at the faces again, only this time there were five faces, but they were all the same, they mirrored my face I stepped back startled. "What is this?" I yelled out at Sage. "What are you doing?" I asked her.

"Shush," she said with her finger to her lips walking away from the well. Her two friends looked down and back up at me then ran off into the woods. Sage looked at me and took off running behind them, I watched as she faded further away into the woods when I could no longer see her. I walked over to the well and looked down again, I didn't see myself looking back up at me the five reflections were gone. When I turned to walk away, the water began to bubble as if there was air blowing from somewhere down in the water.

I stepped away from the well and ran back toward the street; I continued to run all the way to school. When I arrived at school, Fredrick and his friends were standing in front of the school taunting people walking by. I walked past them looking all of them in the eye. "What's up GQ?" Fredrick said laughing with his friends. I walked by them in silence just staring them in the face as I walked slowly away. In my first period class, we talked about our summer plans; Fredrick and his friends laughed and joked around about what they would do over the summer while continuing to make fighting jesters at me.

I didn't feed into it thinking about Sage, what did it all mean my face underwater in the well like it was? I doze off almost in a daydream thinking of my face in the well and Sage running off the way she did when I was tapped on my shoulder by Fredrick. "We're not done, all summer long," he said with a smile. I turned away from him, he tapped my shoulder again. "All summer long," he whispered with a smile. I turned around ignoring him once again when the bell rang; he jumped from his seat rushing to pass my chair following everyone out. I stayed seated until the class emptied.

"Keegan, the bell," the teacher said to me. "Get out of here; you don't want to be late for your next class." I grabbed my bag from the floor and stood from my seat as I began to walk out the bell rang I looked at the clock on the wall ahead of me. "Well, you're late now," the teacher said pointing up toward the bell. "Better rush Keagan, your next teacher might not be as kind as I am," the teacher said erasing the chalkboard looking forward at me. I walked quickly out into the hallways, I began to feel really sick to my stomach I rushed into the bathroom to wash my face.

I began to sweat all over I held my head over the sink holding the faucet dropping my book bag to the floor. The water was cold, but my body felt hot all over. I fell to the floor of the bathroom, sweating and shivering at the same time, I looked up to the ceiling, and the room began to spin fast around and around it went. I closed my eyes and opened them shaking my head to try and get it to stop; I tried to crawl over to the door of the bathroom to get some help.

It was so hard with the room spinning, my stomach aching, and my body both sweating and shivering. I gave up after I began to feel my breakfast coming up from my throat. I crawled over to the toilet stall near the door and began to vomit. I was still shivering and sweating, after vomiting. I lay on the bathroom floor flat on my back looking up toward the ceiling, the room still spinning. I closed my eyes I wrapped my arms around my body as if I was giving myself a big hug.

I wanted to get up from the cold floor of the bathroom but I couldn't. I rolled over on my side hoping that I'd feel better before the bell rang for the next class. People would come in and see me lying here I thought as I tried to comfort myself as the room spin in front of me. I closed my throat again feeling as if I would have to vomit again, soon I heard the bell ring. I opened my eyes trying to focus on the stalls with the door I wanted to get to the stall closest to me. I began to use my hands to slide my body to the stall; the room was spinning and spinning as I moved toward the stall.

Every inch was like torture; my stomach ached; I was sweating so badly that my shirt was completely covered in sweat. When I made it into the stall I curled my legs up and held them to my head with my back facing the tip of the toilet seat. Just as I closed the door to the stall

I heard some other people come in talking loudly, laughing about classes going into stalls and using the outside stalls. Some of them washed their hands, and some of them didn't, I could hear some of them writing all over the walls of the bathroom with markers stretching across the walls as I sat sweating and shivering.

Soon the bell rang again, they all scrambled to rush out, I didn't move from my position on the floor, I sat there taking deep breaths holding my knees to my face. The pain seemed worse; the room finally stopped spinning, still afraid to move. I clutched the toilet paper roller on the side of the stall wall to try and pull myself up from the floor, each time I was halfway up I would slide back down, I was so weak. I couldn't understand what was going on with me. I sat back down on the floor, I can't move; I'm in pain, and I can't move I thought as I looked down at the floor.

I leaned against the wall, closing my eyes, I must have fallen off to sleep because when I opened my eyes, the bathroom was completely dark, I grabbed the toilet paper roller to pull myself up I was still sweating. The pain in my stomach was not as bad as before, I stood to my feet keeping my hands to the stall walls. I can't see what's around me; I began to feel my way out of the stall searching for the stall lock to pull it open. I felt my way around the stall door until I found it; I pulled it toward me and began stepping out of the stall.

I held my hands out in the dark bathroom to find the wall where the light would be, I walked around the dark bathroom tripping over something lying on the floor. I felt my way back up from the floor and walked straight to where I knew I would find the light on the bathroom wall. I walked until my hands touched the cold wall, I felt the door then around until I felt a light switch. Yes, I thought with my hands on the switch, I flipped it upward to turn it on, the bathroom lit up.

As soon as I began to focus on what was around me, I saw standing before me Fredrick; he had a smile on his face with his hands stretched out to me. "Hey GQ," and with a quick slap to my face, I fell to the floor once again this time I began to crawl away from him quickly. I crawled so fast that he couldn't keep up, he ran behind me kicking his legs out trying to kick me in the back. I slid into the stall again this time standing to my feet really quick I was still sweating my hands began to turn black, and the pain in my stomach felt like someone was driving a knife through it and twisting as hard as they could.

Fredrick began to bang his fist on the bathroom stall door really hard then I began to hear banging on all of the bathroom stall doors. Oh no there's more of them out there I thought to myself sweating looking at my hands, I'm going to have to get out of here soon. I looked down at my hands as they began to change, black bladed like hairs grew out quickly. I put them on the door of the stall and pushed against it trying to keep them from coming in, soon I could feel my body making changes bladed like hair ripped through the sleeves of my shirt.

I turned around and looked up and looking down at me was Fredrick and Tessa and a few others they were all smiling. Fredrick jumped down landing into the stall with me. "Hi," he said standing in front of me, then with a quick punch to the face, I was on my back through the door of the stall looking at him standing over me, this time I jumped to my feet as if someone picked me up and held me still. My neck was covered with bladed black hairs and my face also, I felt strong standing in front of Fredrick, and my stomach tingled with excitement at the thought of getting him back for throwing me in the well.

I began rushing toward him, I felt powerful in that moment I had great strength, and I rushed toward him jumping to his throat to strangle him. As I reached for his throat, the others ran for me trying to get me before I could get him. It felt as if I flew to his throat I pinned him up against the bathroom stall and began to choke him. He fought back with fire in his eyes we tossed and turned all over the small bathroom stall trying to turn one another over; I grabbed hold of his throat and shirt and threw him back out of the stall rushing toward him to catch him before he could get up from the floor.

I grabbed him by the throat again, this time picking him up and throwing him across the room as hard as I could, he didn't get up. Soon Tessa rushed toward me and three others, I took them one by one throwing them all over the bathroom hitting mirrors and sinks and stall doors, the strength I felt was so great. I felt like I could pick up a car and throw it, I waited to see if any of them would move.

This was the greatest feeling I'd ever had while fighting them it felt so good. I turned to look at myself in one of the mirrors, I was covered all over with bladed black hairs like feathers, but they were hard, my eyes were completely white with black pupils, I looked very scary. I could see from the mirror behind me Fredrick getting up; he struggled for a minute then in the blink of an eye he was like a ball of fire rushing toward me. I bent down to avoid him, sliding my body over toward the bathroom door, as soon as I turned to look for him; he was there again in front of me.

He pushed me with his flaming hands; I hit the wall, the fire flared from my chest as I fell against the wall. I rushed away from him trying to get free, it didn't burn. I went into a stall near the door as soon as I went in he was in with me pushing me again with his hands on fire, this time I pushed back. When I reached to grab him again the fire from his neck rushed up the bladed black hairs on my arms, I let go quickly. Fredrick tried to grab me as I tried hanging on to his neck with the fire burning up my arms. It began to burn and smell I let go of his neck and stepped back shaking and patting my arms to put the fire out.

As I worked frantically to get the fire out running toward the sink to push down on the faucet I see Fredrick running behind me. I turned to him. He grabbed at me trying to grab hold of me. I jumped out of his way and began to go for his neck once again, quickly before the fire caught me I grabbed onto his neck and threw him with all of my strength toward the bathroom door. He went flying through the door; I turned around quickly turning the faucet water on and wetting my arms to cool the burning from the fire.

I quickly stepped over Tessa and the others to get near the window; I could hear Fredrick walking back toward the door to come back in. I jumped up onto the sink than onto the toilet in the stall and reached for the window. When Fredrick opened the door he looked up at me and began to walk toward me, the fire all over him glared over the walls and mirrors all over the bathroom. I looked back at him before jumping from the window; I fell down outside of the window onto the dirt of the schoolyard.

I ran thinking that it wouldn't be long before Fredrick and his friends would be after me, I was still covered with hair, looking back as I ran. I began to feel sick to my stomach again, sweat dripped from my body as if I had been running for hours. I felt as if I was going to vomit, as I ran I thought about how strong I was in the bathroom, I thought about how they must have feared what I would have done next. I began to grow sicker falling to my knees as I ran clutching my stomach in pain.

I would get up fast hoping that Fredrick and his friends wouldn't catch up to me, I looked back in a panic in pain. I sat on the ground in the dirt of the schoolyard clutching my stomach in pain. When I saw Fredrick and his friends coming from the school, I got up quickly and began to run through the schoolyard, clutching my stomach in pain. I wanted to get to the pathway near the street; maybe someone will see me and help me get to my house, I felt so bad I kept falling to my knees sweating, my body felt weak as I tried to get to the front entrance of the school.

I held onto the railing of the stairs leading down to the front of the walkway near the pathway, the bladed black hairs began to fade away. I looked back to see where Fredrick and his friends were, they weren't behind me, I looked all around me, they weren't anywhere around the front of the school. I walked faster toward the street, when I was close, I stopped near the sidewalk of the school to catch my breath, clutching my stomach coughing and spitting. I felt awful I began to walk slowly toward the pathway. I just need to get home, I thought as I walked slowly down the pathway.

I was almost near the edge of the pathway when I felt a cold wind blowing toward me it was so forceful it almost blew me to the ground. I looked around everywhere holding on to the fence near the trees in the pathway when I was knocked to my knees almost immediately after the wind blew at me. Fredrick and his friends; he pushed me to the ground; I held my hands up this time. I didn't want to fight anymore I was too sick, I was weak, and I couldn't fight another fight like the one in the bathroom.

When he pushed me I fell back onto the fence, I closed my eyes, and I could feel them all taking turns with their forceful hits. Fist after fist punching me in my head and face and stomach, my stomach already hurt badly but along with the punches it felt as if their fist were going all the way through my stomach. They all hit me as hard as they could, I could hear them grunting with each punch. I couldn't fight back, I couldn't move, I bounced back and forth from the fence hit after hit until I hear Fredrick yell out.

"Stop! Enough! GQ," he said coming close to me lifting my chin from my chest. "Have you had enough?" He asked holding my chin in his hand, I opened my eyes looking up at him shaking my head no, and my mouth began to water. I could feel the vomit clotting up in my throat as Fredrick let go of my chin my mouth open, out came the vomit. It spewed out of my mouth like a fountain, they all stepped back. "Ugh!" They all yelled out, Fredrick punched me in the stomach twice. "Can't hold in huh GQ," he said with his hand on my forehead.

The two guys with him held me by my arms; I didn't feel any better after vomiting. I felt as if I couldn't stand my body dropped down as they held me up by the pits of my arms. My head hung low, my chin to my chest, they let go of me leaving me weak to fall forward to the ground face first; I laid there on the ground, I was weak, I felt like I couldn't breathe. I laid there with my hands stretched wide with my face sideways plastered to the sidewalk of the pathway.

They stood around me circling my body as if they weren't finished, I didn't look up I couldn't move. I laid still with my eyes closed, my stomach feeling as if a hole was in the middle of it, burning and twisted in knots. I could hear them beginning to walk away one by one, the sound of their boots sent chills up my spine. Only four of them walked away, I could tell that one of them was still there standing over me. I laid there waiting for the next hit or kick, I know it's coming, I tighten up my fist, but before I allow the hit or kick I turn over, I wanted to face them.

I wanted to make sure I saw the face of the person who did it; I struggled to roll over onto my back. When I looked up there was Tessa she stood over me looking down with her eyes pierced up at mine, she was standing at my feet. She walked up toward my head slowly, she held her foot back from my face, and with a powerful sway of her boot she kicked me in the head as hard as she could. Everything went black, she kicked over and over again soon I was back in the dark tunnel as if I was dreaming.

This time it felt real, I felt as if I belonged there in the darkness of the tunnel. I turned to the walls to look for a way out; hands came from the walls of the dark tunnel reaching out to me in every direction. I tried to run, but they grabbed at me, they pulled me from side to side as if they would rip me apart. I couldn't yell or scream for help, it was as if my mouth was glued shut. I closed my eyes trying to fight my way out of the darkness of the tunnel.

The GQ Ball

I could hear mom calling my name; she sounds so far away. I hear footsteps all around me and beeping noises; I couldn't open my eyes I was no longer in the tunnel. Where ever I was, it was cold, my body shivering from the chill, soon a warm spread came over my body, I tried again opening my eyes this time one eye opened, my vision was blurred, mom stood up over me. "He's up! He's up!" She yelled out. I heard footsteps running toward me, then a snatch at my eye along with a bright light flashing in it.

"Can you hear me Keagan?" A man said to me standing over me listening to my heart while holding my arm. I shook my head yes, I could hear him. My eyes opened up wider, I looked over at mom sitting in the chair staring over at me. She had tears flowing from her face. "Keagan, can you see me?" The man asked I looked all around the room it was still cold. I bald my fists up tight grabbing onto the blanket pulling it up more toward my neck; there were wires and needles all over me.

"What am I doing here in the hospital?" I asked the doctor standing over me. Mom stood up beside the bed and grabbed my hand. "You were brought in by someone, they left you outside the front entrance of the hospital, do you remember, son? Do you know who brought you here?" She asked me. I shook my head no and turned to look around the hospital more. I was baffled, I closed my eyes, leaning back into the pillow; how did I get here? I wondered who brought me to the hospital.

When I closed my eyes I began to remember the fight, I began to remember Fredrick and Tessa. I remember the kick, Tessa kicked me in my head, and I began to see the tip of her boot clearly. I looked over at mom. "What is it son, do you remember anything?" She asked. I shook my head no again, I didn't want to tell her about what happened to me, nor could I explain who brought me here.

I turned my head to look the other way, my head was wrapped in bandages all around my head I looked down at my arms, and they were burned all over my hands and forearms. I pulled up my shirt to see why I was wrapped in a bandage all around my waist. I was so weak I tried to position myself in the bed to turn to look at my reflection in the mirror, but I couldn't. My body ached so badly that I was stiff. "Son, please tell me what happened to you," mom said holding my hand, crying.

"Mom, I got into a fight it was my fault, I should have walked away," I told her looking her in the eye. I turned away after telling her, I was so sick also and weak I thought as I remembered the bathroom and how sick I was before I was caught by Fredrick and his friends there. That scared me I was unable to fight back, I was weak, and I couldn't fight them back. I thought as I closed my eyes. "Keagan, you've been in here now for two weeks, a couple of your friends came by and left these," she said handing me two cards with signatures with names I didn't recognize.

I'd been here two weeks, I thought; looking at the clock on the wall. I took a deep breath sighing loudly they got me that time; they really got me I thought. As I thought about that night, they held me on that fence and beat me until I couldn't stand, I vision when I vomited on them, the continuous beating and that last kick to the head that Tessa gave me. I kept my eyes closed, I won't fight them anymore, and this is getting too dangerous. I'm in the hospital, I could have been killed, I thought as I lay there, this would be it for me.

Mom began to pray for me with her hand in mine, I wanted to snatch my hand away from hers. God knows nothing about this, if he was so great why am I here? I questioned as she continued praying for me, she left soon after she prayed promising to come back later with dad. When she left the room all I could think of was how beat up I was.

I wanted to see what I looked like in the mirror I put my hands to my face; it felt badly especially the knot on the side of my face where Tessa kicked me.

This was truly it for me I'll never fight again, this was really bad, I pushed a button on the bed to get the nurse, she came right in. "Hello young man, what do you need?" The nurse asked. "I wanted to know if you would help me turn over onto my side please, I just want to look out of the window," I told her. "I need to check your vitals and check those burns on your arms first okay, and I'm not sure, but I believe the doctor wants you flat on your back. You had a couple of broken ribs, sweetie," she said coming over to me pushing a machine with numbers on it.

"You scared your parent's young man," she said putting a thermometer into my mouth. "So do you remember how you got here?" She asked, of course, I couldn't answer her I was too busy holding the thermometer in my mouth. "You're a lucky young man," she said as she gently took my arm and wrapped a cold cuff around it. She began to push the buttons on the machine; the cuff began to squeeze my arm tight at the same time it beeped as if it was warning her. She took the stick from my mouth and watched as the cuff slowly began to deflate.

"Good, good, good," she said as she wrote on the paper near the tray by the bed. "Sit up straight young man, I need to listen to your heart-beat," she said helping me to sit up straight. She took her stethoscope and began to rub her hands over the end of it while placing the other ends inside her ears. She was beautiful; her hair fell across my chest as she leaned in to listen to my heartbeat. She then began to rub her hand across my waist. "Does this hurt at all?" She asked me. I shook my head no although it did hurt just a little.

"You can tell me if it does, I'll give you something to help with the pain okay young man." She said walking over to the bottom of the bed, "I think we're all done for now," she said wrapping the blanket tight around my feet. "I'll be back in to check on you in another half hour, but in the meantime, you can push this button right here," she said pointing to the button on the bed. She walked out closing the door behind her. I turned the television on; there were music videos on.

I watched until a tray of food was brought into my room. "Hello, Keagan Phillips, right," the person said holding a tray and a piece of paper in her hand. "Yes, I'm Keagan Phillips," I told her picking my head up from the pillow to get a better look at her. "Good," she said sliding the tray across the bed tray that was hanging over my bed. "Okay Keagan Phillips, today for lunch you have a nice turkey sandwich with a side salad and pea soup, yum right," she said opening her eyes wide. I frown at her a little.

"Excuse me, is there any way I can get an apple? That's all I want is a red apple," I asked her. "I'll check on that for you, but first you should try eating this," she said lifting the tray top. "This is healthy, and you will be able to get out of here in no time if you're healthy," she said placing the top of the tray on the side dresser. I stared at the turkey sandwich and all its fixing packets of mayo and mustard and pickles, tomato and lettuce. Why not I thought, reaching to pick the sandwich up, I began to top it with everything.

I adjusted the bed upward to a sitting position so that I could eat. I ate the turkey sandwich so fast; I must have been starving because when the nurse came in, she noticed everything on the tray was eaten. She came over to me; "Keagan, are you still hungry?" She asked me; when I started to answer the lady who had brought the tray in was at the door. "Look at what I have for you young man," she said holding out a red apple. "Thank you," I told her reaching out for it as she walked toward the bed.

"I guess you do want to get out of here," she said taking the tray up from in front of me. "You finish that, and maybe I'll find you a couple of cookies somewhere after dinner," she said walking out with the tray.

The nurse came over to me; "I need to take your temperature before you eat that," she put the thermometer in my mouth. "You like music huh?" She said looking up at the television, I couldn't answer her with the thermometer in my mouth, I shook my head yes. "Me too, I love music, all kinds but especially jazz," she said with a smile.

"Do you have to go to the restroom Keagan?" She asked I shook my head yes. "Okay Keagan, let me get a small walker, this will be your first time getting up from there since you've been here, I don't want you to fall," she said going to the door. She came back with a little silver bar handle thing with rails on each side and wheels on the bottom. "Is that thing really necessary?" I asked looking over at it. "Oh yes young man, it's very important that you have support, you have a couple of broken ribs sweetie." She said to me bringing the walker close to my bed; she helped me to my feet.

"Here sweetie, place your hands on the rails, and I'll hold on to you from the back of your gown. Now if you began to walk and you're hurting too bad, please let me know, and we'll stop until you can go any further," she said holding onto my gown tightly with her small hands. We walked so slowly to the restroom. After using the restroom she walked me back to my bed. "Do you think I'll be getting out of here soon?" I asked her as she helped me sit gently on the bed.

"I'm going to check on that for you Keagan, but I'm sure you'll be with us for at least another couple of days," she said pulling the covers over me. "Are you warm enough?" She asked. "I can bring you in more blankets if you like," she said walking over to the foot of my bed to write in my chart hanging on the bottom of the bed. "No, thank you," I told her pulling the covers to my neck. I looked over to the window, it looked warm out; I wondered what was going on at school while I'm in here.

I wondered who Fredrick was picking on today. I closed my eyes falling off to sleep; I dreamt about Reese in the dress I bought her for the dance. I dreamt of us dancing together I watched in the dream as she went into the girl's restroom. I watched as they all attacked Reese spitting gum all over her dress and hitting and pulling her hair as she was pushed to the ground of the bathroom floor. She looked up as if she was looking at me.

I woke up in a cold sweat thinking of how angry it had made me that night, thinking of how Reese didn't deserve to be treated that way and how it must have made her feel. I raised the bed up; I wanted to get out of there. I needed to get Fredrick and his friends for what they did to Reese; they pushed her to do what she did to herself. I thought as I sat up looking at the television, soon there was a knock at the door. "Can we come in?" A male voice asked. "Sure," I replied quickly, the door opened slowly.

"Hey Keagan, how are you?" It was Randall, Travis Matthew, and Jacob from GQ club. "Hello, what are you guys doing here?" I asked. "What's with the frown?" Randall replied before answering the question. "Oh I'm sorry, I just had a very bad dream," I told him trying to fix my expression. "Really, what are you guys doing here?" I asked them again. "Well you're a member of the GQ club; we have to check on our own, how are you Keagan?" He asked me slapping my feet.

"You look better than you did before, I came to see you a couple of weeks ago, and you were out of it." "I heard, I was out of it." "Yeah man what happened?" Jacob asked. "You were really messed up, I heard you were hit by a car, were you hit by a car?" He asked. I shook my head no. "You can't remember anything?" Matthew asked. "No, hey did you guys come here to ask questions or what?" I asked looking crossed.

"Oh no man, we came to check on you, see if you were up and ready," Randall said standing at the foot of my bed with his hands in his pockets. "We really wanted to know how you were, I mean we have an important dance coming up, the GQ ball, we wanted to see if you were up for it," Matthew said shrugging his shoulders. "The GQ ball?" I asked

"Yes it's our annual ball we hold one every year at the end of the school year, do you think you'll be out of here, by next Friday?" Randall asked.

"I don't know, I want to be out here now," I answered. "You'll be ready, we've already matched you with a girl from the ladies club," Jacob said smiling. "Oh no, who is it, man," I said shaking my head. "I can't tell you, we want you to be surprised," Matthew said smiling. "So get better Keagan, you can't miss the most important dance of the year," he said slapping my feet with his hand once again. They filled me in on all the end of the year hoopla, the dances and talent shows and the seniors leaving, and us becoming sophomore's this coming year.

It all sounded so wonderful, for a while until I realized that it would mean another year of school with Fredrick and his friends. They joked around for a while about the cafeteria food and the teachers after a while they leave, and the lady with the tray of food came in with my dinner. "Keagan Phillips," she said holding the paper in one hand and the tray across her arm. "You have turkey, potatoes, and gravy with broccoli and cheese a dinner roll and two sugar cookies, two cranberry juices, yum, yum." She said as she slid the tray across the bed tray sitting on my bed.

"Thank you," I told her as she began to leave the room, I was very hungry I ate my dinner quickly. That night mom and dad came in to see me, they told me that I would be going home, the next day I couldn't wait to get out of there. I smiled the whole time they were there. Mom brought a bag of my clothes for me to change into tomorrow. "Thank you, mom, what time should I began to get dressed, what time are you coming to get me," I asked her.

"I'll be here at 10am, for you, the nurse will have everything ready for you to go at that time, all you have to do is get dressed and wait for me," she said raising her eyebrows. "What's wrong mom, you act like you don't want me to leave," she shook her head. "I just want you to be okay, I don't want you to get out of here and go out fighting again. You almost died Keagan, and no one knows how you ended up here," she said looking up at the ceiling. "Mom, I'll be fine, don't worry, I don't plan to fight anymore, I'm done with that."

"You promise son," she said with excitement in her voice. "Mom, I won't make you any promises, but I can't tell you enough how much this has changed me," I told her sitting up. Dad didn't say too much at all he sat there looking out from the window. "Dad, are you okay?" I asked

him "I'm fine son, I just really wish you'd listen to your mother and me sometimes," he said with one hand in his pocket "Dad, I will try to stay away from any trouble," I told him.

The next day the nurse came into my room early, she helped me into my clothes and gave me pain medicine so that I wouldn't be in pain on the way out. When mom came they wheeled me out to the car, I wanted to walk, but the nurse wouldn't allow it. Mom had the car parked close to the entrance door, we drove home in silence. When we made it to the house, she parked the car as close as she could to the stairway near the front door. "Take it easy Keagan," she said as I tried getting out of the car.

"You need to pace yourself," she said running over to the door to help me stand. After we got into the house mom helped me to my room. I laid across my bed thinking about how I wanted so badly to know who Matthew was setting me up with for the GQ ball. I bet it's someone that I don't like, I thought as I laid there in bed. After that day I began to get better and better; I swam for exercise and walked around the block every day for strength.

Soon, I was back to normal running around the block every day sometimes with mom and dad; sometimes alone. I couldn't wait to get back to school the ball was in four days; mom and I had been looking around for the perfect tux for the occasion. Matthew came by a couple of times to make sure I was getting ready. When I returned to school all of my teachers were so happy to see me, in my first-period class my teacher clapped when I entered the classroom.

"Welcome back Mr. Phillips, we missed you," she said writing on the board. I took my seat quietly trying not to bother anyone. "Yes welcome back." I heard behind me; it was Fredrick he placed his hand on my shoulder. "Really glad to see you're well," he said with a grin. I ignored him. I went from class to class ignoring him; I asked to be seated in front of the class in the rest of my classes that I shared with him. I told mom that I wouldn't fight, I'm going to try not to, I thought throughout the day as I passed him in the halls before the bell rang for class.

I watched him at lunch taunting other people along with his friends. They pushed people down; took food from their lunch trays, and tripped some of them down placing their boots on their backs while laughing and digging into their backpacks. When I couldn't take anymore, I walked over to the library until lunch was over. I didn't know how much more I could take. When the bell rang at the end of the day I rushed home, after three days of watching Fredrick and his friends I was sick at the thought of being anywhere near them.

When the night of the ball came it was so intense, I waited at the house for Matthew and Jacob to come by. They had all planned for us to go together in a limousine with our ladies club dates. I was a nervous wreck waiting for them to show up. I paced the living room floor back and forth while mom and dad tried taking pictures of me in the tuxedo it was black and burgundy I looked really nice. When the limo showed up Matthew, Randall and Jacob got out, and the girls got out one by one there was three of them.

I waited to see when the fourth one would get out of the limo soon she got out. It was Sage, it looked like Sage. I rushed to the door, I couldn't believe what I was seeing; Sage didn't go to our school. How did they know her? I wondered; I opened the door quickly looking all around them as they entered the house, mom and dad took pictures of everyone. "You all look so nice," Mom said "Sage?" I asked. She smiled at me and shook her head yes. She looked so beautiful; her dress matched my burgundy tux.

Mom handed me a wrist corsage to give to her, I placed it on her wrist and took her hand as mom and dad took their pictures. We walked out one by one to the limo; we drove off to the school for the ball. When we arrived in front of the school, there was a red carpet stretched out for all of us. It was as if we were royalty, we went inside the dance, immediately Sage and I went to the dance floor. She smiled as we danced the night away on this perfect night.

When the slow songs came on, I held her tight and danced with her, and when the fast ones came on we danced and laughed, no one wanted the night to end. When the dance was over we all walked out to the limo together, the moon lit up the sky; we all waited for the limo driver to pull up. I looked over at Sage; "thank you so much for coming," I told her. "I had such a good time Keagan, you don't have to thank me," she said taking me by the hand. I looked down at her hand then took it to my lips kissing it softly, she smiled at me.

"Thank you Keagan," she said again. Just as the limo drove up, Sage stepped up closer to me and leaned over to my face and kissed my lips it was a surprise. I leaned into her lips kissing them softly everyone began pointing at us laughing. "Alright man!" Matthew yelled out. The limo drove us all home dropping us off one by one at our doors. I was the last to be dropped off; when the limo arrived at my house I got out and went inside. It was dark when I turned on the light in the kitchen to grab an apple; mom was on the kitchen floor.

There were broken glass and dishes everywhere, I ran to mom to try and wake her, but she didn't wake up. I ran to the phone to call 911, the phone wires were cut from the wall. I ran back to mom, I sat down beside her, trying to wake her by shaking her. I sat over her and began to do CPR before I could start she gasped out; "no!" Sitting straight up on the floor, looking around in fear "Mom, it's me Keagan," I said grabbing her by the shoulders trying to calm her.

She pointed to the outside patio; I ran over to the patio windows to see what she was pointing at. Five shadows were standing at each end of the pool; they were dark they stood with their heads down. When I looked out at them, only one of them stared back at me. The face scared me so much that I shut the blinds to the door. I went over to mom and hugged her. "Mom, what happened?" I asked as I held on to her on the floor. "What happened?" She stared up at me without a word.

Come To Me

I held onto mom, she looked as if she had been fighting for a while. She pointed to the sink, and then put her hand to her throat. "Do you need water?" I asked her getting up from the floor to go to the sink. She looked out at the dark shadows outside, I took a glass of water over to her and held it to her lips, her hands shook trying to hold onto the glass. "Mom, what happened? Who are they?" I asked as they began to fade away from the backyard one by one. "Don't worry Keagan," mom said to me in a whisper holding onto the cup in my hand. I placed the cup on the ground and went over to the window.

"Leave it alone Keagan, they are stronger than you are," she said to me waving for me to come back over. "Let them go." I watched them fade away into the darkness. "Mom, what happened? What do they want? Why were they here, are you okay?" I asked question after question with no answer. She looked up at me in silence; soon there was a knock at the door. "I'll be back mom," I told her running to the door. I looked out of the peephole on the door. "Who is it?" I said trying to see who it was I was looking at.

A badge was presented to me outside the peephole. "Can I help you?" I said, still not opening the door. "We need to speak with a Keagan Phillips please." The badge went down; I could see who it was from the peephole. It was Detective Hall and another officer. I didn't want them to come into the house, with mom in the kitchen and the floor covered in glass. I opened the door slowly with only a crack wide enough to see their faces. "Yes sir, I'm Keagan Phillips," I said peeking my head out from the crack.

"Can we come in and talk to you; we'd like to ask some questions about what happened to you a few weeks ago. We missed you at the hospital, you left before we could get back to file a police report." The detective said standing next to Mr. Hall. I didn't trust Mr. Hall; there was darkness all around him. "I can't talk right now sir I'm very sorry, but I'm sick," I said coughing loudly with my hand to my mouth. "Son, it's important that we speak with you, are your parent's home?" Mr. Hall asked.

"No, sir, my mom is at work and so is my dad, you should probably come back when they get home," I told them beginning to shut the door. They stood staring at me for a moment; they looked at one another then back at me. "Son, we just have a couple of questions for you, do you remember what happened or how you got to the hospital?" "Sir, I didn't get your name," I said to the other officer. "My name is Detective Anderson," he reached his hand through the door to shake mine. I looked down at his hand; "sir I wouldn't want to give you this cold I have," I told him.

"It's nice to meet you, Detective Anderson," I said. "I'm so sorry, but I can't talk to you without my parents being here." I closed the door and went back over to mom, she was laying on the kitchen floor blood flowed from her legs and hands "Mom!" I yelled. She opened her eyes wide; I lifted her head placing her arm to her face to let her see the blood. "Mom, where is it coming from? What happened?" She reached over at my head and grabbed a dish towel off the chair and began to wrap her arm with it.

"Keagan, run the water hot, please," she told me pointing over at the sink. I ran over to the sink to turn on the water as she stood up from the floor. "Mom, are you going to tell me what happened here?" I asked her. "Keagan I'm okay, who was at the door?" She asked walking over to the sink. She had cuts and gashes all over her legs she took the cloth from around her arm and wet it with the hot water. "Keagan, please go and get the first aid kit from the cabinet in the hallway. She began wiping the gashes and cuts with the towel. She sat down at the table. "Look at this mess," she said shaking her head.

"I'll help you clean it up mom," I told her sitting the first aid kit on the table. She began to clean and bandaged her cuts. I helped her put them on, when we finished she got up and went to the closet for the broom. "Keagan, can you get the trash for me please?" She asked while sweeping, I brought over the trash can and began to remove the bigger pieces of glass from the floor. "Keagan, who was at the door?" She asked me again.

"It was Detective Hall and another officer; they wanted to ask me some questions about what happened to me. I asked them to come back when you and dad were available to talk to them." "Keagan, why didn't you talk to them, tell them what you know?" She asked. "I don't know anything mom," I told her helping her with the sweeping. "You have to start telling people what's going on," she told me. "I don't trust Mr. Hall, he's Fredrick's dad, and Fredrick's a really terrible person. He does nothing but taunts people at school; he never gets in trouble, and I bet Mr. Hall knows that he does things like that."

"Maybe he doesn't know Keagan, maybe Fredrick is the perfect angel at home. His mom and dad may not know what he's doing at school." "Mom, I don't believe that and Mr. Hall is..." I started to tell her that about the darkness I can see around him when he comes around until I remembered that she wouldn't understand. "Mom it's just something weird about him," I told her taking the trash can from the floor of the kitchen. She stood looking at me with the broom in her hand as I walked out of the back sliding door to the outside trash.

"Keagan, you need to let whatever you think happened with Reese go. It's only going to cause you to be bitter; you're too young to become bitter." "Mom why are we talking about me, I'm not the one who was found on the floor of the kitchen today," I said to her holding the trash can in my hand. "Did I ever tell you that I was in an accident son?" She told me pulling a chair out for me taking the trash from my hands and placing it in the kitchen closet.

"Sit son," she told me. "I know you've been in an accident mom, what does it have to do with what happen here today?" I asked her looking her in the eyes. "Son, after that accident, strange things began happening to me, supernatural things. Things that I couldn't understand," she told me. "I believe I was a little over eighteen when it started, and I can't tell you what it did to me, but I was afraid," she told me taking my hand. "We never thought we'd have to tell our children, but you are different from the twins they don't have what you have."

"I know you don't understand what goes on with you all the time, but son its real, and most importantly you need to know that it can also be dangerous. Some spirits aren't all nice," she told me. "Some of them, want to harm you, those are usually the ones I encounter. It took me awhile to understand what was happening to me, but eventually I put it all together," she told me looking out the window. "And dad?" I asked. "Is he the same way?" She shook her head yes.

"So you know these things about me, but you've never told me. Why didn't you tell me, mom? There have been all sorts of things going on with me, my body changes, and I get strong and weak at times. Mom, why didn't you tell me?" I asked her again. "Your dad didn't want to tell you; he thought it was best you found out on your own, the way we did. You're getting older now." "Mom, but I needed to know these things, I was being picked on every day, and so was Reese."

"I tried to protect her from those guys; I try to protect everyone from them. I'm not afraid mom," I told her. "I know you're not, son, but if you don't know your strength, you can hurt someone or yourself." She told me holding my hand; "Keagan it is Godly, what you have is a gift from God." She says with her hand on my face. "No, mom it's no gift from God, the way these guys beat up on people and just run around fearlessly doing horrible things. It's not Godly, mom, what Reese and I had to deal with every day."

"You say God is good and only does good things, that he can fix things, then why is Reese gone? Why is he allowing Fredrick and his friends to do what they do?" I asked her in an angry tone getting up from the table and walking away. "Mom, I just don't believe it; I won't believe it." "Son, come back, sit down please and hear me out," she said patting the chair next to her. "I want you to understand what's happening to you. I want you to get to know the Lord on your own."

"If you don't believe he's real, I can't make you, but please allow me to tell you these things so that you can protect yourself." She said looking up at me from the seat she sat in. I walked back over to her and took her hand, sitting down next to her in the chair. "Keagan, these things that you are experiencing when you fight or get angry; you may think that they're unnatural, but they aren't. They're natural for you; you have to believe that the good in you over powers what's bad around you."

"If you can use the good to control the bad, you'll be fine, but if you allow the darkness to take over, you may become as terrible as Fredrick and his friends. Your dad and I pray for you all the time even if you don't believe in God we pray that he gives you understanding. We pray that you get what we have; the strength to believe that he will fight your battles when you can't." "Mom, please stop, I appreciate you and dad praying for me, but I think I'll do what I've been doing and fight them back until I can't anymore. If they attack me I have no choice but to fight them back," I told her shrugging my shoulders and walking away from her.

She put her head down as I walked upstairs to my room, tomorrow I have school I thought as I entered my room. We have to turn in our books soon for inventory for the last day of school. I need to get them all together so that I can turn them in. I began to go into my closet to get the books that I don't use everyday I stacked them up to get them ready for tomorrow. When I finished, there were sixteen books. I put eight into my backpack, and I would carry the rest in my arms I thought as I put them neatly in the corner by the door.

So that I wouldn't leave them in the morning, I laid across my bed thinking about the things mom told me. She really didn't tell me too much, she kept dismissing my questions about what happened in the kitchen while I was gone. I laid there thinking of what must have happened in there, something was going on, and she kept it all from me for some reason. I thought as I fell off to sleep. I dreamt of Reese; she was hanging over me as if she was flying. Her red hair hung from her face falling onto mine we looked at one another eye to eye, she smiles blowing me a kiss with her hand.

I reached out to her face to pull hers closer toward mine, and she pulled away. "Keagan, I miss you," she says in a whisper as she fades away into the white ceiling. I jumped up from my sleep reaching for her face; I sat up in my bed. Then standing to my feet I walked over to my desk and pulled out a chair, I began working on some homework that I'd left undone earlier that day. It was 3:42 am, as I worked I began to hear crashing noises coming from downstairs. I stood from my desk chair; I quickly ran downstairs looking for mom.

"Mom, Mom!" I yelled. "Where are you?" I yelled out as I walked all around the kitchen, she was nowhere to be found. I went to the living room, she was nowhere in there, I heard more crashing sounds coming from the back of the house. I went to the back sliding door to look out; chairs were moving around out there, and the wind blew heavy toward the patio table with the umbrella, it was the patio table. It had flipped upside down the glass had shattered all over the patio. I took the broom and ran out to sweep it up before the wind blew it into the pool; I began to sweep all around.

I took the chairs one by one and set them against the wall I was careful not to step in the glass. I went over and took the broken table to the side of the house. As I was walking back over to pick up the broom, I squatted down to pick up the dustpan when I heard the water trickling as if someone was swimming underwater. I took the broom in my hand and stood up; I walked over to the edge of the pool and looked down. It was dark, but I could see a figure in the water, I took the end of the broom.

I put it down in the water reaching to poke whatever it was I held on to the end of the broom as I waved it around in the water. It wasn't touching anything I moved it back and forth, it was nothing, I better go back over and sweep I thought as I began to pull the broomstick back up holding it from the bottom. I pulled it up inch by inch, it was coming up quickly, as soon as I had it above the water in the air something snatched it quickly and pulled me into the water with a big splash. I went burrowing into the water under water I was still holding the broom I turned around and around in the water looking for what pulled me in.

There was nothing until I looked up, and there looking down at me from the edge of the pool I saw Reese I soared to the top of the pool above the water to see if what I was seeing was real. When I came up, she was smiling down at me, with a wave she walked away pointing down at the water. "Wait!" I yelled out to her, but she was gone, I turned to look into the water at what she was pointing at. Again there was a reflection of me in the water, as the light shined down on the water from the moon. I saw the reflection all around me; I hurried over to grab the wall near the stairs of the pool grabbing the broom along with me.

When I got out I threw the broom to the ground, I looked down into the water following the light of the moon to see if the reflections were still there. They faded one by one, I didn't even think about sweeping the glass anymore I ran to the slide in door taking the broom with me I went inside. Closing the door behind me I walked over to the broom closet to put the broom back and noticed a trail of blood, I'd stepped in the glass and cut my feet.

I sat down at the kitchen table to see if I could find the glass. There were big pieces and little pieces I held a napkin from the table in one hand and pulled the glass out with the other. Blood dripped everywhere the napkin was dripping blood also. I couldn't walk on mom's carpet with blood streaming from my feet, I thought as I began to grab more of the napkins. I wrapped my feet up and tried walking without pressing my feet against the carpet to hard. I creep across the carpet slowly hoping the blood doesn't soak through the carpet.

When I reached the top of the stairs, I noticed a little blood on the napkins I jumped across the last stair and into my room falling on my knees. I got up and went to my bathroom to run the water over them and bandage them up. I sat on the toilet wrapping my feet with gauze from a first aid kit I found underneath my bathroom sink, when they were all wrapped I went back to my bed. It was cold in my room freezing as if the window was open; the window had been closed all day. I got up to check to see if maybe mom had opened it while I was gone earlier.

I placed my feet gently on the floor and tip toed across the room to the window to check it. It was shut tight there wasn't even a draft; I tiptoed back to the bed shivering. I wrapped myself in the covers and fell off to sleep. When I awoke the next morning the sun shined right in my face, I got up from bed forgetting about the cuts on my feet. Placing my feet flat on the floor the cuts were closed, but they opened right back up. It felt as if they were being ripped apart; I grabbed the desk chair and sat on the floor.

"Ouch!" I yelled out. "Ouch, ouch, ouch," I said as I unraveled the bandages to check the cuts. I looked over at the books next to the door, oh wow, I have to take those back today, how will I ever make it on these? I thought as I slowly stood to my feet, I took a hot shower and let the water run over my feet, when I got out I dried off. I wrapped my feet back up and put my socks over the wrapping. I went to my closet and began to dress, blue jeans, a baby blue sweater a jean jacket and my boots.

I rushed out walking as fast as I could; I took the books from the floor and my backpack. I walked as fast as I could, with every step I felt the ripping of the cuts on my feet when I reached the stairs I called out for mom. "Mom, Mom!" I yelled holding the heavy books; I wanted her to drop me off at school today. I can't carry these books all the way to school with these cuts on my feet; mom didn't answer me I walked slowly with the books down the stairs. "Mom, mom where are you?" I yelled out.

Still, no answer as I reached the bottom of the stairs, I walked into the kitchen she wasn't there. She'd left a note for me by the plate of breakfast she made; "Keagan, I'm sorry, I had to go and meet your father for coffee, we had some early appointments. I made you your favorite, eat it all before school, I love you son be safe." I put the letter down, I took a slice of orange that she cut and stuffed into my mouth, hugging the books to my chest I went to the door. This would be very challenging, I thought as I shut the door behind me.

It hit my backpack almost throwing me over the porch I caught my-self from falling over clutching my feet to my boots. It was painful; it was a little windy out as I took off toward the path to school. I walked as fast as I could taking a few steps here and there, the pathway seemed further away than usual it seemed to be moving away from me. I wanted to get through the pathway fast; the cuts on my feet slowed me down, and as I began to get close the wind seemed to pick up with every step.

I had the books stacked from my waist to my chin; I was near the entrance of the pathway when suddenly the books were being snatched away from me one by one. A cold wind would come, and with it, a book would disappear from the pile, the wind whistled again and again, and with each whistle, a book left my stack until I only had one book in my hand. I grabbed it to my chest holding it tightly continuing to walk forward, crossing my hands and arms to the book.

The wind was heavier with every step, once when I made it to the entrance of the pathway near where I could see the school, I felt tugging at my backpack. I was trying not to fight anymore, hearing my mom and dad in my head pleading with me to stay out of trouble. I continued forward to the school, when I was grabbed from my backpack and pulled to the ground, I looked up at the trees there didn't seem to be anyone around.

I began to sit up, the books in my backpack were so heavy, I struggled up from the ground standing on my cut up feet it felt as if they were being ripped apart all over again. I held my backpack straps tight to help me get steady on my feet; I looked all around me to see if there were any signs of Fredrick and his friends. The wind blew softly at the trees; I looked around for the books they were scattered all around the dirt near the trees. As I approached the wooded area away from the trees to pick up the books, as I leaned over to pick the books up one by one I was shoved from behind into the bushes where no one could see me.

"I don't want to fight!" I shouted as my face hit the dirty ground. I tried getting up, with my hands to the ground as if I was doing pushups; I pushed myself up turning my head to the side. "I don't want to fight," I said loudly trying to stand to my feet. "Please, leave me alone," I said loudly dusting the dirt from my jeans. I began to walk out toward the edge of the woods near the street. Something pushed me so hard that I flew back into the woods; I fell back up against the tree. After catching my breath I took off running, I ran and ran until I was near the well.

I wanted to get away from whatever it was, I couldn't see it. I ran around the well then back through the trees I could hear the sound of the wind picking up, I ran faster through the trees and bushes only looking back once or twice to check for anyone behind me. When I reached the edge of the woods again this time, I was shoved from the front of my chest. I fell to the ground this time five dark shadows were standing around me I could see them, as they formed a circle around me.

The wind picked up, it blew heavier, I turned around to try and crawl out of the circle, the force from the wind held me in tight grip I clutched onto the dirt trying not to move. I grabbed the weeds in the dirt and held them tight, "I don't want to fight!" I yelled out as the wind blew in my face, soon one by one the dark shadows began to form shoes and clothes then faces. It was Fredrick and his friends they were smiling at the way I looked hanging there trying not to be blown away by the wind.

My clothes began to blow away first my shirt, then my pants, then one by one my shoes. I dug my fingers into the dirt more and more with every heavy blow from the wind. I reached into the dirt for a stronger piece of weed, I felt a big rock I held onto it as the wind blew, I looked up at Fredrick; what next I thought as the wind blew in my face. I watched them look at one another and smile, I blinked my eyes to clear them, and in a flash the wind blew harder than ever. I went flying into the woods near the well again, I had only my socks and boxers on, my feet were burning all cut up in my socks.

I laid there for a second, I didn't want to fight I thought as I tried getting up again I looked behind me and there were Fredrick and his friends running toward me. I didn't hesitate I ran toward the well and jumped inside, I didn't fall in the water I held onto the rusty steal stair and waited for them to come over to look in. I used my bleeding feet to grip the wall when Fredrick came over to the well to look for me. I pushed from the wall and grabbed him throwing him into the well when his friends heard the splashing and yelling they came running over.

They looked down and quickly one by one I grabbed them throwing them into the well, I climbed up using my feet the cuts felt as if they were splitting up. I leap over the wall of the well; I began to run out of the woods looking for my clothes on the way. I put my pants on jumping around in a hurry before they caught me; I tried to grab each book on the way out. Strapping my backpack on I picked up five books from the dirt I was still missing three. They were in the bushes near the edge of the wooded entrance, I walked over to pick them up, and Fredrick was standing there dripping wet with madness in his eyes.

"GQ, do you want me to go after your mom again?" He said laughing. "I don't think you get it, I don't want to fight with you Fredrick, just leave me alone," I told him holding my books in my hands with my backpack strapped around my shirtless shoulders. "I don't think you understand, you don't get it, you and your family don't belong around here, and until your gone," he said coming toward me. "I will continue to do what I want to you," he said hitting my forehead with the palm of his hand. "Do you know what I did to your mom?"

I looked him in the eye not saying a word, "Fredrick, I don't want to fight with you and your friends anymore. I just want to return my books today, I've had enough," I told him backing away from him still staring him in the eye. I backed up slowly and bumped into his friend. "Where do you think you're going GQ?" His friend said holding my backpack from behind, I can't take it I began to feel hot all over and tears streamed from my face. I don't want to fight I thought as I began to feel trapped.

The rest of his friends formed in a circle surrounding me, I can't move I can't breathe my body burned all over like it was on fire. "You can't say anything GQ?" Fredrick asked pushing my forehead again with the palm of his hand he pushed so hard my head flung back and my neck cracked, with tears streaming from my face, I held my head back looking up at the sky, help me I can't fight I thought as I brought my head forward. I could feel my body change; I clutched the books to my chest. "I won't fight!" I yelled out I stomped my feet with every word and the sound was like thunder with every stomp.

Fredrick came closer; I closed my eyes, and soon I felt my shoulder blades spread the hair on my arms changed quickly I was covered in black bladed hairs, and with the hairs, black wings spread from my shoulder blades. Just when they began to spread Fredrick and his friends leap to attack me. I began to spin around striking them with the wings knocking them all to the ground with them. I took the books and threw them one by one, and then I quickly grabbed all of them from the ground sprinting out of the woods. I didn't want to fight anymore I thought as I ran for the entrance of the woods clutching my books.

Almost Home

I rushed from the woods shirtless with the books in my hands. I ran toward the street looking back from time to time to see if they were behind me. When I made it to the street corner, I was panting to catch my breath. I leaned over looking at my bare feet with the books in my hand and my backpack strapped to my shoulders. There was blood running down my face, my feet were covered with blood, and my shoulders felt as if they had been ripped apart at the shoulder blades.

Blood dripped down my back as I stood at the corner clutching the books slouched over staring down at my feet; I couldn't go to school like this. I have to get home to change my clothes, I thought as I straightened up. I looked back one more time and began to run home down the pathway toward my house, I could see from a distance a crowd on the corner near the cross street. I didn't want to run into anyone looking like this, I crossed the street avoiding them. I ran to my house, moms car was parked in the driveway she had come back home since I left this morning.

I didn't go to the front door. I didn't want mom to see me, she would think that I had been fighting; I tried my best not to fight with Fredrick and his friends today. They just wouldn't let up I thought going around to the back patio door to look in the window, there was no sign of mom in the kitchen. I slid the door open, quietly creeping in and looking all around, my feet stamped the prints from the blood with every step. Mom wasn't in the living room nor was she in the back room of the house; I crept up the stairs tip toeing with every step until I reached my room.

When I got into my room I immediately went to the shower to wash off all the blood, when I finished washing, I got out and stood in the mirror. I looked over my body from my head to my toes, I was cut up everywhere, and my feet split open at the bottom. I took Vaseline from the dresser and began to rub it all over my cuts and bruises; it was 8:30 am. I still have time to get to school if I rush out now, after bandaging my cut; I put on a different pair of jeans and nice brown shirt.

I wrapped up my feet and put on two pairs of socks over both feet, I put on another pair of shoes from the shelf of the closet. After getting all dressed I strapped the backpack onto my shoulders and grabbed the books from my desk and began to walk out of the room. "Mom! I yelled. "Mom I need a ride to school, I'm late!" I yelled out looking in every room for mom, she stepped out of the den near the kitchen. "I thought you'd gone already Keagan, you're really late today," she told me reaching for her purse from the table.

"I looked for you earlier mom, you were gone, I needed a ride, we have to turn in our books today," I told her standing steady. My feet burned so badly, I thought about other things to keep my mind off the pain, I thought about how I threw them into the well. It was tough to ignore fighting, I wanted to fight back, but I know it will only get worse if I do, it felt good to try and walk away. Although I had no success, I thought as I walked out to the car behind mom. "Today, I'll pick you up Keagan, you wait in front for me after school, okay son." She told me as we drove off from the house, the winds were still really high out.

Mom had her window down the whole time when we arrived at school; I took a deep breath looking over at the entrance near the stairs. I started to get out sliding my book onto my lap and opening the door. "I'll walk you in, son," mom told me getting out of the car. She came over to my side of the car and grabbed a couple of my books. "Mom, I really can handle it," I told her reaching out to her for the books. "No, son, I'm going with you into the office, you need me to explain why you're late, right." She said looking at me, I shook my head yes.

"Sure mom, you do need to explain why I'm late," I told her as we walked toward the office doors. We walked into the office there was a line from the door all the way to the front desk. Everyone was carrying their books standing in the line talking; they turned to look at us as the door shut behind us. The line moved really slowly, there were two ladies at the front desk checking in each student's books. When mom and I reached the head of the line mom put the books, she was carrying on the table, and I put mine on top. I took the books from my backpack and placed them one by one on the table.

"What's your name son? The lady at the desk asked "Keagan Phillips," mom said looking down at the woman; she began typing my name in the computer quickly. "It says you have sixteen books out, are they all here?" She asked us. Mom began to count them with her finger, I shook my head yes. "I think there all here," mom said putting her hand on her hip looking at the woman. "Okay, let's see here," the woman said taking each book one by one typing the numbers on the back into the computer. "Okay Keagan Phillips, you are missing a World History book and a Literature book." She took her glasses from her face and looked me in the eye.

"Would you happen to know where they are, son?" I shrugged my shoulder, I thought I had them all, but I didn't; I thought about where I left them back in the woods. "Mrs. Philips if he doesn't find each book we will charge a fifty dollar fine for each one," she said placing her glasses on the table. Mom looked at me. "Keagan, do you know where they are?" She asked me. I shrugged my shoulders again. "I think I can find them, mom." Mom turned and looked back at the lady at the desk.

"Tomorrow," she said with a smile. "Okay, tomorrow it is," Mom told her. "Where is attendance, he's a little late today," mom said to her. "I know where it is, mom," I said taking her hand and pulling her toward the other end of the line when we got to the attendance office there was another line. "Mom, I think I just have to sign the clipboard up there and bring a note later," I told her pointing at the clipboard. "No, son, I want to make sure you get a pass," she told me standing beside me in the line. "Do you really think you can find those books Keagan?" She asked me, I shrugged my shoulders.

"I thought I had them all mom, I don't know," I said scratching my head. We made it to the front of the line. "Keagan Phillips," I told the attendance lady. "Why are you late?" She asked. "He had to get a ride to return his books, and I wasn't home this morning." "I see," the woman said turning her chair around to face another woman at a desk across from her.

"In the future Mrs. Phillips, he can't be excused for that, he's to show up on time with or without the books, especially so far into the end of the school year." She says looking over at the other woman while she ripped off the blue slip for class. "Thank you, Ms." Mom said taking the slip from her hand. "Keagan, I have to go now," she said walking toward the front entrance door. "I'll see you after school son, try and get home early today," she said walking and waving her hand at me. I went to my third-period class, they were wrapping up the lesson for the day, the teacher was giving an assignment for homework.

I entered the room and sat down at my desk, Fredrick sat behind me I tried not looking at him. I turned quickly looking straight ahead at the board. "Welcome," the teacher said looking over his shoulder at me with his glasses to his face. "You've missed some things; I'll be expecting you to come back here after school to finish up this lesson." He said to me sitting on his desk holding the chalk in his fingers pointing at me. I raised my hand when he stood up. "Yes Mr. Phillips," he said looking at me crossed.

"I can't stay after school today, I have a track meet, the coach will expect me to be there," I told him looking up at the board. "Maybe your coach won't mind missing a teammate if he knew that the teammate couldn't make it to class on time," he said. "I'm sorry for coming late today," I said. "Sorry doesn't help me when you can't pass a state test," he said sitting at his desk. "Come afterschool or fail the state test next week," he said folding his arms. I had to make the track meet if there's to be a meet against the school that Sage and her friends went to Blair Academy Prep.

The coach has been dying to race against them all season, and I know he wants me to be there. I thought sitting there looking at the teacher. When the bell rang, I sat back and my seat and allowed everyone to leave, when the last person left I stood up and walked over to him. "I know I was late, but I really can't miss the track meet," I told him as he handed me a worksheet. "I'll allow you to slide today, but you have to come in here tomorrow after school, and before you take the state exam I'd like for you to take a practice test. So that I can see where you are with the math portion of it," he said.

"Study that worksheet, and I'll see you tomorrow after school," he said going over to the board erasing it as the bell rang for the next class. "Now, rush, you don't want to do the same thing twice do you," he said staring at the clock. I looked up. "Get out of here young man." I took my worksheet and walked through the door down the hallway, people scrambled all around yelling and screaming through the halls. When I arrived at my fourth-period class Fredrick and his friends were standing in the doorway yelling at another guy's face. "You're an ugly dude, you know that!" Fredrick said to him holding his fist to his nose.

"You think because you've been here for a while that you'll get off easy?" He said as the teacher cracked the door. "He doesn't want it guys," he said laughing. The teacher peeked her head out; "enough Mr. Hall, come into the classroom right now please and take your seat." She said frowning at Fredrick. He stepped away from him and walked slowly into the class giving Mrs. Byrd a very mean stare. "Are you okay Grant?" She asks the guy with her hand on his shoulder. Tears streamed from his eyes. "I don't know what I did to him?" He said looking as if he was terrified.

"Keagan, go ahead, go into the classroom, take your seat until I come in, I'm going to walk Mr. Grant to see his counselor, please let me know if anyone gets out of order before I come back." She told me taking Grant by the arm walking away. "Will do Mrs. Byrd," I told her. I went into the classroom and took my seat, it was really quiet I placed my backpack on the floor taking a notebook out to begin the assignment on the board when Fredrick snatched my notebook and tossed it up in the air.

"You freak," he shouted as everyone else laughed I stood up to grab my notebook from the air. As I got up, he got up with me and snatched me back down to my chair by my shirt. "Freak, sit down," he said grabbing the notebook throwing it around the room from friend to friend. I sat still in my seat; I'm not going to allow him to make me angry. I won't fight him. I thought just get him at the meet, the track meet is where I'll make him pay I thought as I watched them toss my notebook laughing and making jokes.

"Freaks don't get to read and write," Fredrick said as they continued until they heard Mrs. Byrd's shoes clicking down the hall. "It's her, put it down," he said as a friend tossed it over to him underneath the desk it slid right under his feet. He placed his boot on top of it and turned to me. "Keep your mouth shut freak, or you know what's next," he said as Mrs. Byrd walked in shutting the door behind her. "You, come here," she said pointing her finger at Fredrick. "You get a kick out of picking on smaller kid's right?" She said as he began to get up from his seat, he kicked my notebook toward his friend; it went sliding under his boots.

When he approached Mrs. Byrd, she took him by the arm escorting him to the chalkboard. "Did you think I would ignore this, that kid was terrified of you Mr. Hall, just imagine how he felt, she went on to say. "This is what I want you to do aside from the class assignments, and the homework, I want you to write a two-page essay on how it would feel if you were the smallest in your class and someone harassed you." She said standing in his face. "You can give me whatever you want Mrs. Byrd, but I will never do it."

"Oh, I know you won't, but guess what I won't be doing?" She said rubbing her hands together. "I will not tolerate your behavior in my class; you want to disturb the class with the bad behavior you have to get out." She said taking a pad from the inside of her desk begging to write on it. "To the principal's office you go," she said ripping the paper off the pad handing it to him. He refused to take it from her hand; he laughed at her and went back to his seat she kept her hand out looking at him as he walked away laughing.

"Mr. Hall, please do not have me call them in to get you out of here." She went over to the classroom phone on the wall and began to dialing, just as she began to talk, he got up from his seat and walked up to the desk, taking the paper she handed him earlier and walking toward the door. "See all you freaks later!" He yelled grabbing his genital area. "Don't forget freak, we're not done," he said pointing at me. His friends began to clap their hands loudly. "Settle down class, do any of you want to join him?" Mrs. Byrd asked as she walked over to the chalkboard.

"Enough of that charade, let's get started with today's lesson." I watched as Fredrick friend took my notebook and began to rip the pages from it one by one trying to stay quiet. I reached into my backpack to find another notebook to write down the lesson. I didn't have another one to write in I raised my hand. "Yes Keagan." "Mrs. Byrd, can I borrow a piece of paper please?" I asked her, some of Fredrick's friends giggled, Mrs. Byrd looked around at them. "What's so funny?" She asked them. "Keagan, what happened to your notebook?" She asked me.

"Mrs. Byrd, I just forgot it when I was packing my books to turn in," I told her lying trying not to tattle on his friends. I knew if I'd told on them they would really come after me. "Come up here Keagan," she said to me. When I approached the desk, she put her face very close to my ear. "Are these guys picking on you too?" She asked I shook my head no. She handed me a piece of paper, "You can tell me Keagan, I promise I won't allow them to hurt you," she said to me as I grabbed the paper.

"I would like for everyone to work on this assignment quietly until the bell rings. Grant came back into the classroom when we were almost finished he sat in his seat still looking a little shaken. I put my hand on his shoulder tapping him to let him know it would be okay. He turned back to look at me. "Thank you," he said. Grant was very soft spoken, he was a small build his clothes looked really tight, he had huge ears; they stuck out from his hair. His hair was brown and curly he had brown eyes. His eyes looked as if he couldn't open them really wide, so when he looked at you, he held his head back really far.

When the bell rang everyone handed Mrs. Byrd their paper and walked out into the hallway. "Goodbye Mrs. Byrd, thank you," Grant said walking out. "You have a good day Grant," she said taking his paper with a smile. "And Mr. Phillips if you should need to talk to me about those boys, I'm here after school every day," she said waving goodbye. We walked into the hall together. "Hi, I'm Grant," he said when we reached the hallway. "Hello, Keagan," I said to him.

"Are you new here?" I asked him "No, I've been here, I just hid out a lot, you know," he said shrugging his shoulders. "Oh I understand," I said with a smile. "But you can't hide forever," Grant said walking away. I went to the gym; I began to run for it when I saw Fredrick and his friends ahead of me, instead of running into them. I took the long way around to the gym, when I turned the corner on the side of the building, Grant was standing outside of the gym waiting to go in. "They say they will get me later, do you think I have a chance?" He asked me flipping back his hair with his hand, he leaned his head back to look me in the eye.

"You'll be fine," I told him walking past going to change into my track gear. He followed me in looking behind him as if he was being followed; I went to my locker and began to undress. Grant sat down on the bench beside mine, I took my shirt off quickly throwing on my tracksuit, as I was putting my clothes in my locker, Fredrick and his friend s approached us. "Look at what we have here, two fags," Fredrick said walking over toward Grant. Grant began to scoot across the bench fast trying to escape them; he stood up and ran out of the gym.

"What is it, Fredrick? I have a track meet to get to," I told him as he places his arm across my chest to keep me from leaving. I pushed his arm away "I have to go, Fredrick, I don't want to fight," I said putting my hands up in the air. "You pussy," Fredrick said spitting in my face. "Let's go watch this pussy run in the meet," He said walking away laughing. I took my towel from my locker and wiped the spit from my face, it's getting harder every day to keep myself from fighting Fredrick.

I went running out of the locker room to the meet. Coach was standing on the field with all the other runners; he was letting them know the plan for the day. "Fredrick will not be in the meet today due to his behavioral problem this morning," he told us. "Phillips, come here," he said waving his hand at me. "You will be running the long-distance passing to Raymond, you need to be careful do not get ahead of yourself and miss, or we will be disqualified. You got it so keep your eyes on out for Raymond," he said slapping me on the shoulder really hard.

The field was packed, our school on one side and the other school on the other cheering loudly for their favorite runner. I looked around the crowd for any sign of Sage; I waved anyway even though I couldn't see her. When the race started we all lined at the start, coach stood at the start with us looking real serious clapping his hands at us. "Come on Phillips, do this for us, do it for the team," he said clapping as the gun went off. Raymond began running as I waited for him to get to the finish I ran after him taking the stick. I continued on running against the other schools runners this guy was fast I almost couldn't catch him at all.

I slowed until we went around the track then speeding through the crowd I picked up my speed thinking of how disappointed coach would be if we lost to this team. We were the best in our district; it would kill him if I lost this one, the last track meet in the school year. I ran so fast kicking my legs up to my back I held onto the stick as tight as I could as I entered the finish. When I made it the whole team ran over to me grabbing me picking me up from the ground swinging me around in the air screaming and laughing.

Cheering, we had won, we won, I thought as they tossed me around in the air. I held my hands up trying to enjoy the win without thinking about Sage; I wondered where she was in the crowd. When things settled down, we all went to the locker room to change. "We will get our trophies for our wins at a ceremony two days before the last day of school, congrats team, you guys are the best in the district," the coach told us in the locker room. I quickly went to the shower washed myself off and rushed to put on my clothes, as everyone else walked out of the locker room.

I was left putting my shoes on when Grant walked back in. "Hey Keagan, which way do you walk home," he asked me sitting on the bench. "I walk through the pathway near the wood." I told him. "Why, where do you live?" I asked him "I live near the woods across from the little mall and grocery store." "Really, Grant, I've never seen you walking that way," I told him picking up my backpack from the floor. "Yes I know, I wait a long time after school before I leave, I try not to run into your good friend Fredrick," he says sarcastically lifting his eyebrows.

"But since I know you walk that way, you think we could walk together?" He asked. "Sure, why not," I told him as we began to walk from the locker room. "So, what would you do every day after school for so long?" I asked him as we walked toward the back of the field gate.

"I would just do things for extra credit in different classes, why do you think I'm so smart and geeky?" He said holding his hand to his head.

"You're not a geek, being smart is nothing to be ashamed of, at least that's what my parents say," I said laughing out loud. "Parents say the craziest things," he said as we walked through the gates toward the back of the pathway. It seemed like a shorter walk with someone to talk too. Grant talked to me about everything he went on and on until we saw Fredrick and his friends at the end of the pathway. Grant stopped and looked down the path. "What's wrong?" I asked he pointed down the path.

"We don't have to pay attention to them we'll just walk by, and hopefully they'll leave us alone," I told him, but he wouldn't budge as I began to walk further ahead of him. "You think they'll just let you walk by them?" He asked; "they won't, Keagan!" He yelled out to me, turning back toward the pathway to the school. "You need to come with me, Grant!" I yelled "I won't let them touch you, we can't keep running from them," I told him with my back turned to Fredrick and his friends.

Just as I began to turn to look forward, Fredrick was standing in my face. "So you found another geek like yourself to hang out huh GQ, go and get him," he said waving his hand at his friends. "Run Grant! Go into the woods and hide!" I yell out to Grant as they began to run toward him, "Shut up GQ," he said holding onto my shirt. I smiled at Fredrick. "What are you smiling for GQ?" He asked me "Do you really want to know why I'm smiling?" I asked him pulling away from him. I pulled struggling to get free from his grip.

"Let go of me, Fredrick!" I yelled I began to swing my arms around frantically; Fredrick let me go after the swings hit him in the face a few times and I took off running. I ran as fast as I could to catch up with Grant, I promised I wouldn't allow him to be hurt, so I ran into the woods behind him. I told him to hide, when I got into the woods, I watched from the back of a tree branch as they searched around for him in the bushes. I looked around for him too; hoping I'd get to him before they did. I walked quietly toward the lake in the back of the woods; I noticed bubbles coming from the water.

Oh no I thought, Grant's in the water I ran over to the water quickly looking all around for them. I looked down into the water, and there I saw Grant lying straight across the water, trying to stay under, I grabbed him by the arm, pulling him from the water. He came up gasping and trying to go back down I pulled on him, watching as Fredrick stood at the edge of the lake. His face turned as red as a beet, his eyes piercing at us with harmful intent. He looked to his friends standing around; he took a deep breath leaning back as far as he could.

He stood up straight as I pulled Grant back up he spit fire at us, it was a ball of fire coming toward us as fast as lighting. When Grant grabbed me by the neck and pulled me underwater with him, he held onto me tight taking me down deeper as fire struck the water. I stayed at the bottom watching as Grant swam further away under water soon I could see the water swirling around him as if it was going to take him to the bottom of the lake. It twirled and twirled so fast that the lake was begging to swirl around as well, I held my breath for as long as I could coming up only to take a breath and go back under.

I could still see Fredrick spitting fire at us when the lake began to rise; the water began to get high and higher as if it was lifting over Fredrick and his friends. I swam up to catch another breath when I saw Fredrick; he was standing still as if he'd seen something terrifying. He was stricken with fear it seemed, he couldn't move, I turned around treading through the water with my arms to see what it was that terrified him. It was the tallest funnel twister I'd ever seen, with Grant's face, Grant was as tall as the tree's in the woods, his arms were like twisters, and his legs were too.

A twister tornado is what he looked like; it carried him through the water from his midsection as they began to gather together and run away. Grant jumped from the lake toward the woods crushing and mangling everything up. As he walked they began to run frantically through the woods, the wind was blowing, and trees fell down all around the woods. I swam to the edge of the lake to get out; I caught my breath, watching as Grant's twisters tore through the woods after Fredrick and his friends. When I could no longer see them, I stood to my feet and ran the other way toward the pathway to the house.

The wind blew over my face as I ran, imagine that, dandy little Grant can become as big as the trees, I thought as I ran through the woods to get to the pathway. When I made it through the pathway, there was Grant back to normal smiling. "Are you running from me?" He said dripping with water, "Oh no, that was so neat, where did you learn that trick?" I asked him. "What trick?" He said walking alongside me. We laughed, talking about how badly he'd scared Fredrick and his friends, and we were almost home.

Dinner

We continued our walk to school the next day, Grant was quiet the whole way there. He didn't tell me where he left Fredrick and I didn't ask, we made it to school on time. We made it to the entrance of the school, Grant turned to me as we reached the top stairs of the front lawn. "Keagan, please don't tell anyone what happened, don't let them know that I can do that, please," he said holding his head back looking me in the eye.

"Grant, I wouldn't rat you out like that," I told him strapping my backpack on tighter. "It's between us, but tell me, Grant, really, how do you do it, do you know that you can turn or what? I mean how do you do that, it was amazing," I said excited to find out his secret. "It's God Keagan that's all I can say," he said walking away to class. "See you later Keagan, thanks for trying to catch my fall," he says walking away waving his hand. "Can you teach me that later?" I yelled out as I rushed quickly to class.

When I made it to class I saw Fredrick's friends standing in the doorway, it looked as if they were waiting for me. I walked slowly looking behind me to see if anyone else was there they could have been waiting for. As I approached, they began to clutch their fist at me. "Hello GQ, happen to know where we can find Fredrick?" I shook my head no and tried passing them, the tall guy who they called Cody grabbed me by my sweatshirt. "Hey asshole, didn't you hear the question?" He asked me tightening his hand on my sweatshirt.

"Listen, I don't know where Fredrick is, I hadn't seen him since you did this morning," I said slapping his hand away from my shirt. He stepped back then flinched at me. "You little asshole Keagan, Fredrick wants to take his time with you, but I won't waste any, I'm so ready to beat you down loser." He said holding his fist to my face. "You and that little girlfriend of yours are playing a really dangerous game," he said pushing my shoulder and walking into class. I really had no way of knowing where Grant took Fredrick, he didn't tell me.

I know that Grant wouldn't harm him for sure; I thought as Mrs. Byrd walked into the classroom. She came in and shut the door behind her. "Hello class, today we are going to be taking the exit exams, these tests are essential, they let us know how prepared you are for next year." She said taking a stack of paperwork from her desk walking down every aisle tossing one on each desk. When she reached Fredrick's desk, she stood there then turned around in a circle looking for him in the class.

She walked back to her desk holding his test paper in her hand. "Has anyone seen Fredrick Hall?" She asked. No one said a word his friends turned and looked at me. "Mr. Phillips, have you seen Fredrick this morning?" She asked me. "No Mrs. Byrd I haven't," I told her turning my test paper over ready to start. "Are you sure?" She asked. "Okay, we will get started, and then Mr. Hall will need to go to the office to see his counselor to take this test. When I count to three I want all of you to turn your test over and began," she said writing on the board.

"You all have thirty minutes," she said sitting at her desk. "Remember to sign your name on the top of the test," she watched us as we took the test, walking up and down every aisle making sure we didn't cheat. When we were done, we were to turn the test over and hold up our hands for her to pick it up from our desk. My hand went up last, everyone else finished quickly, I couldn't concentrate thinking of what Grant may have done with Fredrick this morning. I raised my hand to ask for permission to go to the restroom.

"Yes Keagan," Mrs. Byrd responded. "I need to use the restroom please," I told her. "Go ahead Keagan, if anyone else needs to use the restroom, please go now along with Keagan, when you come back we will wrap this up for the day. This will be that last test this year," Mrs.

Byrd gave everyone the go-ahead for the restroom we went four at a time. Me, Andrew, Cody, and Thomas, I was reluctant to go with them because they were all Fredrick's friends, but I needed to go bad. They never act out until their around Fredrick any way I thought as we walked down the hall.

We all went to the restroom one after the other I went to a stall I just wanted to use the bathroom and get out as quickly as possible. I used it quickly; when I was done I zipped my pants and walked toward the door. The guys were still inside the stalls using the restroom, when I went to open the door to leave, the door pushed opened toward me hitting the wall the force of the wind from it almost knocked me down. As it widened I rushed to walk out; it was Fredrick standing on the other side of the door with a smile on his face he reached out and grabbed me by my shirt pulling me toward him.

"Tell your bird friend that I'll be waiting for him after school." I tried pulling away from him tugging at his hands. "This time both of you will regret ever crossing me," he said as I walked away. I walked back to class quickly trying to beat them all to class. Mrs. Byrd was standing in the hallway talking to another teacher when I approached the door. "Welcome back take your seat I'll be in there in a second," she told me waving me through. I grabbed a book from the shelf before taking my seat, I wanted to pretend that I was busy reading when Fredrick and his friends returned to class. Mrs. Byrd came in and sat at her desk.

"Keagan, what happened to your bathroom buddies, will they not be returning?" She asked me. I took my book down from my face; "Mrs. Byrd I don't know if they'll be returning," I said putting my book back to my face. She looked up at the clock, the bell rang, and everyone in class jumped from their seats and began walking out. "Keagan," Mrs. Byrd called out as I walked past her. "Is everything okay?" She asked me "Yes Mrs. Byrd, everything is fine," I said as I exited the classroom into the hallway.

I saw Fredrick and all of his friends at the end of the hallway standing around picking at people as they walked by. They laughed loudly and joked at the things they were doing. I looked around the hallways for Grant, he was nowhere in sight, I remembered he told me something about hiding in the library. I thought as I rushed through the crowd trying to get closer to the library, I needed to get there before the last bell rang for the next class.

I didn't want to run so I walked as fast as I could to get there. When I made it to the library, I saw Grant coming out of the two-way doors. "Grant, where have you been" I asked him pulling him to the side He looked up at me with his hair covering his eyelids he tilted his head back to see me. "I've been in there, I don't want any more trouble from them Keagan, I just want to be done with this school year," he said looking me in the eye. "I bet they told you to warn me right?" He asked. I shook my head yes.

"Warn me after all the things I've done. See Keagan, they'll never stop this goes on and on; even when I've challenged them and fought back," he told me as he began to walk forward. "What if I don't hold back Keagan, what if I fought them back and hurt them? Then I'd be the bad one right?" I walked with him he was so frustrated, I didn't say a word until we reached the hallway where we ran into Fredrick and his friends again. "Grant, I know, I'm trying really hard to ignore them too, and they said that after school they're going to get you."

"This time I will help you I won't let them hurt you, Grant, I promise," I told him reaching out my hand for a handshake. "See you later, I'll meet you at the gate near the gym" I told him walking to my class. He shook his head yes, he walked slowly down the hallway with his head down. When class was over I rushed out with Fredrick, Andrew and Thomas following me to gym class, we didn't have to suite up anymore nor did we have track practice.

We all had to meet with Mr. Stewart in the gym classroom; I walked slowly through the crowd of jocks just to avoid bumping into any of them. They looked at me smiling and laughing looking back at Fredrick. "Don't worry GQ, you and your buddy won't ever have to worry about gym again soon!" Fredrick yelled out through the crowd as we all went into the class and sat down; Mr. Stewart came in behind us. "What's the problem, Mr. Hall?" Mr. Stewart asked Fredrick. "No problem Mr. Stewart," he said shrugging his shoulders.

"I saw you talking to Keagan in the hall, what was that all about," he asked him. "There's no problem Mr. Stewart, just ask him, he'll tell you, right," he said nodding his head at me. "You guys seem to have a lot of problems with your peers, you know it follows right, one day you'll be an adult, and the same little guy you picked on in high school will be your boss or your doctor, what will you do then?" He asked him "Mr. Stewart," I said; "there's no problem, can you drop it," Fredrick shouted. Mr. Stewart went over to the chalkboard and began to write summer school rules.

"If I write your name under these rules today, you need to see me after the bell rings. This means that you have summer school this summer and I will be your summer school teacher." He began writing names on the board, the first name he wrote was Fredrick Hall then Andrew Becker, then Thomas Basset, and on and on until he had every one of Fredrick's friend's names beside his. "You'll need to have these papers signed by your parents, if they should have any questions; they can call me here at the school."

Mr. Stewart sat down on the edge of his desk holding the chalk in his hand. "See this is what happens to those who show up unprepared and uninterested in finishing school on time. It is my responsibility to keep you guys on top of the game because you run for me on the track team, and I've failed you, and you've failed me. Now we have to play catch up all summer long," he said shaking his head. "Do you know I planned to visit Maui this summer to catch some waves," he said clutching the chalk in his hand and standing from his seat.

The bell rang soon after he got up, I walked out of class there wasn't to many of us who escaped summer school, there was little crowd leaving the gym class. I walked down the hallway quickly going to meet Grant to tell him the good news about Fredrick. It would be something we could laugh about on our walk home; when I caught up to him he was already waiting by the side fence. "Hey Grant, you been waiting long?" I asked him walking up to him. He shook his head no. "Will you be able to come over for dinner tonight?" He asked me.

"Oh I don't know Grant, I need to ask my parents about tonight," I told him as we walked through the brush of the canyon leading us to the side of the woods. "Hey Grant, something really funny happened today," I told him. "What was it, what happened?" He asked. "Fredrick and all of his buddies were called out for summer school in the gym by Mr. Stewart, can you believe it?" I said laughing. "Mr. Stewart gave them this really long speech about how when they get older, guys like us will be their bosses and doctors and what will they do then.

It was entertaining to watch them squirm as he went on to tell them about themselves." We laughed I made faces showing Grant the face each of them made when he called out their names. "Do you think they'll be in summer school all summer?" Grant asked. "No, it only lasts for three weeks," I told him as we walked on. "But Grant you should have seen their faces," I laughed out loud thinking about it Grant, and I made it to the gate we went through the hole in the gate one by one.

"Do you think you'll be able to come over tonight?" He asked me again. "I don't know, you can come over to my house, and I'll ask, and if I can, I'll walk home with you," I told him as we walked through the brush of the path. Grant kicked rocks as he walked dust kicked up with every rock. Grant began to talk about God and the Bible, as he babbled on about how God created everything on earth I daydreamed about having dinner with his family, I wondered what it would be like.

When we made it to the fence we both threw our bags over the fence, then we began to climb over. We jumped down onto the ground and picked up our backpacks instead of us splitting up Grant followed me to my house. "How long have you lived over here?" Grant asked. "For as long as I can remember," I told him. "But you didn't go to elementary or junior high school with us," he said looking up pulling his bangs back with his hand to see my face. "I went to private school in elementary and junior high.

"Oh I see, how was that, I mean did you have lots of friends there?" He asked. "I did, a couple of them go to Kennedy High with me, but they don't talk to me now, they're close friends with the jocks," I told him. "Oh that's too bad, you're a nice guy Keagan, I'm glad we met," he said as we walked up to the front door of my house. "You're not bad yourself, Grant," I opened the door with my key and went inside. "Come on in," I told him. "Is your mom home Keagan?" "I don't know," I put my backpack on the floor and walked through the house, I went into the kitchen.

"Mom, are you here?" I yelled out grabbing an apple from the bowl on the table "Are you hungry Grant, would you like a fruit or something to drink?" I asked as I walked away looking for mom. He grabbed an orange from the bowel he straddled his backpack onto his shoulder tightening the straps. "You're welcome to sit your backpack down on the floor by mine if you want," I told him. "Wait here okay, I'm going upstairs to see if she's in her room okay," I told him. "Okay, can I sit in here?" He asked pointing to the couch in the den.

"Go ahead I'll be right back," I told him running toward the stairs. "Keagan, I'm going to have to go soon, my mom will flip if I don't show my face before the sun goes down," he tells me peeling the orange. "Go ahead and call her, tell her what's going on." I went upstairs and found mom in her bed laying down sleeping, I tapped her on her feet. "Mom," I said in a whisper. "Mom," I said again. She looked up at me. "Hello Keagan, I didn't hear you come in, is everything okay?" She asked.

"Yes mom everything is fine, Grants downstairs, and his mom wants to know if I can have dinner with them tonight." Mom sat up on the bed; "Keagan, what time is it?" She asked me; squinting her eyes. "Mom it's a quarter till 3," I told her. "Okay son, just call me when dinners over, and I'll come pick you up, I don't want you walking from there late in the evening," she told me laying back down. I ran downstairs to tell Grant that it was okay I could go he was sitting on the couch waiting, eating his orange.

"Hey, it's okay I can go, did you call your parents?" I asked him "I did," he said holding his last piece of orange standing by the door. "If you're up for meatloaf and mashed a potato that's what we'll be having," he told me. "What's for dessert?" I asked him. He shrugged his shoulders we don't have sugar in our house, sweets aren't allowed." "No sweets, no apple pie or cookies?" I asked as we walked out of the door. We walked toward the gate.

"Let's take the street way to my house, it's not very far from here I just live around that corner," he said pointing down the street. "Oh okay," I said running toward the street corner. We made it to Grant's house quick; he placed his backpack on a swing on the porch. The house was so old the paint was peeling off it must have been white paint, but it was peeling so bad you could only see pieces of it and wood.

When he opened the door for us to go inside you could smell the meatloaf baking from the doorway. Inside his house was old fashion also the furniture had flowers all over it and wood around the edges of it. There was soft music playing on the radio near the couch it was gospel music, Grant showed me his room. He had a small bed a dresser to match and blue blankets and pillow cases, there was posters of different super hero's all over the walls, a chair sitting under a desk. He had a small library of books near his bed.

"Do you want to wait here?" He asked me; "or would you like to go into the kitchen and wait?" "I don't know, are you going somewhere" I asked him. "We always pray when I come home from school, would you like to join us?" He asked me smiling. "I know you're not into that kind of thing." I shook my head no. "Go ahead I'll wait in here," I said sitting in his chair. He walked out shutting the door behind him; I went over to his library to see what books he liked to read. He had a collection of bible book stories and a collection of encyclopedia.

He was really into reading; he had a lot of mysteries on the bottom shelf all by the same writer, I began to hear whispers coming from the other room. I walked up to the door and cracked it opened just enough to see into the living room. I looked out of the crack; they were on their knees kneeling down on in front of a big cross on the wall near the window in the living room. They were lined up side by side; his mom prayed out loud while they held their hands to their chest with their heads down.

When it was over they all stood to their feet, I closed the door softly as Grant walked toward the door, he opened it and came inside. "Okay, dinners ready Keagan," I pretended to be reading a book from the shelf. "I know you were watching," Grant said as we walked out of the door. We went into the kitchen and sat at the table, there were five plate settings. "Sit there," Grant told me pointing at the seat near the end of the table, soon we were joined by his mom and dad and his younger brother Max.

"Hello, Keagan nice to meet you," Grant's father said to me shaking my hand. "Do you like broccoli?" His mom asked. "Yes, ma'am I do," I told her lifting my plate for her to put broccoli on it. "So son, how long have you been going to Kennedy high school?" His father asked. "Just this year," I told him. "Do you like it?" His mom asked. "It's okay, aside from the jocks pushing everyone around, I love my teachers," I told her. "You're the first friend Grant has ever brought over," Max said. "You are his friend, right?" He asked me.

"Yes I am, he's a good friend," I told him taking a sip of water from a glass sitting in front of me. Grant didn't say much at the table he ate quietly as his parents went on asking me questions as we ate. "Do you and your family go to church at all?" His father asked. "We do, my mom and dad go a little more than me, but I do go with them sometimes," I told them. His mom offered me more mashed potatoes. "No thank you," I told her going on, eating the meatloaf. "Did Grant tell you about our Bible studies? We do Bibles studies after dinner every night," his mother tolds me.

"No, he didn't tell me anything about it," I told them shaking my head looking at Grant. "Well, now we're in the book of Job, we study from the Old Testament, do you read your Bible at all son?" His father asked. I didn't want to answer any more questions about the Bible nor did I want to talk about God, I began to shake my head with every question. "Okay, I get it," his mother said beginning to clean the table. "You're not interested in Bible studies are you?" She asked me taking my plate.

"No, I'm not ma'am." "Okay well, did you want to stay in Grants room until we're done or did you just want to sit and watch us tonight?" She asked as everyone scattered around her helping her collect the plates and cups from the table. "I'd really like to call my mom so that she can come pick me up ma'am, dinner was delicious, thank you so much for having me," I told her excusing myself from the table to follow Grant to the phone to call mom. As I told mom where to come get me Grant and his family gathered around the living room, setting up for their Bible studies.

I waited in a chair by the door. Mom showed up minutes after I hung up with her, she came to the door; Grants mother went to the door and opened up. "Hello again Karis, how are you, come on in, we were just about to have Bible studies, Keagan tells us that he's not interested in Bible studies at all," She tells mom at the front door. "Really, yes he's funny when it comes to things like that, thank you so much for having him, Grant is always welcome to come over," she told her as I stood up from the chair. "Goodbye, Grant I'll see you tomorrow."

"Sure I'll come by in the morning we can walk the long way," he said as mom and I walked out of the door. "Thank you goodbye," Mom said again waving her hand goodbye. Mom drove me home talking about church and Bible studies. "Keagan, those stories in the bible are very good ones, you're missing out you know," I shrugged my shoulders. "You don't believe me?" She asked looking over at me as we pulled into the driveway "Yes, I believe you, mom, I just don't believe those stories," I told her getting out of the car.

"You're missing out son," she tells me as we walk up to the door together. "Mom, what did you have for dinner, did dad make it today?" I asked her walking into the kitchen, I saw on the table two glasses and two plates. "Dad was here mom?" I asked "Yes, but he was called back to the hospital," she told me. "Aw mom I wanted him to remove the tape from my nose, it feels better now, I think it's healed up," I told her grabbing an apple from the bowel on the table taking a bite.

"No son, you still have a bit of time left to wear it," she told me taking a basket from the floor heading down to the laundry room. "Mom it's healed," I said walking up to my room. "Keagan, what did you have for dinner," she asked following behind me with the basket. "We had meatloaf and mashed potatoes and broccoli," I told her. "Sounds delicious," she said. "What about you and dad, what did you have?" We had steak and potatoes and carrots."

I went to my room took off my clothes and showered, I thought about Grant and his family as I put on my pajamas. They were a little too religious to me, maybe they'll tell him he can't hang out with me now because I didn't stay for Bible studies, I thought as I laid in bed covering myself up. There was a bible on the table near my bed, I almost never look at it, mom had left it there for me to read long ago but it didn't interest me. I started to reach over for it to look through, but I didn't I turned over and went to sleep.

The next day I was awoken by the loud knock on my room door. "Keagan, it's me, Grant, your mom said I could come up, are you ready?" He said. I sprung up from the covers looking at the clock. Oh no! I thought my clock didn't go off this morning, I'm late. I thought as I got up running to the bathroom. "Hey Grant can you wait for me downstairs I'll be there in a second," I told him scurrying around my room for my clothes and shoes.

I brushed my teeth and washed my face quickly throwing on my clothes as fast as I could, I put on my shoes as I walked out of the door. I went downstairs looking for Grant. "Hey Grant, I'm ready," I said kneeling fixing my shoelaces, I looked around. I didn't see him. "Hey, Grant!" I yelled out "Grant! Where are you?" I shouted I grabbed a piece of toast from the plate mom set for me at the table with breakfast. When I noticed Grant outside in the back sitting on the patio chair, I slid open the door.

"Hey Grant, I'm ready," I told him standing in the doorway; he got up and walked over to me. "You ever feel like this is going to be one of those days?" He asked, "One those days, no what do you mean?" I asked as we walked toward the front door. "Just one of those days, don't you feel it?" He asked. "No I feel great this morning, don't you?" "It's not one of those feelings?" He told me as we walk out of the door. "Let's not walk the long way around," he said to me. "The pathway" I questioned.

"Yes, I have a feeling that we need to walk this way," he said walking toward the pathway. "Okay," I said smiling. "Man, Grant dinner was nice." "Yes, I'm sorry you couldn't stay for Bible studies," he said as he walked on beside me through the pathway. We were halfway through when we noticed Fredrick on the corner near the edge of the walkway. I thought you said this was the way we needed to walk?" I said to Grant as we approached him, Grant and I walked past him not saying a word.

"Don't worry Keagan he won't touch me, see that car over there? "He said pointing at a car parked on the other side of the road. "Those are his father's police friends, he won't touch us," Grant said with confidence. As soon as we thought that we were in the clear of Fredrick doing anything wrong he ran up to Grant and pushed him to the ground and began to kick him with his boots. The car parked on the side of the street drove off as if the men inside didn't see anything. Fredrick kicked and kicked at Grant; I ran over and pushed Fredrick away.

"Get off him! Get off him!" I yelled pushing him away from Grant. Grant got up from the ground and ran into the woods; Fredrick clutched his fist and began to hit me as hard as he could in my stomach. I bent over holding my waist. "You stay out of this GQ," he said in my ear clutching my shirt. "Stay out of it!" I shook my head no as I watched him run into the woods after Grant. I knew he would never let Grant get away with humiliating him the way he did that day in the woods. I stumbled behind him to catch up with Grant.

"Grant!" I yelled out. "Grant, where are you!" I yelled looking all around the brush there was still trees lying around from when Grant chased them through the last time. Soon I heard scuffling around and yelling; I ran through the woods following the sounds. I found Grant surrounded by Fredrick and his friends they had him surrounded Fredrick was beating and kicking him all over with his hard boots. I tried to get in to help him, but they pushed me around hitting me to keep me out.

I fought them, but I couldn't get in to help Grant, soon I saw Grant crawling around pulling at the dirt underneath him to get away. He crawled and crawled until he reached a big rock sitting still in the dirt. He grabbed onto the rock holding onto it tight both his arms straddled around it tight while Fredrick continued beating him and kicking him. Grant's hands covered in blood it dripped down the rock, he went to kick Grant in his head once more, and Grant was like the rock.

His body turned as hard as the rock; he was still, the rock was covered in blood, soon we all heard rumbling, an d the ground under our feet begin to shake as if the earth was to break open. The rumbling was loud; I looked all around me every rock on the ground beneath us rolled toward Grant. When they all hit him, they formed into an even bigger rock, so big that you could no longer see Grant; Fredrick and his friends stood still watching for what was next in shock. Fredrick looked at me, his face turned as red as fire, his body began to become engulfed in a flame of fire.

He shot fire out at the rock, but it didn't budge, the rumbling noise was so loud by then that I covered my ears and began to run the other way. I looked back to see what would happen as the rock grew; I hid behind one of the standing trees looking to check on Grant. The rock burst open into what looked like millions of pieces, rocks rushed out covering the sky in the woods. They begin to fly out at Fredrick and his friends everywhere, they flew past me too. I held onto the tree tight hoping I didn't get hit. I could hear them all yelling and screaming to get away from the rocks, but there was no escape. The rocks flew out everywhere; I closed my eyes until it was over.

Last Day of the Year

After the rocks fell all over Fredrick and his friends, I ran through the rubble sliding and slipping on the rocks to get out of the woods. I didn't look for Grant nor did I waste any time getting out of there, I feared what Grant had done with the rocks. I knew that someone had to have been hurt badly, I ran out of the woods to get to school as quickly as I could. When I made it to school, I sat on the steps in front of the school to catch my breath, I waited until the bell rang to go to class when the bell rang I got up to walk to class.

"Hey, Keagan" I hear as I walked past the office. "Hey wait up." It was Grant he ran toward me smiling. "Hey you left me back there, did you see what I did to them?" He asked me walking quickly behind me. I shook my head yes. "You might be in some trouble Grant, I think someone got hurt that time," I told him as we began to part ways. "Don't you get it Keagan? They can't be hurt, they can't feel, they are not of this place," he said pointing out toward the sky.

"Don't worry about it; I didn't hurt anyone I'm sure they'll be here today. I only slowed them down," he said walking away. "See you later, Keagan," I waved to him and walked to class. As I walked up to Mrs. Byrd's class, I saw Fredrick and the rest of the jocks standing by the door the only jock missing was Andrew. I walked up slowly up to the door passing Mrs. Byrd on my left. "Coming in a little late huh Keagan," she said smiling.

"No Mrs. Byrd, I'm on time," I said looking at my watch. "I know," she said putting her arm around my shoulders. "Keagan you're one of my best students, you'll do well if you just stay out of their way," she said looking at Fredrick and his friends. "I try Mrs. Byrd, I really wish it was that easy," I said walking into the classroom with her as we pass

Fredrick and the jocks. I noticed scar's and cuts scratches all over their faces Cody was holding a bloody cloth over his hand.

I passed them as they stopped Mrs. Byrd, "Mrs. Byrd, we have to go to the nurse's offices, we were attacked on the way to school." They told her as she walked past them. "You boys need to come in, I will see what I can do about the nurse after we talk about these test scores and non-test scores for you Mr. Hall." She said pointing at Fredrick with the papers in her hand. "These test scores will tell you if you will be taking this particular English class next year again. If it should read that you have a below average score I will see you again next year, you didn't pass my class," she said beginning to pass the papers out.

"But Mrs. Byrd I'm bleeding out," Cody told her holding up his arm covered in the bloody cloth. "Cody Stanford, please keep your mouth shut and wait until I'm done, and I'll see about you getting to the nurse," she said passing out the last couple of papers. She walked back down to her desk Mrs. Byrd wore a long shirt and sandals with a tight shirt, and a scarf wrapped tightly around her neck, she had a lot of different colors a green skirt, a yellow shirt an orange scarf, and orange sandals. She was always wearing a scarf.

When she went back to her seat, Fredrick immediately raised his hand. "Yes, Mr. Hall?" She asked him. "Mrs. Byrd don't you think you're being a little harsh, we came to class on time, all we want to do is get treated for our wounds. I mean there should be some kind of punishment for bad teachers who don't care about their student's welfare." "Mr. Hall enough, I've heard your plea, you and your friends made it here on time today, but how many days have you disrupted my class coming in late? I think you guys can wait it out," she said putting a book in front of her face.

I could tell that Cody was becoming irritated he swung his hair back from his face over and over again with his breath. He wore a black sleeveless vest with baggy jeans and a pair of black long leather boots.

He tapped his feet under the table and flung his hair back as if he was in pain; blood spots were all over his face. "You know what, I've failed anyway, fuck you, Mrs. Byrd!" He shouted standing from his seat throwing his paper up in the air. "I'm out of here, I hated your class all year long," he said walking toward the door.

"Does anyone else want to join Cody Sanford?" She asked standing from her seat with a frown on her face. "There's the door," she said walking around the class down every aisle. "I have tried to be as lenient as I could with you boys," she said looking at Fredrick and the rest of the jocks. "I can't take any more of the crap," she said. "Raise your hand if you received a below average," she walked back up to the front of the class. "If you did, when the bell rings, please don't leave the room, I will ask that you stay in your seat when the bell rings," she waved her hands in the air with a smile.

"I know that some of you are anxious about the summer that will be our last assignment of the year. I want you all to write an essay explaining what you will be doing this summer and how important the next school year will be for you; what will you hope to accomplish as a sophomore this upcoming year. Tomorrow we will focus on that." When the bell rang I left my seat with my paper in my hand, my score was proficient I don't have to take her class over. I was so happy about it too, as much as I liked Mrs. Byrd I didn't want to have any classes with Fredrick next year. I thought as I walked down the hallway to my next class.

"Keagan!" I hear from down the hall, it was Grant running toward me. "I'm going to have lunch on the lawn today, do you want to come?" He asked with excitement in his voice. "I want you to meet a good friend of mine," he said smiling and running ahead of me, he was in a hurry to beat the bell. "I'll be by the tree in front of the cafeteria," he said as he faded into the crowd, I just shrugged my shoulders and shook my head. I didn't know what to really think of Grant; he was sometimes very scary than sometimes confident with no fear.

He dressed like he didn't have a mirror in his home, always wearing pants that hung above his ankles and a tight sweater that hugged his waist. His hair short and dark bangs hanging over his sleepy eyes, I wondered about his eyes all the time. I wanted to ask him why are they closed like that, but I thought it to be rude so I will never ask him. I went to my next classes, there wasn't much to do, the teachers seemed to be as anxious as the students, and we were all ready to end the school year.

In class, everyone talked about summer vacations, where they were going and how much fun it had been to go there again. I had very little to share we had only one trip before, and it was my grandfather's lake house. I don't remember what went on there that summer when the lunch bell rang, I ran out of class looking for Grant. I really wanted to meet this new friend of his I had never seen him with anyone other than me, I walked over to the cafeteria first to find him; I went to buy lunch.

They had all of my favorite burgers and fries, no veggies for me I thought as I stood in line to pay for my lunch. I noticed Fredrick and the jocks at a table in the lunch room, playing around throwing food at one another and laughing. I paid for my food and went out to the tree in front, Grant was there with a tall girl; way taller than him. I walked over to them holding my tray. "Hello Grant," I said sitting my tray down on the grass by the tree. "Keagan, this is Hanna Brown, I wanted you two to meet.

Hanna comes to vacation Bible school at my house in the summer. I wanted her to tell you how fun it is to learn all the Bible stories before you turn me down," he said with a smile. "Hi Keagan, did I say your name right?" She asked. "Ke-Keagan, that's right, right?" She said reaching out to me for a handshake. "It's very nice to meet you," I said with a smile I began to eat my fries crossing my legs, placing my tray in my lap. "You know I'm not going, right Grant no matter who you bring over to meet me, I'm just not interested in it at all," I told him eating my fries.

"Would you like some Hanna?" I offered her my fries. "No thank you Keagan, can I ask why you feel that way?" She asked me. "Sure, but you won't like my answer, you know, I mean it's good that you guys enjoy it. I just think it's a waste of time," I told her taking a bite of my burger. "Are you sure you don't want any?" I asked waving my burger around to them both. "No thank you," Grant said. "I think I will have some," Hanna said taking a piece of it with her hand.

"Thank you," she said taking it to her mouth. "You're welcome," I told her. "Keagan, you really don't know what you're missing you'll learn so much, and we have so much fun. Grants parents are so great, every story is worth hearing, you should give it a chance," she said standing from the grass taking a napkin from my tray. "May I?" She said as she wiped her hands and mouth with it. "Well, I have to go, Grant, it was so nice to meet you Keagan, I really hope to see you at Grants for Bible studies this summer," she said with a smile.

She walked away, through the crowd. "One day she will marry me," Grant said as she walked away. "Really, she's like five feet taller than you," I told him. He held his head back watching her walk away trying to focus on her. "It doesn't matter how tall she is, I'm going to marry her one day," he said smiling. I stood up from the grass and walked my tray over to the trash can near the window where the jocks were sitting.

They were all throwing food around laughing and joking, they didn't notice me staring at them until Fredrick stood up from the table. He caught my eye pointing his finger at me with a smile; I turned my head quickly as if I didn't see him. I walked away going back over toward the tree where Grant was waiting for me. "Will you be able to come to Bible studies with us?" He asked again. This time I shook my head no, we walked over to the stairwell near the office soon Fredrick and all of his jock friends were standing around us.

We continued to walk away from the lunch court. "Just don't say a word," Grant told me as I begin to ask if there was a problem. "The best thing to do is walk away," he said proudly. I was growing tired of it, we couldn't even share lunch in the lunch court without being hassled or picked on. I know I said that I was never going to fight again, but I couldn't stand it anymore. Cody pushed me in the back really hard. "GQ, aren't you going to tell me where to go?" He said laughing.

Grant shook his head no at me before I could answer him; we continued to walk toward the hallway to the classes. "It's best we don't fight here," Grant said holding his head back. "I know Grant, we can't fight here, we will get expelled and next year will be the worst for us," he told me as we walked to class. We parted in the hallway Fredrick and his friends walked behind me. I really hope that I don't have any classes with him next year I thought as we went into class. It was fifth period Mrs. Green's class when Mrs. Byrd came running into our class. "I need to see Mr. Hall," she told Mrs. Green.

"Mr. Hall, go ahead," he frowned as he left the classroom. "What is it now?" We heard him say to Mrs. Byrd as he holds the door open. "You have to go to the auditorium after school for testing; you've missed the most important test both of them. The exit exam for math and English or you will not enter into the next grade level," she told him with her hands folded into one another. "Mrs. Byrd I can't come after school, I explained that to you already," he told her letting go of the door walking back to his seat.

"Mr. Hall, are you refusing to come after school to take these test?" She asked; peeking her head into the door. He looked at her and shook his head than shrugged his shoulders with his hands out. "Okay, I'm so sorry for disrupting your class Mrs. Green," Mrs. Byrd said closing the door giving Fredrick a glare with her eyes. When the bell rang, everyone got up from their seats quickly. "Remember there is no homework!" Mrs. Green yelled over the crowd, I had to turn in my GQ sweater today we were no longer wearing them on Fridays.

We were planning for next year; I would ask Grant if he would like to join GQ with me for next year I thought as I walked into the classroom. The class was filled with guys from the year before, I sat down when the bell rang, and the teacher began to explain why the students from the year before us were there. "Hello young gentleman," he said loudly trying to throw his voice over all the noise in the classroom. Some of the students were familiar with the students from last year because GQ was a mixture of all grades from 9th through 12th grade.

"Some of you may know these nice gentlemen from last year, they have moved on to college. I was honored when they called me to visit. They wanted to share with all freshman students the benefits of continuing your high school journey in this GQ class," he said with his hands in his pocket as he walked back and forth from one end of the room to the next. One of the college guys stood up in front of the class. "Hello gentleman, my name is Braxton, I first joined the gentlemen's club in my freshman year as well, and it was a great experience for me.

I learned to live a certain way, carry myself differently; I know that you're wondering what makes me any different by being in the GQ club. For starters, going to college was a bit different for me I was able to engage in the elite clubs that I wouldn't have had the opportunity to join had I not did my four years in the GQ club." He went on and on about staying in GQ for the rest of our high school years, when he was finished speaking our GQ instructor walked around handing our schedules for next year. I raised my hand with a question.

"Mr. Cain if I bring someone to join, would they have to join before the school year ends or can they join at the beginning of the school year?" I asked looking at the schedule he handed me. "Mr. Phillips it depends on who you have in mind if the person failed any of his exit exams. He will not be able to join because he'll have to take extra classes during the school year to help him pass those exams," he told me as he walked across the room picking up the schedules from the guys who already had filled them out.

"You can have the person come in after school I'll go over his schedule with him and let him know whether or not he can join us. "Thank you, Mr. Cain," I said checking the box where I'd stay in GQ another year. The bell rang and the guys from the college stood at the door shaking everyone's hand and answering any questions anyone had for them. I rushed to meet Grant I wanted to bring him to the class to meet Mr. Cain before we left school. We all left our GQ sweaters on the desk in front of the room. I rushed into the hallway looking for Grant, the crowd covered the halls.

I look all around me as I walked toward the lockers on the walls ahead; I spotted Grant at the edge of the hallway standing talking to Hanna. "Hey GQ, are you going to the end of the year party tomorrow night?" I was asked by a guy I didn't recognize. "Hey my name is Keagan, and you are," I said with my eyebrows raised. "Sorry dude, I'm Rich I don't go here, I was just in your GQ class, one of the visitors from the college," he said with a wink. "We're giving a party at the college for all of you guys, you should come, everyone's going to be there," he said shaking my hand.

"Relax dude, I'm just a messenger," he said walking away. "Hope to see you and your friends there," he said pointing at Grant and Hanna. I walked over to Grant; he was still talking to Hanna when I approached him. "Hello Hanna, hi Grant, I've been looking for you," I told him. "I was wondering if you may be interested in joining GQ, for next year" I asked him. "GQ, um I don't know Keagan, don't you have to dress up for that?" He asked me. "Yes but only on Monday's and Fridays," I told him.

"It's not that bad, and we'll have a couple classes together, come on you should try it." "Yes, you'll look nice in that sweater," Hanna said agreeing with me that Grant should join. "He says we should come to his class so that he can look at your schedule and help you get in for next year," I told him. "Go on, you should try it," Hanna told him smiling. I could tell that it was all Grant needed to hear, Hanna's approval made my convincing Grant much easier. Of course, she only had to smile, Grant was blushing the whole time, I don't think he heard anything more after she told him he'd look good in that sweater.

"Well let's go, Mr. Cain is waiting," I told him. "Do you mind if Han-na comes along, I'll be walking her home today?" Grant asked. "Sure, why not," I told him as we walk down the hallway to Mr. Cain's class. "Hey did you hear about the party they're having at the college, it's the end of the year party, have you ever been?" I asked. They looked at one another; "Keagan, we're not allowed to go to parties, only the ones that the church gives," he told me.

"I've been before, they're cool," Hanna says smiling. "You have! You've been before?" Grant asked with a surprised look on his face. "Yes I am allowed to go to parties," she said to him. "It wasn't bad I went last year with a couple of my friends," she said as we approached Mr. Cain's class. "Mr. Cain this is Grant he's interested in joining GQ next year," I told him. Mr. Cain reached out to shake Grant's hand. "Hello gentlemen, you will love GQ, son," he said pulling him over to his desk to talk to him. He looked back at Hanna and me with his head held back to see through his hair.

"Do you think they'll make him cut those bangs off?" Hanna asked as we waited at the door. "Do you think he'll look better without them?" I asked her smiling with my hands in my pocket. "I don't know, but I know he'll be able to see better," she said laughing loudly. "Well his eyes look closed even with his hair back they seem sleepy," I told her. "Yeah, but he opens them when he wants to," she told me. "So, are you going?" she asked. "Where, "To the party, the college party" She asked.

"I don't know, I've never been to a college party before, what do they do?" "It's the same as any party, play music dance, chat, hangout, it's a little wilder than a high school party, and sometimes they have drinks." "Drinks, alcohol drinks," she said. "Oh, I don't know if my mom and dad will allow it." "My mom and dad didn't know when I went," she told me. "Hey, can you tell Grant that I'll catch up with him later. I really have to go home, this is taking a long time," she said walking away waving her hand.

"I'll tell him," I said to her. When Grant was done, Mr. Cain came over to me, "Thank you so much Keagan for bringing Grant in to see me. I think he'll make a wonderful addition to our GQ team," he said putting his hands into his pocket. "You two young men enjoy your summer," he said walking us out of the door. We walked down the hallway, the halls were dark everyone was gone except for a few teachers. Tomorrow's it; there will be no more school after tomorrow. I thought as we walked down the hall. "Hey, where'd Hanna go?" He asked.

"Oh yes Hanna, she told me to tell you she'd catch up with you later, she had to get going. She couldn't be late," I told him. "Do you think she likes me?" He asked me. "I don't know she seems a little advanced for you," I told him as we walk out toward the pathway. "Advanced, what do you mean advanced?" Well you know, don't get offended okay, please don't. I just think that she's a little bit more outgoing than you are." "You don't think I can handle outgoing or something?" He asked. "No I'm sure you can handle it, I'm just saying you don't want to be with someone you can't take to a party right?" I asked him.

"I can take her to a party, just not a college party," he said sounding cross. "Are you going to the party?" "I think I might go and check it out, I just want to see what goes on at a college party," I told him. "It does sound a little fun," Grant said. We walked down the pathway, no one was around it was quiet except for the cars passing us in the street. We didn't see Fredrick and his jocks anywhere; we talked about the summer and our plans for next year. We were so caught up in our conversation we didn't even realize that we were so close to my house.

When we made it to the sidewalk near the crossing to my house, I noticed Sage standing near my porch. "Hey there's your friend," Grant said looking over at her, we crossed the street quickly. "Hey Sage, how are you?" "I'm good, hi," she said to Grant. "Grant, Sage," I said introducing them. "Do you guys want to come in for a while?" I asked. "Well, I have to get home," Grant said. "Do you mind coming with me to walk Grant home?" "Sure why not," she said holding her straps to her backpack. I put my hand on her shoulder to take her backpack.

"I can put this in my house if you want," I told her holding her backpack in my hand. "Sure, that will be fine," she said. I ran up the stairs to my house, opened the door with my key. I didn't look inside for mom I placed her backpack on the floor near the door and closed the door quietly, I didn't want mom to know I was home yet. I ran back down the stairs. "Okay, I'm ready," I said as we begin to walk toward the street to Grant's house. "So are you guys going to the party tomorrow night?" "Oh, you heard about that?" I asked her.

"Yes, they do it every year at the college, are you going?" "I don't know if I'll get to go," Grant said as we arrived at his house. "See you later Grant," I told him watching him walk up to his stairwell to his door. He waved his hand good bye. Sage and I turned around to walk back toward my house. "So, how have you been?" She asked with a bit of shyness in her voice. "I've been okay Sage, how about you? I haven't seen you in a while, what have you been up to?" I asked as we walked.

"I've been a little busy at my school; I came over today to tell you that I made the varsity cheer team for next year." "Wow really, that's a big thing huh?" "Yes, it is; I thought I'd never make it, I'm not as good as the other girls." "Why would you say something like that? I'm sure you're great at cheering," I said to her. She looked at me and smiled.

"You're so funny Keagan," she said skipping around me. "Do a cheer for me?" I asked her as we approached my house.

"Right here "Yes right here, it's just us go ahead, I want to hear how you made varsity," I told her smiling with my arms folded across my chest "Okay," she said looking all around to make sure no one else was watching her. "Ready! Okay! Go! Win! Fight! Blue and gold is dyna-mite! Go! Win! Fight! She jumped up high with every word cheering in front of the house I watched her as she clapped and cheered. After she jumped up the last time, she turned to me and stood still looking up at the window. "Um Keagan, is that your mom?" She asked.

"Yes, it is," I said waving at mom. "Come in, do you have time to have a snack with me?" I asked walking up to my door. "I have to give you your backpack anyway, so come in for a while," I told her opening the door, mom stood by the window as I walked in. "Hi mom, you remember Sage right, I took her to the GQ ball." "Oh yes, hi Sage, so you made the cheerleading squad huh?" She asked. "I made the varsity team today," she told mom. "Good for you sweetie, that's great, would you like a snack?" She asked Sage.

"No thank you, Mrs. Phillips, I really can't stay, I have to get home," she told us taking her backpack from my hand. "I'll see you later Keagan," she said holding on to the doorknob. "Hey, I'll walk you out," I told her walking behind her. I walked her down the stairway. "Sage, if I go to the party, will you dance with me again?" I asked her, she looked at me and smiled. "Sure, I will, if you come," she said. She reached over my shoulder and hugged me. "Goodbye Keagan, see you later," she said running toward the stop light at the end of the corner.

I walked back into the house; mom was sitting on the couch in the den area. "So, a party huh?" She asked. "Mom, how'd you hear?" I asked her grabbing an apple from the bowel on the table. "I hear it all," she said smiling. "You know you have to ask your dad if you can go," she said getting up going over to the kitchen table. "I know mom, I'll ask him at dinner," I told her biting my apple. "What's for dinner mom?" I asked her. "I don't know son, I think we'll be having leftovers, I'm not feeling well," she said taking a cup of tea from the counter.

She walked up to her room, I walked behind her, then the doorbell rang, I ran back down the stair to see who it was. I looked into the peephole on the door, it was Detective Hall again, I opened the door. "Hi, how can I help you?" I said biting my apple. "I need to talk to you about that day in the woods son, are your parent's home?" He asked peeking through the door opening looking around. "No sir, no one's home right now," I told him. "Isn't that your mother's car?" He asked me pointing at her car.

"Yes sir, it is, but she's not here at the moment," I told him. "Well, son, I really need to ask you why you were seen running out of the woods that day?" He asked me. I shrugged my shoulders. "I have to go," I told him. "I'll tell my dad you came by again," I told him trying to close the door on him. "Listen son, tell your mom and dad we must speak to you soon, you need to explain why you were running out of the woods that day." "Sir, I'll tell them, and my dad and I will come see you," I said with a smile closing the door.

I walked over to the window watching as they got into the police car parked in front of the house. The phone rang, I ran over to answer it. "Hello," I said. "Hi Keagan, it's Grant, I think I can get away and go to that party tomorrow night, can you go?" "I don't know, Sage says she's going. I would like to go just to dance with her," I told him. "Yes, and I want to see Hanna," he says.

"Man you're stuck on that I'm telling you, Grant, Hanna's out of your league, let it go," I told him laughing. "So see you tomorrow maybe we can leave for the party from your house," he said. "Yes after school we'll come here change then off to the party, maybe I can help you look a little cooler," I said laughing hanging up the phone. Tomorrow the party, I thought as I walked up the stairs to my room.

Party Night

The next day would be the last day of school, Grant came over really early, I watched as mom opened the front door for him. "Good morning, Mrs. Phillips," he said walking into the house. "Good morning to you Grant, would you like some breakfast?" She asked him closing the door behind him; I peeked over the railing of the stairs to see what he was wearing today. He wore the same colors every day, the brown colored khakis hanging above his ankles and the old man shoes.

Brown with dark laces, he had on a baby blue sweater today with a yellow colored scarf. I rushed back to my room to finish dressing, I shook my head thinking of what Grant was wearing, but I guess he's comfortable like that, I thought as I put on my clothes. I wore a pair of dark colored jeans, a fitting black and red shirt with a pair of black boot cut to my ankles I put on a cardigan sweater on and went down-stairs. Grant was sitting at the table with my parents when I got down there. "Hey, are you ready?" I asked him standing behind his chair. He shook his head no, turning to look at me with his mouth full of food.

"Aren't you going to eat something Keagan?" Mom asked me. "No thank you, ma'am, I'll just have....." I was about to say an apple when dad shoved one in my face. "Keagan Phillips, one day you'll have to eat more than an apple for breakfast," he said with a smile. I took a glass of juice from the table and gulped it down quickly. "Grant, we have to get going," I told him. He shoved what was left on his plate down into his mouth, and we rushed out of the door. "You think we'll make it to school before the bell rings?" He asked me.

"Sure we will," I told him as we walked off from the house; we went toward the pathway near the street. I saw across the street Mr. Hall in a police car watching us walk across. "Don't look, but that's Fredrick's dad over there, did you know his father was a policeman?" He asked me. I shook my head yes as we walked by him trying not to stare at him. "Yes I knew he was a cop, he keeps coming by my house asking about that day in the woods." "What's he asking you for?" He asked looking up at me. "He claims that someone saw me running from the woods after it happened." "Really, that's odd, did someone see you?" He asked me.

"I don't know I was running," I said as we passed the car almost at the edge of the street we could see a crowd of people standing ahead of us. "Oh no, who's that?" Grant said looking afraid to continue the walk to school. "It's no one man, come on we have to get to school, don't get afraid now," I told him continuing to walk. When we made it to the edge of the corner, there was Sage and a group of her friends. "Hello Keagan," she said with a smile pulling her hair from her face. "Hi," I said continuing to walk to school through the crowd. "Hey wait up," she said chasing me.

"Do you mind if I walk you to class?" She asked me grabbing on my shirt. "You in a hurry" "A little bit," I told her. "We don't want to be late today, it's the last day," Grant told her. "What are you doing here, don't you have school today?" I asked her. "No, our last day was yesterday, I thought I'd come hang out here with you guys." She said looking back at her friends who were staring at me as if I was food from the kitchen. "What if you stay out today and hang out with us," she said. "No thank you," Grant said quickly.

"We have to go today; didn't you go to your last day of school?" He asked looking crossed at her. "Yes I did," she said with a bit of anger in her voice. "Our school let out a little earlier every year, we're private," she said standing next to Grant with her hands crossed. "We have to go," Grant said walking ahead of me. "Are you coming, Keagan? We don't want to be late," he said looking at me with his head leaned back.

"It would be nice if you came with us to the mall," Sage said to me in my ear as I began to walk away she grabbed onto my arm. "No, I better go," I told her peeling her hand from my arm. I walked quickly to catch up to Grant. "Hey, Grant what was that about, why were you being so mean to Sage?" I asked him as we walked into to the school front entrance. "You don't know her, she's hanging around you for a reason, and it's not a good one," he told me walking with his hands in his pocket.

"What do you mean, she's always been nice, hey Grant, you don't know everything okay. I like Sage she's a good person, what's your problem man?" I asked him as we walked apart from one another. "I'll see you after class," I told him as he walked to class in the other direction; he waved his hand up at me. That day everyone had parties in their classes Mrs. Blanchard gave a party for his students with pizza and sodas from class to class. We celebrated the last day of school, in Mrs. Byrd's class we had sandwich wraps she brought in lots of tasty snacks and treats to go along with them too.

Fredrick and the other jocks horsed around in class throwing food at one another when Mrs. Byrd wasn't looking, she was so busy talking to everyone about their summer, explaining to them about how important it will be for them to go into the next grade with greater expectations, she ate while she told us stories about herself as a high school kid. "I was just as shy as any young girl could be and look at me now," she told the other girls. When the bell rang, she stood up, holding her wrap in her hand. "You guys take care of yourselves over the summer."

A lot of the other students went over to her giving her hugs and talking to her Fredrick winked his eye at me. "You know you want to hug her GQ, go on you wimp do what you do best," he said as he stood by the door with his jock friends. I went over to Mrs. Byrd and hugged her looking back at Fredric with a smile. "Thank you for everything Mrs. Byrd," I told her walking away. I passed Fredrick and his friends. "It's nice that I can give her a hug unlike you," I said smiling passing through the crowd.

He watched me as I walked down the hall looking for Grant. "Hey, have you seen Grant?" I asked his friend Hanna. She shook her head no. I continued to walk down the hall. When I arrived at the end of the hallway I saw Sage and all her friends through the crowd, everyone was throwing papers everywhere in the air. I looked through it all trying to get past the crowd to greet her, I waved as I walked. "Hey, have you seen my small friend Grant?" I asked her. "Sure, he just walked past me I thought he went..." She said pausing pointing her finger over her shoulder.

"Oh I don't know he was just there, he couldn't have gone that far," she said following me toward the end of the building. She put her hand on my shoulder. "So you're still coming to that party right?" "I am if I find Grant," I told her walking fast around the building. "He's your date or something?" She asked. "What kind of question is that?" I asked her stopping in my tracks. "No, he's my friend I'm supposed to help him get ready for the party." "Oh I see," she said. "Did you need me to come along, I know a lot about fashion," she said holding onto her shirt.

"No thank you, I think I can handle it," I told her walking back toward the front of the building. "There you are," Grant says. "I've been looking for you, I waited in front of Mrs. Byrd's class for you to come out, and you never did." He told me holding his hand on his head. "I was looking for you too, are you ready?" I asked him as we walked toward the side gate to go home. "So will I get to help you?" Sage asked. "Uh, no thank you, I got it," I told her as we walked away.

"Your loss," she said walking back toward the door near her friends. "See you later, at the party then," I told her walking with Grant. "She's going to the party?" Grant asked. "Yes, she says that she wants to help me get you ready for the party too, I told her no, I knew you wouldn't fall for that," I told him laughing. "No way, I don't think Sage likes me anyway" he told me. "You think I can wear something gray, I like gray and black," Grant said as we walked through the pathway toward the gate.

"I thought you' want to wear something cool like the things I wear," I said smiling. We made it through the pathway quickly when we came to the fence he climbed over first; I went right after him, we both walked toward my house first. "Do you think your parents are going to freak when they hear you're going to a party at a college?" I asked him as we approached my house. He shrugged his shoulders. "I think they will," I told him as I opened my front door. The house smelled of soup, like a veggie soup.

"Yummy Keagan, is your mom making soup," He asked me "I don't know let's go check," I told him shutting the door behind us, I walked toward the kitchen with Grant tailing behind me I grabbed an apple out of the bowel on the table. "Hello Mrs. Phillips," Grant said to mom. I went over to mom and kissed her cheek. "Hi mom, how was your day?" I asked her. "It was good, son, and yours?" She asked. "It was great, the last day of school, you know."

"I know son, what are you planning to do for the summer?" She said with a smile. "Mrs. Phillips we asked if he wanted to join the vacation Bible studies class and he declined." Grant told her before I could open my mouth to tell mom what I wanted to do for the summer. "No mom I won't go, I plan to work on my running, track practice starts in the summer," I told her. "And I'm thinking of other sports also, mom," I told her eating my apple. "The Bible studies sounds so nice, don't you think, son?" She said placing a spoon in the soup pot.

"It smells so good mom," I told her walking away. "What are you two up to for the rest of the day?" She asked me. I turned back and went toward the kitchen, I peeked my head around the corner to see her reaction when I told her I wanted to go to a party. "Mom, I was invited to a party at a college by a friend, Sage, you know Sage, the girl I took to the GQ ball." I told her, she put the spoon down and walked over to me. "Son, you know you have to ask your dad about that, a college party… I'm not sure about that," she said with her eyebrows raised.

"Mom, it's not going to be so bad, I won't even stay long. I just want to see what it's like that all" I told her walking near the stairs where Grant was standing. "Grant's going with me, I'm going to help him dress for the party," I told her as we walk up the stairs. "Keagan, I don't know if your dad will allow it, so don't get your hopes up," she tells me watching us walk up the stairwell. We went into my room; I went straight to my closet. "Have a seat over there," I told Grant. "What color would you like to wear?" I ask him.

"Um, I like red," he told me looking himself over up and down. "You like red?" I said from inside the closet. I flipped through the hangers in my closet I had jeans, sweaters, shirts with and without designs. I wore a lot of different things, but not a lot of red, I had one red t-shirt. I grabbed it from the hanger along with a pair of jeans and a red and black sweater. "Here try this stuff on," I said throwing it toward him; I grabbed a pair of my boots from the floor of my closet. I had the perfect boots to match his outfit.

"Here and try these with it," I told him going back to see what I could find for myself. I closed the closet door so that he could change in private. "Hey this actually looks really good on me," Grant yelled out. "Good, do you have on the shoes and everything?" I yelled back. "Yes I do, I look really nice," he said. I came out of the closet; I wore a green shirt with a design on the front and black jeans and green and black boots. "Hey you look nice," I told him as I walked toward the mirror. He looked totally different all dressed up. "Do you think Hanna will notice me when she sees me this time?"

"Grant, Hanna's going to think you're someone else," I said smiling in the mirror. "I brushed my hair backward then forward, he walked over to the mirror. "Should I do anything different to my hair?" He asked with his head held back, trying to see from underneath his long bangs. "No, I think its fine," I told him. "Maybe just brush it just a little away from your face so that you can see a little better right," I told him handing him the brush. He began to brush his hair I went back into my closet to get my black leather jacket, to put it on.

"Alright, we're ready to go," I said looking in the mirror once more, Grant looked at his watch. "It's still really early, I have to go home and tell my parents about this, and I know my mom will want me to eat dinner before going out." "Okay well, let's head over there, just don't get your clothes dirty," I told him as we walked toward the door. "Boys" Mom yelled before we made it to the hallway "Yes, mom!" I yelled back. "You come down here to the kitchen please," she said. "Yes, mom," I said as we entered the kitchen.

"Son, I talked to your dad, he wasn't happy about you going to the party, but I told him what you said. That you wouldn't stay long and you just wanted to see what it was like, he says he wants you home by eleven no later. Do you understand son?" She said holding her small bowl of soup in her hand. "We are going to Grant's house to ask his parents for permission, tell dad thanks for me, please. I will be home by eleven," I told her as we walked to the front door. "Goodbye Mrs. Phillips, I'll see you later," Grant told mom as I open the door.

We walked down to Grant's house; his parents were outside in the yard working in the rose garden. "Hey, Grant were you been? School let out over an hour ago," his mom asked lifting her sun hat from her face to look up at us. She blinked her eyes to get a good look at him. "Nice clothes son, where did you get them from?" His father asked with a stern voice. "Oh I just borrowed them from Keagan," he told them looking down at the boots he was wearing "Where you going, in those nice duds?" His mom asked.

"Well that's kind of why I came home; I was invited to a party." "Where is this party?" His father asked digging deeper into the dirt with the hoe in his hand. "It's the last day of school type of thing," Grant said nervously. "I will only be there until eleven o'clock dad I promise it will be okay, Keagan's going with me." He told his dad nervously rubbing his hands together. "Son, you know we don't do those sorts of things," his father said. "A party Grant, since when have you liked parties?" His mom said looking down at the dirt in the garden.

"Mom, I know I've never asked, but it's really going to be a nice party. Hanna's going to be there also, can I please go, please?" He said now putting his hands in his pocket holding his head down. "You really want to go, son?" His father asked. "Yes dad, I do." "Well it must be a good party because you never asked us about any parties before," he said hoeing the dirt in. His mom looked up at me. "I think it would be good for you, I think you'll have fun too." "You go ahead son, but be here at home no later than eleven, by the way where is this party going to be? I'd like to drop you off there," he said standing up tall holding the hoe.

"It's at the University dad, you know downtown," he told him holding his head back to look at them. "Oh we know that one for sure, we've been to those parties when we were younger," they said laughing and smiling at one another. "You have?" Grant asked. "Yes, son, actually that's where your mom and I met, at a frat party in my dormitory," Grant's dad said smiling at his mom. "Sure son, you don't think we've always been this boring now do you," he said beginning to ploy through the dirt with the hoe again.

"Now go on eat some dinner, and by the time we're finished up here, it'll be time for the party, you guys don't mind me dropping you off do you?" He asked with a smile. "No sir, not at all," I told him. As Grant began to walk toward the house to have dinner before we go, his mom made a meatloaf with mashed potatoes. I didn't eat much of it, I sat there and watched as Grant ate through his whole plate and started eating more and more. "Do you think she'll dance with me?" He asked. "Who" I asked him.

"You know who," he said with his cheeks full of food he smiled with potatoes flowing out through the middle of his lips. "Oh Hanna, huh sure she'll dance with you, do you know how to dance?" I asked him. He shrugged his shoulders. "I don't know how to dance, I mean I've danced at the GQ ball with Sage before, but it was nothing fancy," I told him. "Just a little moving my body around to the beats I hear," I laughed along with Grant. "Show me the moves to the beat." "What beat?" I asked him. "Make a beat in your head," he told me.

"Go on you can do it," he said slapping my arm from his chair. I stood up and started to mumble a song from my head, I moved my body around. Grant began to laugh potatoes spewed from his mouth. "You know what Keagan, I think you should stick to just talking to the girls, please don't dance with them," he told me. "Oh, you can do better?" I asked him. He shrugged his shoulders. "Okay hot guy, get up and do your thing then," I told him pushing his chair for him to get out. He kept eating as I tugged at his chair.

"Okay, okay!" He said getting up from the table; he walked over to the stereo on the cabinet and turned it on. He began to do all this dancing; I was baffled Grant could really dance, like the guys on television. He had rhythm and was on beat; oh my I thought he's going to show me up at this dance. I ran over to the cabinet and turned down the music. "Grant, you have to show me how to do that?" I asked him, he looked up at me. "Okay just watch and do what I do," he said wiggling his hips around and moving his feet.

We practiced until his father walked in with his mother following behind him; Grant quickly turned the music off. "Why did you turn it off, son?" His father asked. "Oh the song was over," Grant said sitting down on the couch. "I saw you from the window son, nice moves," his mom said smiling. "You think you're a good dancer, son, you should see your mother and me, I bet that's where you get it from," his dad said moving around the floor dancing. "No dad, I'm not a good dancer at all," Grant told them smiling.

They went to the back of the house and after a few minutes came back out cleaned and ready to take us to the party. "You guys ready?" His father said dancing to the door. "Come on son let's get this party started." We laughed as we walked to the car. On the way to the dance, we saw groups of kids walking together to the college laughing and talking about the party. When we pulled up in front of the party there were crowds of people everywhere, I doubt we would find Sage and Hanna in the crowds. Grant and I got out of the car; he was nervous and so was I.

We walked up to the front of the door through the crowd and knocked, after the first knock the door went flying open. "What are you guys stupid? Come on in," a guy said to us holding a cup in his hand. "You don't have to knock at a college party, come, come talk to me," he said as he grabbed me by the neck and pulled me close to his mouth. "Over there is the booze, and over there are the girls," he said with warmth coming from his breath. "Go, go ahead pick one," he said laughing.

Grant looked at me and shook his head, of course, we didn't know there would be drinking. We walked around the house rooms looking for Sage or Hanna. "There are some rooms upstairs, are you guys looking for someone?" A girl asked us standing by the stairwell railing. I shook my head yes, music was playing loudly. "Who is she?" She asked me yelling over the music. "Um… before I could finish my sentence, she pulled me toward the middle of the room where everyone was dancing.

"What's your name?" She asked as she pulled me into the circle and began to dance in front of me. "I'm Keagan," I told her yelling over the music, she put her mouth to my ear. "Who are you?" She asked again this time putting her ear to my mouth waiting for an answer. "I'm

Keagan," I yelled into her ear. "Hi Keagan, I'm Tracy," she said snapping her fingers and twirling around in front of me. "Where do you go to school Keagan?" She asked me still yelling and dancing around me.

"You know what?" I said looking around the room, I lost sight of Grant. "What!" She yelled. "Um I came here with someone, and we're supposed to meet up with some friends, do you mind if I leave to find them?" I told her barely moving my feet dancing with her. "I know who you're looking for Keagan Phillips, I know all about her," she said spinning around in front of me. "You know who I'm looking for?" I yelled out. She moved in close with her mouth to my ear. "You're looking for Sage Jennings, and she's looking for you," she said in a whisper.

"You know her?" I asked "Of course I do she's my sister," she said smiling and dancing. "Your sister, really, well where can I find her" I asked politely, she shrugged her shoulders as if she didn't know. I walked off leaving her in the middle of the room to dance alone; I walked into the hallway and ran into Hanna. "Hi Hanna, have you seen Grant at all?" I asked her. "He would be back there," she told me looking back pointing to the dark hallway. "Thank you, how's your night going?" I asked her. "It's going fine," she said pointing at another guy across the hall.

"Oh, I see," I told her walking away. "You're just going to leave me dancing?" She asked running behind me. "I have to find my friend now, I'm sure he's been looking for me," I told her going across the room scanning for Grant or Sage or anyone familiar. I was tapped on the shoulder really hard by the time I reached the den area of the house. I turned to see who it was and my eyes were covered by two cold hands. "Guess who?" A soft voice said I turned all the way around. "It's Hanna, right?"

"Yes your right, it's me," she said smiling. "Hey where is Grant, I've been looking for him, he got away from me after we danced," she said smiling. "Oh you've been dancing with him tonight, I bet you didn't expect him to move the way he did right?" I said to her smiling. "No he took me by surprise, I want to dance again, so let's find him," she said. We began walking around looking for Grant when we heard a horrifying scream down the hall way, we looked at one another and ran toward the scream, everyone else ran as well.

We ran down a stairwell everyone tripping over one another to get to the screams when we made it down everyone was standing around one another trying to look over each other's shoulders. Hanna and I pushed our way through the crowd to see what was going on; when we made it almost to the front we saw that people were surrounding a circle of people. I peeked through the crowd, and there were Fredrick and the jocks.

They had Grant pinned up against a wall choking him, and they had Sage on her knees in the middle of the room two of them held her arms while she sat on her knees. She was crying, and her top was off, and one by one Fredrick and his friends were taking their pants down standing in front of her face one by one, she was screaming out for them to stop, she held her head down to her chest and screamed out. "Please stop! Please stop!" I saw Grant and ran toward him they tried blocking me from getting to him I pulled at them one by one; they held him up higher up against the wall.

I could see Grant getting madder and madder, he kicked out at them, but they didn't budge. While we were busy trying to get Grant free Sage cried out; she screamed so loudly that the basement walls cracked everyone covered their ears except for Grant and me. The guys who were holding on to Grant dropped him to the ground and turned to see what was going on with Sage. They let her arms go, and she curled to the ground in a fetal position, she screamed more then complete silence hit the room everyone began to scream out.

"Look! Look at her!" They yelled out and began to run back toward the stairs, her body turned as if it was water the room began to fill with water, everyone ran toward the stairs, but the water flowed quickly toward them. When the room began to clear of some of the people the water began to swirl up back toward her it swirled and swirled until it stood her up. Her naked body was of water, and she stood firmly standing in front of Fredrick she smiled at him and his friends. She stuck out her hands as if to shun them, and soon the water sprayed out at them as if it was coming from a hose or a fire hydrant they went flying across the room.

Grant and Hanna ran for the stairs I ran behind them, the jocks in the room were being tossed around by the water as if they were leaves from a tree flying in the winds of winter. I stood back waiting for her to render them from her wrath, but she took her time twirling them across the room over and over again. Fredrick tried to fight back with his fiery arms, but to each of his attempts, she sprayed him harder and longer. When she stopped, she screamed out again so loudly that the basement walls cracked opened to the outside.

They laid there holding their ears as she screamed and ran out through the hole in the wall to the back of the house. I ran out behind her, it was dark I couldn't see where she went at first until I looked down for her footprints. I followed each one and found her in the woods curled up in a ball crying, her hair was soaked, her body shivering, she looked up at me. "Keagan I'm so sorry," she said to me, I took off my jacket and covered her bareback. "Why are you sorry? You have nothing to be sorry for," I assured her helping her zip the jacket.

"Are you going to be okay?" I asked her. She looked up at me and grinned a little, then shook her head. "I think I'll live," she said. "Do you mind walking me back to find some pants or something before my father comes? I don't want to go back in there could you get them for me?" She asked me. "Sure, just stay put, I'll get you a pair of pants, stay right here okay, don't move," I told her. "These will keep you warm until I come back." I said pushing the leaves on the ground all around her, she smiled at me I got up and ran as quickly as I could to get her a pair of pants.

When I got back to the college, there was a crowd of people leaving and standing around. I put my head down and walked through the crowd quietly, when I made it into the house I snuck around snooping around each of the rooms in the house for a pair of pants that will fit Sage. Finally, I was in one of the rooms, there was a guy and a girl making out on the floor I saw the girls pants on the dresser, I grabbed them and ran for the door. I ran and ran until I reached the spot where I left Sage, she was gone "Sage!" I yelled out. "Sage, where are you!" I yelled out looking all around the woods the leaves were wet with her body prints where I left her.

"Sage! Sage!" Where could she have gone? I began to walk back to the college when I got there Grant was standing in front waiting for me with Hanna. "Is she going to be okay?" Hanna asked, I shook my head I don't know, I held the pants by my side still looking out into the woods. "Hey, hey" I heard a whisper. "Over here, please," I heard I looked toward the darkness by the wall of the college, and there she was waiting with my jacket on in the dark. I walked over to her; "what happened?" I asked handing her the pants. "They came looking for me, I had to leave," she told me putting on the jeans, zipping them up.

"Thank you so much Keagan," she reached over to me and kissed my cheek. "I promise I'll get your jacket back to you," she said running off into the woods. I walked back over to Grant as I walked up to him his father pulled up to get us. "Dad, Hanna needs a ride home," he told his dad. "No problem son, get in you guys," he said smiling; we all got in and fastened our seatbelts. "So how was the party?" He asked.

"It was cool, dad." "Yes cool, lots of excitement," Hanna and Grant told him as I looked out of the window toward the woods as he drove away. I thought about Sage, I hoped she made it home safely, I don't know what to think about tonight, I thought as Grant's father pulled up to my house. "Thank you, sir, see you two later," I told Hanna and Grant. "Yes, see you later," Grant said. Hanna waved her hand goodbye. What a night I thought as I approached my door.

Summer Time

I didn't see Sage after that night for a while, although Grant came over every other day still trying to get me to go to vacation bible studies. I would decline every time; Hanna and Grant became very close after the party. They'd spend almost every day together; she did attend vacation Bible studies, there were at least ten people who came to the vacation Bible studies from our school. One of them was a good friend of Fredrick's a young jock they called Matthew.

Grant would tell me that he wasn't there to do Bible studies but to study them. I never understood what he meant by that, and I never asked. Grant was always saying things to me in code as if I would understand him. I often wondered what happened to Sage after that night in the basement, I know she was embarrassed and wanted to run and never look back. I'd look for her around town in the mall, sometimes when I would shop with mom, I was sure I'd run into her by now, but I hadn't.

I even tried calling her, she never picked up the phone for me, I got her mom on the phone most of the time she'd say, Sage wasn't there and didn't know when she'd return. I'd call her at least twice a day trying to catch her on the phone; track practice was to start next week. Maybe I'd see her there, sometimes some of the girls from the private school would come hang out at the school. Especially during football practice, they didn't have a football team over there. They had a lot of different sports, but they didn't have football, I hoped that she would come.

I just wanted to make sure she was safe; I wanted her to know that I didn't look at her naked body that night. It had to have been awful what she went through that night, I thought as I began to look through my closet for my track shoes and my tracksuit. I would run on junior varsity this year. It would mean I would be a step ahead of the freshman coming in this year, mom knocked on my door. "Keagan are you okay in there?" She asked me. "Yes mom, I am, I'm just in the closet."

"Can you come downstairs for a second; I have something to show you?" She told me at the door. "I'll be right down mom," I yelled out from the closet. I hurried down after putting my things on the chair, to see what mom had to show me. I ran down half the stairs until I heard a familiar voice I slowed down to see if what I was hearing was real. It was Sage she came over to see me I tried walking slowly to keep my cool, as I approached the front door I jumped down from the last two stairs hitting the front room floor lightly.

"Hey, Sage, what brings you by?" I asked turning to look at her in the doorway. "She wanted to give you something son," Mom said holding my jacket in the air. "Oh yes, that's it I came by here to return your jacket, I know it's been a while. I'm sorry my family went to our summer home for a few weeks," she told me smiling. "I did get some messages from you." "Your mom right, it was her who answered the phone?" I asked her. She shook her head no. "It was the housekeeper, did she say she was my mom"

"No, she didn't, she just kept telling me you were gone and she didn't know when you would return. She wasn't rude or anything, she was very pleasant," I added trying not to get the housekeeper in any trouble. "You are so sweet Keagan, thank you so much for helping me that night," she said whispering so that my mom wouldn't hear. "It's okay Sage, I'm just glad you're okay. I hadn't seen you around or anything I didn't know where you went that night, you ran away into the woods, and I couldn't go after you because Grants father showed up to pick us up from the party.

I didn't know what to think, I thought maybe you were mad at me or something," I told her. "Would you like a seat?" I asked walking toward the living room. "No thank you, I just wanted to return your jacket to you," she said smiling. "So you didn't want to come see me and hang out?" "No, I'm sorry, I can't, I have to get back home," she told me walking toward the door. "So are you and your family going on any vacations this summer?" She asked me.

"No, I don't think so my sister and brother and coming in from college next week, and we'll probably visit the lake house in Michigan," I told her as I held the door open for her to walk out. "Oh, Lakehouse, that sounds so cool, do you guys stay out there long?" She asked standing by the door. "Usually we go at the end of summer and stay at least two to three weeks." "Oh I see, do you ever invite friends up?" She asked me smiling. "No I've never invited any friends up, it's kind of like a family thing," I told her.

"Oh I see, well it sounds like a nice place to go Michigan on a lake, sounds perfect," she smiled again and walked out the door. "So, I guess you have a lot to do this summer then, huh?" I shook my head. "I don't have too much to do, I have just been hanging out around the house mostly, and the only visitors I get are Grant and Hanna. Sometimes, and they only stop by for a while before vacation Bible studies, are you interested in going?" I asked her. "Oh no, I can't go, oh and hey I wanted to ask you about that, how'd you end up with Grant as your friend?" She asked me holding onto the door handle.

"It's a crazy story, you know Fredrick Hall right?" I asked, "Oh yes, let me guess, he was bullying him and you helped him out, am I right?" She asked. "Yes, you're right," I told her with a smile. "Yes they'll never learn," she said walking down the stairs from the porch. "Well, I will see you around Keagan, thank you again," she said walking away, a couple of her friends was standing at the curb waiting for her. "Goodbye Sage," I told her closing the door. I walked back into the house, mom was in the kitchen cooking, I walked in and sat at the table.

"So, what was all that about?" She asked. "What was all what, mom?" I replied. "You and Sage, did you dance with her at the party?"

"No, something happened to her at the party something bad, mom. She's really a nice girl, I like her, I want her to be my girlfriend this year in school, and do you think she likes me?" I asked mom eating grapes from a bag she had sitting on the table. "Of course she likes you, you're a very handsome young man and all that great personality," she said smiling.

"Who wouldn't like you?" "Well mom, the guys around me seem to have more going for them, and girls fall all over themselves to be with them." "And they don't fall all over you?" She said standing with her hand on her hip. "Come here son," she pulled me from my seat, we walked over to the living room mirror, and she stood me in front of it. "Look at yourself," she took my glasses from my eyes "You are a very handsome young man, those eyes that dimple in your chin, your simply breathtaking sweetheart.

The girls would be crazy if they can't see that," she said. "Mom you have to say that to me, you're my mom." "No son, I wouldn't tell you any lies, you're as handsome as they come, and there is absolutely no reason why this year you and Sage can't hang out or become boyfriend and girlfriend," she said. "But you're still you, it's always better to wait until college to date someone." "College mom, no way that's a long time from now," I told her smiling. I sat back down at the table and begin to throw grapes in the air waiting for them to fall in my mouth missing almost every time.

The doorbell rang again. "Get that Keagan, I bet it's for you," she said standing over the kitchen sink. "Okay mom, I'll get it." I got up from the table and walked to the door, still tossing grapes in the air. I didn't even ask who was there or look in the peephole; I tossed a grape as I opened the door. Grant stuck his head in and caught the grape coming down. "Hey Keagan, how are you today?" Hanna asked. "I'm good, what brings you guys here?" I asked her. Grant was chewing the grape.

"Do you have any more of those anywhere?" He asked me still chewing. "That was good," he said swallowing. "Yes, they're in the kitchen, mom Grant wants some grapes!" I yelled as he walked in. "Come in, you guys," I said holding the door all the way open, we walked back toward the kitchen. Grant walked ahead of Hanna and me. "What were you doing today? You missed a great Bible study, we're reading about Paul, it's really very interesting," Hanna told me as we walk toward the kitchen. "I bet," I said sitting at the table across from Grant.

"So, what are you guys up to for the summer?" Mom asked them setting the table with plates and napkins. "I made some pasta and pizza, would you guys like some?" "Sure Mrs. Phillips, I'd love some," Grant said. "Sure, I'd like some too," Hanna told her grabbing a plate from the pile. "I'm just preparing for next year, I hear being a sophomore is even harder than being a freshman," Hanna said as mom placed the pizza on the table. "Really, well I'm sure you guys know how to stay out of trouble, just do your school work and try not to follow the bad crowds," she told us handing each of us a slice of pizza.

"Have you heard from Sage at all, that was terrible what happened to her," Hanna said. "Sheesh" I said to her, looking at mom while her back was turned to us getting drinks from the refrigerator. "Oops I'm sorry," she said as mom walked over with juice in her hands ready to pour. "What happened to her?" Mom asked quickly looking at Hanna. "Um, Mrs. Phillips did you make this pizza yourself?" Grant asked quickly turning the focus toward him. "No, it came out of a box," she said looking back at Hanna; I stared at Hanna to warn her not to tell mom what happened to Sage that night.

"Nothing happened, ma'am," she said looking at me. "Oh it's a secret huh, well I hope she's okay, whatever it is," she said walking out of the kitchen. "You kids enjoy the pizza, eat as much as you like, try the pasta too." "Thank you, Mrs. Phillips!" Both Hanna and Grant yelled out. "You're very welcome, have fun guys," she said walking up the stairwell. "So, what are your plans for the rest of the summer?" Grant asked me. "Oh, I start practice tomorrow, aren't you playing a sport this year?" I asked him. "Me!" Hanna said.

"No Grant, aren't you playing a sport?" I asked again. "I'm planning to play basketball," Hanna said. "Have you played before?" I asked her. "Yes at the rec center, I've played every summer just about, you should come see me play sometimes," she said to me eating mom's pasta. "Oh, then you are better at it than me huh." "I don't know I've never seen you play before," she said. "Grant use to play until he was tired of me beating him all the time, he's a bit of a poor sport," she said laughing.

"Huh, Grant?" Grant lifted his head from his plate chewing; he looked at her and smiled. "I only let you beat me because I knew you'd cry if you lost the game," she said laughing. "We should have a game when we finish up here, are you guys up for it?" I asked them. "Sure why not, where will we play at?" "Right in the front, your hoop is good enough," Hanna said. "But don't you want some other competition? If we go to the rec center we can get an extra player to play with us," Grant said.

"Okay let's do it then," I said grabbing my plate walking it over to the sink with my cup. "I'll go and change, do you guys need to change into some playing gear?" I asked them. "Do you have any gym shorts I can borrow?" Grant asked. "Sure, what about you Hanna, are you comfortable wearing what you have on?" I asked her, she stood up from the table with her plate in her hand and pulled her pants down a little grabbing a pair of shorts she wore underneath her pants. "I come prepared," she said laughing walking over to the sink.

"Let's get this game going, come on Grant, you can change clothes upstairs," I told him walking out of the kitchen. "Hanna you can wait in the living room," I told her. We went upstairs and changed Grant wore my basketball shorts and a t-shirt I had in my drawer. "Thank you man,

I appreciate it, I'm going to return your other things as soon as my mom washes them," he told me as we walk back down to get Hanna. We headed out of the front door on our way to the rec center which was down by the grocery store where Reese and her father used to live.

I often wondered what happened to her father, Reese was all he had. When we passed their house, I saw the old couple who would always be outside when I'd come to pick up Reese. "Hello son, how have you been?" The little old man asked me. "I'm good sir," I said as we passed one another, I stared back at the apartment building that she lived in, I missed her all over again. Memories of her went through my mind as we walked together in silence until it was time to cross the street. "Are you okay Keagan?" Hanna asked putting her hand on my shoulders.

"I knew Reese, she was such a nice girl, it's very sad what happened to her," she said walking across the street; the sign blinked as we walked across the crosswalk. "It shouldn't have happened to her that way, she didn't deserve any of it," Grant said shaking his head. "It was a complete surprise when she killed herself," I told them. "I mean, I knew that they were taunting and teasing her, but I didn't know how bad it was, I didn't know that she needed me more than she did. She never asked me for anything except for my friendship, I feel like I failed her," I told them as we approach the rec center. I stood at the top of the stairwell to think about Reese a bit more.

"You were a good friend I'm sure, maybe there were things she just couldn't tell you, girls are different Keagan believe me. There are lots of things I wouldn't share with you and Grant, I just wouldn't. I'm sure she just couldn't share certain things with you, it wasn't your fault I'm sure," she said grabbing me by the arm pulling me to go up the stairs. "Come on let me teach you some things that girls will share on the basketball court," she said laughing. "Don't be sad for her just pray for her soul," she told me holding onto my arm as we walked into the gym.

There were guys and girls everywhere with basketballs bouncing them around the court, there were four hoops, and two games were going on. "Come on Grant let's go get a ball," Hanna said to Grant pulling him toward the door opening in the middle of the room. "Stay here Keagan, stand over there near that hoop save the spot for us," she said. "Okay!" She yelled out walking away. "Okay," I told her standing up against the pole underneath the hoop. There were so many people playing basketball yelling and scuffling around the court I watched intensely as the game at the far end heated up.

There were a lot of guys and girls playing a serious game on that end. One team was really aggressive they hustled around the other team really fast as if they were really playing for a championship or something. It was so intense I didn't pay attention to anything else that was going on around me I watched them until I heard Hanna yelling at Grant to hustle up the ball. She was laughing at him, turning all around with the ball holding her hand out to him. "See, little one, try me," she said twirling running all around him. "Heads up!" She yelled out tossing the ball to me, I jumped away from the pole, running to catch it.

"Hey, you really can play huh," she said as I dribbled all around her and Grant, we horsed around until a group of guys and girls came up to us. "Let's play a game of five on five," the tall guy said holding his hand out for Hanna to toss him the ball, she tossed it over. "I got you, and you and you over there and you let's hustle," he said as everyone else began to spread out around the court to play "Hustle!" Hanna yelled out, I was playing on the tall guy's team. "I'm Patrick that's Mat, that's Harrison, the other ones are Rick and Eric," he said as he helped me block the other players.

We played against Grant, Hanna and three other girls, their names were Candy, Sharon, and Jenna. The game was getting intense the girls seem to be better at hustling than we were. Hanna made so many baskets I was losing count. She was as good as she said; she ran fast and shot from afar, she knew how to dominate on the court without being selfish with the ball. In the end, her team won they had 33 points over our 15 it was awful. "See I told you not to try me," Hanna said standing around still bouncing and tossing the ball to the hoop.

I walked over to the water fountain to get a drink of water when I noticed Sage standing in the doorway. She was laughing, oh no, I thought as I leaned into the fountain to sip the water, she seen that. She waved at me, I waved back, and when I was done I turned around and started to walk back over to Hanna and Grant. "Oh don't be embarrassed" she said walking up behind me. I turned to look at her. "I'm not embarrassed at all, Hanna's a great basketball player, she caught me off guard this time," I told her smiling.

"No she's good, I can't believe how badly she beat us," I said walking over to them watching Hanna show off more. Grant stood back watching her toss the ball through the hoop over and over again. She shot the ball into the basket; making us all look like amateurs, we stayed there playing around the court for a while before walking back home, it was beginning to get dark out the sun was going down when we walked out of the rec center. "Are you guys walking me home first?" Hanna asked us. "Of course we are," Grant told her.

"Even though you're a handful on the basketball court, you're still a lady," Grant said smiling at Hanna. It was like he was glowing when he was around her, he was so in love with Hanna, but she didn't seem to act as if she knew anything about it. She would laugh and smile with him, and that was all; he'd get as a response, they hung out together a lot though. She was just so much taller than Grant and so different. "We should go the short way around," Hanna said walking across the street, we followed her, she had to live somewhere close to Grant because she was always at Grant's house.

"Where do you live?" I asked her. "Just a few houses down from where the small church is, on the corner near the edge of the street," she said. "You guys don't have to walk me all the way," she said as we followed her. "Why not, it's really no problem, right Keagan?" Grant said looking at me. "No problem," I said walking faster than them to get there quicker. "So, you and Sage, your girlfriend" Hanna asked. "No, she seems a little shy to me, does she go to Kennedy High with us?" "No, remember she goes to private school downtown," I told her.

"Oh yeah, is that where you met her?" She asked me as we walked on to her house. "Here we go," she said stopping pointing at her house. "This is it, I thought you lived up a little further, nope this is it," she said staring at the house. Kids were hanging out everywhere on the porch and in the yard playing. "How many children does your mom have?" I asked her. "I don't know, I've never met my mom," she said walking toward the house. "Keagan this is a group home for teens, she doesn't know any of her real family, this is it for her," Grant told me as we watch her walk up to the house.

"I didn't know that," I told him, the kids in the yard were playing kick ball they watched as we begin walking away after Hanna went inside. "Wow, I feel bad for her," I told Gran.t "Why, she knows Jesus, she's a very smart girl, you should be more worried about yourself. Hanna's going to be fine, she's been through a lot, but she's always in prayer about it. At some point you just have to give all the bad things to God," he told me as we walk. "What does that mean Grant? Give it all to God; do you really believe that he cares enough to look out for us?" I asked him looking cross.

"He does Keagan, you just have to believe that he does," he said. We walked down the sidewalk in silence for a while until he saw a truck drive by with a sign on it that read, "Vacation Get Away!" "Look Keagan, you'll be getting away soon right?" "Yes I will, Torch Lake, Township Michigan," I told him with excitement. "I haven't been there in years, but I'm so excited, I plan to go out on the boat this time, hey do you think your mom and dad would allow you to come with us?" "I don't know, I can ask them, but don't you need to ask your parents first, it is a family vacation right?" He asked.

"Yes, but I don't think they'll mind if I bring along a couple of friends, it's a bit boring out there," I told him. "Well, here we are, this is you," Grant said pointing at my house. "I'll ask my mom and dad about you going, maybe we can even get Sage and Hanna to go with us, it's only for two weeks," I told him as I walk up to my door. "Bye Grant, I'll see you later," I said waving to him. "When I got into the house no one was home I went into the kitchen to see if mom was there she wasn't, I looked all around the house for her, but she wasn't there.

"Mom" I yelled out but nothing, I went over to the phone to call dad to see if he knew where mom might be when I noticed a note pinned to the refrigerator door. "Keagan there's food in the oven for you; I'm filling in at the hospital for a sick nurse. I'll be gone until midnight, dad should get home before me," the note read. "Lock up the house, Love you, mom." I put the letter down on the countertop and walked over to the oven to see what she left for dinner. There was a plate of food it looked like pasta and sauce, I reached in and pulled it out.

I took it over to the table grabbing a fork from the drawer and a cup to have a drink juice. I sat down at the table and began to eat, it was so quiet in the house, I sat there eating my pasta thinking about Hanna. I was so surprised that she was in a place like that; she seemed to be okay with it. I don't know what I'd do if I didn't know my mom and dad, I thought as I looked out of the window watching as the sky turned dark. The kitchen light was the only light on in the house, I finished up my food and my drink and placed it in the sink, running the water hot to wash it and put it away.

I wondered if mom and dad would mind if I'd have company on vacation, the twins are going to be with us, but that doesn't mean that I'll be entertained by them. Maybe mom and dad will think that way as well

I thought as I turned off the water, placing my plate and fork in the dish rack. I walked over to the light and dimmed it. I went through the house turning on and off lights to lead me to my room. It was so dark and quiet in the house as I walked through to my room. When I made it to the top of the stairwell I heard a loud crash in the kitchen it sounded like glass crashing against the floor.

I turned on the light leading down the stairs and ran down, I turned on the light in the kitchen, my plate was shattered all over the floor. "What the..." I shouted I went over to the cabinet to grab the broom when all the cabinets opened, and the lights went out. All the of the glasses and plates came flying out of the cabinets at me I stood straight up as they hit me in the dark. I walked toward the light to turn it back on while the glasses flew out at me, the lights wouldn't come on, I stood by the table waiting for the glass to stop. I tried not to panic thinking about what was happening in the kitchen, I held on to the chair by the table until it stopped.

When it did, I went back over to the light this time when I flipped the switch it came on, it began to get brighter and brighter. I turned it down, and it came right back up really bright, I dimmed it again a third time, and again it was turned up to the brightest level. I left it and went over to the cabinet for the broom when the broom closet opened on its own. I turned to look around me, at my glance I saw five guys standing around me, and the room went black again when it went black this time I was able to see them surround me.

They spread out their arms squatting in front of me leaning toward me with their necks sticking out I didn't move. I couldn't understand what was happening, what was going on? I thought standing there waiting for their next move, I stood still like a board it was intense. I could hear the glass around my feet crackling as I moved in it in fear. They stood there for a while; I just watched them, then the phone rang, and the light came back on, and they were gone. I looked all around the room for them, they were nowhere around I turned around looking out of the window.

The phone was still ringing, running through the glass I looked around the whole house while the phone was still ringing. My heart was pounding heavily as if it would jump from my chest after I saw that they had gone. The phone stopped ringing I went into the kitchen and began to sweep up the glass; the phone began to ring again, this time I ran to it. "Hello," I said picking it up. "Hello Keagan, how's everything going tonight?" It was, mom, I was silent for a minute looking out of the window.

"Hello, hello Keagan, is everything okay son?" Mom asked as if she thought I'd hung up on her. "Hi mom," I said with a pause "Hello, son, what's going on, is everything okay?" "Yes mom, yes everything is fine," I told her still looking around the house. "I'll be home, in two hours son," she told me starting to sound panic. "Mom I'm okay, thanks for dinner, it was good," I hung up the phone and walked over to the kitchen. I quickly sweep the floor and ran up the stairs to my room; I turned on the light and laid across my bed waiting for mom.

Torch Lake, Township, Michigan

Mom came in later that night and dad came in, right after her, she came into my room. "Keagan are you okay?" She asked me peeking through my door. "I'm good, mom," I said sitting up from the bed. "Did you eat your dinner?" She asked me coming in looking around with her arms folded. "Keagan do you ever clean this room son?" "I do mom, I clean it all the time." "It doesn't look like it," she said with her arms crossed leaning to look into my bathroom. I stood up from the bed and shut the bathroom door and the closet door too.

"How was your night?" She asked "It was okay mom, just a little weird at the end of the night," I told her walking toward my desk. "Your brother and sister will be here soon," she said smiling. "Are you excited?" "I am, mom, I'm very excited, I haven't seen them in a while." "They are going to be so surprised at the way you've grown up; maybe you can talk to them about some of the things you've been going through at school," she told me walking toward the door to go out. "Good night Keagan, I'm tired, see you in the morning," she said closing the door.

I sat down at my desk to read a book; I couldn't sleep at all after what happened I could see them staring at me in the dark again every time I closed my eyes. I don't even know what to think of it, I open a book one of my favorites; The Count of Monte Cristo. I read until my eye lids were heavy from trying to stay up, I must have fallen off to sleep in the chair. There was loud knocking on my door, "Keagan, Keagan, are you up?" It was dad; my neck hurt so bad my back slouched against the seat of my desk. "Hey Keagan, are you up, you have practice today, son!" Dad said still knocking.

"I'm up dad," I said rubbing my neck the pages from the book were stuck to my face as I lifted it from the desk. "I'm up dad, don't worry!" I yelled out. "Okay son, Grants downstairs waiting for you to come down, he says he's walking with you to practice," he told me walking away from my door. I pilled the papers from my face and walked into the bathroom to brush my teeth and washed my face I did it quickly. I dressed and went downstairs to meet with Grant. When I got down there, he was sitting at the table with mom talking to her about the Bible.

"It's about time you showed up down here," Grant said chewing mom's breakfast sausages. "I had to change into my gym clothes," I had a bag full of my track gear in my hand. "Keagan, you need to have a little breakfast before you leave," mom told me handing me a plate of food. "No, thank you, mom, I'm just going to have a banana and an apple, do we have bottled water?" I asked her going over to the cabinet. "Look over in the pantry," Mom told me handing me two bananas.

"Son, be home early today;" just as she said that the doorbell rang. "Remember we have to pick up the twins from the airport tonight," she reminds me. "Thank you so much for breakfast again Mrs. Phillips, it's always the best food I've ever eaten aside from my moms of course." Grant told her as we walk toward the door, when I opened the door, Hanna was standing with her back toward us; she turned around quickly. "So were you guys just going to leave me out today?" She asked. "I was just about to go walking toward your house to see if you were hanging out there.

I didn't want to ring the doorbell because I couldn't tell if anyone was up, it was so quiet," Grant told her pushing the door open wider to see her. We stepped out onto the porch. "Yeah, we're not allowed to get up around there until about 9am in the summer because the group leader says she needs her rest. The summer is the worst for her because no one goes to school and she has to deal with us every day." Hanna walked alongside us, talking about playing basketball the whole way to the school. "So Keagan, did you talk to your parent's yet about allowing us to come along with you guys to the lake?"

"No, I haven't talked to them yet, they both worked late last night," I told them. When we made it to school, the jocks were already getting dressed in their track gear. "Oh no its, Travis," Hanna said turning her back to them. "Who's Travis?" Grant asked. "He lives in the group home, he just moved in from a foster home," she says. "I used to be in the same foster home with him." "What happened there?" I asked her, her face went from happy to really sad. "Too much happened there Keagan, I can't tell you anything that didn't happen," she said walking up to him. "Hi Travis, how are you?" She said hugging him tightly.

"Hi! How are you Hanna, how have you been? I was so worried when I didn't see you anymore; they just told us that you had to leave. They didn't tell us where." "I live in the same group home as you; I sleep on the female side." "Oh I see, did you know I was there?" "I did, but I thought you needed time to get settled in." "I'm so happy to be there, the group leaders seem to be really nice," he says to her standing close holding her by the waist side. "It was so nice to see you," he hugged her really tight.

Grant started to get upset. "Oh let me introduce you to my new friends, this is Grant and Keagan, they have been nothing but nice to me since I've met them." She says smiling while we shake hands. "Hello, nice to meet you guys, which one of you thinks you can outrun me?" He asked smiling; I pointed my finger at my chest. "I'll give you a fighting chance, but after that, you're on your own," I told him walking into the locker room to change. Grant stood there looking at them with a frown on his face, he looked so nervous; this guy Travis was very tall.

I could see why Grant would be intimidated, I hurried and changed and ran onto the field. The coach was already there waiting with his whistle. "Do you think we can hang out a little after practice is over?" Travis asked Hanna as he ran onto the field. "Sure, why not," she said shrugging her shoulders, I watched Grant get so angry. He walked away going to the other side of the field to sit on the bleachers across from everyone else. We ran lap after lap until coach said to stop, then we practice relay racing 100 and 200 meters sprints, and cross country.

By the time we were done the sun was setting. "I walked over to Grant before going to change, Travis ran over to Hanna after talking to the coach. "Hey Grant, what's wrong man?" I asked him while tying my shoe. He shook his head looking over at Hanna. "Man, Grant you have it bad for her, I'm so sorry about that man. You shouldn't get so upset about it, it seems like he's known her a very long time. I'm sure they just want to catch up on things," I told him.

"Come on, walk me to the locker room, try not to let it bother you. He's just her friend, see look, they're just talking to one another, nothing serious," I told him as we walk past them. I waved at Hanna. "Hey, see you later Hanna." "You guys are still walking home with me, right Grant?" She asked standing up smiling; Grant lifted his head and pulled his hair from his face. He had a big grin. "Yes, we're walking home with you," he said to her walking into the locker room with me. "I'll wait out here man," Grant told me as I go for my bag in the locker.

"So, what do you think happened to her, there in the foster home?" I asked Grant. "Probably really bad things, when she first came to Bible studies she would cry a lot, almost every time. She never said why, my mom would always comfort her, and told her it would be okay." "Did she ever talk about your mom about what went on there?" I asked him. "No, but it must have been very bad because she cried a lot." "I bet, we are lucky, we have parents," I said as I walked out with my bag strapped to my shoulder.

"You ready," "I am," Grant says as we walk out of the locker room talking. "Hey over here," Hanna called out from the back gate, she was standing there with Sage and a lot of other people from school, we walked over to where they were. "Where did you guys come from?" I

asked Sage and her friends hugging her hello. "We've been here all
along; you were so busy running you didn't even notice us." "Wow,
really, it's really nice to see you, Sage," I said to her. We all began to walk
through the back gate toward the pathway in a crowd, everyone talked
about everything.

We talked about school and summer trips; we could see the jocks
standing around the pathway playing around as we walked up toward the
street. Sage clammed up a little, looking nervous about seeing them, I
grabbed onto her hand as we walked past them. At first, I thought we
wouldn't have any trouble until we passed them and they threw a rock at
Sage hitting her in her back. "Are you okay, Sage?" I asked. "Yes, I'm
fine, let's just go Keagan," she said. I couldn't just go I felt so bad for
her, after what happened and what she did to them in the basement.

They still want to taunt her, I turned to them. "You want to pick on
someone, pick on me," I said running up to Fredrick and grabbing him
by the throat. "I'm so sick of you putting your hands on people who
can't fight back! You want to fight someone fight me!" I said to him still
holding his throat, everyone grabbed my arms. "No Keagan! I'm okay I
promise, just let go!" Sage yelled out. Grant grabbed me by the waist.
"Come on Keagan, let it go." "You can't do this man," Travis said
grabbing my hand from Fredrick's throat I stood back.

"I'm telling you, Fredrick, it's not going to happen this year, I will
make sure of it," I said pointing at him. He stood there, him and the
other jocks. He stuck his finger out at me and mocked me, while they
stood there laughing. I could feel my body began to change quickly, my
heart pounded in my chest as if it was going to come out of it. "I mean
it," I told him. "I mean it," he said back. "Shut up, you pussy" He said
running up to my face. "I'm tired of playing around with you; you'll get it
this year if you cross me again.

Don't you ever put your filthy hands around my neck again, or I'll
make sure you never use it again." He said standing so close to my face

that I was going cross-eyed trying to stare into his eyes. "I'm not afraid of you," I told him while everyone tried pulling us apart. They pulled me away from him; all the other jocks laughed and mocked everything I said as we walked away. "Man Keagan, I didn't know you had it in you," Grant said. "I've never seen you get that upset before, wow," he said again as we walked toward the street.

"Are you okay?" Sage asked me. "I'll be fine Sage, I'm sorry I got that upset, really I am." It had been a while since I'd gotten that upset, I'm just so sick of them always picking at us. We can't continue to let them do that without any consequences. It's so unfair; I can't even imagine how they're going to treat the freshman coming in next year. They don't know what they're in for, I thought as I walked with them; holding onto Sage's hand. We walked all the way to the edge of the pathway that way until we both realized that we were holding hands. She looked down at my hand, I looked at her.

"Oops, I'm so sorry," she said snatching her hands away from mine covering her mouth. "You don't have to be sorry Sage," I told her. "Yea, that was awful what they did the other night, sometimes you need a good friend to hold your hand," Grant said walking behind Hanna and Travis. They walked ahead of all of us talking and laughing, Grant kept looking at me every time they laughed. He was so upset I could tell, but he humbled himself for her sake. "Remember they're just catching up," I told him.

We all stayed by the edge of the street talking about what we were going to do when I leave for vacation. "Keagan, make sure you ask your parents tonight, I really want to go to the lake with you!" Grant shouts. "Hey, you're going to a lake house, where?" Travis asked. "It's in a small place, in Michigan called Torch Lake, Township; we have a house there," I told him looking across the street to see if mom was coming out to her car yet. "Is it nice out there, do you guys go every summer?" He asked me. "No, we haven't been there since last year," I told him.

"We go about every other year," I told him. "You have to ask if we can all go up there this summer Keagan, wouldn't that be cool you guys?" Travis asked everyone. "Man, that would be the coolest thing; do you, guys have a boat too?" He went on asking. I shook my head yes. "We do, I'm going to learn how to sail this summer too," I told them. "Maybe I will ask if you guys can come along," I told them getting ready to leave. I walk away thinking there joking about going. "Don't forget to ask," Grant says again as I begin to say my goodbye's to everyone.

"I'll see you guys later, I have to go with my parents to pick up my brother and sister from the airport. See you guys later." I crossed the street waving back at them, Sage stood in front of everyone just staring across at me. I really liked Sage; she was so sweet I thought as I walked into the house. "Are you ready son?" Dad said. "We need to hustle, you know how the airport is, let's get going son," he said again as I ran upstairs to grab a jacket. "I'll be right down dad, I promise, just one second," I told him.

I ran up to my room and grabbed my jacket from my desk chair and ran back down really fast almost tripping over my feet on the last step. "Hey son be careful please, no more hospitals for a while," dad said holding his chest as if it hurt him. "Okay dad," I said catching my step as I stumbled toward the door holding my jacket in my hand. "Karis, we're leaving now!" Dad yelled out to mom. "I'm coming, honey!" She yelled back when mom came into the room she had her scarf wrapped around her neck tighter than I'd seen it wrapped before.

We walked out to the car. "Mom is your neck okay?" I asked as I sat down in the back seat. "Yes, its fine," she said pulling it down a bit with her hand. "Is that better?" She asked with a smile. "Much better mom, I thought you had a cold or something," I told her as we drove off to the airport; it was a long ride from the house. When we made it there, we parked in the lot across the street and walked over to the airport where they would be arriving. It was so crowded in the airport; we waited near the exit where the twins would come out.

We waited for a while before we saw the notice on the screen above the seating area that told us they would be late because of a delay in New York. We would be there another hour before they would make it in. "Let's go have some dinner," dad said pointing over at a restaurant near the front of the airport. There was a strip mall with different restaurants dad wanted to eat some barbecue; we walked over to the barbecue place near the exit doors. We all ordered the same thing a barbecue beef sandwich and a coke a cola drink with potatoes it smelled so good.

Mom and dad sat side by side while I sat across from them, we ate as soon as the waitress brought the food to us. "Are you ready to see your brother and sister?" Dad asked me. "I am, it seems like I hadn't seen them in so long," I told dad. "You think they've changed a lot?" mom asked me. "I bet they have, they've been away they probably changed a lot," I told them while looking at the clock. "I am so eager to see them," I told them looking over at the clock on the wall. "Dad, I wanted to talk to you about the trip to Torch Lake," I said looking at dad.

"What is it, don't tell me you don't want to go with us," he says. "No, dad sure I want to go, it's just that my friends were wondering…" "Oh Keagan, before you say another word, you do know that it's in Michigan and we will be driving there, it's a really long drive." He said looking over at the clock. "I know dad, they were just wondering if they can come along this time, I would like them to because I'm learning how to sail and they can keep me company. Before you say no dad please think about it," I begged him. Dad shook his head and looked at mom. "Mom, just think about it; don't say no already, please."

"Keagan, how many of your friends want to go, this is a family vacation you know that right?" "Grant's the only one who wants to come so far, and you guys know Grant he's a good guy, mom you like him right?" I asked trying to convince them to allow Grant to come along with us. "You should have asked us a little earlier Keagan; we can't make a decision like that overnight. We'll be leaving for the lake in a week, his parents need more time to make a decision like that, don't you think?" Dad said looking over at me.

"Okay dad," I got up from my seat and took my plate over to the trash. Our hour was almost up it would be time to walk back to the exit for the twins to come in; I started walking without mom and dad. I know mom and dad wanted it to just be us, but I did want some company it would be fun. I had some time to think it over, it would be cool to have all of my friends come, Hanna, Sage, Travis, and Grant, of course. Hanna and Travis have never been on a trip like this it would be so good for them.

They'll get to leave and see things they've never seen, I thought as I walked ahead of mom and dad. When the twins plane came in, Kristine ran out of the terminal to greet us she hugged mom and dad for a very long time. Kristopher was cool, he hugged mom and gave dad and I a hand shake, and dad grabbed him and hugged him anyway. We left in the car after getting their luggage; on the way home, they talked about college and how they had so much fun there. "Mom, dad, guess what?" Kristine said to them.

"Yes." "What?" they replied. "I have a surprise; my friend from college is coming over tomorrow she lives here too, is it okay if she comes along with us to the lake house?" She said smiling. "You do remember that this is a family trip right?" Dad told her in a stern voice. "Dad, but we're older now, I have some buddies who want to come along too," Kristopher said looking over moms shoulder from the back seat. The car went silent for half the trip home. "I hope you'll think about it," Kristine said as we pulled into the driveway at the house.

"Home Sweet Home" Kristine said when she grabbed her bag and jump over Kristopher's legs to get out of the car. She was different, she was loud, and she didn't bit her tongue at all to talk. "Come on dad open the door, I can't wait to get in, I missed home so much," she said jumping up and down like a kid in a candy store. "Okay, okay, calm down sweetie, I'll open up," dad said putting the key to open the door she was still jumping up and down when the door opened. Kristopher shook his head at her, we watched her go into the house, and she threw her bag to the floor and jumped up and down.

"I'm home, I'm home, I'm home" She shouted. "Calm down," Kristopher said putting his bag on the stairs. "I'll go get the rest, dad," he took the keys from dads hand and walked out to get the bags. "You want to help me?" He asked me. "Oh sure," I said to him following him out of the front door to get the bags. "She's scary huh dude?" He asked as I helped him get the bags from the truck. I shook my head yes. "Dude, do you talk at all?" "I do, I'm just a little tired, I had track practice today," I told him.

"Oh you run track now, yea mom told me about that, how's it going?" He said patting me on the head. "It's going well, I'm pretty fast, I think." "Oh yeah, well we have to see about that, I bet money you can't out run me," he said to me carrying the bags up the stairs into the house. "You think mom and dad will allow my friends to come to the lake?" "Who are your friends?" He asked me. We put the bags down on the floor and walked to the kitchen where everyone else was, you could hear Kristine shouting a cheer.

"What's going on with you guys in here?" I asked taking an apple from the table. "Nothing much your sister was just showing us what kind of new cheers she's been learning at school," mom said smiling. Kristine stood in the middle of the kitchen with her hands on her hips "Fight! Fight! Win! Win! Go, Team, Go!" She screamed out. She was so loud I covered my ears while she went on cheering the doorbell rang. "I'll get it," I said walking to the door. I opened it, it was Grant. "Hey, you're back, I've been waiting and waiting to hear from you, can you come out? Hanna wants us to come over for a while."

"I don't think so," I told him taking a bite of my apple. "Come in, I want you to meet my brother," I told him. "Are you sure, I don't want to intrude," he said walking in any way. "No one will mind, come on we're all in the kitchen." We walked back to the kitchen, Kristine was still cheering until she noticed me enter the kitchen with Grant. "Hey who are you, kiddo?" She said out loud. "I'm Grant Keagan's best friend," she immediately began to cheer about Grant. He looked over at me.

"This is my brother Kristopher," I said. "You should sit she's going to be doing this all day." Kristopher told him. We stayed in the kitchen eating and talking for hours; it was dark when Grant went home. Mom and dad helped Kristopher and Kristine to their old rooms, I went into Kristopher's room to talk to him and help him put his things away. "Do you have a girlfriend, dude?" He asked me as I handed him the clothes from his bag to hang up. "No, but I like a girl named Sage, she's beautiful, and sweet too," I told him.

"Have you asked her out on a date, yet?" "No, but I took her to the school dance last year, and we talk all the time and hang out I'm hoping that mom and dad will allow a few of my friends to go the lake with us I want her to go too," I told him. "Do you think you can ask them to let them go? There's just four of them" "Yeah maybe I will, a few of my friends are coming out too, there's plenty of room. I don't see why they won't allow it," he said taking his suitcase and throwing it into the closet. "There, all done." "Do you have a girlfriend?" I asked him as we walked out of the room.

"I do dude, her name is Jennifer, she's gorgeous, see look," he said taking a picture from his wallet. "She is pretty," I told him walking out of his room. "I know right dude, and she's coming out to the lake so you'll be able to meet her and tell me what you think of her," he says smiling. "Well, they'll allow you guys to have company there because you guys are in college," I said. "Dude, they'll allow it you just have to use your head." We came to the end of the hallway where my room was. "Good-night dude, see you in the morning."

"Goodnight Kristopher, see you." The house was still loud when I went to bed, Kristine's voice carried as she told mom stories about her dates and her friends on the cheer team. I fell asleep listening to her loud voice. When I woke up the next day they were all downstairs having breakfast; dad and Kristopher had already been up early, they had gone for a run before breakfast. "Guess what son, you've convinced me, I am going to let you have a few friends go with us to the lake, but you have to have their parents call us, and we need a written letters giving them permission to ride there and back.

We will be staying for two weeks, son, and I will need those letters a week before the trip," he said with a smile taking his coffee cup from the table, walking up to his room to change for work. "Thank you," I whispered to Kristopher, he winked at me and ate his eggs. "You boys did a good job conning your dad, but I'm still not completely on board yet," mom said smiling. "Yes, I saw that wink," she said walking over to Kristopher kissing his cheek.

"That's good looking out for your little brother." "Mom, I just don't see why it would be a problem, I mean I have guests coming out, and so does Kristine, so why shouldn't he have a few friends come out? And mom, you know how boring that place can be, we have to break tradition this time just to spice it up, have a little fun. You know mom, you and dad should invite some friends up too," he said smiling taking his plate over to the sink.

I got up from the table, I needed to go get Grant and to tell him the good news. "Mom, is it okay if I tell Grant now?" I asked. She looked at me with her arms crossed. "Go ahead Keagan, invite him to go son, but remember what your dad said. They need to have permission, and their parents have to call," she told me with her eyebrows lifted.

At Torch Lake, Township, Michigan

The twins settled in really well over the week, Kristine finally stopped cheering loudly around the house. Kristopher took me all around to the malls; even though he had a girlfriend he claimed to be in love with, he'd flirt with all the girls in the mall. Grant and Hanna would meet us there; we'd walk around the mall and shop all day. Kristopher would come to track practice with me every day after the mall. We had a week to go before we would leave for the lake house, Grant had permission to go and so did Sage and Hanna.

Travis was told he couldn't go with us because he was just getting settled into the group home and they didn't know his behavior very well. Everyone was so excited about going, especially Sage. "When do we bring our things over?" Grant asked me at the mall. "It will be another week before we leave," I told him. He was so excited to go; Kristopher would kid around with him teasing about the way his eyes would light up when we talked about going to the lake.

On the way home from practice, Kristopher drove us to a burger place where the girls come out with your food dressed in little skirts and crazy hats. When we pulled up and parked a group of girls came running toward us screaming for Kristopher. He was so popular around town, and he'd only been in town a few weeks, Kristopher dressed so cool. The girls would hug all over him and kiss his face; it was like they would be fighting over him. He was a six feet 4 inches, tall, dark-haired jock, but his attitude was different from the jocks at our school.

He didn't bully anyone or try to hurt anyone; I wanted so badly to ask him about the jocks at our school. Like why do they pick on other people or why they are so rude but I thought it to be a little offensive since he was a jock himself. I really admired him though, I would watch him, then later I'd go to my room and talk to the mirror the way he would talk to the girls we saw that day. He was definitely a suave one. We would hang out at the burger place every day just to be around all the girls and eat.

They would always give him free burgers and fries for us; he knew some of them from high school. It made hanging out there even more fun because they'd talk about what Kristopher was like in high school. That was always so interesting to me because he had it a lot better than I did. He was a part of the in-crowd. He didn't hide out from anyone, and all the girls loved him. I loved listening to the stories they would tell about him, my big brother was a jock but a good jock in high school, and this year when we return to school.

I wanted to be like he was in high school, really cool I thought as I watched him talking to all the girls. We were all packed by the weekend; we would leave Sunday morning at 5am. Dad rented a van that carried as many as 24 people, Grant brought his things over on Saturday night, and he planned to stay the night until we leave. Dad was to pick up the girls from their houses around 4 in the morning. It was a lot of work getting everything into the van mom and Kristine took so many bags, mom packed food and dishware too.

When Grant's parents dropped him off that night, mom and dad offered them dinner and wine, we all stayed up talking and laughing around the pool in the backyard, Grant went swimming with Kristine. Kristopher talked on the phone to his girlfriend all night; I don't think he took a breather at all from talking to her. He was making sure she was able to get to the lake house without any problems, his friends from college were coming out too, mom would have a houseful of people there.

"Well, thank you for coming by, try not to worry so much about Grant, we'll take good care of him," dad told Grant's father. "Thank you, we really appreciate you guys letting him go along with you on this trip, it's all he's been talking about," he said shaking dad's hand. "Yes, he's so excited, I don't think he's rested properly since you told him he could go. He's been reading books about Michigan all week," his mom said hugging my mom on the way to the door.

"Well, we plan to have a lot of fun out there this summer, everyone wants to bring along a friend, and we figured, why not allow Keagan to have some friends to go along with us this time?" She told her standing at the door. "Come here son, come give me a hug goodbye," Grants mother said to him holding out her hands to him at the door. "Goodbye mom, I'll miss you," Grant said kissing his mom's cheek; his dad grabbed him by the shoulders.

"Son, you behave yourself, listen to Mr. and Mrs. Phillips, don't be afraid to ask them questions if you need something." "I won't, dad, I'll behave myself too," he told his dad. He walked them down to their car and hugged them both, and waved as they drove off. "Are you okay, son?" Mom asked as he came back to the house. "I'm fine Mrs. Phillips; can I go back to the pool?" He asked. "Only for a while sweetheart, we really have to get some rest, we'll be on the road early in the morning," she told him. "Maybe just an hour longer"

"Thank you, Mrs. Phillips," he said running to the backyard jumping in the pool, I changed into my shorts and jumped in with him. Kristine was still swimming around in the pool singing, she loved to sing. It was beginning to get dark when mom came outside. "It's been over an hour Grant, Keagan, it's time to get out, please get out now, take a shower and get in bed, please," she said peeking her head from the sliding door. We got out of the pool and wrapped up in towels left for us on the patio chairs.

We grabbed our towels and went inside, Kristine went into her room to shower and change, Grant and I went up to my room. "Go ahead Grant you can shower first, I'll wait out here until you're done," I told him wrapping myself tighter in my towel. It was a bit chilly in my room I went to the window to shut it when I heard a splash in the water by the pool. I looked down to see who was getting into the pool, there was no one there, I sat down to waiting for Grant to finish, I thought about when Reese would come over and get into the pool without asking.

I vision her out there smiling, swimming around in the pool; she would always come up from the water with a smile. I stood at the window for a while not looking out, but just standing there thinking about Reese. So many things went through my mind when I thought about her. I thought of the day she hung herself from the church, I don't know if I'll ever attend church again. How I wish there were something I could have done for her to prevent what happened. The thought of her doing what she did never cross my mind. I never knew why she did it, and it haunted me every day. I thought standing there holding onto my towel.

"Hello, hello can you hear me, Keagan," Grant said standing by the bathroom door. "Are you okay man? You look like you just lost your best friend you're up for the shower man, are you okay?" Grant asked again. "I'm okay, I was just thinking of someone," I told him walking toward the bathroom. I got inside the shower, it was really hot, I let the water run over my face and hair for a while before washing my body. When I was done in the shower, I put on my pajamas and lay across my bed. Grant was sitting at my desk looking through my book collection.

"You read a lot Keagan; do you ever do anything else?" He asked me. "Sure I do, I'm always doing other things." "The Count of Monte Cristo," he said holding the book up turning the pages. "Yes it's my favorite, have you ever read it before?" I asked him. "No I haven't, it looks very old." "It's old, but it's a great book, you should take it out to the lake with us and read it when you get a chance to read," I told him throwing a pillow over at him. "Here you go, there are some blankets in the closet you can sleep on the other bed by the wall," I told him covering myself laying my head down on the pillow.

"Good night Grant, Torch Lake tomorrow," I told him turning my head from him. We were awakened the next morning by dad's loud knock on the door; I think it might have scared Grant. He jumped up looking around squinting his eyes. "Hey, what happened?" He said lifting his head up from the pillow. "Who's there?" He said. "It's my dad, we have to get up," I told him sitting up straight. He covered his head with the pillow. "Already, no way, we just went to sleep," he said smothering to himself with the pillow; I threw my pillow at him.

"Get up, Grant we have to get dressed, we still have to pick up Hanna and Sage, he quickly jumped from the floor. "Hanna," he said smiling going through his bag next to him to get his toothbrush. "I thought that would wake you," I said laughing. "Man, you're pathetic," I told him laughing. We put our clothes on quickly, we rushed downstairs. I grabbed the book for Grant to read on the way there. "Hurry you guys I would like to be on the road before traffic gets started," dad said holding his bag in one hand and bananas in the other.

"You didn't forget anything did you honey?" Mom asked him holding a bag in her hand and her purse on her shoulders. "Okay, I think I have everything," Kristopher said standing on the stairs. "I grabbed the safety kit from the cabinet upstairs and the one downstairs too; I locked all the doors and the windows. Once we're out we just need to turn on the alarm and go," he said rushing everyone out. Kristine came running out from the room downstairs. "Hey don't forget about me," she said holding up her bag in her hand.

"Come on sis would I forget my better half," Kristopher said grabbing her bag. We went out to the van, dad had parked in the driveway, we were all still so tired from the night before, Grant and I guided dad to Hanna's then to pick up Sage. We had to go all the way on the other side of town, dad got out each time with us. He greeted Hanna's group leader with a handshake, when we arrived at Sage's house he greeted her dad with a handshake also.

I carried Sage's bag for her, she looked like she had been sleeping all day her face looked rested, and when she got inside the van I introduced her to Kristine and Kristopher. "So you're a cheerleader too huh?" Kristine asked her, she sat down next to Hanna, placing her bag in between her feet on the floor. "Yes, my second year," she told Kristine. "I've been cheering for six years now, I love it, do you know this one?" She asked beginning to cheer. "Wait! Wait!" Kristopher yelled out.

"We are not going to listen to you cheer all the way up to the lake no way, no way Kristine please," Kristopher said out loud. "I can do what I want Kristopher you're not going to stop me from cheering on the way. Mom, please tell Kristopher to mind his own business, if he doesn't want to hear me cheer put his headphones on and ignore it!" She shouted out looking Kristopher in his eyes. "You need to stop with the cheering just for a while Kristine it's a little early for it, sweetie, when we get to the lake, you can cheer all you want I promise," dad told her.

"Okay dad, only for you," she said kissing his cheek. She rolled her eyes at Kristopher and sat back into her seat. "Do you think it will take us all day to get there?" "It will take us one day and about 15 hours," dad said to us. "A whole day, dad?" Kristopher asked. "Yes son, one whole day 15 hours "I don't remember it taking this long before," he said putting a pillow under his head. "Yes it's always been a long ride, but one with a rewarding ending," he said as we drove along.

Everyone was really quiet through the morning sleeping on and off and mom and dad which switch positions. He drove about ten hours, and she drove ten hours, and when we reached the rest stop they talked about Kristopher driving at least ten hours, and dad would drive us the rest of the way. At each stop we would use the restroom and eat, it was so beautiful; the scenery, we drove through the mountain. We passed through Arizona, New Mexico, Arkansas, and Missouri, the ride was long, but the way my mom and dad and Kristopher drove made it look a lot easier than it was.

We talked and looked out the whole time; Grant took a lot of pictures. "This is great, Mr. and Mrs. Phillips, thank you so much again," he told them almost every time he'd snap his camera. "You don't have to say that every time," Kristopher said. "We know you're Grateful," he laughed at him and teased. "Dude, you're really a weird one," I hit him with my elbow when he said that; it was one of those offensive things that always hurt Grant's feelings at school. "Hey, what was that for?" Kristopher said to me.

"Don't say that to him, he doesn't like it," I told him in a whisper. "Why? He is really weird," Kristopher said loudly I looked at Grant, he was offended. He put his camera away and covered his face with his jacket for the rest of the day. We finally arrived at the lake at ten at night; we all were a little off with the time; the difference was three hours. We all grabbed one bag and went to the lake house, it had been cleaned up for us; the lights were on, and the food was brought up dad paid the caretaker when he arrived.

"Hey David, how are you?" Dad said shaking the man's hand. "Hey, long time, no see," he said smiling. "Yeah, I had to go around the back to check the water pressure for you, it's good, everything is ready to go, everything's working properly, sir." He said with a smile walking alongside dad into the house. "You must have taken the long way in, I was expecting you hours ago," he said to dad. "No, I have the family with me this time, it was a lot of stopping and going, if you know what I mean," he said to the man laughing.

"Come on in, and meet my family," dad said he introduced us all as we all walked in holding the bags not knowing where to place them. "You guys can put your bags in the rooms down the hall. Keagan, you and Grant will stay in one room and Sage you and Hanna can stay in the room across from our room," mom told us, we walked in back. "This place is so beautiful Keagan, you're so lucky," Grant said walking around looking out of all the open windows. "It's breathtaking," he walked behind me almost tripping over himself, trying to rush.

"I want to take pictures outside and inside for my parents," he said rushing into the room to put his bag down. "That would be nice, but don't you want to come out to see my boat?" I asked him. "Sure, I do," he said dropping his bag on the side of the bed. We both took our jackets off and ran out of the room quickly. "Don't go out there just yet, Keagan," dad said with a stern voice. "I know where you're headed, son, you have to wait until I'm ready to go out there, I don't want you messing around with the boat without me," he said.

"Have a seat, we'll have plenty of time tomorrow to see the boat, son." "Aw, dad why? I'm fine, can't Kristopher come along, I just want to show it to Grant." "No son, tomorrow," he said turning his glass of wine up. "You boys should go fishing with me and your dad this week, we'll be catching some good flounder," Mr. David said. "You catch fish out here too?" Grant asked almost yelling. "That really sounds awesome Mr. Phillips and Mr. David, I'd be so honored."

"Good, son, just be ready at 3 am, that's when all the good catch is out," Mr. David said handing dad the glass back. "Michael, I'll see you tomorrow, you guys enjoy," he said walking out of the door with his hat in his hand. "Thanks for everything," mom said to him waving goodbye. It was midnight when we finally settled in, dad and Kristopher brought in the rest of the bags and the cookware mom brought with her. No one wanted to sleep because we'd slept enough on the way, but dad wouldn't allow us to go out.

It was too late, and we have all of tomorrow he told us. I unpacked my bag and gave Grant the book, and the girls cheered in the room with Kristine until they fell asleep. I couldn't sleep; I sat with Grant in the sitting room looking out at the sun coming up over the lake early in the morning. He read out loud so I could hear him as if I hadn't read the book before, I didn't stop him until the sun began to rise higher. I closed my eyes as soon as the sun shined brighter through the window; I dozed off into a deep sleep.

"Keagan, Keagan wake up," Grant shoved me over and over again. I was so tired that I didn't budge; I heard him, but I couldn't move, it had been a long day and night. I rolled over on the couch by the window and fell off to sleep. He knew I wasn't going to get up to talk to him at that point; he began to talk aloud as if I would respond. "Well I guess I'll just have to enjoy this sunrise all by myself," I heard him rambling on about taking pictures of it. "I can't wait to get up and enjoy the day," he went on and on, I covered my ears with the couch pillows until I couldn't hear him at all anymore.

It worked, when I woke up in the morning, he was lying across the floor with his camera strapped across his neck sleeping. He must have fallen to sleep taking pictures all morning, I tapped him on the shoulder, but he didn't move. I walked over him to get by; I could hear everyone up in the kitchen; dishes clinking and doors opening and closing as I made my way through the hallway to see who was in the kitchen. I didn't smell anything cooking, so I knew it wasn't mom, I peeked inside the kitchen door.

"Hello mom, is that you?" I asked softly yawning and stretching my arm "No it's the boogie man," a voice said back to me, it was Kristopher. "What are you doing in here Kristopher?" I asked. He laughed at me. "I'm making me a quick breakfast shake," he said cracking two eggs and pouring the yolk into a glass. "What are you doing?" I asked him. "Haven't you ever had one of these?"

"No I haven't, what is it?" I asked him. "It's a protein shake, two eggs, yogurt, strawberries, canned peaches and powered protein," he said standing over the counter about to start the blender. "Please tell me you don't drink that stuff every day?" I said standing in front of him trying to keep my glands in my mouth to stop reacting to what I was hearing. "You should try it, you see these abs" If you want to be something like me you have to yolk up," he said starting up the blender, it was so loud. I shook my head.

"No thank you, Kris I'll just have this apple." "No, no Keagan, you have to at least try it okay, just give it a chance. It's the perfect way to start your day, I promise you'll want another one after this," he said handing me a glass with a straw. "Go ahead, try it, I even added bananas this time," he took his glass up and clashed it into my glass. "Bottoms up," he said taking the glass to his lips, I lifted my glass and took a sip, at first it seemed a little bitter then it was sweet, but it was a little slimy made me feel sick, I put the glass down.

"It's okay Kris, but I can't drink it all," I told him walking over to the sink to sip the water from the faucet. "I will," Grant said walking into the kitchen holding his camera around his neck. "Here you go, drink up," Kristopher told him holding the glass up to his face. Grant gulped it all down without even frowning; he placed the glass down on the table. "That was a great protein shake, thank you," he said sitting down at the table. "So what are we doing today, are we going out on the boat?" I shrugged my shoulders.

"Yes we are, dad will be up in a little bit, he'll want us to be dressed by the time he gets up, so you guys need to go get dressed and remember its summer. We don't need to wear pants and long sleeve shirts," he said walking out of the kitchen looking at Grant. "Did you bring shorts?" I asked him. "Of course I did, I brought two pairs of them, how about you, did you bring shorts?" He asked me. We left the kitchen when Kristine and Sage came in. "Is Hanna up yet?" I asked them. "I don't know if she is, I didn't check to see if she was before leaving the room," Sage said picking up a piece of bread from the plate on the table.

"Can I toast these?" She asked Kristine. Kristine walked over to her and took the bread from her hand and placed it in the toaster. We all devoured breakfast, rushing afterward to get dressed for the boat ride today; when we were all ready, dad called us out to the den. "You guys need to make sure if you can't swim to wear a vest, and everyone needs to know the safety rules," he ran down the rules while we walked out of the door. We went to the boathouse; everyone was amazed at how big the boat was, Hanna couldn't stop waving her hands across the boat.

"This is so great," she said as we got in one by one climbing the stairs, it was so beautiful. "Dad, can I start her up?" Kristopher said jumping ahead of me to get to the steering wheel. "No Kristopher, dad promised me that he would teach me how to drive the boat," I said pulling on his shorts. "You can do it on the way in, son," dad said to Kristopher walking ahead of us to get to the front to steer us out. The doors opened wide, and we were on our way out.

"This is so great," Grant said holding up his camera taking picks of the house as we sailed away, the scenery was so beautiful; it was so early in the morning. The fog was still lifting from the water, as it lifted the sun rose more and more. We sailed further out, dad allowed me to stir us for at least three miles before he took over. We were going south to a small Township marketplace, dad wanted to get some shopping done before Kristopher and Kristine's friends showed up. Mom never thought we had enough; it took us two hours to get to Township marketplace.

When we pulled in there were other people there at the docks pulling in too, "Hey Phillips, you have a group this time, what's the occasion?" An old man with a long mustache said; he wore long boots with ties hanging from them really long. "No sir, a family vacation extended that's all," dad told him. "Looks like some fun to me," the man said helping us tie the boat onto the poles. "Excuse me, sir; can you take a pic of all of us before we leave the dock?" Grant asked holding out his camera.

"Sure son, get in there," the man said pushing Grant's shoulder for him to get back on the boat with everyone else. We all stood still as boards waiting for the old man to get the hang of using the camera. "Everyone, say, Township Lake," the man said holding the camera to his face. "Township Lake!" We all yelled out. "This will be a really nice picture," he said handing me the camera. "Thank you so much, sir, you have a nice day," Grant told the man as we walked away in a crowd. "Where is this place?" Sage asked.

"It's so quiet here, where are all the people?" Hanna asked as we walked down the streets looking into all the old shops, there was little to no people out; one or two people in each store we walked by. "This town is tiny not many people live here population only 4000 people," dad told us. "That's why it's the perfect vacation spot for us," he said as we entered the small grocery store, this store was called Township Market. They sold everything in it, from household needs to food and supplies, mom and dad grabbed a lot of things candles and bags of fruits and veggies too.

We all left the market carrying two or three bags for mom and dad. When we made it back to the boat the old man was standing at the end of the dock with another old man waving at us. We approached them with all of our bags. "Hello how was your shopping? This is my brother Sam Phillips; I don't know if you remember him, but he's a repairman. He came out to your house a few years back to help with some electrically issues you were having back then.

He just wanted to say hello," he said as we all got back into the boat one by one with our bags. "Yes I remember, hello Sam, how are you?" "I'm okay sir, work is a little slow around here though, if you need any help with anything just let us know," he said shaking dad's hand. Dad got into the boat and gave them a wave goodbye, and we sailed back to the lake house. On the way in, there was a small boat sailing in front of us with two people on it. They kept looking back at us; Grant took pictures of them as we sailed by.

"Hello," Hanna said to them, as we passed they didn't say hello back nor did they wave at us. Instead, they pointed at us until we could no longer see them on the lake. We arrived at the lake house, by me steering us into the boathouse the doors opened wide, I sailed us in. It felt so good, it felt like I was flying the wind blew in my face. I loved to turn while everyone held on tight to the handrails as I steered us into the boathouse going as fast as I could.

Township Lake Day Two

We all settled in that day after the boat trip to Township marketplace. We put away the groceries with mom; afterward, she made lunch for everyone. It was tuna fish sandwiches and potato chips, with fruit juice. "Pass the bread please?" Sage asked Kristopher, I noticed her laughing and talking to Kristopher a lot. Kristopher was a charmer; he tickled her and played around with her a lot. "You want bread?" He asked holding two pieces of bread in his hands and pretending to talk with them.

"Here you go," he said throwing the bread onto her plate. "Hey be careful," I told him looking cross. "When do you think we can go back out on the boat again?" She asked Kristopher. "We can go out as soon as you like, I can take it out as much as I want," he told her. I shook my head no. "He can't Sage, don't believe him, dad won't allow it," I told her looking at him crossed. "Dude, I was talking to Sage, you aren't a part of the conversation, right Sage?" He said winking at her. "Can you stop that," I said to him.

"What dude, you can't handle a little competition huh?" He said to me putting jam on his bread. I'm starting to feel like how I feel at school with the jocks; Kristopher was a pain at times. I couldn't wait for his friends to show up so that he could leave my friends alone. Our second day together and he was already making me and Grant feel like we didn't belong. "Dude, she's not your girlfriend right?" He asked me looking at Sage; she shook her head no, walking away with her sandwich to sit out by the lake with mom and dad.

She waved at Kristopher as she walked out, he gave her another wink, I waited for her to turn her back before I threw a chip at Kristopher. "Dude, don't get your pants in a bundle, I'm only kidding around little brother, you know I have a girl," he told me throwing a handful of chips back at me. I went out to the back where mom and dad were sitting talking to Grant about the history of the lake. Pretty soon we were all out back with mom and dad watching the ducks in the lake, when we were all done dad got up, taking his plate into the kitchen.

"Hey, guys how about another ride on the boat across the lake?" "Yes, dad" I yelled out "Can I drive out of the boathouse dad, can I?" I asked him excitedly. "No, dude you drove in, I'm driving out," Kristopher said while everyone walked out to put their things on the boat. Kristopher and I argued all the way to the boathouse when we made it to the edge of the boathouse. "Dude, you can rock paper scissors me for it," Kristopher said holding his hand out. "No way, never," I told him running jumping on board the boat.

"Hey Keagan, be careful don't hit anyone with your shoes please," dad said as I took a seat right beside him. "Dad, I'm ready to get us out of here," Kristopher said taking the wheel. "No son, I'm going to do all the driving since you two can't stop fighting about it," he said turning the key to the boat. "See what you did dude," Kristopher said as he took his seat next to Sage. He sat down so close to her, smiling at me; he turned to her. "You smell so good Sage, what are you wearing?" He asked her, as dad pulled the boat out turning.

I got up holding on to each rail; I managed to get closer to them to sit in between them. I tried squeezing in between them, but Kristopher kept hitting my hip moving me back where I was. Grant took pictures of everything even of Kristopher fighting with me. As soon as the boat was out far from the boathouse Kristine began to sing, Sage and Hanna clapped and sang along with her. They sang old and new songs, dad made me come close to him to hold the stirring wheel whenever he needed a rest. He taught me to maneuver the boat around the lake; soon I was on my own.

Dad just sat back relaxing with mom, I went from one end of the lake to the other, when he wasn't watching Kristopher would try and take the wheel from me. "Keagan, you need to really pay attention," he'd say to get dads attention trying to make him worry. "This is really serious, dude," he'd say at every turn, we sailed to the end of the lake and dad took the wheel from there. He took us on the other side of the lake where there was a row of small cottages all the same color they were all empty, but they looked very nice surrounded by the lake and many trees.

"Dad, look there's no one there anymore!" Kristopher yelled out. "Son, just steer the boat, no horsing around," dad stood up from his seat and walked over to us, he took the wheel. "Dad, what's wrong?" I asked him, Grant snapped pictures quickly while dad turned the boat around sailing away from the cottages. "Dad, can we go over there and look around?" Kristopher asked. "No son, its best we don't," he said sailing the boat further out away from the cottages.

As we turned from the cottages, I saw out of the middle cottage window a man staring out from the window watching as we left the area. "It looks like they upgraded them, there's new paint on them, dad, are they renting them out or something?" Kristopher asked while I watched the man watching us. Grant took pictures of the cottages until we sailed too far away to see anything anymore. "The windows were new too, dad," he said I looked over at Grant.

"Did you see that Grant?" I asked him as we moved further out, he shook his head no moving his camera down from his face. I looked over at Hanna and Sage they shrugged their shoulders at me as if they didn't see anything. "Keagan, son" Dad called out to me loudly. "When we pull in, you and Grant jump out at the edge of the dock and help me and Kristopher tie the boat down." "You got that Grant?" I yelled at him. "On the count of three please jump; 1, 2, 3." We jumped into the water it was as high as our knees; we tied down the boat together.

When we were done we helped everyone out, I grabbed mom and Hanna's hand, Grant helped Sage and Kristine. "Thank you ooh, ooh!" Kristine sang her way off and on the boat that day; dad looked at me as I became annoyed by her singing. "What can you say Keagan, she's a cheerleader studying music in college, what do you do?" He said shrugging his shoulder smiling at me. I wanted to shush her, but I knew mom would yell at me, I covered my ears as we walked with our bags toward the house.

Mom began to prepare for dinner, this time dad was doing the cooking; he tied an apron around his waist. He began to take pots and pans from the cabinets turning the barbeque pit on to get ready to place meat and veggies on the grill. This was different because dad never cooked at home; he started with chicken and beef skewers. "Come on Keagan, help your papa, we're making skewers, you start chopping for me, here grab the knife. Chop these red peppers, this bell pepper, and these pineapples, after that toss them in this bowl of goodies I have over here. It's a little lemon juice, Cajun seasoning, and salt and a little something special to make the taste pop."

Dad was pleased about cooking; it was weird. I tied an apron around me and begin to chop, Grant ran over to me, tapping me on my shoulder. "Hey Keagan, Mr. Phillips, can I help?" He asked. "Sure, but will you need the book while you help?" I asked him smiling; he couldn't put the book down. He read it everywhere we went, he also carried his camera everywhere he went too. He placed the book on the table and went to wash his hands; he put on an apron and joined me chopping the skewers.

When dad was done chopping the meat, he handed it over to us along with long wet wooden sticks. "Here you go, now this is the easiest part of this, you place the peppers and pineapples after every piece of meat, then place them into that pan over there. Right after I will put them on the grill," he told us walking away with a pan full of nice looking steaks and potatoes. "I'll put these on until you guys get done with that," he walked outside onto the patio; he placed the steaks on the grill.

It began to get smoky out back, mom sat in the chair looking out at the lake, she watched dad on and off. "Just relax Karis, I'm good at this too, I promise you'll love dinner tonight," he told her. "Okay Michael, "she answered back with a smile. "I'm going to set the table, are you sure there isn't anything else I can help you with?" When the steaks were done dad placed them in the oven to bake, we took the skewers out to him. He allowed us to lay them on the grill one by one; it was 5:30 pm when we heard a loud knock at the door.

"I got it, I got it," Kristopher yelled out running to the door with his shirt off, and his shorts still wet from the water in the boathouse. "It's for me," he said looking out the window, he went to the door soon after, in an excited rush. He opened the door really wide. "Dude, come in, where have you been?" He asked the guy standing in the doorway, his hair was so long at first he appeared to look like a girl, but he didn't wear a shirt either. "Where's everyone else? I've been waiting for you guys all night," he said to him going out of the door with him.

"Dude, we need help with stuff on the truck, can you help us get everything down, we got lost coming up here dude. It was a long ride," he said to Kristopher. Kristopher left the door open wide, I took the hand mittens off and the apron and followed behind them to the front of the house. I wanted to see who was visiting him; I stood at the front of the house staring out at them. They were all jocks all of them except for the girl, wore very long shorts and sandals.

Two of them had long ponytails; I guessed the girl was Kristopher's girlfriend she ran to him jumping up high to grab his neck, kissing him all over his face. She was very beautiful; she wore a small jean shirt, a brown tank top that was cut off so you could see most of her stomach. She was barefoot with an ankle bracelet on; I stared at them as they stood around the giant king cab truck talking about the trip down here. The truck was shining it looked new; he had a pair of jet skis on the back and lots of baggage.

"Keagan, come over here dude, help us out," Kristopher called out to me, I ran over to him with no hesitation. I wanted to see the inside of this huge truck. "Hey little dude, I'm Harvey, but my good friends call me Harv, this is Cody, Cedric and that's Jennifer. We all call her Jeni for short, what's your name dude?" He asked me shaking my hand. "I'm Keagan, very nice to meet you, Harv," I said to him staring at the truck wheels. "It's nice isn't it," he said with a smile.

"Dude, after we get everything down, he'll let you go inside, but for now let me show you guys where you'll be staying," Kristopher said to Harv. "Follow me," he walked them around to the guest house. "Now Kristopher, will your parent's mind about Jeni staying here?" Harv asked him. "No, there are three rooms here and a den; she'll have her own room. They're fine with this, come on dude don't worry about it," he said to them as we entered the guest house. It was really dark inside Kristopher flipped on the lights, as we walked in; it was nice and clean in there.

"Wow!" Everyone said all at once, looking around the house; we placed the bags at the door as they ran all around the house. "Man, this is fabulous, Kristopher, I have to meet your parent's, they must be so rich," Cody said looking in the kitchen and the bedrooms. "No, believe it or not, my father's grandfather left this to his son, and he left it to my dad, it's all inheritance." "Well lucky him, what did they do for a living?" Jeni asked. "They were all surgeons," Kristopher replied looking around, Jeni ran to him and hugged his neck.

"Thank you for inviting us again Kristopher this is awesome," she told him holding onto his hand. "You're very welcome, thank you for showing up," he told her kissing her on the hand. "Let's go meet mom and dad, mom's been asking me about you all year," he told her as we walked out of the guest house. "Is your sister here?" She asked Kristopher. "Yes and all she does is cheer and sing, please say you won't be joining her."

"Well, we are cheer buddies; she's also in my choir class." "Yes, I know, but can you please encourage her to save it for choir practice and the game," he told her. "Sure, I'll try and keep things quiet for you, baby," she told him kissing his cheek. "Hey be careful with the kissing mom and dad doesn't know that we've gone there yet," he told her as we walk up to the door. "Here goes nothing," Kristopher said opening the door. "Follow me." We went to the back where everyone was watching waiting for the barbeque to be done.

"It smells so good in here, doesn't it?" Jeni asked looking at the other guys, who followed Kristopher looking nervous. "Hello mom, hello dad." "Hi, come on back," dad said waving them to come to the back patio area near the lake. "The chairs are over there and down there if you like. I'm Mr. Phillips Kristopher's dad, that's his mom, Mrs. Phillips, that's his sister, oops, you guys already know her. These are Keagan's friends, here's Grant, Hanna, and Sage."

Everyone waved and said hello promptly as Kristopher showed them around the lake. "You have a very beautiful place here Mr. Phillips," Harv told dad standing with his hands on his hips staring out at the lake. "Thank you, Harv, I try," dad told him walking back over to the grill. "Keagan, Grant! Come help me take the skewers off the grill, we can set everything at the table now. Dinners done, grab the corn Sage," he said walking with the mittens on his hands grabbing a pan full of steaks from the oven.

"Grab those dinner rolls please, Karis come, sweetie, where would you like these?" Dad asked mom. "Just sit them in the middle," she said staring at the table settings. "Come on everyone let's eat." As soon as we all sat down to eat there was another knock at the door, everyone looked at each other, and we all wanted to eat quickly. "Is anyone going to get it?" Dad asked. "Dad, can you bless the food first?" Kristopher asked.

"I'm starving," Kristine said. "I'll get it," Grant said getting up from the table. He quickly walked over to the door to answer it, we all watched, waiting for him to open the door. "Who is it?" Grant yelled out. "It's us open up." It was a group of loud girls yelling, Grant looked at us. "Go ahead open up. He opened the door wide. "Hi, we are looking for Kristine!" They all yelled at once, Kristine jumped from the table and ran screaming. "Oh my God! They're here dad!" She yelled running jumping into the crowd of girls.

"Hi you guys, come in!" She shouted. "You guys were supposed to be here yesterday, what happened?" She asked them escorting them all into the kitchen. "We got lost driving up here, it was a long ride, and Patricia drove most of the way. Hi, I'm Angel, this is Stephanie, Kayla, Rachel, and Patricia, we call her Patty. Nice to meet everyone," she said pulling a chair toward the table. "Oh yes, I'm sorry, have a seat, Grant, Keagan, go grab some chairs and a couple of tables from the side of the shed out there. Looks like we'll have lot's more company," dad said.

"Hun, can you bless the food now?" Mom asked him. Dad sat down and gave a very short blessing, with all that was going on around the house; his nerves seemed to be in a bundle. "Kristopher, is there any more room in the guest house?" She asked. "Dad, they can sleep in the den, the girls can have the rooms," Kristopher said to him. "Relax dad, it will be okay there's plenty of room in the house for everyone," Kristine said. We sat down and ate dinner, Kristine and her friends talked the whole time about cheering and how they have to go camping soon.

She went on and on about it as we ate. "You guys have any bags in the car?" Kristopher asked them getting up from the table and putting his plate in the sink. "We do, I'll show you where, when I'm finished," Angel told him. Kristopher and Harv went outside to wait for the girls to finish. When they finally came out Harv was laying on the rocks in the yard, Kristopher was laying on the ground with his head resting on another rock. "Hey, you guys ready?" Angel asked them.

"We've been waiting out here for hours," Kristopher said standing up from the ground. "Calm down Kris, you've only been waiting for 15 minutes," she said to him. "Come on don't be a punk," she said smiling at him. "Do you guys wear shirts around here?" "It's 93 degrees out, why would we?" Harvey said taking the bags from the little mini truck Angel drove. "This is a nice little truck you have here," Harvey said to her. "I borrowed it from my brother, I can't complain, it got us here," she told him walking away following Kristopher to the guest house.

"Hey, how about a campfire tonight, doesn't that sound great? Mmm, under this lakeside moonlight, aw just beautiful. You think everyone's up for it?" She asked as they approached the guest house. "Oh my God!" She screamed out loudly, Harvey dropped all of the bags on the ground. "Gees woman! You scared the heck out of me, what did you yell like that for?" He asked her with his hand over his forehead. "This house is gorgeous, Jesus, Mary!" She yelled again. "Angel, I haven't even opened the door, what are you thinking? Cut out the yelling, please?" I said.

"It's just so nice, I can't wait to see inside," she said jumping up and down with the bags in her hands. When Kristopher opened the door, she ran in dropped her bags and took off running all around the house. Kristopher and Harvey dropped the bags near the door, sat down on the couch and waited for her to finish running all around the house. "Are you ready to go back, we have a long day ahead of us tomorrow," Kristopher seemed very annoyed by her.

"I'm ready," she said grabbing a sweater from her bag. "So, how about that campfire, I mean, I know we're not at camp, but we have the perfect setting for a campfire in the back looking out at the lake. Roasting marshmallow's over the fire on the patio," she told us as we walked back to the lake house. When we got back, everyone was sitting around outside playing charades with mom and dad. "I guess there will be no campfire tonight, huh," Harvey said to her going over to the other jocks sitting next to them.

Grant seemed very uncomfortable around them; he hardly said two words after dinner. He sat out back with us, but read the whole time and when someone asked him a question his reply was, "huh." As if he didn't want to answer them. "Are you okay, Grant?" I asked him, I knew that he never liked being around jocks; they made him very uncomfortable. "I'm good Keagan, don't worry," he told me pulling his hair from his face. Tonight he wore a long jacket over a big shirt that wasn't fitting.

He wore long shorts and sandal with socks, I didn't help him pack, so I had no idea what he brought for the trip. I knew he was feeling uncomfortable because I was a little uncomfortable myself around them. It was a little bit better when Kristine's cheerleader friends showed up, they began to act as if we weren't there when they saw them come into the back. "Are you feeling okay Grant?" Mom asked him, everyone seemed to have been thinking the same thing. While everyone else was laughing, talking, and playing charades he was sitting almost with his back turned to us barely saying a word.

We all went to bed late that night, it was a long night. Mom and dad made sure everyone was where they belonged at night. They walked over to the guest house to make sure the girls slept where they were supposed to sleep, and the boys stayed in their places. We would be in the lake house with mom and dad, so it wasn't a concern where we slept. When they came back inside from checking everything out in the guest house, Grant was still up, he had a night light hanging over his head reading the book on the couch when they walked in.

"Will you be up late?" Mom asked him. "No ma'am, I only have a few pages in this chapter left Mrs. Phillips, can I stay up to finish it please?" He asked mom. "Sure, but just a little while longer," she told him walking away. "Are you absolutely sure you're okay?" "I am Mrs.

Phillips, I'm okay, as soon as I'm done with this chapter I'll go right to bed." The next morning everyone woke up and came over to the lake house where mom was cooking breakfast. There was a woman in the kitchen with her, she had long black hair her skin was very shiny brown like clay.

"Keagan, this is Patelli, she cooks over at the diner in town sometimes. I asked her to come help us since there's so many now," she told me as I walked into the kitchen. "Hi, how are you? I'm Keagan," I said going to shake her hand; she wiped it with her apron. "Nice to meet you too," she said going back to cooking. "Tell everyone to get washed up for breakfast, do you mind walking over to the guest house to get your brother and his friends?" "No problem mom, I just need to wash up a little," I told her going back into the hallway.

I knocked on the door where Sage and Kristine were, I knocked for Hanna, I kept walking down the hall. I knocked for Grant, I went into the bathroom washed when I came out everyone was in the hallway looking around for me except for Grant. "Good morning, guys mom will be serving breakfast in about twenty minutes, can you guys wash for breakfast, she likes to eat on time," I told them looking in the room for Grant. "Has anyone seen Grant, this morning?" I asked. They all shook their heads no. I looked in the den and the living room area, no Grant. I wondered where he was I thought, looking all around the house.

I grabbed my sweatshirt from the chair by the door, I put it on; he couldn't have gone far, I thought, throwing my sweatshirt over my head and walking out of the door. I went over to the guest house first; I knocked on the door hard I knew they wouldn't be up. "Hey, who is it?" A voice yelled out as I knocked continuously really hard. "It's Keagan, open up please," I told him. "Hold on dude," he yells back, I could hear him scrambling around in the room moving things and shushing someone. "Hello, I'm still out here, open up!" I yelled into the door.

"I'm coming dude, hold on!" The voice yelled back, when he opened the door, he stood in the doorway with one hand on the door handle and the other holding up his pants. One of Kristine's friends stood beside him with a very long t-shirt on. "Yes, dude, how can I help you, what are you doing here so early?" I walked into the house. "Where's my brother?" I asked looking around the house. "Have anyone seen my friend Grant?" I asked. "Uh dude no one has seen your friend, maybe he's still sleeping."

"No, he isn't, Kristopher!" I yelled out knocking on his door. "Kristopher, mom is cooking breakfast, get up, and come over," I told him knocking really hard on his door. "Dude, what are you doing here, tell mom I'll be over soon!" He yells back out at me. "Go away, we will be over in about ten minutes," he told me yelling. There were clothes all over the floor; girls underwear hung from the light fixture. It looked as if they were up all night playing around; I walked over the blankets and clothes to get to the door.

"Dude, I don't remember seeing a friend of yours last night, is this a real kid you're looking for?" Harvey asked as I went to the door. "Of course it is," I said shaking my head leaving the house. I began walking back over to the lake house when I hear rustling around behind me in the bushes. I stopped and looked around, it was probably just an animal rustling around, I thought as I walked on. "Hey, Keagan!" I heard.

"Are you looking for me?" It was Grant. "Hey, where have you been?" I yelled walking toward his voice; he came out of the bushes near the small bridge on the other side of the lake. "Where have you been, Grant?" I asked him. "I went for a run, with your dad, he's ahead of me," he told me wiping sweat from his forehead with the bottom of his shirt. "You didn't ask me if I wanted to run?" "Yes, we shook you, but you didn't budge," he told me as we walked up to the lake house.

They were already eating when we got into the house. "Get washed up please, we've been waiting for you guys," mom said standing at the door. "Yes hurry, we're going on a boat ride today," Kristopher said lifting his plate from the table walking out back. Grant went to wash in the back I washed in the hall; we made it to the table just in time for juice and toast to go cold on us. Everyone else began to get up from the table, putting their plates in the sink, they all went to wash.

"We're wearing ski suits and swim suites today, so no long pants Grant," Kristopher told us "I am trusting you Kristopher; you guys can have the boat today to go out on the jets skies. I'm expecting you to be safe" "We will be, dad, you can trust me," Kristopher told him. Dad handed him the keys to the boat, he helped mom clean while everyone went to get dressed. When they were done, we all walked over to the boathouse, mom and dad walked with us. We had a freezer chest full of food and beverages for the ride, Kristopher and Harvey tied the jet skis on. We were off for the day, as we sailed away from the boathouse Grant clutched his book looking back at mom and dad waving from the boathouse.

Township Lake Day Three

We sailed out that day everyone ready for fun, while Grant held his head into the book ignoring his surroundings, everyone else yelled. Laughing and singing while Kristopher took off fast toward Township downtown area. "Where are we headed captain!" Harvey yelled out to him. "I figured we go into town grab some more drinks if you know what I mean," he said to him. Grant immediately looked up from his book. "Hey Kristopher, your father said no horsing around on the boat."

"Hey Geek, you mind your business, what I do out here my dad doesn't have to know," he told him looking over at Harvey and Cedric. "Yes, you're lucky to be on this ride, relax and enjoy or get tossed out," they told him laughing. Grant turned to his book and clutched his camera strap as they pulled into the Township downtown pier. "We're here! Everyone off," Kristopher said. "I'm staying in the boat," Grant quickly replied. "No, you're going with us, we're all getting off this boat," Kristopher told him. "Yes, so let's go, dude," Harvey said pulling him up from his small seat on the boat.

"I hope you don't plan on giving us too much trouble, we hate troublemakers," Cedric told him. "Hey Cody, you wanna remind him how we treat troublemakers at our college," he said. "Leave him alone, or we'll remind you guys how we treat people who mess with us," I told him slapping Grants shirt away from his hand. "Oh, you guys think you can take us on?" "Just don't start any trouble and there won't be any," I told him jumping from the boat. The two old men that dad met with the other day stared on at us as we left the pier.

They followed us into the small mini-mart. "Hey, you fella's need some help?" The old guy asked Kristopher. "Sure we do, can I talk to you a minute over here?" He said waving his hand signaling him to come to the side of the building where no one could see them." I could see him whispering to the old man, the girls walked into the mini-mart and began to pick things up. They played around with each other, with lipsticks and perfume samplers. I turned just in time to see Kristopher hand the old man money by shaking his hand.

"Nice to see you again," he said as the old man walked away. "Come on you guys, let's get back to the boat," he said rushing everyone back. "Did he do it; is he going to get it?" Harvey asked him. We walked back to the boat everyone took their places on the boat. Sage lay across the bench with her legs hanging off the edge of the boat with her sandals on. She wore bikini top and short brown shorts. I caught Cody staring at her from time to time; he was quite the jock, flinging his hair around staring at her. She acts as she doesn't notice, but she does.

She smiles at them both, him and Kristopher whenever they acknowledge her. Now that Kristine's friends have shown up she smiles at them a bit more, especially when they practice cheers. I was beginning to feel like this all was a bad idea, bringing my friends out to the lake. Mixing my friends with Kristopher and Kristine's; Grant was barely talking anymore, Hanna hung out with the jocks more than any of us. I had an awful feeling about this day when the old man finally showed up; he was carrying a brown paper bag.

You could hear the water jiggling around in the bag as he came closer to us. "Here you go, son," he said reaching to hand the bag over to Kristopher before snatching it back clutching it to his chest. "Now wait a minute, son, you know the rules, promise this is kept between us, now money," he said holding out his hand again. "Sure Mr. Sam, do I ever get you in any trouble? This is always between us," Kristopher told him grabbing the bag handing it to Harvey and Cody. They immediately checked the bag.

"Good job dude!" Harvey yelled out. "It's time to party!" Cody yelled out jumping up and down in the boat. "Alright let's get this show on the road," Cedric said going up to the front of the boat with Kristopher to start the boat. Grant looked over at me. "Kristine, would you like one?" Cody asked her. "Sure, I would!" She yelled back. I sat down next to Grant, he looked at me. "Do you think this is a good idea?" "I don't, I think we might be in some trouble," I told him looking over at them as they put their cans together as a toast to the ride. Sage and Hanna watched everyone dancing around them singing, they looked out of place until Jeni took Sage by the hand.

Helping her up from the bench "Come on let's dance" She said swinging her hand up and back, the music began to play from the bottom speakers on the boat. Soon everyone was dancing around except for Grant and me. "Crank it up, Cody!" Kristopher told him taking his drink back gulping it down while steering the boat. "I'm going to the bottom man, I don't want your dad to be angry at me," Grant said taking his book and camera leaving. "You coming?" I shook my head no, I was afraid to leave Sage and Hanna, I sat watching. We went in circles then down the bank of the lake where those old cottages sat.

"Man, this is good; this is good, let's just dock over here!" Harvey yelled out to Kristopher. "Alright man." Kristopher turned the boat so hard that Kristine and her friends began to hold on to one another laughing. When the boat came to a complete stop, their alcohol began to spill all over the floor of the boat. "Hey! Please be careful!" Kristopher yelled out. "We'll clean it up man, don't worry, it's just like always," Cody told him grabbing a towel from the bag on the side of the boat. He placed it into the water and wet the bottom of the boat floor.

"Cedric, go get the soap from the bottom man, hurry," Harvey said. Kristopher docked the boat right in the middle of the cottages where there was a small amount of wet dirt, the dock wasn't very big at all, the jet skis stuck out far into the lake. It was really warm out still; Harvey and Cody began to change into their wetsuits. "Hold on!" Kristopher yelled out. After tying the ropes onto the dock, he jumped on the Jet Ski. "Come on Sage you want to take a ride with me?" He asked here.

"No, she doesn't," Jeni said angrily at him for asking. "You're just going to ask her right in my face?" She asked him taking his hand for him to help her up; just then Grant came up from the bottom of the boat with his camera. "Kristopher, what are we supposed to do while you guys have fun on the jet skis?" I asked him as he began to kick up water from pulling off from the deck on the jet skis. "I don't know? Find something to do, it's not my problem," he told me standing up on it parking next to Harvey.

"Read with your friend!" Cedric yelled out, they all began to laugh. "Oh really funny," I said picking up the bottle of alcohol that he left on the deck near the boat; I threw it toward him crashing it on the side of the jet skis. "Cut it out Keagan!" He yelled out jumping up to dodge the bottle. "We're not going out too far, why don't you and your little girlfriends find something to do?" He said as he sped off with Jeni on the back of the Jet Ski. We sat on the edge wooden dock watching them ride back and forth doing tricks, they yelled and screamed loudly.

Grant sat quietly reading his book with his back turned to us. Sage and Hanna sat close to me while Kristine and her cheerleading friends drank their bottles of beer, cheering loudly. I looked over at the cottages from time to time to see if the old man would show his face again. He may have been just a drifter or something, but I know I saw him there before. I watched intensely, the places looked so inviting; they were clean and well kept. I wanted so badly to go look inside them. "Hey Sage, let's go over there," I said pointing over at the cottages.

"No, Keagan your dad said we should stay away from there," she said shaking her head. "We're just going to look inside," Hanna said looking over there. "Don't you want to see what's inside?" I asked her. "No, I don't," Sage answered. "Well, I do," Hanna said walking over to the cottages, I followed behind her. "Wait up Hanna, I'm coming too," I told her picking at the bushes of weeds growing near the dock. "What do you think is inside?"

"I don't know, it just looks nice, let's go see," I told Hanna as we begin getting closer to the cottages. When we came up closer, the windows went up, and the doors begin to open and shut, Hanna stopped in her tracks. "Did you see that Keagan?" She said her eyes widen with fear. "I did, are you afraid?" I asked. "No I'm not afraid, come on let's go," she said walking slowly toward the cottages. The doors and windows slammed down harder and harder with each step we took toward the cottages. "No, I'm sorry Keagan I can't go over there," Hanna said walking backward backing away from them.

"Aw I thought you were brave," I said running up toward them. "It has to be some kind of prank house, there's nothing to be afraid of right, come on, come with me." "No Keagan, I can't go ahead, I'll stand right here and wait for you," she said to me. "Go ahead, go see." Just as I walked up closer to the cottages the windows and doors stopped banging. "Now do you want to join me, Hanna?" I asked her walking up closer. "No, look Keagan!" She screamed out, I turned and looked the old man stuck his head from the window staring at us.

"Be careful Keagan, come over here quick!" She yelled. I stopped moving, the man looked harmless, I just wanted to see inside the cottages. "I just want to see what's inside," I told her going toward the cottage in the middle of the row. "Good luck Keagan, I'm going back to the dock," she told me walking away I walked up to the cottage door before I could open it, it opened. "Can I help you, young man?" "I just wanted to see inside sir, are these places lakefront rentals?" I asked him trying to sound like I was interested in renting a cottage.

"No son, they are not," he stood in front of the door looking at me crossed. His eyes were red, he wore a long colorful shirt with green pants, and he was barefoot. He kept his hands behind his back. "Do you need anything else, son, there's no one here, do you want to come in?" He asked me. I looked back over at Hanna, she stood right at the edge of the hill were the dirt met the dock. It seemed as if she was so far away from me. "You're welcome to come in," he said moving one hand in front of him waving me in.

"No thank you, sir, I just wanted to ask you if they were a rental, that's all," I said backing away from the door. "Okay young man, come back when you want to come inside, I'll show you inside," he told me smiling. "You can come back young man," he said again opening the door; I backed away more and more when I saw him go in. I turned around running toward Hanna. "Hanna, Hanna!" I yelled out. "There's a man inside there, he told me to come back when I want to look inside," I told her. We went back and sat down on the dock with everyone else waiting for Kristopher and his friends to stop show boating around on the jet skis.

They switched up, now Cody and Cedric rode around the lake each with a different cheerleader on the back. "You're next they'd scream out as the approached the deck. "Hey, I'm going to pull you guys on the boat as fast as I can." "That's not a good idea Kristopher," Grant said standing up from the deck. "It's really not a good idea Kristopher," I told him standing. "You shouldn't Kristopher." "Just get the ropes for me, it will be okay, come on Keagan, Grant, help me untie these," he said pulling away at the ties on the dock metals brackets.

"I won't even go that fast," he said when they were all untied. He jumped inside with Jeni. "Stay over there on the deck," he told me as I tried to jump inside with him. "Kristopher, you've been drinking, please let me drive for you," I told him trying to get in. "No, Keagan just stay there!" He said yelling and pointing at the deck. "I'll be back!" He pushed my hands away from the boat and began to hook the jet skis up to the boat he took off with Cody and Cedric tied to the back of the jet skis. They went as fast as they could go on the jet skis, the jet skis jumped up away from the water high off the lake water.

We could see Harvey and Jeni standing by on the end of the boat to untie them when Kristopher was ready. They went around in a circle going as fast as he could take the boat, water sprayed up and on us as he flew by. Kristine and her friends cheered them all on each time the boat came by spraying water on us. "Go, Kristopher! Go!" They yelled out, this went on and on until Cody went flying into the air, the jet skis flipping him over and over. "Oh no!" Kristine yelled out, her friend went flying through the air; the jet skis ejected them both from it.

The girl who was riding on the back went flying through the air, Harvey jumped in the lake after the girl, trying to help her up from the water. Kristopher turned the boat around to pick them up, when they got inside the boat; Kristopher took the boat and turned it again going around the lake to find Cody. Cody flew so far away from the boat. When we couldn't find him, Kristopher brought the boat over to the dock and tied it to the deck. We all looked out into the lake for Cody. "Oh no, where is he!" Kristopher yelled out.

"Cody! Cody!" We all yelled out for Cody the water was still "Cody!" Kristopher yelled and yelled. "We have to do something Kris, come on man!" Harvey said running around the dock kicking the dirt. "Come on man, come on!" Cedric said. Kristine and all her cheerleader friends were holding on to each other crying. "Kris, what are we going to do? What are we going to do?" Harvey was so scared; Grant sat back on the deck and watched. Hanna walked all around the front of the lake looking in the water for him everyone else began to search further out into the water. "He has to be out there somewhere," I said to Kris.

"Try not to panic you guys, come on let's keep searching." I walked around the lake looking for him with everyone else, the sun was going down. Kristopher began to panic, even more, walking around shaking his head. "Dad is going to kill me, man; he's never going to trust me again. We have to find him guys, come on, please!" He said walking around the lake; Cedric went back into the water along with the cheerleaders that were with the Kristine. "Stay together guys, please, two at a time, don't get lost in the water." We looked around everywhere, by nightfall we were all exhausted.

Some of us laid in the boat and watched the sun go down, some of us sat on the deck, and some of us sat near the dock. Harvey was still searching for Cody when we heard footsteps coming behind us, we all turned around to see who it was. We didn't see anyone walking toward us; everyone who was in the boat jumped out. "Dude, what was that!" Cedric yelled out. "Maybe it was Cody, man, look down there, that's where I heard the sound coming from." "You look down there, you guys look over there," Kristopher said.

"Are you sure, you guys heard something?" Harvey ran over and asked us. "Yes, now come on Harv, we have to find Cody, we can't leave here without him," Kristopher said in a panic. "Maybe we should get inside the boat and start looking all around the lake, if we stay around here we may not ever find him," Grant said grabbing his camera and book. "This is so bad," Sage said. "This is bad, look over there!" She yelled out pointing in the direction of the rocks near the edge of the lake, all that time we were looking for Cody; he was lying on top of the rocks.

We all ran toward the boat jumping in, Harvey and Kristopher untied it as fast as they could. Cedric jumped onto the jet skis and went as fast as he could to the rocks, Kristopher got the boat started, and we went as fast as we could over to the rocks. "Try not to go too close, don't run into the rocks," Grants said just ease up toward them, or we could really be in some trouble. "Shut up man, I need to concentrate," Kristopher told him. "I know how to handle this boat; I don't need your help." We approached the rocks right after Harvey did, he had Cody straddled across the Jet Ski.

"Man he's not okay; I don't know what to do!" Harvey yelled out. "Kristopher, please, help him." Kristopher pulled the boat up close to the jet skis; we all helped him pull Cody onto the boat. "Does anyone know CPR?" Harvey asked in a panic, he hopped inside the boat. Everyone tried to see what was going on in the boat Kristopher pushed everyone back. "Everybody, relax, just relax, he's bleeding somewhere." He began to peel the wetsuit off Cody. "Hey Harvey, don't just sit there help me!"

Cody had a really big gash on his head and a huge gash on his stomach. "Go get the first aid kit, Kristine, go get it now!" He yelled out to her. "Okay!" She said running down to the bottom. "Is he breathing, man?" Harvey asked as Kristopher checked Cody over, everyone stood around pacing around the boat. Kristine's friends were crying holding onto each other, while Grant, Sage, and Hanna sat on the bench watching. "Keagan, grab those flashlights, hand them to everyone, please," Kristopher told me.

"Quickly get them, we have to see what's going on, I can't see," he said in a panic. It was getting darker by the second; I went into the storage on the side of the boat and got all the flashlights I could carry. I rushed them out to Kristopher. "Turn them on hurry!" He yelled. I passed them all around to everyone, I held the one I carried over Cody. "Is he alright?" I asked Kristopher. "He's still bleeding," Kristopher said holding a towel over his stomach. "If we don't get him to a hospital soon he won't make it," he said in a panic.

"Go ahead Keagan, you have to drive us into to town, go get up there," He told me pointing to the steering wheel of the boat. Harvey held another towel over Cody's head to try and stop the bleeding. "Kristine, help him," Kristopher yelled out. Kristine and I went over to the front of the boat. "Kristine, I don't have my glasses, I can't see ahead too well," I told her turning the key to the boat. "Don't worry I can help you." As we begin to pull away from the rocks, everyone flashed there flashed lights toward the darkness to guide us through.

Looking ahead I couldn't see anything, Kristine steered with me. "Don't get scared okay Keagan, just stay on the path." It was so dark and quiet, we could hear the water as we maneuvered the boat through the lake, and we were surrounded by darkness. "Keagan, watch out!" Kristine yelled she startled me so that I pushed the boat's gas lever to go faster I almost rammed into what was ahead of us. "What is it, stop Keagan!" She yelled out again.

"I'm trying!" I told her slowing the boat down. "What is it? Did you see something?" I asked her. "I did, over there," Harvey said pointing his flashlight west of us. "Do you guys see it, in the water?" "What is that?" Kristopher said standing up from holding the towel on Cody's stomach. "It's there look!" Kristine said. She walked away from the steering wheel of the boat and went over to the back of the boat. "Kristine, what's wrong?" There was a boat ahead of us with men standing in it. When I took the boat up further, I could see what she saw, there was a group of men in a boat.

They shined a bright light on us, it was so bright that we all tried covering our eyes; I rubbed mine and tried to see past the lights. "What do you want?" I yelled out. I took the steering wheel and began to steer it in a direction away from the light. I managed to get the boat to turn the other way; they turned their boat in the same direction. "Keagan, we have to get out of here, Cody's still not saying a word his breathing is shallow. Let's get out of here man!" Kristopher yelled out to me. "I'm doing the best I can Kristopher, these guys won't get out of my way!" I yelled out to him.

Harvey came to the front of the boat and started to throw the beer bottles at them. "Get out of here! Go!" He yelled out, but they didn't budge. "Man, we have to get out of here!" Kristopher yelled out. It was so quiet on the boat Kristine, and all of her friends went down to the bottom along with Sage and Hanna. Kristopher didn't want the girls up on top anymore, we didn't know who these men where. Grant and I stayed at the wheel while Harvey and Cedric tried throwing things out at them from the front of the boat.

"You guys need to get us out of here quickly!" Kristopher yelled out. "We're trying!" I yelled back at him, I moved the lever for the boat to move forward. I had to get the boat through these guys somehow, as I moved the boat forward trying to maneuver through the water Cedric turned the flashlight he was holding toward them. Harvey turned his flashlight too. "Go Keagan, Go!" Kristopher yelled out I went as fast as I could following the light that Harvey and Cedric provided for me. I began to see the light up ahead of us.

"Kristopher, we're almost there!" I yelled back to him. "Hurry up Keagan, there's blood everywhere," Kristopher said. We begin to get closer to the lights ahead I pulled the boat up as close as I could to see what was ahead of us. We were in the middle of Township Lake Marketplace; Harvey shined his flashlight on all the signs ahead of us searching for the one that read hospital. "Where is it? Where's the sign!" Kristopher yelled. "Oh there, there it is, Keagan, turn the boat, turn it east hurry!" Kristopher yelled out to me.

"We're almost there, hold on Cody," Harvey said. His body was trembling; he still hadn't opened his eyes or said a single word since we'd picked him off the rocks. When we spotted the sign that said hospital I sped up, I didn't hesitate to place the boat anywhere near the dock. We all jumped out as soon as we were close, we quickly tied the boat onto the hooks on the dock. "Get him!" Harvey yelled. "Hurry, grab him!" We all grabbed him; Grant and I took him by the arms, and Kristopher and Harvey grabbed him by the legs.

"Hurry up!" We all stepped off of the boat carefully trying not to hurt Cody any more than he'd already hurt himself. "Are you going to tell the girls?" Grant asked. "We don't have time for that, Grant, come on we need to get inside." Once we made it up to the hospital entrance we knocked on the door; it was a tiny hospital, the windows were small. Harvey knocked so hard on the door that the knob fell off; the windows shook with every knock. We were getting tired trying to hold him up; we all held onto him until the door opened. "Hello, how can I help you?" A very old man said at the door.

"My cousin, he needs help, he was thrown from a jet ski onto a big rock!" "There's only one doctor in this town, and he's out of town," he told us holding onto the door. "Please, sir, my cousin could be dying! He's been bleeding for hours, please, sir can you please call him!" He yelled at the old man to get help. "Kristopher, you have to call your father, he's a doctor man, please call him!" "Harvey, he won't be able to get across the lake, we have the boat remember?" He told him.

"Kristopher, maybe you should call dad, he's going to find out anyway," I told him as the old man opens the door wide for us to bring in Cody. "Go ahead lay him down over there, I'll see what I can do to get the doctor here," he told us grabbing a book from the shelf. There was one hospital bed in the back and three other rooms that were closed off; the shelves were old and dusty. It looked as if the hospital was hardly used, while we waited for the old man to make the calls. We talked about going back to the boat to tell the girls that someone was helping us.

"Should I go out to them?" I asked Kristopher. He shook his head no; Harvey didn't say too much at all, he held onto Harvey's hand. We were all covered in blood; Harvey's hand was covered in blood. "He's so cold man, he's cold," he cried holding Cody's hand. Kristopher got up and checked his pulse. "Harvey, he's still here, he's still breathing man, don't worry okay, he's going to get someone here," he told him. "I'm scared man, he's the only family I have beside my father," Harvey cried and cried Grant got up and went toward the door.

"I'm going to check on the girls, I'll be back," he said going out of the door. "I'm scared for him, what if he doesn't make it through this?" "My dad will kill me, I'm responsible for him, he's younger than me. I'm going to be in so much trouble," he said crying out. Grant walked out, I followed him, I just couldn't watch Harvey crying. He was so sad I began to get sad along with him. "I'll be back," I told them I walked the other way into the room beside the entrance to see if there was a phone. I had to get a hold of dad; he might be the only one who could save Cody's life on the lake.

I turned the light on in the room, there was dust everywhere, there was an old telephone sitting in a pile of papers on the top of the desk near the wall. I went over to the phone, there were spider webs all over it, I wiped them off with my shirt and picked up the receiver. There was no dial tone, I hung it up and began to walk away. Wait, I better check the phone lines, I thought walking over to the wall, the cord was hanging down from the wall it wasn't connected to the phone.

I plugged it into the wall and picked up the receiver, there was a dial tone. I got the operator on the phone. "Ma'am, please get me the Phillips place across Torch Lake please, Township Lake," I told her. "Hold please," she said. The phone began to ring immediately "Dad! Dad," I said as soon as he picked up. "Keagan, where are you guys? Where are you guys at? We've been worried sick," he said. "Dad, please don't panic, please, we're at the Township Marketplace, is there any way you can get here, there's been a terrible accident," I told him in a rush.

"What happened, Keagan?" He asked me frantically "Dad, I can't explain it all now, but Kristopher's friend Cody was thrown from the jet skis, we're at the hospital, can you get here dad?" "I'll get there son, I'll get there as soon as I can," dad said. I hung up the phone and went back into the room where Harvey and Kristopher were. I didn't tell them what I did; I knew Kristopher would be mad at me. We waited for the old man to come back in the room.

"The doctor will be here in a couple of hours," he told us, he checked Cody's pulse. "I'm a nurse, I'm going to start an IV on him, he's a little cold," he said covering him with a blanket. "Do any of you know what his blood type is?" He asked us. Harvey shook his head no, soon after that we heard a knock at the door, it was the doctor. The old man rushed to door when he opened it, Kristopher's eyes widened so big, I thought they would pop out. "What happened here?" Dad came in yelling, mom followed behind him, they began to work on Cody fast, pulling his clothes off.

Dad checked him over while asking us what happened. "Keagan, go out to the boat, get your sister and all your friends, come in here and sit down, all of you," he told me with a stern voice, I rushed to get them leaving Grant sitting in the room with them. "Son, I'm very disappointed in you," dad said to Kristopher. "He smells of alcohol," mom said looking toward Kristopher, they worked on him for what seemed to be hours. We all stood by waiting for word that he was okay when dad came out of the room and told us the news.

Township Lake, Tragic Night

Dad worked on Cody all night with mom by his side, we all stood by watching as the night grew into the morning. No one said a word, each time dad looked around at us we would all put our heads down. "I need to use the restroom," Grant whispered to me. "Do you think you could ask your dad if I can go?" He said. "Go, and Keagan, you go with him," he said before Grant could even finish his question. "Thank you, sir," Grant said standing, waiting for me to show him the way.

I had no Idea where the bathroom might be, this place we were in was dark and dim, and everything around us was ancient. We would have to ask the man who let us in the hospital when we first arrived. We didn't see him anywhere, we decided after looking all over the cold dim hospital for the man, that we would just search using the signs on the walls. Some of them were covered in dirt; some of them had letters missing from the spelling. "Hey Grant, do you see that?" I asked him, we came to a turn in the hallway where there was a sign with a drawing of a man, on the other side a drawing of a woman.

"I think we're in the right place, that means women's and that's the men's," I told him walking toward the signs. "Are you sure Keagan? It just looks like a bad drawing to me," he says following me wiggling all around. "Do you think you can stop that?" I asked him. "I really have to go, if I don't go soon I'll wet my pants," he told me wiggling. "We're going in there then, because there are no extra pants around here," I told him leading him into the restroom. We were far away from the room that everyone else was in, it was so quiet.

"Can I help you boys find something?" A heavy voice asked. Grant and I jumped with fear; Grant clutched his chest jumping almost from his shoes. "You scared us," he said holding my shirt with one hand and the other to his chest. "I'm so sorry; can I help you fellas with something? It's only me," the little old man said. "Yes, we were looking for the restroom," I told him. "You're heading in the right direction, just follow that path and then to your left and there it is," he said smiling. "Thank you, sir," I told him looking to see if he was following us.

"Thank you, sir," Grant said excitedly about finding the restroom. When we opened the restroom door, it was filthy; the walls were covered in old wallpaper, it smelled so bad. I almost wanted to hold my breath, there were only two toilets, and one was covered in feces and smelled of old urine. "I can't, I'll wait for you outside Grant, I can't be in here I will vomit," I told him walking back out. "Wait, don't leave me, please?" Grant asked me holding the midsection of his pants wiggling even more. "I'll just use it right here, I won't even go near the toilet, please don't leave me in here alone," he said.

"Okay, then I'll stand by this door and hold it open, go ahead go to the toilet. Please don't make this place smell worse than it already does," I told him holding the door open. When he was done, we walked out toward the hall where we came from backtracking our steps. It was so hard to believe that this place was a bathroom. "Grant, keep up," I told him. "You keep falling behind, I don't want you to get lost in here," I told him as I walk ahead of him. We made it back to the room where dad and mom were working on Cody.

We took our seats back around the table where everyone was waiting for mom and dad to finish; they seem to be finishing things up. "We need to get him to a hospital close by, he's lost so much blood, he may not make it through the night," I heard dad tell mom. "Do you think we can get him there in time?" "We have to try." Dad took a needle and laid it near the table were Cody's lifeless body laid. "Grant, Keagan, I need your help," dad said waving us over. I think he was so angry with Kristopher that he couldn't say a word to him.

"I need you two to help me get him into the truck out there; it has Tate's Lake Transportation on it. I need you two to carry him like your own lives depend on it. I'm going to carry his legs; you two carry his upper body, Kristopher, Harvey you two take him at the sides. Place your arms underneath his back and lock them together so that they won't move while we walk out of here." Dad's hands were covered in blood, his shirt too, he was sweating so badly that his back was soaked with sweat as if he'd been running all night.

I've never seen him work so fast. "On the count of three, we all pick him up, 1, 2, and 3." We carried him out to the truck; it was a huge gray truck, mom had laid a blanket on the bed of the truck. She spread it to cover the whole back bed after we laid him there she covered his body with another blanket. "You guys can't all fit in here, I want you to go back inside the hospital and wait for me or mom to return. I do not want you to take the boat back across the lake without one of us," he told me in a stern voice. He looked really crossed at Kristopher.

"You are in charge Kristopher, please do not leave until we return," he told him pointing at his chest. "We will let you guys know when to leave here, but for tonight you stay here, is that understood, Kristopher?" Dad said in a stern voice. "Yes dad, I got it, we're to stay here until you call us in the morning," Kristopher said to him. "Dad I think you should allow Harvey to go into the city with you, Cody's his cousin, he needs to contact his family," I told dad. "Come on son, he's right, you need to come with us," dad told him rushing him to the truck.

We all watched as the truck took off into the quiet, dark town, Grant and I walked back into the hospital, Kristopher sat outside on the steps. We could tell that he needed a moment to himself, we opened the door and went inside, and Sage and Hanna were lying across the chairs leaning up against one another for support. "When will we get to leave?" Kristine asked. "Where did they go?" Hanna asked. "They took him into the city to be treated, dad said for us to wait here. He'll call us in the morning, he doesn't want us to leave," I told her.

"I'm starving," Hanna said. "Let's look around, maybe there are some vending machines around here," Sage said. "Look around you, this place doesn't even have a proper waiting room for patients. You can look around if you like, but I'm staying right here," Cedric said holding onto the rail near the chairs. There was dust everywhere, just as Sage and Hanna were about to get up from their seats, the old man came into the room. "Would you kids like some candy or water?" He asked us, the scrubs he wore were so dirty, they were covered in blood and dirt.

I shook my head no fast. "No, thank you," Hanna said quickly. "Hey speak for yourself, yes I would like some water and candy please," Sage said to the old man. "No one else?" The man asked as he walked away. "Okay, I'll be right back with your candy young lady." "Excuse me, sir; we would also like some candy and water please." "Okay got it," he said walking away. "Don't you guys feel a little weird in here, I mean it's so dim and dirty," Cedric said to us. "It's just an old place, doesn't look like anyone really comes here for treatment at all," Grant said.

"Can you blame them, look around here, this would be the last place I'd come for help." "Hey, do you think Cody will be okay?" Kristine asked. "He lost a lot of blood, you guys should be praying for him," The old man said as he walked back into the room. "Here you guys are, cool water in a bottle and lots of candy," he sat a bag of candy on the table and another bag full of bottled water. "Thank you, sir," I said to him everyone grabbed the candy and water except for Cedric when Kristopher walked into the room he stared at us.

"Where did you guys get the candy and water?" He asked. "The old man brought it out," I told him; he took a candy bar from the table. "What year do these things expire, did you guys even look?" He asked us looking all around the candy bar wrapper. "There really good, try one," Jeni told him putting an unwrapped candy bar to his mouth.

"No, thank you," he said walking toward the chairs to sit with Kristine. Whenever he would get afraid or worry he would cling to Kristine for comfort, I knew he had to be afraid.

Dad was angry with him, and his friend maybe seriously hurt, all because he didn't listen to dad. He sat quietly next to Kristine; she didn't sing nor cheer at all. The room was quiet Kristine's friends were quiet, hugging one another sharing their jackets to keep warm. The old man came in and out of the room to check on us from time to time. "I'm going out to the boat to lie down for a while, I can't sleep in these chairs, does anyone else want to join me?" Kristopher said standing from his seat. "I will," Cedric yelled out.

"Me too," Grant said holding up his hand "We can all go out there, there are blankets and pillows in the bottom," Kristopher said. "There's enough room for us all to sleep on the boat," I said walking outside, it was cold, and fog covered the dark sky's we could barely see where we were heading. There was a small light near the pier where the boat was docked. "There it is over there," Kristopher said pointing toward the light. We could hear the water splashing against the dock and the boat. "Stay together you guys," Kristine said.

"Do you guys think this is a good idea? I mean your dad said to stay in the hospital, I want to sleep, but it's really foggy and dark out. Maybe we should go back," Grant said. "No, we're almost there, don't be a pussy Grant, come on," Cedric told him looking back at him. "Hey, don't call him names, I'm starting to feel the same way, we can barely see out here," I told Kristopher. It was so quiet out; except for the water hitting the boat we heard nothing.

"If you guys shut up and keep walking we'll be there in no time," Kristine said walking ahead of all of us. Jeni held onto Kristopher's arm as she walked, Sage and Hanna stayed close everyone walked close to one another. When we approached the boat Grant helped the girls in one by one, I stood outside making sure no one fell down or was missing. When we were all in Kristopher went down to the bottom of the boat, we all followed behind him. It was so cold, it wasn't spacious down below, and we had to lie close together just to fit.

It was so dark; when Kristopher turned the light on we could see where the pillows and blankets were. "You two share this one, and you guys share this one," he said handing out the blankets and pillows to us. We had to share them between us, when we all lay down, Kristopher turned off the light. "Good night everyone, let's all just go to sleep, this night will be over if we get to sleep now," he told us placing the cover over his head. "You're right, I'll be so glad when it's over, I pray to God that Cody's okay," Grant said.

"Yes, I'm praying for him too," Hanna said. "Yes, please pray for him," Kristopher said turning over to go to sleep. I couldn't think of any prayer to say, I just hoped he'd be okay "Good night everyone," I said out loud. "Good night, Keagan," all the girls said to me at once; everyone fell to sleep quickly. I couldn't sleep; I laid there thinking of what happened that night in the water with those men. They were blocking the way out, I wondered about them. Who were they; did they want to help us at all? I laid there with my eyelids heavy, I wanted to sleep, but I couldn't, for a while.

I watched the small window, I just stared out at the light in the fog, and soon I was falling off to sleep when my eyes finally closed. The boat began to rock with the wind, it rocked back and forth slowly, it woke me. I looked out at the light and fell back off to sleep, the rocking went from being a slow rock to a violent rock, and quickly I sat up. "Kristopher! Kristopher, get up, get up!" I yelled. "Something's going on," I shoved his back; I shoved Grant's back and Cedric's too. "Wake up you guys something's wrong!"

No one moved; I shoved at them and shoved at them, while the boat shook us violently. I struggled to get up on my feet to go up top to see what was going on, I didn't hear any wind blowing nor could I see anyone from the small window. "Help you guys, get up, come on!" I yelled at them. "What's wrong?" Grant said getting up holding onto the wall keeping himself from turning over while the boat shook us back and forth. I screamed out to the others to wake up trying to get past everyone without falling down as I made my way to the top deck of the boat.

It was still shaking violently when I got up there, I tried to hold on to the benches without falling down, but it shook me all over. I flipped around, I fell from one bench to the other, I could hear everyone else trying to get up when I went flying around the boat. Suddenly it stopped and with the jerk from the shaking my body went flying toward the steering wheel. I flew head-on, the shaking was completely gone, but I was dazed from the hit to the steering wheel, everything around me was a blur.

Suddenly I saw in front of me a bright light flashing, my head began to spin, it was as if I was on an amusement park ride, everything went black. When I came to the fog was lifting, the mist from the morning dew was falling on my face. I sat up on the floor of the boat; looking around for the others I didn't see anyone at first. When I stood to my feet I could see underneath the bench Grants shoes hanging out, I went over to him. "Grant, Grant!" I yelled out rubbing my head. "Grant, can you hear me?" I asked him.

"Huh, huh, Keagan, is that you?" He answered. "Yes it is," "What happened Keagan? How'd this happen?" "I don't know," I said rubbing my head looking around the boat. Suddenly I realized we were no longer at the dock near the hospital, we were on the sand by the cottages. "What the hell happened last night?" Kristopher said coming from the bottom of the boat holding his head. "You didn't feel it?" "We were shaking, the boat was shaking, I tried to wake you guys up, no one would budge," I told him.

"What was it the wind?" He asked me. "I don't know what it was, but I know it was powerful, it shook us all the way over here," I told him. "Well, we better get back to the hospital, dad will be so upset if he comes back and we're not there," he said. "You're so right, but look," Grant said pointing down at the boat, there were holes all around the boat, the holes were so big they went from the bottom to the midsection of the boat you could see the wood inside. "What the hell! What the hell man!" Cedric screamed out.

"Man, we can't go anywhere with the boat like this," Kristopher said. "Look!" Kristine screamed out. "Look over there." Two old men were standing on the hill near the edge of the lake, they didn't say a word, they didn't move. They just stared at us. "Hey, excuse me!" Kristopher yelled out. "Can you help us with something?" He yelled. The men didn't say anything they walked away together, one of them was carrying a stick in his hand waving it back and forth. "Kristopher, maybe we need to ask someone else, they don't look too friendly," Kristine told him "Who else Kristine? There's no one over here, but us, can't you see that?" Kristopher said to her in a panic.

"I have to ask for their help, come on Cedric, come with me to talk to them," he said to Cedric. "I can't go, man, it's creepy, why didn't they answer you? I'm not going over there," he told him. "Man, this is no joking matter, we have to get back to that hospital before my dad comes back I'm already in enough trouble for what happened to Cody, now come on!" He demanded him. "No, dude, I'll stay here with the girls, I'll protect them." "Why don't you take the Jesus freak and your brother," he said pointing over at Grant and me.

"You're a pussy," Kristopher said grabbing his sweatshirt from the floor of the boat, walking away from us, Grant and I ran behind him. "Kristopher, don't get angry, it's okay, we'll come with you," Grant told him. "That guy is beginning to make me wish he'd been on the Jet Ski instead of Cody," Kristopher snarled. "No don't say that everything will be okay," Grant told him as we walked up to the cottages. When we made it up to the cottages, Grant stood back while Kristopher and I walked up to the middle cottage in the row.

The windows were open; we could see inside them clearly, Kristopher knocked on the door hard. No one came, there was no sign of the men anywhere, "Kris, let's just go, no one's answering," I told him trying to pull his hand away from the door. "Keagan, there has to be someone here, we saw them come over here, where could they have gone?" He said looking all around through the windows. "Come on Kristopher," I said pulling him away.

It was quiet as we walked away from the cottage as we turned the corner; the men were standing right in front of us. "What can we help you with?" One of them asked. "We have a problem with our boat, we need to get back to the hospital in the Township Marketplace, and can you help us get back over there?" Kristopher asked. "We don't leave the cottage," he told Kristopher. "I will take you to get help," he said walking alongside us. "No thank you, we can find help on our own," Kristopher told him.

"I can help you, follow me," the man said standing in front of us as if to stop us from walking away. The other man stood behind Kristopher. "We are fine thank you, if you guys can't help us we'll go and wait by the boat, someone will come along soon. I'm sure," Kristopher walked around the man standing in front of him. He grabbed onto his arm, and the other man closed in on him leaving him no room to move, Kristopher turned to look at me. "Run," he said in a whisper, they grabbed Kristopher by the arm guiding him back toward the cottage. I started to run toward the hill when four other men ran out toward me, I ran as fast as I could.

"Grant! Cedric! Help! Help!" I yelled running as fast as I could toward the boat. I couldn't see them over the hill, but I know they heard me yelling, when I approached the boat I waved my hands at Kristine, she looked over at me wondering what I was doing. "What is it? Keagan! What's going on?" She yelled back at me "Hurry," I said. "Get them down!" I yelled for her to take her friends and go down to the bottom of the boat, at least they won't get a hold of the girls. "Go, Kristine, Go down!" I yelled, she looked harder noticing that I was being chased.

I saw her frantically rushing everyone to the bottom "Keagan, what's up, what's going on!" Cedric yelled. "Get out; we have to get to him!" Grant yelled out at him jumping from the boat running toward me. "What happened?" Grant asked me running alongside me. "They have Kristopher in the cottage." "What do they want with him?" "I don't know, I just know we have to get back there." Grant ran alongside me until we approached the cottage, Cedric was being chased around the hill by the two of the men only one of them followed us to the cottage.

"What do you think they want with him?" He asked as we approached the cottage looking in the window for Kristopher. "I don't know, we just came to ask them for help, I told Kristopher not to come ask them, but he did anyway. I don't know what they want." We heard Cedric hollering out for help, we ran to see where he was, we ran around the hill looking for him I went one way, Grant went the other way. "Do you see him?" I yelled out to him looking at the back of his shirt. He shook his head no, Grant was so afraid I could see him walking backward checking all around him to see if someone was going to attack him.

"Keagan, over here!" He yelled out. "Keagan! Over here, please hurry!" He yelled out, I ran toward his voice, when I approached him he turned to me looking as if he'd seen something awful "What is it?" I asked him. "What's wrong, what happened?" I asked him, he shook his head and turned away from me. I walked around him to see what he was looking at, it was Cedric, he was lying in the dirt faced up. He had blood all over his face and shirt; I walked over to him staring down "What happened to him, Grant?" I asked.

Grant shrugged his shoulder turning his head unable to look at Cedric anymore. "Come on Grant, help me get him to the boat, we have to hurry and come back to look for Kristopher," I told him trying to pick Cedric up by the shoulders. He was so heavy, his body was still warm. "Come on Grant, help me," I told him in a panic. "We'll just have to pull him there, he's too heavy," I told him looking around to assure we weren't being watched by the men of the cottage. "You aren't pulling him, help me, Grant, before they come back.

Hurry!" I said sliding him over the dirt as fast as I could toward the hill. "I am going as fast as I can," Grant explained. When we reached the top of the hill, we could see the boat. "We're almost there Grant, don't get tired on me," I told him dragging Cedric across the dirt. As soon as we approached the bottom of the hill, Cedric shook his head. "Ouch, what happened, what are you guys doing?" He asked looking over at me. "We're taking you to the boat can you walk?" I asked him. "Yes, yes I can," he said trying to stand, sliding in the dirt.

"You sure?" Grant asked. "I don't want to let you go until you're sure that you can stand," he told him. "Grant, just let him go, he says he can do it, let him do it," I told him worried about Kristopher. "Where could he be, I let go of Cedric's arm, he stumbled a few times before standing firmly on his feet. "What happened to me?" He asked wiping the blood from his face with his shirt. "We just found you over there bleeding face down in the dirt; you don't remember how you got there?" I asked him.

"I don't, where's your brother dude? I'm so ready to get out of here and go back to California, what the hell man," he said looking around. "Why don't you just go back to the boat while we search around for him, the girls are there in the bottom of the boat, they'll need to know what's happening out here," I told him pointing to the boat. "I want to stay and help you dude's find Kristopher," he said stumbling around holding his head. "No, we'll be fine you just go ahead go back to the boat, there's an ice pack there in the cooler put some ice on that if you can," I told him pointing at the bump on his head.

"Come on Grant, let's go," I said walking back toward the cottage's, we approached the cottage in the middle. "You go that way Grant, I'll meet you back here in 20 minutes," I told him with my hands on my hips watching as Cedric stumbled toward the boat. "Wait, Keagan, wait we need to do something so that we'll know that everything is okay while we search," he told me. "What do you think we should do?" I asked. "How about clapping, or stumping." "We wouldn't be able to hear one another doing that."

"Let's just count to three and yell out our names, if I don't hear you yelling your name, I know you're in trouble if you don't hear me yelling my name you know I'm in trouble. Deal?" I asked him. "Deal," he said. "Now let's hurry, dad might be back already from the city," I told him running toward the side of the cottage's, I looked all over. I didn't want to go inside, but I had to. I had to get in there and look for Kristopher, I walked into the first one, it was empty, and very clean. I went into every room; there were only pictures on the walls no furniture at all around each room, just weird pictures of many different faces.

I counted to three and yelled my name as I went looking around the rooms. I could hear Grant loudly as he searched the back of the cottages I went from cottage to cottage looking through, and through for any signs of Kristopher. I walked out of the third cottage, and I heard Grant yell his name followed by a very loud sigh, I ran out of the cottage around back as quickly as I could to get to Grant. That sigh sounded bad as if he was startled, I looked around back there was no sign of him anywhere. I waited to count to three, I yelled my name and waited for him to yell his, I could hear my heart beating so fast in my ears in silence.

I waited in a panic, suddenly I heard Grant yell out my name. "Keagan, come quick!" He yelled "I didn't know where he was I was back and forth up and down the back of the cottages." Where, where are you?" I yelled. "Over here Keagan, hurry!" I stopped again trying to follow his voice I turned in circles; it was coming from far away. "Where are you Grant, help me find you!" I yelled out. "I'm here Keagan, come here!" He yelled again I turned toward the trees behind me and there I saw him standing there waving at me.

"Come quickly!" He yelled. I rushed over to him I ran so fast I could hear the wind whistling in my ears when I made it to him. I stood with my hands to my knees bent over to catch my breath. "Grant," I said gasping for air "Grant, what's wrong, why are you over here? We were only supposed to check the cottages, you've come out too far," I said looking up at him. "I know, I know but," he said upset putting his hands on my shoulders. "Keagan, come follow me please," he said squeezing my shoulder.

I stood up and followed him into an open area in the woods there were three trees as tall as the sky's they were crossed like the letter W in the middle of the trees. Kristopher was strapped with his arms crossed over his head and his feet crossed over one another with no clothes on. Blood fell from his face, his head lay to his chest as if he was dead; there were cuts on his legs dripping onto the tree, I was so startled I put my hand to my hands.

"Grant!" I screamed out pointing up at him "My brother Grant, my brother!" I yelled out. "No, Keagan, no, you have to quiet down, they may still be around here," he said pointing at a painting easel with a stool sitting close by. There was paint next to it as if someone had been doing a portrait of Kristopher. I ran toward the painting, Grant ran behind me, the painting was of Kristopher in the tree. I took my hand to it, smearing the paint all over destroying the portrait, punching a hole in it and threw it to the ground kicking the stool and the portrait all around. I yelled out grunting in anger, suddenly we heard Kristopher trying to yell out my name. "Keagan, no, come over here, hurry," he said lifting his head slowly.

Leaving Township Lake

It took us a while to get Kristopher off of the tree; we used ladders we found in hidden behind the trees in the back of the woods. We carried Kristopher to the boat almost dragging him, he bled everywhere. His naked body was covered in blood dripping in the dirt as we drug him toward the boat. We each had him by the shoulder, when we made it to the boat we grabbed his legs, holding his back and shoulders; we slid him over the boat railing. Grant and I immediately ripped apart the cooler getting the first aid kit, we used the ice packs on Cedric's head, and we cleaned his wounds with the alcohol pads and the gauze to keep the wounds from bleeding out.

"Keagan, we can break these and use the pieces to patch the boat, is there a hammer or something around that we can use to nail it?" He asked me, I ran as fast as I could to the bottom of the boat grabbing dad's toolbox, I brought it up and handed it to Grant. "Here you go, there has to be something in there that would help patch it up. "Hurry Keagan, Grant said handing me a hammer and nails; we patched the holes in the boat as quickly as we could. Kristine and her friends finished cleaning up the blood from Kristopher and Cedric, she held onto Kristopher so tight. She helped him put on his pants and shirt, when Grant and I were done we jumped out of the boat and began to push it back into the lake.

"Just go to the lake house Keagan, don't go to town, dad will be at the lake house by now, I'm sure of it, let's go Keagan," Kristopher said. "Grant what do you think, Lake House or hospital?" I asked him. "I say go straight to the lake house also, we need to get back to see what's going on with Cody." We sailed off into the sun that day it was still hot, the sun was high in the skies over the lake, and no one said a word the whole time. Kristine and her friends didn't cheer nor did she sing.

She cried silently, as she watched Kristopher staring at his wounds, tears streamed from her face. Jeni rubbed his back and kept watching out for bleeding. "We're getting close!" Grant shouted. "Just a little while longer, and we'll be there." We sailed for what seemed to be hours before we saw the boathouse, as we sailed up closer to it everyone began to get happy. Everyone was sitting up watching the dock as we pulled in, when we pulled up close everyone began to jump out before we put the boat in the boathouse. The truck that they took Cody to the hospital in was sitting in front of the lake house.

We tied the boat, securing it in the boathouse while everyone helped Kristopher out. Cedric was able to walk, but with a limp. There was still dried blood on his head, there was blood all over Kristopher's face also as we walked him into the lake house. "Mom! Mom!" I yelled out as the door opened "Mom! Are you here?" I yelled "Yes, I'm here! Oh no Keagan, what happened, where have you guys been? Your father spent half the morning looking for you and your friends," she said looking at Kristopher and Cedric's head. "What happened to them?" She asked. "Mom, is dad back with Cody and Harvey?" I asked her, she shook her head, she walked away to get a washcloth for Kristopher and the Cedric.

"Come, boys, Kristopher can you walk?" She asked him. "I have to stitch you two up, especially you Cedric, come on," she said helping Kristopher to his feet. Kristine helped pull him up to his feet; they walked them to the bathroom, where he sat on the toilet while Cedric sat on a stool near the bathtub. "I'll stitch you up first," she said. "Mom, where's dad?" Kristine asked "He'll be here in a little bit; I need for you and your friends to go back to the guest house and pack your things. Pack everything because we're not coming back here," she told them looking serious.

"We're leaving mom?" I asked. "Yes son, we are, I'll let your father explain everything to you when he returns," she said cleaning Kristopher's head with peroxide. She cleaned it over and over again with a cotton ball before she began to stitch it. Kristine and her friends left the room. "Do we bring everything back here?" Kristine asked. "I don't know exactly what your father wants us to do yet, but I do know we need to pack." "Okay mom, I'm going," Kristine said to mom she came back and forth trying to get an explanation from her.

When mom was done putting stitches in Kristopher and Cedric's head, she walked them back into the front room. "You guys sit here until your father shows," she told Kristopher. "I'll get someone to pack your things for you," she told them going to the kitchen to get them a glass of water. She took some pills from the cabinet. "Here take these, there for pain, you'll need them," she handed each of them two pills and a glass of water, as they were taking the pills dad and Harvey showed up.

"Hello dad," Kristine said to him as he walked in. "Hi sweetheart, how are you?" He leaned into her and kissed her face. "I'm okay," "Do you have your things packed, are all your friends here?" He asked coming toward the den area. "They're still packing dad, but they'll be over soon," she said. "Good, I need to talk to all of you." Harvey stood close to dad, he didn't say a word his eyes were red and swollen. "Harvey go have a seat son," dad told him. "I'll get you something to drink," mom said going back into the kitchen.

"Do you want something cold or warm?" She asked him "Anything, ma'am, I'm thirsty," he said leaning back into the chair. He wasn't himself at all, quiet and sad, when everyone else came back from the guess house, dad told us to all have a seat in the den. He and mom came in soon after we were all sitting, dad stood in front of us. "We are leaving the lake this evening, your friend didn't make it to the hospital, he died on the way there, and there was nothing they could do for him.

The head injuries were too severe, I'm so sorry you guys," he said walking over to Harvey putting his hand on his shoulder.

"Harvey will be riding with us, is there someone who can drive his truck for him?" He asked. "I will, Mr. Phillips," Cedric said. "Are you sure you can drive all the way?" Mom asked. "I can help him," Kristopher said standing to his feet. "I can too," Jeni said. Harvey began to cry, dad patted him on the back and hugged him; we all hugged him as we began to get our things together. Jeni cried loudly, Kristine and her friends all packed into Harvey's big truck, while Grant and Hanna packed their things in dads van. By the time the sun was going down we were all packed into the van and trucks.

We were leaving the lake house before we left dad waited for the caretaker to come. He greeted him and gave him an envelope. "I'm so sorry for your loss," the man said shaking dad's hand. "Drive safely, I will be praying for his family," he said as dad walked away. "Grant, do you think his family knows already?" "Yes, I'm sure they do," he told me looking sad. "He's going to be fine now," Grant said, it was a long ride from the lake. Everyone was so sad and quiet, no one said anything all night when we stopped at rest stops for food; hardly anyone wanted to eat. We switched drivers and continued on home, still in silence.

Harvey sat in the back of the van holding a necklace that he took from Cody's neck. He stared out of the window from time to time, he cried off and on. "Wonder why he didn't go back when they took Cody back?" I asked Grant. "He probably wanted to get his truck home safe, I don't know," he said. Hanna got up from her seat and went back to sit with him, she hugged him and held his hand. Kristine and her friends did the same; Harvey was surrounded by the girls. They comforted him the whole way home.

This time Grant didn't get angry at Hanna, he looked sad enough to go join them to comfort him too. I sat back and thought about getting home, I wondered what they would be planning for his memorial. I could tell that dad was a little upset at us for taking the boat out he was keeping his cool on the drive only asking who was there when the accident happened. No one wanted to answer him but Kristine, she told him we were all there, but we didn't see what happened or how he hit the rocks.

It was 11 am when we made it home, it was hot out, and everyone parked their cars in front of our house. There was a car parked outside the driveway already waiting for Harvey, it was an uncle, we all got out and went inside. Harvey's uncle wanted to talk with us about the accident, when we got in everyone went toward the kitchen for a drink it was really crowded in the house. Mom went around trying to offer everyone something to drink and eat, while Harvey's uncle sat in the living room with him waiting to talk to us. Dad took Kristopher by the side to talk to him about the accident; I could see him eyeing Kristopher the whole time until he pulled him away.

I wanted to stay close to see what he'd say about what happened. "Tell me what happened out there son?" He asked. "Dad, we were all playing around, we raced. I drove the boat recklessly, while Cody and Harvey were racing me on the jet skis, things got out of control," he said in a whisper. "Out of control because you guys were stoned out there? I asked you not to play around with the boat son, I asked you to be careful, not careless, now look at this mess!" Dad was shouting, but in a quiet whisper, you could see that he was angry.

He talked to him in a tone I'd never heard before. "Do you know I had to call that kids uncle and tell him that his nephew had died, over the phone. I had no explanation why. He was torn apart, son, what were you thinking?" He asked him. "Dad, I'm so sorry, I wasn't thinking, I'm so sorry, we tried to get him to the hospital, we did dad. He was bleeding a lot, we tried to wake him, he didn't wake up. Dad, please forgive me," he said holding onto dad's hand. "Please, dad." "Son, I'm not the one you need to ask for forgiveness, that man in there is hurting over a kid he took care of all his life, he's sad and hurt.

You need to go in there and explain to him why he's gone son, try and do that," he told him. I watched as he wiped his eyes, he walked over to the hallway near the living room and stood there watching Harvey and his uncle holding hands crying. Harvey tried to explain what happened, but he couldn't explain without crying in between each sentence. When Kristopher stepped into the living room, he just stood in front of them without a word. He didn't say a word until Harvey's uncle lifted his head up, looking him in the eye.

"Sir, I'm so sorry about what happened, we tried to get him to the hospital, but it was too late. Sir, please forgive me, I'm so sorry," he said with tears streaming from his face. Harvey's uncle stood up and hugged Kristopher. "Son, this wasn't your fault, I know you guys did everything you could son," he said patting him on the back. "Everything will be okay, son, it will," he said still hugging him patting his back. Kristopher cried along with Harvey, everyone hung around the house waiting for instruction from dad.

Hanna was picked up by the group leader, Grants parents picked him up shortly after, they all wanted to know about the trip, but we couldn't explain. No one wanted to talk about what happened out there, almost everyone left. When it was time for Harvey and his uncle to leave dad walked over to him and hugged him. "If you need anything at all, please call me and let me know, please, and please let me know about the funeral arrangements I want to help in any way I can sir." Dad told him. "Thank you so much, Dr. Phillips," he said shaking his hand again. "Please call me, Michael, please," he said walking him to the door. "I will be in touch," he said standing outside the door.

"Good bye sir," dad said shutting the door. The night was so quiet, dad helped mom clean up the house. They hardly spoke a word to one another; she kissed him from time to time: you could tell that dad was still upset at the whole issue. I offered to help them clean, but dad told me to go upstairs not to worry about it. When he was done, he came up to my room to get my side of the story. "Keagan, tell me what happened out there," he said sitting on the desk looking me in the eye. I sat in the chair looking for something to read, I wanted to get my mind off the whole trip. It was a terrible trip from the start.

"Dad, I really can't tell you much," I told him. "Keagan, were they drinking out there?" He asked me. Oh no, I thought this is what I didn't want him to ask me. "You might as well tell me, son when they do his autopsy they'll be able to tell. Just tell me the truth." I shook my head yes. "I knew it!" He yelled. "Were you drinking too, son?" "No dad, I don't drink, I just watched, I tried to tell them not to dad, I did," I told him "How did they get the drinks?" He asked me.

"Two old men in town took their money and went to buy it, I don't remember their names, but you know them, dad, they're your friends." "Okay, I see," he said standing with one hand over his mouth and the other on his hip. "I will handle all this after we get this kid buried," he said angrily walking out. Maybe I should have lied to him. I thought dad was so upset. We woke the next morning to mom cooking, the house smelled of coffee and sausage. Mom would clean and cook when she was upset, she didn't say a word to anyone.

When we came down to eat she sat at the bar stools near the window not saying a word. We ate in silence. "Mom, is there any more juice?" Kristopher asked her, she turned to him and pointed at the refrigerator. "Mom, you're not talking to me either? I didn't do anything," I told her placing my plate in the sink. "I'm just praying for you guys," she said. "Your father is really upset with you guys. I can't understand how you guys allowed that to happen!"

"But, mom, I didn't, they're not my friends. They're Kristopher and Kristine's friends," I said walking to the back patio. "You were there too Keagan, do you guys even know what's going to happen now? People are going to think it was our family who was careless! Your dad allowed you to take the boat out for a day and someone died! They died Kristopher," she said crying. "I just want to know what you were thinking; drinking and playing around in the water!" She said throwing her dishtowel into the sink walking away. "I'm sorry, mom," Kristine said running after her.

Kristopher stood up and went to the trash throwing his whole plate in, "I can't do this anymore." He said coming out to the patio with me, he pulled a chair really close to the edge of the pool and took a cigarette out of his pants. He lite it and began to smoke; looking at me shaking his head. "Keagan, you know I'm so jealous of you, if you had done something like this, it would be looked over. They wouldn't do a thing to you, you'd still be around here laughing and smiling. It was an accident man, that's all it was," he said puffing the cigarette shaking his head. "I was only trying to have a little fun," he said crying smoking his cigarette.

"Kristopher, it was an accident man, please don't blame yourself," I told him. "No Keagan, dad will never forgive me for what happened," he said. "He will get past this, it's going to take some time, but he will forgive you." I sat with him for a while inhaling his smoke, the doorbell rang. "I'll be right back Kristopher," I got up and walked into the living room to the door. "I got it, mom!" I yelled out. "Who is it?" I asked before looking out of the peephole, it was Grant. He was holding a bowl of something in his hand.

"What do you want dude!" I yelled out. "Hey, it's me, Keagan open up," he said looking up at the peephole, I opened the door quickly. "Keagan let's take this to Harvey's uncle's house, do you know where they live?" He asked me standing in his high water khakis. "I don't," I told him. "Let me see what you have here," I said taking the fruit bowl from his hands "Hey, no Keagan, that's for Harvey's family, don't open it," he said worrying I would open it up. "Come in we're out back at the pool," I told him turning around toward the back sliding door I noticed Kristopher was gone.

The chair was still there but he was gone, I looked around the room for him there was no sign that he went inside. I placed the bowl of fruit on the table. "Kristopher!" I yelled out. "Mom is Kristopher up there!" I yelled out. "No, he isn't!" She yelled back. "He didn't come up here!" She yelled at me. Grant walked toward the chair as I turned back toward the sliding door to see where he could have gone, I watched as Grant jumped into the pool with everything on. He didn't say a word he just jumped in, I ran and jumped too, Kristopher was at the bottom of the pool.

Grant grabbed him, trying to pull him up, but Kristopher began to fight him trying to stay down in the water. He pushed us both away, looking at us in the water trying to keep his self under. We came up for air; mom was standing at the end of the pool. "Mom, Kristopher he won't come up, mom!" I yelled out I begin to cry, mom jumped in going straight to the bottom toward Kristopher pulling him up, when she brought him to the surface he wasn't breathing. She began to do CRP on him crying and pumping his chest.

"Come on son!" She yelled out. "Keagan, go call 911," She said, soon Kristopher began to cough loudly. "Let me go, mom, let me die, I don't deserve to be here mom!" He said crying. "It was all my fault" he said crying, mom held onto him until the ambulance showed. They checked him out and left, mom was so upset she cried; I called dad. He came home immediately when they left Kristopher went to his room, Grant was still dripping wet.

"Come on, I'll get you something else to wear," I told him. He followed me up to my room dripping all over; dad followed us up heading toward Kristopher's room. "Son, what were you thinking?" He asked him with the door opened; Kristopher was lying across his bed still all wet crying. "Dad, I'm so sorry, I should have listened, now

Cody's gone, Harvey's lost his cousin because of me!" He cried. "Son, you can't change what happened, you can't. All you can do now is learn from it, they'll bury Cody in two days; his uncle wants all of you guys to be there. I don't want you there blaming yourself, you all made the decision to go out that day and play around on the water. Stop blaming yourself son," he told him standing over the bed.

"You did all you could to get him help, right?" He said. "He's gone; you all need to live for him. When you go back to school tell what happened so that it can help someone else to make a better decision," he told him. "Son, you can't carry this in your heart, you have to let it go, look at me. And killing yourself is never the answer to anything, be strong for your friend Harvey. Imagine what he's going through, they were like brothers, they grew up together in the same house," he says as he hugged him.

After that day, we saw more and more of everyone who came on that trip with us. They would come by; everyone planned to bring something special to the funeral for Cody. Kristine and the cheerleaders made little notes that they planned to put in the pocket of the casket. Harvey's uncle wanted us all there early, he wanted everyone from the college there especially the jocks that played sports with him. Our household was still a bit quiet, especially after what Kristopher did. Mom kept a close eye on him and Kristine hardly ever left his side.

Grant and Hanna wanted to attend the funeral although we hardly knew Cody; we wanted to go to the funeral to share our condolences. Mom and dad would be in and out of the house they did everything they could to help Harvey's uncle with the arrangements. They even ordered the flowers and offered to pay for all of it; I think they felt guilty because it was our boat that it happened on or something. Kristopher kept telling them that it was his fault, every day when the time came to bury him.

Everyone from college came to our house to meet Kristopher and Kristine there were so many people. Some of them came crying; some came asking about the boat trip. They wanted to know how it happened; they'd heard all sorts of rumors about it. "We heard he was thrown from the boat." "We heard that he fell onto the rocks trying to dive into the lake." I heard them whispering all sorts of things. "I can't take it!" Harvey told Kristopher as he waited for a car to pick him up from the house.

We all followed the car to the church where they had a memorial ceremony. They had pictures of Cody everywhere; they showed a video of him while music played until everyone was seated. Once everyone was seated the organ player began to play music as the church stood for the preacher to come in, the choir sang loudly. Everyone from the college was crying, they were holding onto each other crying. I sat next to Grant, and Hanna. Kristine sat next to mom and dad, and Jeni sat close to Kristopher.

The ceremony was long; two of his best friends got up and spoke about him. All of the coaches from the college got up and spoke of him, he was in almost every sport there was. When his uncle got up to speak, he cried with every word he spoke. We could hardly understand him. When it was over, we all walked past the casket. Everyone who wrote a note placed inside the pocket of the casket. On the way out, they gave everyone a little obituary with his picture on the front of it. He looked very nice dressed in a suit and tie, maybe they were school pictures.

Inside it was pictures and stories of his young life and more pictures of him from high school to college. He was an athlete almost all his life, it seemed from the obituary. But most of what I read said he was a really good guy. When the funeral was over everyone went to the burial grounds where he would be laid to rest beside his mother who died very young from a disease in her lungs. Harvey's uncle stood near the casket for a very long time after they laid the casket down into the ground.

They stood there together just staring down into the casket, it had been a very long day.

We went from the burial grounds to Harvey's uncle's church hall where they served everyone dinner and cake. All of the jocks stood around talking about what a great football player Cody would have made. They shared their stories about him having quick hands in baseball and fast legs in basketball. Kristopher hardly said anything to anyone. He sat in the back of the church looking at the nice statues they had out in the churchyard; I walked over to him. "Kristopher, are you okay?" I asked with my hand on his shoulder, he turned to me looking very sad. "I am little brother, I am okay," he said.

"Do you need anything; I can get you a drink?" I asked him. "I don't need a drink, I just need a little space, do you mind?" He said with his eyebrows up in the air at me. "Oh I'm sorry, I didn't mean to be intrusive, I'll go wait for you in the kitchen. That's where I'll be if you need me, okay," I told him, walking backward to the kitchen. I noticed dad looking around the room, he may have been looking for Kristopher, so I went to him. "Hey dad, Kristopher's over there," I told him. "I wasn't looking for him, son, I was looking for your mom. Have you seen her?" He asked me.

"I haven't dad, not since the burial grounds, I thought she was sitting next to you at the table?" I asked him. "She said she was going to get a drink, but I didn't see her over by the bar or anything," he told me. Soon they were serving food to everyone, and the pastor asked that we stand and pray over the food before eating. We all stood and began to pray, while our heads were down, I could smell mom's perfume walking up close to me. She took my hand holding it so tight in prayer that I was pulling it away from her.

When prayer was over, dad stood between mom and me. "Where have you been, Karis?" He asked. "I was in the chapel praying that's all," She told him sitting down at the table. Everyone ate and said there goodbye's. Harvey's uncle came up to dad when the room was almost clear. "Thank you so much, Michael, I will be in touch about that project overseas next year." He told dad giving him a firm handshake. "You think, you'll be ready for that?" He asked dad.

"Sure I will I'm always up for a challenge," he said walking us to the door of the church kitchen. "Goodbye Mr. Kimble, I hope everything goes well for you and your son," Dad told him. We went home that night in the car together, dad dropped Grant and Hanna off first before getting us home. "That was a lovely ceremony," mom said to dad. "Yes, but he was so young Karis, can you imagine, if it were us," he said opening the door to go inside the house.

Kristopher still didn't say a word; he placed his suit jacket down over the chair in the living room and walked up to his room. "He'll be fine after he gets some rest." Kristine said. "Yes, maybe he is a little tired," mom said going to the kitchen. "Did you want some tea, honey?" She asked dad, dad shook his head yes. We walked over to her and hugged her. I sat down at the table with Kristine when we heard Kristopher coming down the stairs. "Dad, I'm not going back to college," he shouted. "What are you saying, son?"

"I'm not going back," he said again walking back up the stairs mom and dad looked at one another. Dad went walking behind him upstairs. "What will he do without college?" Mom said sitting down at the table with her tea. Just then, the doorbell rang, Kristine went to the door; it was Grant and Harvey. "Come in," she tells them. "I left my bag here with Kristopher, is he here?" Harvey asked. "Yes, he's upstairs; this is a bad time can you come back?" Mom asked.

"No ma'am, I'm not returning to school I need to get my bag from him; our flight leaves tonight," he told her looking sad. "You're not returning to school?" Mom asked him, he shook his head no; dad came down the stairs with Kristopher following behind him. "Can I talk to you? I just have a minute," Harvey asked Kristopher; they walked into the backyard and sat at the patio table to talk.

Back on Track

When the time came for the twins to return to school, Kristopher refuse, Kristine went back to college alone, mom and dad didn't argue with him. They barely spoke to him about his decision at all. Harvey left town to go back and live with his uncle in New York. Kristopher spent most of his days around the house out at the pool, smoking cigarettes on the patio. Mom didn't like that he was doing those things at all. Mom knew there was something wrong with him; it was as if she tiptoed around him.

I overheard mom and dad talking about him going to see someone a professional therapist because he has a lot going on, mom would say. "He's smoking too much, and he only leaves his room to eat and go out to the pool. He never wants to talk about what happened at the lake, it had been two months since the accident. He has yet to mention what happened," mom would say to dad. "Karis, don't get upset, it may take him some time to get over this, he is still in the grieving process" dad would tell her.

"Do you see him every day Michael? He's not even bathing Michael; he's not even getting out of bed some days. Have you gone to his room Michael, please talk to him?" She asked dad as they sat and talked at the table. I stood by the door waiting for Grant to show up, we were going to the school today for orientation. We also have a meeting with the coach after we take our photos for the new school year. "So dude, you're really going to wear that to orientation huh," Kristopher said passing me on his way to the back patio to have a smoke.

"What's wrong with my outfit?" I asked him. He didn't say a word; he looked me up and down and continued walking by toward the back patio. I didn't say a word back to him, these days he's really mean, he just walks around the house looking lost all the time. When Grant showed up he asked to come in to say hi to mom, but I rushed him off, I didn't want Kristopher to say anything mean to him. "Mom, I'll see you later!" I yelled walking out. "I wanted to say hi, Keagan."

"Not now, maybe when we come back." We walked halfway through the pathway when Hanna came walking behind us. "Hey you guys wait up," she said catching up to us. "You guys excited about starting a new school year?" She asked holding a plastic bag full of fruit. "You want some?" She asked holding it in front of Grant and me. "No, thank you," Grant said. "Sure," I said taking one from the bag. "I'm excited about sports this year, I'm trying out for football," I told her. "Football really Keagan, so you're not doing track?" She asked me.

"Oh yeah, I'm doing track, I just want to try something different this year." I told her as we begin to get closer. "Oh no, here goes nothing," Grant said as we approached the edge of the sidewalk near the school entrance, there were Fredrick and his friends standing near the railing. "So you've come back for more huh, I heard you killed a guy on a lake trip," Fredrick said smiling. I walked past him not saying a word. "Not this again," Hanna said. "Just don't say anything, just keep walking," Grant said walking by fast. "We shouldn't have to deal with him, this year," Hanna said.

"Hello again, losers," Fredrick said balling up a piece of paper and throwing it our way. We managed to walk away getting to the lines where we would have to turn in our orientation packet. "Come stand in this line," Hanna said "I want you two to meet my friend," She pulled my arm toward the line in the middle. "Come on don't be shy," she said dragging me over. The school was packed, there were kids everywhere laughing and joking around in the line. I stood next to Hanna and Grant.

"Keagan, this is Riley, Tate, and Leland they all live there in the group home with me. They will be playing football also," she told me. "Nice to meet you guys," I said shaking their hands. "So, you know

Travis too?" They asked. "I do I met him before we left he's cool," I told them. "Have you played football before?" Tate asked me. "I haven't played, but I can't wait," I told him smiling. Tate was very tall but big, he wore a big gray t-shirt with a pair of jeans and white tennis shoes, his voice was soft.

He was as big as an elephant but gentle. "I can't wait to play," he said. "I'm going to play lineman," he told me. "I'm going to go out for quarterback," Leland said standing beside me. "What position are you going to play?" He asked me. "I don't know yet," I told them as the line moved forward, everyone carried their packet to turn in and get the classes they needed. I had mine tucked underneath my armpit so my hands would be free, we were almost at the window where we would hand them over when Fredrick snatched my papers from my arm.

I reached out to grab them back quickly, he pushed me back with his hand, and his friend grabbed it from him and began to open my envelope with my information in it. "You want it you have to work to get it," Fredrick said as his friend tore out the information inside. He began to read off the information line by line as I struggled to get by Fredrick we wrestled and wrestled. He pushed me I pushed at him my arms swung all around him trying to reach the papers. He moved all around me pushing me, grabbing my sleeve twisting me to the ground by my shirt.

It was really hard to get around him, we tussled around the line pushing other people over and pulling on each other. "You're still a little strong aren't you," Fredrick said as he dragged me around by the shirt. "You're weak Fredrick, and later I'll show you how weak you really are," I told him as I struggled to get up. "Oh, you mean you'll have some balls this year huh." Suddenly Grant grabbed his shirt and pulled him down to the ground.

"He will have balls, we'll both have some, and this year we'll be sure and teach you a good lesson about control." He told him helping me up from the ground. "You're going to need all the help you can get this year GQ," Fredrick said walking away with his friends. We made it to the window; after all, Grant handed over his packet first, and then mine. "Is everything in your packet filled out, make sure these classes are the ones you want because after next week there's no turning back. It'll take another semester before you can change them," the lady at the window told us as she looked them over.

"You boys both have GQ, and you're doing sports, Mr. Phillips," she said looking up at me with her glasses. "Yes, track and field and football," I told her. "You can only do one at a time," she told me "And because you have GQ you might only get to do one each semester," she said handing me the packet back with my schedule on top. "Look them over, over there and choose wisely, remember it will be another semester before we can change them again." I took the packet of papers from her and went to a bench near the office door to look them over.

"Man, this is a mess, I can't play football if I run track, because I'm in GQ," Leland said looking over his packet too. "Did she tell you the same thing?" He asked me. "Yes, she did." "Well, I'm choosing to stay in GQ, I was in it at my other school, and it was cool," he said scratching on his paper with a pen drawing a line through the page. "I think I'll do the same," I told him drawing a line through mine as well. "The team will just have to make it through the season without me, they're going to have a hard time winning this year," he said walking back toward the line.

"See you in GQ club, there's a meeting in two days, wear your sweater," he told me looking back waving his papers into the air. I walked back over to the line after looking at my paperwork one last time to make sure that I had everything right. I did want to play football badly, it just didn't pan out I thought as I entered the line again hoping it would move faster this time. It didn't, more and more people showed up to get there classes for the new school year. As I was moving forward, there was a tap on my shoulder.

"Hello son," a manly voice said to me, I turned to see who it was, it was Mr. Hanson. "Hi Mr. Hanson, how are you? It's so good to see you," I told him excited to see him there. "Yes son, same here, it's really good to see you too." I looked around to see why he was there I don't remember Reese having any siblings. "Are you here signing someone into school or something?" I asked him. "Oh no son, I will be teaching Algebra here for a couple semesters," he told me. "Algebra, oh that's cool Mr. Hanson, it's really nice to see you," I told him shaking his hand.

"Well Keagan, you have grown too son, I will see you in Algebra class maybe," he told me walking away. "So does that mean your teaching tenth graders?" He shook his head, yes, walking off with another teacher. "See you, Mr. Hanson!" I yelled out to him. It was really good to see him; I hadn't seen him since Reese's funeral. I didn't think he'd be the same after that, but he seemed okay. "You know him?" Riley asked me standing close to me in the line. "I do, he's a good guy," I told him as we move closer to the window.

"Then you should do well in Algebra huh?" He said laughing. "I doubt I'll do well, but I'll try," I told him. We were almost at the window when I heard Grant calling out for me, I looked around, and around I didn't see him anywhere. "Do you hear that?" Riley asked me. "I do, but I can't get out of line now," I told him. "Then don't, he's probably just playing around," he said as he made it to the window. He handed his papers and the lady looked them over.

"Thank you, next," she said reaching out for my papers "Here you go, ma'am," I said walking away quickly before she could say anything to me I ran off to find Grant. I looked everywhere, there were people everywhere, but I didn't see him. "Anybody seen, Grant?" I asked as I ran through a crowd of guys he knew. "No, uh un," they all say at the same time. "Have you seen Grant?" I asked Hanna. "Um, yes, he was over by the vending machines a few minutes ago," she said pointing toward the vending machines in the back of the office.

"Thank you," I said running toward them, I didn't see him there, I went to the back of the gym to see if he was there. Oh no, I thought what if they have him and they're beating him up. I thought as I looked around the school for him. "Hey, you looking for Grant?" Tate yelled out to me standing near the gym bathroom. "Yes, have you seen him?" I asked "I have, dude, don't panic, he told me he was going home. I think he walked that way," he said pointing toward the back gate; he held a cigarette in his hand.

"Thank you," I said running toward the back gate my heart raced as I ran thinking of what they could be doing to Grant. Fredrick promised him he'd get him and I can't allow it this year I thought as I ran through the canyon toward the side of the school gate. I didn't see him out anywhere, I ran to the front of the school all the way around to the pathway we walked every day. No Grant. Okay now, where else could he be? I thought as I ran down the pathway, I'll just go to his house, he has to be there. I thought as I went running down the street, I saw a couple of guys from school on the corner near Hanna's group home.

"Hey, Travis did you see Grant come down this way?" I asked. "No, I haven't seen him at all, maybe he's at the school," he told me. I shook my head no. "He could be at his house," he says. "Yes, I'll check there, thank you," I said walking past. I walked down to Grant's house there weren't any cars in the driveway I walked up to the door. I knocked twice no one came I stood there for a while before his mom came to the door. "Ma'am, I'm looking for Grant, is he home?" I asked. "No, Keagan I thought he was with you at the school," she said to me wiping her hand with a towel.

"He was at the school with me, but he left before me," I told her. "Oh, I see, well I'm sure he's probably still there, it's not like Grant to leave and not tell you where he's going you're his best friend." She said putting the towel into her pocket looking out of the door for him. "Okay, I'll go back to the school, but if you should see him before I do can you please tell him I'm looking for him?" I asked her. "I sure will don't worry he's probably in the band room at the school he loves band," she said with a smile closing the door. I went walking down the street where I ran into Travis again.

"Hey, I'm going up to the school did you want me to walk with you?" "Sure why not," I told him walking really fast, we made it to the school really fast it was like we ran there, Travis went to drop off his packet. I went into the school band room, there was no one there; there was no one in any of the classes. I walked by I decided to go back out toward the gym when I heard Grant calling out for me again, it sounded as if it was coming from the bathroom. I went running I slammed the door to the wall rushing in.

"Grant, where are you?" I yelled out, I went into every stall. "Where are you, Grant!" I yelled. "I'm here Keagan!" He yelled. "Where? I don't see you man, where are you!" I yelled out. "You have to come out, Grant!" I yelled I heard a loud noise coming from the walls outside the bathroom I ran toward it. "Grant is that you!" I yelled walking toward the sound on the outside of the wall. "Grant, Grant!" I yelled, Grant was hanging upside down with both his hands and feet tied together against the wall.

"They tied me up here," he said looking at me upside down. "It was Fredrick and his friends, this is what I get for threatening them I guess," he said. "I don't know what to do if I just cut the ropes you'll fall to the ground," I told him. "Wait here I'm going to get help." "No! No! Keagan, do not leave me here, they're coming back," he said looking straight with his eyes. "Hurry, just get me down the best you can!" He yelled. "Okay, okay," I grabbed the top of the rope trying to find out where the knot was.

They tied it so tight I struggled to untie it, but I couldn't. "Just go Keagan, just go!" Grant screamed as they approached us. "No, I won't leave you here, they'll just have to try and tie me up too, I won't leave you," I told him. "GQ, you just can't get enough, can you?" Fredrick said pushing me back onto the wall holding me by my shoulders. "Maybe I can't," I told him pulling his shirt to get him off me. His friends ran toward Grant hitting him repeatedly as his body tied up from the wall swung all around.

Punch after punch Grant took, I struggled to get away from Fredrick I began to punch at his face as hard as I could; hitting him in his eye and nose, he laughed at me. "GQ, please tell me you can do better than that," he said spitting on the ground. "That's all you got?" He took me by my shirt and threw me toward the ground trying to kick me as I fell. I pushed away using the heel of my feet to help me move away faster, I stood to my feet once I was away. "Come on GQ; show me something new, I've waited all this time for you to come back to school. It's going to be a long year if you keep this up," he said throwing punches at me.

I threw them right back, hitting him once or twice with each punch, he just laughed at me coming at me harder and harder the next time. I wanted to get away from him to help Grant, they were still hitting him swinging him around, and his body hit the wall hard. They each took a turn at him; Fredrick fought me and fought me trying to knock me back to the ground. I took my fist and hit him as hard as I could, when he fell to the ground I ran toward Grant to try and catch him before they threw his body to the wall again.

As I ran Fredrick grabbed me by the ankle trying to keep me back, they had Grant's body holding it far from the wall about to push him hard and let him go. "Don't do it!" I hear someone screaming. "Don't you dare," I looked up it was Riley; they stopped and held him looking to see who it was. "Let him go!" He yelled. Fredrick stood up. "What if we don't want to," he said to him. "Then you'll find out why they made me come to your school," he told him standing in his face looking him eye to eye.

"See, I know what you do, I know your type, beat them up and laugh, right?" He said. "Yeah, well do you know about this?" Fredrick said punching him in the stomach, Riley didn't budge it was as if Fredrick didn't hit him. "Do it again loser, I enjoyed it," he said staring him in the eye. His eyes were red like fire when he said it, "Go ahead, hit me again, this time I might scream for you," he said Fredrick balled his fist and began to hit him. He grabbed his hand and squeezed it as hard as he could; we all stood still watching what would come next.

Fredrick's hand turned to fire, but Riley didn't budge he began to blow on it. He blew ice, and then he blew ice at his face softly. "You like that loser, if you don't leave here now, I'll turn you all into ice!" He yelled at them. "Leave now!" They all looked at Fredrick as if they didn't know what to do, Fredrick began to run the other way, and they all followed him running away from all of us. Riley and I began to get Grant down from the wall, he held him up while I figured how to get him out of the knot. "Thank you so much man, thank you," Grant said to Riley as we worked on getting him down.

"You handled that well," Riley said to me as I untied the knot. "There I got it." We held onto Grant as he fell to the ground to his feet. "Thank you again, guys, that was close," he said standing with his hands on his back. "Are you okay, do you need help walking home or any-thing?" Riley asked. "No, I think I can manage," Grant said; we walked through the back gate to the canyon, Riley followed behind us. "Do you live around here?" I asked him. "No I don't, I have to ride the city bus, I live across town."

"Oh, I see," I said. When we made it through the pathway Riley walked ahead of us, he seemed to be in a hurry. "Hey Riley, thank you again, dude, that was awesome what you did." "No problem, where I went to school someone was always picking on me, I'll help you again in a heartbeat," he said waving to us. "You think we should wait with him at the bus stop?" Grant asked. "No, he seems to be okay," I said waving at him. "Come on let's get you home," I said walking beside him. "You think that scared him enough to leave us alone this year?" Grant asked.

"I don't think anything will ever scare Fredrick enough to leave us alone. He's always going to find some way to pick at us and if not us he'll pick at the rest of the dudes at school that he thought are too weak to defend themselves. It doesn't matter he'll always come back to try us," I told him as we approached his house. "Well, good thing we have each other right?" Grant said smiling. "And now maybe Riley too," Grant said going up the stairs to his door. "I'll see you tomorrow; will you come with me to track practice?" I asked.

"Sure I will, come by and get me this time okay," he said smiling at me. "No problem Grant, I'll be here as early as 7 am," I told him walking away; his mother met him at the door. "See Keagan I told you you'd find him," she said waving goodbye to me. "Hey, you left me," Travis said to me as I walked by. "Yeah I'm sorry, dude, I found Grant though he's fine," I told him. I made it to my house soon after, Kristopher was sitting on the porch smoking a cigarette.

"Dude, you've been gone a long time, how was the orientation?" He asked as I begin to walk up the stairs. "It was good." "You meet any nice girls there?" He blew smoke in my face after each question. "I didn't meet anyone new," I told him. "Dude, don't you want to sit out here with me, I mean where do you have to be? Mom isn't finished cooking yet," he told me blowing smoke in the air. "Naw, I think I'll go inside and help mom."

"Okay dude, don't ever say I didn't want to spend time with you." I walked past him going into the house, mom was cooking, I sat at the table. "Mom, do you think Kristopher will ever be the same again after what happened?" I asked. "He just sits around here all day, is he ever going to work or do anything?" "I don't know Keagan, sometimes things can happen in someone's life, and it will set them back. That's why you have to be really careful of the choices you make in your life because you'll never know." "Are you happy about the choices you've made, mom?" Mom didn't say a word she looked sad for a moment then happy again.

"No Keagan, I don't regret any of the choices I've made at all." "That's good, mom," I told her going over to her giving her a big hug. "Thank you mom, for always being there for me," I told her, just than Kristopher walks in sliding his feet. "Aw, mommies little baby," he says going to the refrigerator. "I just want you to know that it doesn't last, dude, you can't be a mama's boy forever," he told me drinking from the container of juice then burping out loud. "Really dude, grow up," he said putting the container back and walking out of the kitchen.

"Don't you think about anything he said, he's just jealous because you're the baby." Mom hugged me tight and let me go. "So, how was orientation?" She asked. "It was good, the counselor told me that I can't play football and have GQ." "Oh good son, I didn't want you playing football anyway, it's way too dangerous, do you still get to run track?" She asked. "I do mom, I almost chose football over track mom, good thing I didn't. "You did good, son," she said handing me an apple.

"Before dinner mom," I bit into the apple and walked up to my room. "Dinner in 10 minutes, son" She yelled up to me, I ate my apple sitting at my desk looking out at the pool in the backyard. Kristopher was sitting out on the edge of the pool again; he was just staring at the water as if he would jump again. I wondered if they did something to him before tying him up in that tree, he was acting so strange. I just stared at him kicking his feet in the water sitting on the edge. I ate my apple watching him, as I bend my head down to take another bite.

He stared up at me and began to laugh loudly, he didn't take his eyes off me laughing and swinging his hair back. I spat the apple out into the trash and threw the rest away. It was a horrifying look he gave me, when

I looked out of the window again he was standing looking up at my window. He flung his hair back smiling up at me, he walked away coming back into the house, I ran out of my room down to the kitchen. "Mom, mom!" I yelled on my way down. "There's something wrong with Kristopher!" I said approaching her in the kitchen.

"What's wrong with him?" She asked. "Yeah, what's wrong with me?" He said winking at me. "That look you gave me in the window, you know what I'm talking about Kristopher, what's wrong with you?" I said standing next to mom. "Mom, there's something wrong with him." "Keagan, calm down, there's nothing wrong with him," she said holding onto the towel in her hand. "See you later, dude," he said walking past me. "Keagan, what's wrong with you saying that about your brother?"

"Mom, there is something wrong, he gave me a really scary look, it was like evil mom," I told her in a panic. "Keagan, sit down it's time for dinner," she said walking over to the stove. I pulled out my chair about to sit down when I saw Kristopher standing against the wall staring at me. "Mom!" I yelled out jumping from my chair running over to her, he began to laugh loudly coming out from the wall. "Dude, you're so scary," he said laughing standing at the table. "Kristopher, stop it, why are you scaring him like that, leave him be!"

"You boys sit down for dinner now," mom told us. While eating dinner, I didn't say a word, I watched him closely. Every time he'd make contact with me, he'd roll his eyes back and stick out his tongue. I would pretend not to notice, eating my food as quickly as I could, so that I could leave. "May I be excused, mom?" I said standing from the table with my plate in my hand. "You're done? That was fast, did you even swallow?" She asked. "Yes, I did mom, can I be excused?" I asked again.

"Sure son, can you clean your room before bed tonight?" She asked me. "I will mom," I told her placing my plate into the sink. "See you later dude, much later," Kristopher said looking at me as I walked past. I made it to the stairwell and looked back at him; mom was by the sink putting her plate away. He turned to see if she was watching then flipping his hair back again, he looked straight at me and gave me the same evil look as before. I ran the rest of the way up to my room; I grabbed the phone from the stool in the hall and slammed my door going inside.

I dialed Grant's number as quickly as I could. It was ringing, his father picked up. "Hello, may I speak to Grant, please?" I asked him in sort of a whisper. "He's in the shower at the moment; did you want to leave a message?" He asked me. "Um sir, can you please have him call me as soon as he gets out?" "Sure son, Keagan, right?" He asked. "Yes, this is Keagan," I told him I hung up the phone and sat it near the desk. I began to straighten up my room like mom asked.

I kept looking back at the phone waiting for Grant to call back, I knew Grant could help me, I thought. He knows about these things, spirits, and things. I cleaned all around my bed picking up dirty clothes and shoes I had laying around. I went to place them in the closet when the phone rang, I ran for it. "Hello, Grant." "No, this is Jeni; may I speak to Kristopher please?" She said. "Um, I'm waiting for a phone call," I told her, she was silent not responding when I heard heavy breathing. "Dude, hang up the phone, I got it, your phone call will have to wait,"

Kristopher said on the other end of the phone. "I really need to talk to Grant," I told him. "Dude hang up!" He yelled at me; I held the phone for a while before hanging up. "Don't make me come up there," he told me in a really mean voice, I hung up the phone. I sat on my bed, I bet Grant's going to call me soon I thought looking around my room, and soon there was a knock at my door. "Dude, open up, there's a phone call for you," Kristopher said. I opened the door quickly thinking that Grant was on the phone, he pushed me with the phone in his hand.

"Dude, don't you ever do that again, when I pick up a call you hang right up." He said looking me straight into the eyes; I took the phone from his hand. He stood there watching me. "Thank you, you can go now," I told him holding the phone to my chest. "No, I'm good right here," he said staring at me; I put the phone to my ear. "Hello," I said waiting for Grant to speak. It was quiet. "Is he there?" Kristopher said standing in my face. I shook my head no and handed him the phone back, he pushed me down to the bed pressing the phone against my chest.

"You little shit; you and your friends think you're tough? The next time someone at school does something to any of you, and you threatened them, you'll have more than just me to deal with," he said whisper-ing in my ear. His breath smelling of smoke and his hair falling over my face, his eyes looked of pure evil. "Do you understand me, you little shit?" He asked. I was stiff, I couldn't move, Kristopher wasn't himself at all. I shook my head yes, he stared at me a while longer, then moved off me slowly not taking his eyes off me. "You remember what happened to that little bitch you use to hang out with, right?" He said turning away toward the door, he took one last evil look at me and shut the door.

Rage around Me

That night, I slept with the lights on. I tossed and turned and watched my door, I can't be afraid of him I thought. He was my brother, would he really hurt me? I thought on and off throughout the night, I dared to call Grant when he could pick up the phone and listen in on our conversation from the other room. I couldn't wait to get to Grant's house the next day. I got up so early in the morning rushing through the room getting dressed, I didn't even say goodbye to mom or dad.

I rushed out of the house to go to Grant's house; I ran the whole way there when I saw that his mom and dad were gone. I knocked so hard on his door I thought for sure his neighbors heard me. "Grant! Grant! Come on, open up!" I yelled out. I could hear him coming to the door, I heard him removing the locks. He opened the door; he was wearing a pair of very short pajama pants and a small shirt. "What's wrong Keagan?" He asked.

I rushed inside shutting the door behind me placing the lock back on. "Grant, there's something wrong with my brother, he threatened me about us." "Us? What do you mean, what are you talking about?" He asked walking toward his room. "Wait a minute Keagan, I have to wash my face, stay calm," he said with his hair in his face, leaning his head up to look at me. "Grant, what do you think is wrong, I mean he really threatened me. He called me a shit, and said that if we planned on fighting back in school this year, we'd be in even more trouble. How does he know what's going on at school?" I asked him in a panic.

"What do you mean, he knows?" Grant said brushing his teeth at the sink. "He knows Grant; I think something happened to him at the lake" "The Lake?" "Yes, the lake, I mean doesn't it make since we pulled him off that tree, he was strapped there for a while. How do we know that they didn't do anything else to him while he was up there?" I said. "That painting, we didn't take it, we should have taken it," I told him. "Keagan, calm down please, you're becoming irate," Grant told me looking up at me from the sink.

"You don't even know if he's playing around with you or not, your brother plays around a lot," he told me. "Maybe he's just trying to scare you," he told me standing straight up. "No, Grant I'm telling you, it's not him, my parents can't see it, and if you don't, believe me, I'll just find someone who will," I told him about to leave. "Wait, Keagan, I'm not saying that I don't believe you I'm just saying that you have to be careful. Especially if something has possessed him, have you ever heard of demon possession?" He asked me. "No, I haven't, what is that?" I asked him walking over to the stool near his room.

"Wait, let me get my Bible," he said running out into the living room area, his little pants were falling down as he ran. "Um, Grant, before you come back you think you want to put on a pair of pants!" I yelled. "Oh yeah, hold on, don't go anywhere!" He yelled out to me. "I'll be right there!" Grant had all these weird pictures all over his room. I looked at them thinking about how weird I've become hanging around him and Hanna. "So tell me what he say to you, what makes you think that there is really something wrong with him?" He asked me opening his Bible now wearing a pair of high water jeans.

"I was watching him from my bedroom window he was laughing as if he knew I was watching. Then, he turned to me giving me an evil look; it was like he was looking through my soul. I took the phone to call you, I waited for you to call me back but someone called for him. After he talked to Jeni, he came up to my room and shoved me onto my bed pressing the phone into my chest. He whispered in my ear and threatened me; he said we'd all end up just like Reese. He called her a bitch Grant, it was horrifying," I told him.

"Well let's see, I really hope there's nothing wrong with him, Keagan. For your family's sake, he could be dangerous, what else did he do?" He asked going through his Bible looking for scriptures to read to me. "Grant, I can't explain it, but I know there's something wrong, someone's living in my house inside of Kristopher, and I'm afraid of it. Something in me can feel that he's really dangerous" I told him "Okay let's see here" Grant said holding his Bible close to his face.

"I know that there's something in here that can tell us whether or not he's really possessed. Maybe he's just trying to scare you," he said looking up from the Bible at me. "Keagan, don't you think your parents would notice if there were really something wrong, especially something like that?" He said. "No! Dude, come on, are you going to help me or not? I didn't come over here to hear this, there's something wrong with my brother, he's evil. There is evil inside him right now, and before he does something crazy, we really need to do something," I told him sitting down in his mother's rocker.

"Now, help me find something in here." He went on flipping through the pages of the Bible. "Oh, here's something, hold on. Matthew 12:43, The Return of the demons. It describes a demon that left a man, presumably because of an exorcism. He returned later with seven other evil spirits to repossesses the person. However, there is no mention of any of the exorcisms by Jesus or his followers having produced only temporary cures," he looked up at me. "I think this is telling us that maybe it did happen out there on that lake."

"What else does it say, what else is there? I don't get what that's trying to tell us." "Okay, let's look for more, hold on," he said flipping through the pages of the Bible. "Okay, okay, in Acts 19:13, the demon-possessed man exhibited superhuman strength. He turns seven Jewish exorcists beat them and expelled them from the house with their clothes ripped off. The evil spirit had apparently recognized that the exorcists were not Christian. He refused to follow their command."

"Grant, you're reading a lot about exorcism, I don't know much about getting a demon out of anybody, do you?" Grant flipped through the pages of the Bible again. "Hum let's see, if you really think that Kristopher possessed with evil, then these are the things that we should be looking for. Did he have supernatural strength when he pushed you onto the bed? Did he seem to be stronger?" He asked me looking up at me. "Well he's always been pretty strong, but there's just something weird going on with him, I don't know." I told him rubbing my head.

"Why don't we go over to your house? We'll just observe him for a while, and if he is possessed with something we'll use this to get it out of him," he says holding up the Bible. "Okay, are you coming today?" I asked him. "I guess, I can, but remember we have to pick up our school schedules today. Hey, don't you have a meeting for track today?" He asked. "I do, I ran out of the house so quickly, I forgot to grab my gym bag. We'll have to go back there to get it, then you can see for yourself what I'm talking about okay," I told him standing from the chair. "Are you coming?" I asked him.

Grant stood up; "Keagan first let me warn you. Demonic spirits are so dangerous, if he is really possessed with some kind of spirit, we can't take it on alone. We have to find someone of great faith and strength in God to help us. There's no way we can do it, so I'll come with you but only to see if he's really possessed. We won't try and fight it out of him, okay," he said brushing his hair back. "Let's go, Grant, the meeting is in an hour," I told him. We went walking back down to my house to get my gym bag.

Grant seemed so nervous about going to my house, maybe I shouldn't have shared that with him, I thought. We made it to my house, he just stood in front. "Are you going to come in?" I asked walking up to the door. "Wait Keagan look up, look up," he said rolling his eyes up not moving his head at all. "What is it?" "Just look up," he said in a whisper, I looked up at the window above the porch. Kristopher was staring down at us with a big smile on his face as if he knew we were coming. He laughed at us and pointed down at us, then suddenly stopped.

He motioned his figure telling us to come in, with the look of pure evil on his face. I stood back looking at him from the porch; I looked over in the driveway to see if mom's car was there, she was gone. "Come on Grant, we can't allow him to scare us, and I have to have my gym bag today," I told him holding onto the rail. "I have an awful feeling about this Keagan, why don't you just go inside grab your bag and come right out," he says still looking up at Kristopher with only his eyes.

"Oh, come on Grant don't be a coward, what can he do to the both of us, we just go inside I grab my bag, and we leave. We'll ignore his words if he has any" I told him turning the doorknob slowly, here goes nothing I thought as I stepped inside. I looked back at Grant. "Come in," I said waving my hand at him to follow me in. "Don't be afraid, he's not going to hurt us, I'm sure," I said whispering. He followed me in, I ran upstairs as fast as I could to get my gym bag, it was sitting in the chair next to the desk.

I snatched it off and turned back to go out, Kristopher was standing right in front of me blocking the doorway with this evil look on his face. "Where do you think you're going?" He asked me. I held my bag close to my chest. "So you went and warned your friend huh, good, good," he said shaking his head. "Because this year you two little cunt's better think twice before interfering. Make sure you tell him to mind his own business, walk away from what he thinks he can change. Or I'll make sure you two get the worst of it," he said with his hands on my bag squeezing it.

"Kristopher, I'm not afraid of you, I'm not afraid of what's inside you either," I told him looking him in his eye. "You're not scaring me, Kristopher, I know you're only acting out," I told him hoping he'd back off. He looked up at me frowning, and then his frown turned into laughter very loud laughter. I tried pushing past him to get through the door. He held me by my shirt bringing his face close to my neck blowing air from his nose. "I won't hesitate to hurt your little nerd friends." I stepped back away from him grabbing his hand away from my shirt, dropping my bag grabbing his wrist with the other hand.

"I'm not afraid of what you are Kristopher, I won't let you hurt my friends." He pushed me back onto the wall near my desk holding me by my shirt. He held me up high then tossed me to the floor near my bag as hard as he could. He gave me an evil stare then began to laugh loudly walking away from the door. I picked up my bag and ran for the stairs; Grant was not waiting downstairs where I left him. I searched the house quickly, clutching my bag. "Grant, where are you! I yelled out.

"Over here!" He said coming from the living room. "What were you doing over there, did you hear what happened, and did you hear what he said to me up there?" I asked him. He shook his head yes. "I heard everything, he's bold the devil is always bold," he said looking up at the stairway. There was Kristopher, standing near the railing looking down at us laughing swinging his hair around. "Let's get out of here," Grant said going to the door, we both dashed toward the door trying to open it up. It wouldn't unlock we twisted the knob and turned the locks over and over again looking back at Kristopher making sure he didn't come down to us.

"Come on Grant," I said running toward the back patio door. "Come on!" I yelled. Kristopher stood up there looking down at us while we panic. He laughs loudly shaking his head at us. He tried to get out of the patio door but it too wouldn't allow us to open it, we ran back to the front door. "Grant twisted the knob, we tried getting out, but it was stuck. We looked up at the stairwell for Kristopher; he was no longer there. "Grant stop," I told him. "Don't make a sound," I needed to know where he was. I didn't want him to sneak up on us, Grant looked so afraid he was shaking with fear.

"Grant, don't move," I told him. "Stay right here," I began to walk up the stairwell, and I began to hear Kristopher making noises. It sounded as if he was throwing things around, I ran up to the top of the stairs to see what he was doing. As soon as my foot touched on the hardwood hall floors, the noise stopped. "I knew you would come," it was a voice I'd never heard before. I looked around me this voice sounded raspy and old. "I knew you'd be tough enough to come up here," the voice said again.

Still, I didn't see anyone; I began to turn back to the stairwell to go back down to Grant. I didn't want to see who it was, my skin began to crawl just hearing the voice. I turned walking toward the stairwell I walked backward not turning my back on the hallway "Keagan!" Grant screamed out, I turned to look at him, he pointed up, I looked up. Kristopher was hanging from the ceiling crawling around me with his neck hanging down and his hair hanging from his face. I ran as fast as I could down the stairs, tripping over my feet half the way down.

"Go! Go!" I yelled out to Grant. "Get out of here!" I yelled out, Grant turned around twisting the doorknob to get out, "Grant! Grant! Open it! I yelled out at him "Keagan, I can't get out." We both stood still watching Kristopher crawl all over the ceiling coming toward us. Grant closed his eyes tight, he didn't want to look up at Kristopher, I watched him. I couldn't tell what he'd do next. When he made it over to us his neck fell, he looked at me, then at Grant over and over again. He did a full circle around us then flipping over falling down right in front of us laughing loudly.

And in that raspy voice of the old man, he began to quote what Grant read to me from the Bible earlier that morning. "Return of the demon, Matthew 12:43 described a demon who left a man, presumably because of an exorcism. He returned later with seven other evil spirits to repossess the person. However, there is no mention of any of the exorcism by Jesus or his followers, having produced only temporary cures." His eyes rolled back, he swung his hair around and fell to the floor onto his back. Grant and I looked at one another, I didn't want to touch him, and neither did he.

We stood over him staring in silence, suddenly the door opened, and his eyes opened looking up at us. "Leave!" He roared in the raspy voice of the old man. We didn't hesitate we both ran, I grabbed my bag on the way out from the floor. We ran all the way to the school without a word to one another, when we arrived at school, we both sat on the stairs near the entrance. "Keagan he's in him," Grant said. "He's all in him, what are you going to do?" Grant asked. I shook my head.

"What are you going to do, about what?" It was Tate he was standing behind us, we looked at one another. "Nothing, never mind," Grant said standing to his feet. "Hey Keagan, I'll catch you later okay, I have to go see my band teacher," he said rushing off. "So what's up Keagan, you guys look scared or something, what happened?" Tate asked. "Oh nothing, everything is fine," I told him clutching my gym bag getting up from the stair. "I have to go to the track field," I told him as I begun to walk away.

"Me too, wait up," he whistled really loud and waved his hand out. "Track field come on!" He yelled out, Leland and Riley came running over. "You guys like to be early, we still have ten minutes," Leland says. "Yes, the early bird catches the worm," Riley said. "Whoever makes it to the gym first gets my candy bar," he said holding up a chocolate bar. "On your marks, get set!" He didn't get a chance to say go before we all took off running. "I strapped my bag on my shoulder giving them a little head start, and then I took off behind them.

I caught up quickly leaving them all behind me, when we all made it to the gym Riley pealed back the candy bar opening it up. He stretched his hand out toward me as if he would give it to me then snatched it back. "I just can't dude, I'm so hungry right now," he said smiling taking a bite from the candy bar. "You're too funny, dude," Leland said laughing. "I didn't want it anyway," I told him placing my bag on the bench in the locker room.

"Dude, I don't think the coach wants us to suit up today," Riley said still eating at the candy bar. "Yes he does, today we start conditioning for the new season," Leland told him taking off his shirt "Really, because I didn't bring my gear." "I have extra," I told him throwing a pair of shorts and a t-shirt at his face knocking the candy bar from his hand. "Thanks, dude, now we're even," he said taking his clothes off to change. "You can keep those too," I told him. "Ready when you are," I said to them running in place.

"You guys better be ready today," Leland said. "I'm always ready," Riley said as we all went running out toward the field. We were met by Fredrick and his friends on the way out. "Going down to the track fellas?" Coach said walking up behind them "Yes sir," Riley said. "Okay, looks like you guys are ready to start the season, we're off to a good start everyone's here, new and old," he said following us down to the track with his whistle. I tried to keep my mind on the field; I didn't want to think of Kristopher at home on the ceiling.

I didn't want to think about Fredrick and his friends today, or what they did to Reese. I just wanted to run, once we were on the field, we began to do workups over and over again. We stretched and ran around one another for what seemed to be hours, after all that we ran the field for another hour. Then practiced relays between us all, when we were done, we went into the locker room covered in sweat. "Good job guys," the coach said walking alongside us into the locker rooms. "Let's bring that same motivation back onto the field again tomorrow," he said going into the back office.

I began to take off my shorts and shirt and head to the showers; I was too sweaty today to leave without a shower. There was a line of people waiting to go into the shower room it went from the edge of the doorway all the way down to the last bench. I stood there for a while, and then walked away, I couldn't wait any longer, I needed to get home to mom. I don't know what's happening with Kristopher and I didn't want him to hurt mom. I changed quickly and placed my bag in my locker then went looking for Grant.

I don't know if I can get him to go back to the house with me, but I'll try. I went to the band room looking for him; there was no one inside there. All the equipment was put away neatly as if no one had ever been in there today, I ran back out down toward the stairs. "Hey, are you looking for Grant again?" Hanna asked. "Yes, how did you know?" I asked her "Because you're always frantically searching for him. He's sitting on the stairs over there. Did you pick up your schedule yet?" She asked me. "No, I'll get it later," I told her.

"He looks a little worried today, is everything okay, he barely spoke two words to me today," she said looking worried. "I don't know, I'll ask him," I told her walking past her, I ran toward the stairs to get Grant. "Hey, Grant! Let's go," I told him standing behind him. "Are you ready, come on," I said again tapping his shoulder. "Yes, I'm ready," he said standing to his feet. "Why are you in a hurry, what's wrong?" He asked me. "I want to get to my house before mom comes home, what if Kristopher hurts mom?" I told him walking as fast as I could toward the pathway.

"He won't show himself around your mom," Grant told me struggling to keep up with me. "What makes you say that, why wouldn't he show himself?" I asked him. "He's not going to let your parent's know who's inside him, so calm down," he said catching up to me. "No Grant, you don't understand, I don't think that he's afraid of them either. I don't think that it would matter a bit whether or not it's mom or dad," I told him.

"Didn't you see what he did in front of us, he was crawling on the ceiling, he didn't care that we saw him there." "He was just letting us see the power in him; he wants us to fear him Keagan that's all. He wants us to believe that nothing is greater than the power of evil. We can't act afraid of him or run when he allows us to, one day soon we'll have to stand up to him," Grant said as we approached the house. We could see Kristopher in the window; he was smiling at us as we walked up to the door.

When I opened the door, he was standing next to the table laughing with mom. "Isn't he funny, mom," he said laughing with her. "He is, son, that whole dance was hilarious," she said laughing standing over the stove. Kristopher turned to me and smiled. "You guys ready to eat, Grant are you staying for dinner?" He asked. Grant shook his head no. "I have some things I have to do tonight with my parents," he said backing up toward the door. I grabbed his shirt. "Yes, Grants staying for dinner, what do we have, mom?" I asked.

"We will have roast beef tonight with potatoes and carrots," she said smiling. "Hey Grant, what's wrong, you look a little worried, is everything okay?" Mom asked him. "I can't stay for dinner Mrs. Phillips, not tonight. I have a lot to do at home," he said walking toward the door; I followed him to the door. "Hey dude, you're the one who says we can't be afraid, you're acting like you're afraid," I whispered to him. "I'm not afraid Keagan; I just need to go home. He's not going to act out in front of your mother, he'll act normal now.

He knows that we know about him," he said looking over at Kristopher. He watched us and talked to mom, at the same time. "He can hear us, he knows our every move, so there is no need to whisper," he told me opening the door. "Goodbye Mrs. Phillips, goodbye Kristopher see you all later," Grant said closing the door behind him. I began to walk away from the door when there was a knock, I went back to the door and opened it, it was Grant. "Keagan you need to pray and believe right now, it's critical," he told me in the crack of the doorway.

"What are you talking about Grant, you know I can't do that. "You can, you have to Keagan, or we will be in way more trouble than you think," he said looking up over my shoulder. "What, what's wrong?" He raised his eyebrows looking over my shoulders; I turned around to see what he was looking at. It was Kristopher standing behind me looking over my shoulders. "What are you doing?" I yelled out. "It's time to eat dude, what are you two whispering about out here, you really can't stay huh Grant," he said looking down at Grant.

He shook his head no and began to walk away from the door. "You sure!" He yelled out. Grant waved his hand continuing to walk away from the house. "Come on dude dinners ready now," he said holding the door open for me to move away from it, I walked in front of him to the kitchen, we sat down for dinner. "Will dad be here later mom," I asked. "Of course he'll be here late tonight, why Keagan is there something you need?" mom asked me. "How was track practice?" She asked.

"It was interesting we have some new team members," I told her. "Oh yeah, new runners huh, how many?" "There's just three, Riley, Tate, Leland, they can all run fast too," I said to her. "Oh good, you guys needed some new runners, right?" "Well, everyone was good we didn't need them, but it makes the team stronger I guess," I said eating the carrots on my plate. Kristopher stared at me giving me an evil look. When mom wasn't watching, he would give me evil looks while he ate bit after bit until he was finished.

I wanted so desperately to tell mom that there was really something wrong with Kristopher, but I knew she wouldn't believe me. "Mom, do you know anything about the cottages across from Torch Lake?" I asked her, Kristopher put his fork down and looked at mom and me. He got up and took his plate over to the sink. "What are you talking about, what cottages?" "You know the cottages across from the lake, the one's dad warned us about?" I told her.

"No, I don't know why your dad would have warned you guys about it. Everything around the lake seems lovely to me," she said going over to the sink to wash the dishes. "I stayed in my chair eating while

Kristopher went upstairs to his room. I thought I heard him going up the stairs, but when I got up to put my plate away, I notice him standing on the side of the wall staring at me. I was startled by him, I almost dropped my plate. He looked as if he wanted to grab me; I walked my plate over to mom, then sat back down at the table closer to mom this time.

"You don't want a shower?" Mom asked me. "Oh, know I'll wait for you to go up," I told her playing around with the napkin holder on the table. I didn't' want to leave mom down here alone, and I don't want to deal with Kristopher. I waited while mom finished the dishes, when she was done she shut off the light in the kitchen; we walked upstairs together for bed. Kristopher was no longer behind the wall; I looked all around downstairs for him. I went into my room after watching mom go into hers, I needed a shower badly, I was sweaty and smelly, I sat down at my desk to catch my breath.

It felt like I had been holding my breath all that time around him, I sat there dosing off to sleep with my shirt off. A loud knock on the door startled me up from the desk. "Who is it?" I yelled out "It's me Keagan; I just wanted to let you know that they've called me in for a midnight shift at the hospital. I'm filling in for someone who called off," mom told me. "Can I go in with you, mom?" She opened the door. "What, you want to go to the hospital with me while I'm working, no Keagan, what's wrong, why don't you want to stay here with your brother?" She asked me.

"Oh nothing mom, I'll be fine, go ahead," I told her putting my head back on the desk. "Are you sure Keagan? Because you don't seem sure about it" "I am, mom don't worry, go ahead and go to work," I said to her. "Okay son, just get you a shower and get you some sleep you look a mess," she said kissing my head "You smell," she said laughing shutting the door. I listened for her walking to the door leaving the house, I got up soon after and took my pants off and got into the shower, the water was warm.

I washed my body than my hair, as I washed my hair the water began to get hotter and hotter, I turned the knob to make it cool, but it wouldn't move. I washed the soap out as fast as I could. Then, tried to turn off the water, it wouldn't turn off, I reached for my towel, and began to dry my hair and face when I took the towel off my face, the bathroom went black. It was dark I got out of the shower wrapping myself with the towel. I went for the light switch on the wall, I flipped it up and down, and the lights still wouldn't come on.

I felt my way through to my room with my hand on the wall looking for my other light switches. I flipped them up and down, they didn't come on, what was going on, I thought as I walked over to the door. I opened it to see if mom had left any lights on in the house, the hallways were very dark. I stepped out feeling around the wall for the light switch I flipped it up and down, it didn't come on. I grabbed the phone from the table next to the door and went back to my room to call Grant. I picked up the phone, there was no dial tone, I started to sit down on my chair at the desk when it was pulled from me, I fell to the floor.

I looked up five dark shadows were surrounding me all I could see were their eyes piercing at me, I turned over onto my stomach clutching my knees together in to my arms. I don't know why, but I began to recite verses from the Bible. I repeated the verses over and over not looking up at the dark shadows. They stood in a stance as if they were going to attack me; I could feel their evil around me as I laid there on the floor.

I didn't know if any of them was Kristopher or not; I was afraid. Soon, I heard the voice of the old man speaking out, then a big hand squeezing the back of my neck picking me up from the floor. "Now you're afraid," the voice said; it was Kristopher holding me in the air by my neck.

Omega

That night I turned, it was if my body went numb. It was as if my world changed, I closed my eyes as he held me up and my body turned. I was covered in a shield made up of hard blade-like feathers. They were all black my eyes turned white, and my shoulder blades were white. It was as if I was a different person, I looked down at Kristopher, I didn't see my brother, I didn't see a close friend who I laugh with. All I saw was an enemy, all I felt was despair and defeat, my body flexed immediately I began to fight for my life. My shoulder blades split open, I grabbed Kristopher by his ears pulling him up to me.

The room was still black as we fought; I began to defeat them, the lights flashed on and off. The room walls sounded as if they were expanding, the noise from Kristopher's mouth was of pure evil. He didn't stop attacking; he gave me no chance to get away. I fought my way around the room, the window opened and shut, the doors opened and shut as went toe to toe in the darkness. It didn't stop, I threw him around until he held onto me, when he pinned me to the floor.

My voice changed as of a great horn, when I opened my mouth it was over with; the loudest horn you ever heard, and he was gone. The lights came on in the room, the windows and doors secured. Everything went back as it had been before Kristopher came into my room. I laid on the floor naked no longer covered in the black bladed feathers. I crawled over to my bed; the room was torn apart as if someone had run through it with a truck.

I didn't even put any clothes on I laid in bed with the covers over me, thinking God what's next. I fell off to sleep that night only for a while, mom came in and woke me standing over my bed watching me as I slept, I grabbed the covers to my neck. "Mom, what are you doing in here?" I asked her. "I'm just checking to see if you're okay its 9:45 you were supposed to be gone now right, and what happened in here Keagan, you have to clean this room," she said walking out.

I jumped up from my bed holding the cover over me running for the closet to change. I needed to get to Grant to tell him about last night, school will be starting in a week. I needed to get to the school to pick up my schedule too. I rushed out of the house soon after putting on my clothes, I didn't tell mom goodbye, and I didn't look around the house for Kristopher. I didn't want to see him after that night. "See you later!" I yelled out before closing the door, I ran down to Grant's house passing Hanna and Travis on the way.

"You're in a hurry today," Hanna said as I ran past them. "Yes, I am!" I yelled back when I made it to Grant's I knocked on his door really hard. "Grant! Grant! Open up," I yelled Grant came running to the door removing all the locks opening it quickly. "What's wrong now?" He said as I pushed my way in. "Last night, Grant, last night, he attacked me, but I turned, I fought him back. It was strange because I felt like I'd left my body. I was no longer there, Grant you have to explain to me what's happening to me."

"You have to come to Bible studies; you need to familiarize yourself with the Bible." He took a little Bible from his pocket pants. "This is the only thing that will save you from evil, these days you have to have some of this," he said slapping the Bible to his hand. "Seriously, Grant, I need to know what's in there." "You do Keagan, I'm not joking it's all we have." "Really, all we have." "Yes, believe me, if I didn't know what's in here my days would have been a lot longer dealing with Fredrick and his crew at school.

Do you really believe that all they are at school are bullies? They are much more than that; they are hate, pain and fear. They are the evil that keeps people like me and you from ever moving forward in life. Remember what happened to Reese?" He said really serious.

"Remember what they did to her, they didn't care, she killed herself because of what they call bullying, and taunting. She felt she had no one, no one at all, but if she had just had a little of this, she would have made it through it." "I think you're wrong Grant, I never had any of that, and I've survived it. I fought them back."

"Yeah because of him you fought them back, come on dude, you really think he's not in you? Okay, I'm not going to say a word, I just dare you to read some of this every day, and tell me then if you're really on your own," he told me walking away from me. We went on through the week, I started to attend some Bible studies, but it just didn't make too much sense to me. Every time I'd attend I left with the same thoughts. Who is this God, and why should I go on believing in him? It was a no-win situation for me.

We began school on a Tuesday weeks later. I had most classes with Grant this year, and GQ was much more interesting than it had ever been. Riley and Leland were in it along with Tate and Travis. It was really cool walking around every Friday with our sweaters and slacks on. Mr. Hanson was my Algebra teacher he was actually really nice, he didn't mind if my work were late. He'd just ask me to stay later just so he could know that I was getting it he'd say. I never had too many classes with Grant; I've now learned why they called him a nerd.

He was somewhat of a little-gifted genius, he knew everything in all the class especially Algebra and science. There was nothing he didn't know. School started off terrific this year, I didn't have too many classes with Fredrick. The ones I did have with him Leland and Tate had too, and for some reason, he didn't bully anyone around them. He didn't even talk much around them. School was going fine, while in my home Kristopher became more and more lost.

He'd gotten so distant, he wouldn't talk; he didn't eat much, and he only left the room to use the restroom or smoke. He was unkempt his body smelled really bad, mom and dad took him to the doctors a lot.

They didn't know what was wrong with him, the doctors claimed he'd suffered some kind of mental break down and that it would be left up to him whether or not he wanted to snap out of it. They gave him pills to take every day and told them to monitor him because he acts as if he didn't want to live anymore.

Grant mentioned every day that he was possessed and we should make sure, that we are aware at all times. He said that at any time the devil would get mad if he couldn't use him the way that he wanted, and would explode inside him causing more rage in our home. He was so serious, always reminding me every day to pray for protection for my family. Kristopher never attacked me again, after that night he didn't even look at me too much, it was as if we were living with a stranger.

The school's first pep rally was coming up this Friday. This would be my first time attending any football games or Pep Rallies. There were signs up everywhere around the school all week; the cheerleaders shouted cheers for a month before the Pep Rally began. Fredrick was a football player this year among other things, he still picked on everyone. "You're going to the Pep Rally right?" Tate asked me in science class I looked over at Grant.

"Yes, we're going," I told him smiling. "Good, we're all going to the game afterward, right?" He said. "I guess so, right Grant?" "I don't know Keagan, I'm not sure," he said. "Oh, come on Grant, what are you afraid of?" Leland asked. "If anything goes down we all have your back," Riley said making smoke with the bottles of the liquid concoction he poured in one drop after the other." "Be careful!" Tate yelled out. "Dude, you're going to blow us all up one day," Leland said standing way far away from him.

"I'm not afraid of anything; I just have this bad feeling about that Pep Rally." "Dude, you sound one hundred years old," Leland said mocking him. "I just have these really bad feeling fellas, something's going to happen, don't you young fellas go to that there Pep Rally," he said. We all began to laugh loudly, everyone except for Grant. "I'm not trying to be a party pooper, but I'm telling you guys that night is not going to be a good one." He said reading his science book with his head down and his hair draping over his eyes.

"Dude, how can you be reading with your hair like that?" Tate said laughing. "Believe me I'm reading," Grant said flipping his hair back. We all went from science class to Algebra together Mr. Hanson would always catch us talking and telling us to always pay attention to the details in the lessons he gave and maybe we'd learn something. He would say that almost every day.   It was Thursday when the announcement went over the loudspeaker reminding everyone about Pep Rally.

When the principle was done with the announcement, everyone shouted and screamed about it in class. Mrs. Trembles told us to quiet down. Most of us did, but that didn't stop the wild bunch in the class from screaming out "Pep Rally! Yeah!" They screamed until the bell ring when Mrs. Trembles dismissed the class, they were held behind to get a detention slip for the day. Everyone pointed and laughed at them. "Grant so are you going or not, I can pick you guys up after school from your house the pep rally starts at 7 pm," Leland said walking out of class with us.

"You drive?" I asked. "Yes, I got my driver's license last year I'm a senior this year," he said. "Oh, I didn't know, why are you still taking these classes? These are sophomore classes," I said looking at him funny. "You don't have a driver's permit?" He asked me. "No, I don't I haven't even taken a class yet," I told him. "Riley has a permit, but his parents are afraid to get him the other lessons because they don't want him to drive," he said laughing. "Hey, don't laugh at him," Tate said. He's just on the slow track to riding."

"Come on Grant; say you'll go with us to the football game and the pep rally?" Leland said. "No, I don't feel good about this, you guys go on. Have fun for me too," Grant said looking away from us. "I'll see you guys later," he said walking to his next class. "Hey, Grant, wait up," I said following behind him. "Hey, don't you want to go to the Pep Rally with me? We do everything together, come on man, it will be fun. We hardly do anything fun anymore, and I need this," I told him while we walked to our last class together.

"It's not going to be a good day Keagan, something bad will happen," he told me. "Maybe just think about it overnight, okay Grant please, I don't want to go without you," I told him as we split up at the end of the hallway. "See you after school," I told him walking away, at the end of the day he waited for me at the stairway near the entrance of the school. "Hey Keagan, look over there," he said pointing at Fredrick and his friends. They were surrounding a new freshman grabbing at his backpack throwing his notebook in the air while the boy chased his things crying.

"You see that they're still messing with the new ones," Grant said. I ran toward the crowd surrounding the boy, I snatched the backpack from them giving it back to the kid they were taunting. "Hey, GQ is here to save the day again," Fredrick said standing with his hands in his pocket. The others kept taunting the boy pushing and shoving at him, Fredrick spit at me missing my face by an inch. "You really don't know when to quit huh GQ? You really don't value your peace do you?" He said. "Come on you guys, I'll get him later," he turned away quickly.

Wow I thought, he didn't even try to attack me this time. "No, he didn't," Leland said. "And he won't as long as we're around, he knows what it is," Tate said laughing. "He doesn't want to get iced." They all began to laugh loudly staring at Fredrick and his friends walking away. "Come on you guys need a ride home?" Tate asked. "Sure why not," I said "No thank you, I'm not allowed to ride home with anyone other than adults," Grant told them walking toward the pathway.

"Are you serious, dude?" Leland said. "Well come on Keagan, I guess you're the lucky one," Tate said walking toward the parking lot. "No, I can't let Grant walk alone." "Aw dude really, he's not walking alone though see Travis is walking with him," he says. "No, I better walk with him too," I said to them. "I'll see you guys tomorrow alright" "Alright dude see you tomorrow then, man that Grants so serious huh," Riley said. "Walking instead of a ride," he said shaking his head. "You have to be kidding me," Leland said.

"Wow, that dude is serious, has he always been that way?" He asked me as I walked away "Yep!" I said running to catch up with Grant and Travis. Hanna caught up with us too. "You two hear about the pep rally and the game tomorrow? Are you guys going?" She asked hoping that Grant would say yes he was going, this year she was the one wanting to date Grant, his interest was somewhere else, he didn't pay any attention to her like he'd done in the past.

"I don't think I'm going," Grant told her "No, why?" She asked frowning up at him. "I just don't think it's a good idea, as we approached my house I could see Kristopher from the window watching out for me as he did every day since the evil had taken over him. "See you later Grant, see you, Hanna," I said walking to my door. I went inside my house only to find mom scrubbing the floors on her knees with a bucket of water and a hand towel. She scrubbed all over; there was vomit all over the floor of the house.

"Mom, what happened to the floors?" I asked her. "Kristopher's sick, he's been vomiting all morning," she said scrubbing away at the floor. "Well, mom let me go change, I'll help you clean this up," I told her. "You don't have to," she said to me looking up. "Just go check on Kristopher for me, I think he may have a fever." "Okay," I said walking past her to toward the stairway. I looked up as I began to walk and Kristopher was standing at the top of the stairwell on the edge of the first step. He smiled, his face turned to pure evil. "Help me," he said to me in the voice of the raspy old man's.

His body twisted around, he fell as if he was pushed down the stairwell I ran up to catch him, but was unable to reach him in time. Mom heard the fall; she got up from her knees running over to us. "Keagan, what happened" She screamed out. "I don't know mom!" I yelled. "He said help, then he fell down" I told her. "Keagan, run to the phone call 911, please call them, hurry!" She yelled at me, I ran to the phone and dialed 911 a woman quickly came on the phone asking me what my emergency was.

"My brother fell down the stairs, I don't know if he's breathing." "Tell them he's barely has a pulse, they need to hurry!" Mom yelled out to me "Did you hear that?" "Yes, son is that your mother?" "Yes ma'am it is, can you please hurry?" I told her again. "The paramedics are on their way she said reciting my address to me." "Thank you." "Your welcome is your mom giving him CPR son?" She asked. "Yes she is," I told her, I could hear the sirens coming down the street, I went to the door.

"Son, the paramedics, should be there now, can you open the door for them?" She asked me. "Yes," I said to her opening the door. "Where's your emergency?" a team of paramedics asked me. "He's over there with my mom," I told them they all rushed in, running to aid Kristopher. There was blood coming from his mouth, mom explained to the policeman what happened. She told him he'd been sick all day and missed his step falling down the stairs. That's not what happened, but I guess she didn't want them to know what really had been going on with Kristopher.

"Keagan, I'll be going to the hospital with Kristopher, I'll have them page your father when I get there. You stay here and clean up for me okay," she said crying. "Okay mom," I told her kissing her cheek, I watched as they rushed off in the ambulance. I shut the door turning looking at the mess that mom left all over the house. It would take me all night to clean this mess I thought as I went to the kitchen for an apple and a glass of water.

When I walked back over to the floors all of the spots began to look as if it was blood not vomit. I dropped my apple and glass of water, running for the door, stopping myself at the porch. I'm going back in I have to clean this mess; it couldn't be blood I thought walking back into the house. I looked around the room walking over to the bucket mom left on the floor, the water didn't look like blood it just looks dirty. I took the bucket cleaned it out filled it up and began to scrub the floors until everything was up and cleaned.

It may have very well been blood, but I ignored it thinking about how fun the Pep Rally would be tomorrow. To keep my mind off what could have been happening to Kristopher. I stood to my feet looking up at the stairs where he fell, how he asked me to help him right before he fell. I don't know how to help him I thought, carrying the bucket to the back room where there was a bathroom. I poured the water into the toilet, it looked as if I was pouring a bucket of blood, the phone rang as I finished up, I ran to get it.

"Hello," I said. "Hello Keagan, did you clean up everything?" She asked. "Yes mom I did, how's Kristopher?" I asked her. "He's stable Keagan," she said getting quiet "Keagan, tomorrow the pastor of the church will be coming over to pray with us, I want you to be there," she told me. "No mom, I have a Pep Rally at school to go to, you know I'm not into that mom." "Keagan, please just this one time for me," she said almost begging me. "Please, we have to do this for Kristopher." I paused in silence.

"What time will he be coming?" I asked. "He said he'd come around seven thirty." "Mom, I can't, seven thirty is when the rally starts then the game. Come on mom any other time, but not tomorrow please," I said to her. "Okay Keagan, you can't be there then have fun at your pep rally," she said hanging up on me, I put the bucket up and went up to my room. I was about to get undressed to change when I heard something fall on the floor downstairs, I ran down to check on what was going on. The bucket was near the stair flipped over, it was as if I hadn't just cleaned the floor, it was again covered in blood, I knew that this couldn't be real.

I took the bucket up from the floor took it back into the bathroom filled it with water, when I came back out the floor was clean again. I took the bucket back and emptied it, I went back up to my room, and shut the door and staying there until I heard mom and dad come in. I waited to hear her call me to ask why I hadn't cleaned the floors, but she didn't say a word. Instead, there was a knock on my door. "Mom, is that you?" I shouted out. "Yes," she said opening the door. "Thank you for cleaning up for me, are you sure you won't join us tomorrow Keagan, we really need you to," she said.

"Mom, I can't, you know it's not my thing," I told her. "Well clean your room for me at least, he will be blessing the house again," she told me. "Okay no problem," I told her. "What time will you be back from this pep rally?" She asked. "It's over at ten." "How will you be getting home?" She asked. "I don't know yet, mom but I have a friend who drives now, his name is Tate." "Does he have a valid license?" "Yes mom, I'm sure he does." "Okay son, just be careful with who you're getting into a car with, please," she says kissing my head.

"Mom, how's Kristopher doing, is he going to be okay?" I asked. "Yes he'll be fine, he'll be coming home tomorrow, clean your room son," she said closing my door. I walked around the room picking up my things; I thought about Grant, he doesn't want to come with us to the pep rally. I wondered why, if Hanna couldn't get him to come then no one could. I'm going to call him as soon as I'm done to see if I can convince him to come along, I thought cleaning my room. There was peace in our home now that Kristopher was no longer there, it felt better and smelled better throughout the house.

I hoped when he came home that he'll be back to normal. No more moping around here unkempt and no more evil I thought. When I was done, I sat down at my desk to read a book from my bookshelf, books always made me feel better. I don't know what to read I thought, looking the bookshelf over, huh I've already read most of them I thought. I looked down on my desk, the Bible was staring back at me, I picked it up flipping through the pages.

I guess I will start here, Grants always raving about how good this Bible is, I began to read from the back I started with the book of Revelations. I read until my eyes began to become blurry. Revelations was so interesting, this story may have been one of the greatest stories I've read in a while I thought, dosing off trying to read more. I was tapped on my shoulders by my mom, "Keagan, get into the bed son, you can't sleep like that you'll hurt your neck." I picked myself up from the desk, my face was plastered to the pages of the Bible mom peeled them off page by page.

"You must have been really tired, what's this?" She said picking the Bible from my face. "You're reading the Bible son, good job," she said smiling leaving the room. "Did you learn anything," I shook my head no, I walked over to my bed with my clothes on I laid in bed covering myself. I fell off to sleep thinking of the Bible, what did it all mean, was it just a book or did it really happen and why should I believe in God, why should I? He's never done me any favors, I thought as I fell off to sleep.

When I woke up the next morning I could hear mom and dad downstairs talking loudly. I rushed around the bathroom to get dressed, today was Pep Rally. I couldn't wait, when I ran downstairs mom was cleaning dad was helping her. I'd never seen them so happy cleaning together. "What mom, no breakfast this morning?" I said watching them both work their way around the house. "Nope son, you're on your own."

"Have an apple, son, isn't that what your use to?" Dad said throwing me an apple across the room. "Good catch son, we'll see you later, son," mom said coming over to me kissing my forehead with a rage in her hand "Really, no breakfast huh?" I asked. "Get out of here son, have a good day, pep rally today, right?" "And don't forget that your brother comes home today, at least be on time to see him return," dad told me as I grab my bag from the floor on the way out. "See you guys later."

I went running down to Grant's house all ready to talk him into going with me to the pep rally when I went to knock on his door. He opened it wide wearing a school jersey with a nice pair of jeans that were fitting; they weren't high waters at all. His face was painted in the school colors, for once he out dressed me, I was surprised, he jumped out at me "Pep Rally today!" He said. "Are you ready Keagan?" I was so stunned at him, I couldn't say a word. "So what do you think about my new look?" He said stepping outside the door holding his backpack to his side, posing. He even had new shoes on.

"Wow Grant, what a change," I said. "What happened?" "I went shopping, and mom threw away all my old clothes," he told me jumping from each stair on the way down. "Let's get this day started! He yelled out "It's Pep Rally Time! We walked to school with Travis and Hanna. "So you're going now huh Hanna said unable to take her eyes off him as we walked "I almost didn't recognize you," Travis told him "Yeah, I was hoping for that kind of response," Grant said laughing.

"Come on dude, tell me what happened?" I asked as we approached the school. "I just felt like fitting in, if only for one day," he said. We walked up the stairs. "I'll catch you guys later," Grant said so confidently. Everyone was staring at Grant as he walked through the hallways. They waved at him and smiled as if they didn't know who he was. "See you after class, Keagan; we're all going to hang out at the park around the corner until the pep rally starts, would you like to come?" Tate said. "No, I can't I'm going to go home to change then come back to school for the pep rally," I told him.

"Dude, you're killing me, you have to go home?" "Yes, just for a while, I'll come over to the park if you guys are still there when I come back." "Okay dude no problem, see you at the pep rally," he said running off to class. Everyone was so hyper screaming and yelling through the halls about the pep rally. It would be the first football game of the season against one of the local private schools. Everyone was wearing a school t-shirt or a jersey when the bell rang at the end of the day people were running everywhere.

I went looking for Grant, I found him talking to a girl who was in our science class. Her name was Katherine, she was tall and beautiful. Her hair was so long it fell to her waist in one braid. "Nice to meet you, Katherine," I said waving walking away. I began to run all the way to my house hoping that the pastor would be there already to bless the house. When I got inside mom and dad were sitting in the living room, mom was crying. "Keagan, Kristopher's no better than before, in fact, he's worse." Just as she said that I heard moaning and loud thumping coming from upstairs.

"What do you mean, mom?" I said looking up at the loud sounds, she shook her head. I just wanted to get out, I didn't want to be there anymore, I ran up to my room trying to close my ears from the sound of the loud thumping and moaning. I changed and ran back down; as I ran out of the front door the pastor was coming in. "On your way out son?" He asked me standing at the door. "Yes sir, I can't stay, I'm sorry," I said running out.

"Good bye, son," he said waving as he went inside, I didn't want to be there. I had a really a really bad feeling there, I thought as I ran through the pathway I saw Leland and Riley standing near the trees. "Hey, Keagan, what's up, what are you running for?" They asked. "You look scared is everything okay?" Riley asked. "Everything is fine," I told them walking by fast; I didn't go to the park instead I went to the locker room in the gym and just sat until the pep rally started. I didn't look for Grant nor did I sit with him I had this bad feeling in the pit of my stomach the whole time.

When the pep rally started the band played, the crowd yelled and screamed out for our school, the cheerleaders cheered, it was a very loud event. I sat in a crowd of people that I didn't know when Grant noticed me he walked up to me from behind tapping my shoulder. "Hey, dude, what's up?" He asked. "Why are you sitting way over here? We're over there," he said. "Yeah, I know," I told him.

"Dude, what's wrong?" I could barely hear him over the crowd when they introduced the football team I stood up and walked away, I couldn't stay. I had to go home to see how mom and dad were doing. This time I ran through the back entrance of the school through the gate and the woods. I needed time to think about what I felt, this was a long way home, I thought as I walked through the woods. Quickly, my mind took me through the events of that day at Torch Lake, when we found Kristopher. I vision him hanging naked from that tree-shaped of the W.

What did I miss there, why would they hang him that way and leave him for us to take him? I thought about what I read in revelations that night, if it is evil in him and if I believe in God, could I get it out of Kristopher? Could I help him like he asked me? I began to run to my house as fast as I could, when I arrived at my house, I saw Kristopher standing in the window looking down at me. I entered the house immediately, the house was dark I couldn't see a thing I went to flip the switches for the lights, on then off they didn't come on.

"Mom, Dad!" I yelled out, no one responded to me as I continued to yell out for them, I began to walk to toward the stairwell. As soon as I approached the first step the lights flickered on and off, I looked up, Kristopher was standing at the top of the stairs laughing in an awful raspy loud groggy voice. As the lights flickered on and off Kristopher began to recite the verses from the book of revelations that I fell to sleep reading the night before.

"I am the Alfa and the Omega the Beginning and the End, who is and who was and who is to come. The Almighty," he said walking down toward me. My mind went blank, I stood still there hoping he'd stop; the lights flickered and flickered as he recited these words in that loud raspy voice of the old man. I couldn't see around me, I couldn't yell for mom and dad. As he approached me, my body changed; over and over again it felt like chills coming over my body up and down me. I was covered again I could feel it, it was hard to see anything, but I could feel it.

He made it down almost to the last step he looked me in the eye and began to laugh loudly. The lights turned on completely, I squinted to adjust my eyes. When I opened them wide, I noticed that there was blood everywhere the walls were covered in blood. Kristopher stood in front of me as if he was being held his head was hanging low as he laughed loudly. He picked his head up and looked at me then turned his head quickly looking over toward the living room laughing loudly and pointing.

I turned to look at what he was laughing at, mom and dad were hanging as if he'd pinned them to the wall naked and bloody. I tried running to them when he grabbed onto my neck still laughing loudly. He took me by my throat dragging me to the kitchen where I saw the pastor on the floor with his cross in his hand. He was covered in blood, there was a W on his forehead painted in blood I closed my eyes. "Worthy is the lamb who was slain to receive power and riches and wisdom and strength and honor and glory and blessings," I yelled out this verse from the Bible over and over again.

He held onto my neck tight as if he wanted to squeeze the breath out of me. We began to fight all over the house; he threw me to the wall the blades on my body were of steal. The walls cracked, he kept coming at me he didn't let up this time. "Shameless of you to think you will ever win," he said to me in that raspy voice of the old man. I stood before him; running toward him to catch him by the neck this time. The blades on my body cut through his skin like knives when he grabbed hold of me this time.

I heard a voice tell me to run him out, take him out into the woods and slay him, hang him back on the tree. It said to me, I allowed him to grab onto me, I hit him as hard as I could. He fell back onto the floor; I began to run to the patio door. I opened it running out of the side gate as fast as I could in the darkness toward the woods when I made it to the woods I waited for him.

I waited covered in my blade like feathers, I was completely black, I looked at my body as if I could see myself the blades were so black I could barely see them. I ducked down into the center of two logs when I heard him coming for me, his large feet crumbled the dried leaves as if he wanted to warn me he was there. When I heard him close, I stepped out, standing right in front of him. "Here I am," I said standing at attention. He rushed to me grabbing me by the throat, I grabbed at his throat, we went flying all over the woods fighting.

I fought him in the darkness as if I was fighting for my life, after being thrown clear across the woods near the well I almost gave up. I curled up in a ball of defeat; I was done with my head between my legs catching my breath. Suddenly I hear thumping and groaning coming my way, it was like thunder burrowing over my head, I dared to look up when I did there was Grant, Riley, Leland and Tate. "Need some help huh Keagan?" They said looking down at me. "Trust us we've been here," Tate said. "My mom and dad are gone," I told them.

"I know dude, I'm sorry." "Let's put this demon to rest," Grant said running over to him. They had come to rescue me; it would be the hardest fight we'd had to fight yet. We joined together to defeat the evil inside of Kristopher, he tossed us around laughing asking for more. We had to attack him together, forming a circle around him smashing down on him holding him to the ground. Tate sprayed him with ice; Leland's hair grew like a weed making a rope to tie him up with. Grant stripped him down before we could tie him up.

Leland ran through the woods pulling the trees together to form the W, he hung from at Torch Lake. When he was done, Grant stood up in front of his tied naked body. "Our Father, who art in heaven, hallowed be thy name. Thy kingdom, come, your will be done, on earth as it is in heaven. Give us this day our daily bread, and forgive us our trespasses as we forgive those who trespass against us. Lead us not into temptation. But deliver us from the evil one. For yours is the kingdom the power and the glory forever Amen!" He recited it over and over, Kristopher was strapped to the tree unable to move he struggled and moaned loudly as Grant recited the prayer over and over.

He growled at us from time to time until he was weak, we all joined in reciting the prayer as we watched the evil inside of Kristopher grow weak. We were all on our knees in prayer together tears flowed from my eyes as I watched my brother try to get away from the evil inside of him. His voice would go from the old man raspy voice to Kristopher's. His face changed over and over again as we prayed. We continued to pray through the night until the sun came up, Grant stood to his feet. "We have to leave him here," he said looking up.

"We can't take him down, once the evil is spilled from his blood he will be unleashed by God." Kristopher cried out; "Keagan help!" He said crying. "I have to get him down from there," I said to them. "No Keagan you leave him!" Tate says holding me back by my legs; Leland took me by the arm. "Come on Keagan we'll take it from here you go, go home to your mom and dad," he said pushing me away. "No, Keagan don't leave me! Don't leave me here, help me, brother, help me!" Kristopher cried to me as I was pulled away.

I could still hear him hollering for me to come help him, I cried going to Tate's car parked close by the woods. "We will take care of him don't worry Keagan, don't worry he'll be okay," Leland told me placing me into the car. "Get home!" He said. Tate pulled off heading toward my house, when we arrived at home there were police cars everywhere people were standing around our house looking through the windows and doors. I jumped out of the car running to see what else was wrong. I had forgotten what Kristopher had done at the house earlier as the police carried large bags out of the house.

"What is it, what's wrong?" I yelled out I could feel the, blades on my shoulders lifting ready to change. "Son, do you live here?" A policeman asked me holding out his hand to escort me inside. "I do," I told him pushing my way through the door. "Son, where were you tonight?" He asked. "I was at my school's pep rally," I told him. "You've been there all this time?" "Yes sir, um sir where are my parents?" I asked. "Where are my parent's?" I asked again. "Son," He said with his hand to my shoulders.

"Your parents are gone, we are trying to figure it out, and we're trying to piece together what happened here. Are you familiar with the pastor, we found him over there in the kitchen," he said staring at me. I couldn't catch my breath, I couldn't see I couldn't move, mom and dad were gone I thought, gone. My head began to spin; I stood from the seat in front of the Policeman. "Son, please don't go anywhere," he said walking over to the kitchen I looked over at the walls covered in blood.

I was so angry; I could have ripped the skies from the sky, why would God do this to me? Why mom and dad? I thought standing there. My shoulders began to rise, I felt warm all over, there is no one of a higher power that would do this. Take all I have, I thought. I walked over to the kitchen and looked around; there on the floor in a pool of blood was the Bible that the pastor carried in with him that day. I took it and flipped through the pages, the blood seeped through onto my fingers, I stood up, I looked at the policeman.

I ripped the pages one by one out of the Bible my body felt as if it was on fire I walked out to the patio. I threw the Bible into the pool, "Who is this Alpha, who is this Omega, where is he, what will he do now!" I yelled out. "Come please show me! What will you do now?" I stood there screaming out; my scream sounded like a horn out to God, the anger in me took over. "Where are you?" I yelled out. I took off running through the side gate away from everyone; I had to run to Kristopher.

I had to get him from the tree, I no longer wanted him to be free of the evil after what happened to mom and dad and the pastor. I ran through the darkness of the woods to find him, I made it to the tree where I'd left them; no one was there, no one. The tree-shaped of the W waved back and forth I ran through the woods in search of Kristopher, Tate, Leland, and Grant. "What! What will you do?" I screamed as I stood near the well thinking of mom and dad.

"I won't believe, I won't!" I screamed out loudly through the woods. Suddenly I was surrounded by everyone; Tate, Kristopher, Grant, and Leland. They stood together in front of me, the sky changed as they recited to me from Revelations. "You are righteous, O Lord, the one who was and who is to be; because you have judged these things."

"For they have shed the blood of saints and prophets, and you have given them blood to drink. For it is their just due." I heard the words coming from them loudly; the sky changed as my body did; still, my anger rose over God's words. I rushed toward them but was snatched from my feet and thrown into the well.

About the Author

K.C McGee born March 7th 1972 to Mr. & Mrs. Ernest and Ruth Love. While her journey has been altered throughout her life she pressed forward raising her nine children, she pursued her career as a Novelist while working and studying Behavioral Health at UCSD, she is now on her journey to becoming a well-known novelist captivating readers with her five book series and more, building her legacy for her children. Today she is a published Author pursuing her dream.